Praise for *The*

'*The Longest Fight* is all about pain — hiding it, inflicting it, feeling and not feeling it. The view we get of the ring, the lives of the boxers, and the austerity of post-war London are stunningly real. And that is its wonderfully original touch – we see outside of the ring, there are sisters, lovers, aunts and wives. The voices ring so true it's as if we are back in the 1950s, right in the stinking, rat-infested under-belly of the capital. We get to smoke, eat and yearn with these characters, to know what a hole in your shoe really means, and what it's like to lose – and, occasionally, to win. It's a world in which dreams of escape soar, thrilling and captivating us, but it's a world where getting hit and staying down is not an easy option.'   Derek Neale

'Atmospheric and elegant storytelling with a strong sense of authentic detail in everything from the sootiness of the post-war London air to the glamour of a nightclub. The characters are rich and alive, including the unforgettable Jack Munday, whose youth and adult years are expertly interwoven in a taut exploration of how or how much an individual can overcome a damaged past. An intimate and original view of the world of boxing and the men and (importantly) the women involved in it.'   Linda Anderson

'Emily Bullock's pungent, punchy prose vividly describes a world of hard knocks and high hopes in post-war London. *The Longest Fight* is a wonderfully compelling, atmospheric first novel.'   Andrew Cowan

'*The Longest Fight* tells a gripping and nuanced story about boxing and London in the 1940s and '50s. Emily Bullock brings a new sensibility to the way the sport is evoked and has produced a boxing novel that is both compelling and original.'   Kate Pullinger

THE LONGEST FIGHT

I love you so much.
Hope this book inspires
you to do great things.
♡Maja

I think you should
read this...
I wish we could
match each other in
commitment.
F. Flyth

★ ★ *The* ★ ★
LONGEST
FIGHT

EMILY BULLOCK

First published in 2015 by

Myriad Editions
59 Lansdowne Place
Brighton BN3 1FL

www.myriadeditions.com

1 3 5 7 9 10 8 6 4 2

Excerpts taken from *Boxing* by A.J. Newton,
reproduced with kind permission from
Bloomsbury Publishing Plc

A CIP catalogue record for this book is available
from the British Library

ISBN (pbk): 978-1-908434-53-1
ISBN (ebk): 978-1-908434-54-8

Designed and typeset in Palatino
by Linda McQueen, London

Printed and bound in Sweden by
ScandBook AB

For Robin
Always in my corner

PROLOGUE

Meet John James Munday. Jack the Silent Killer to those who read the cheap ink papers. He is a man who could knock you down; not today because his hands are strapped behind his back. And never again once he steps into that final rope. We only have a few minutes left. The guard checks his watch.

I remember the first time I saw Jack in here. Being sealed behind these stone walls makes most men small. But not Jack. Even now he stands the tallest of all. His white shirt does not cover his wrists and the metal cuffs bite his skin. Jack stares straight ahead.

This plain brick cell is unlike any other in Pentonville. It has two doors: one for the taking in and one for the taking out. Yellow tiles blank as a new page. All graffiti quickly scrubbed off the walls: there is no humour in reading another man's thoughts at a time like this. No windows, no draughts; I cannot hear any breathing, everything is still. Life left outside those iron doors.

Fingernails scrape against metal as the unseen jailer pulls back the bolts. Some noises you can never forget, like a screaming baby, the echo of laughter. The door slowly opens; it cannot be slow enough for Jack. He turns and nods to me, he is too close: is that a smile? It is too late to ask questions now. But I remember the things we spoke of.

There is nothing more alive than a boxing match. Jack told me all about it. He talked about the bubble of anticipation in his gut, one of life's surprises about to happen. Only sometimes in a match there are no winners. The jailer counts us in;

1

we will be one down when he counts us out. Twenty paces and we are in the centre, not the dead centre, of the pale green room, and it paints us all with its sickly tinge. The doctor stands to the left. The guards step back, their duty done. Two men, one old and one young, in dark blue suits, clean-shaven, buttoned-up to attention, step forward. Jack strides to the wooden platform. No one follows him.

He stands by the rope as the men strap his legs together. The brown serge rucks around his ankles. Jack is at the end of the fight now. All he said was, *I done it*, and he has never told them anything else, not at the trial, not in the cell. The guards have been taking bets all day. They know that the threat of that most final of silences will make most men talk.

I step forward until my polished shoes touch the lip of the platform. The black leather book falls open in my hands, *Watkins & Co. Bible Factory* embossed in gold on the inside page. The scarlet-dipped edges flutter apart and it sounds, for a moment, like the beat of a bird's wings. Jack glances up to where the sky should be. Silence. Mine should be the only voice left to speak.

When we first met in here, Jack asked me if I wanted to know the truth. I said it was not my place to judge. They whisper it at night, he said, asking him did he do it? If I were a gambling man I would put a bob down that he will not say a word, although like you I do not know the outcome yet.

The white cotton hood comes out of the younger man's pocket, a crisp crack as the starched edges settle like a dove on his arm. Two minutes left if Pierrepoint's weights and measurements are correct, and they always are. Jack took a wager too: *you can't go against a holy oath*, he said to me. Some say it takes a brave man to face death, but it takes more courage to look back and see where it all started. Jack named the year, 1953, but really it began long before that…

I

★ COURAGE ★

'*Learn to submit yourself to punishment, and you will often be able to weary an opponent who is infinitely stronger than yourself, until the joyous moment when he leaves an opening and you step in to do your share of the fight.*'

Boxing, A.J. Newton

– PROGRAMME –

Friday, May 22nd 1953

North v South

Grand 10 Rounds National Contest

PAT O'CONNOR

Kensal Green

versus

JOHNNY HALL

Sutton

6 Round Contests

## BILL MADDOX	## FRANK BULL
### Enfield	### Lambeth
versus	*versus*
## CHARLIE PETCHER	## ERNIE DONALD
### Kingston	### Harrow

Special Notice
Free Seats For Patrons.

Seats for this Hall will be given away at each show to holders
of lucky programmes. All programmes are numbered;
please check your number with those called from the ring.

ONE

Jack looked up at the painted advert on the dirt-slicked brickwork. Take Courage. The gas flames at the end of the street flicked blue shadows across the letters. He straightened his tie. And he wondered for a moment if life was as layered as those bricks, each join carefully worked into place with the next. Each one over with the ringing of the bell and on to the next round. He rubbed his thumb in the palm of his hand and crossed the road to the gym. His nose twitched against the sour stink of the Grand Surrey Canal. Someone had a sense of humour, as there wasn't anything grand about the back end of Camberwell.

The doors slammed behind him. Men stood around the ring, packed tight like traders down Waterloo Market, eyes and ears open for the prize. The fighters' shadows fell on to the crowd, casting a darkness that wiped out features, turning faces into skulls.

It wasn't the fight Jack was interested in that night. He had been watching the red-haired boy for a couple of weeks, first training down the gym, then out in the booths at Rosehill. It paid to keep an eye out for talent; there wasn't much fight left around those crumbling streets. He didn't have one decent hitter left on his books. Jack shrugged off his jacket, slung it over his shoulder. He was tall enough to see over the wall of macs and overcoats, his long legs giving him a few inches on everyone else, and probably thin enough to slide in between them. But he kept to the back, eyes searching the corners of the gym not the ring. No one else thought to turn their heads from the fight.

Light leaked from under the store-room door. He made his way towards it; the floorboards creaked like his knees on a damp day. Only a couple of years past thirty but already he felt the cold creep of age. He eased the door open an inch. Inside, old rolls of canvas were slumped against the flaking walls, but the boy had cleared a space for himself. A thick rope hung from the middle of the high ceiling, a bag, big as a man's body, suspended on the end, sawdust and stitching swirling about. The boy was punching smooth and fast. Each throw timed to graze past leather, the updraught of air swinging the bag. What if Jack had left it too long? Timing was everything, any decent boxer worth his silks and leathers knew that.

'Ain't going to get much return out of that old bag, are you?' Jack raised his voice above the cheers from outside, walked around to stand in front of the boy; he looked younger up close, probably no more than seventeen, eighteen at most. Not a cut or bruise on him. White-faced, pink-cheeked, but his breathing came steady and slow.

'Newton said… no one'd mind… me using it.'

The muscles on his arms tightened into ridges as he shrugged. Jack resisted the urge to pinch the boy's thigh and measure for fat.

'Newton's only the caretaker. Suppose you're not signed up for membership, then?'

Jack took out a cigarette. Hot smoke kept his voice steady and his hands busy. The boy kept moving, hair standing up as if lightning was about to strike.

'Spider said… he'd sort it.'

'That your mate?' Jack dropped ash on the floor.

The boy nodded, pressing his thick lips together until they turned white.

Jack caught the bag. 'Listening to other people's never going to get you nowhere. Your mate's been telling you porkies. No one gets to use the equipment, less he's signed up.'

'I can't… afford no subs.'

8

The boy had nothing to lose; that would up Jack's cut. He let the bag rock free again. 'Ever tried the fairs?'

He had seen the boy himself: one time he landed a punch so quick and straight that half the crowd at the booth didn't even know why the gypsy in the ring dropped to his knees and bounced forward on his head. Jack didn't feel old when he saw a left hit like that.

'Won me fights... I had down there... but the lads take a cut. The purse don't stretch far.'

The boy nodded as he spoke; he was Irish not far back. The voice south London but a soft turn to his vowels and a face just stepped off a farm: milk round.

'I should tell the management straight – it ain't allowed, you being here. But suppose I could square it?' Jack pulled down hard on the cigarette.

'What... you want to... do that for?'

He wasn't suspicious, just interested. The perfect combination: a killer in the ring but soft enough to mould and train up. Jack wanted to laugh – his luck was changing.

'Someone did the same for me long time back, helped me out. It'd just be a loan, and I get it back out the winnings.' He dropped the cigarette to the floor, ground it out.

'Spider... wouldn't want no one... getting a cut.' The boy landed hooks, slicing up under the bag. It crashed against a mouldering pile of mats, tumbling them to the floor.

'I'm not talking about Sunday afternoons down the fairground – they're full of pros fallen on hard times and gypsies bred not to care. An old one-two job. Only the booth owner wins at them things.'

Jack spun the bag back to the boy; leather whirled its way around them both. The boy knocked it off course with a left, didn't even break his rhythm. He weaved in and out of the tight circling, tying it in knots. Jack held his breath, certain any moment someone else would come in. If one of those punches landed it could smack the bag off its hook, crumble plaster from the ceiling, and deafen the noise from the ring.

He grabbed the bag, held it still. 'I'm talking about real battles, no more pissing around with mates. Go professional, make a life out of it.' He offered the boy a cigarette; he shook his head. 'What you need is someone in your corner.'

'Spider sees me right… I told you, he's a mate.' The dark patches of sweat swelled together, turning the boy's grey woollen sweater black.

'Your parents like the idea of you getting knocked about the head for fun? Turn pro, put some real work in it and you could be sending money home, not living on floors and under bridges. Make 'em proud.'

'How… d'you know me family?'

The boy stood up straight; Jack had found his soft spot.

'London's not such a big old place. I heard they're good sorts.'

'I'm the oldest now. My brothers died.'

'My brothers are gone too. They all look up to you, don't they?' Jack dropped his voice low and soft, drawing the boy closer.

'They've gone… back to Ireland. I want them to be proud… what you said.' He didn't even question how Jack knew so much about him.

'You need taking care of. A proper manager could do that.'

'That what you are?'

'As it happens, I am, but you'd take a lot of work and money. Not sure that's for me. You'd be good though.'

'You think?' His eyebrows lifted closer up to his hairline. It wasn't disbelief.

'A lot of work.'

'I work hard.'

'I'd have conditions.' Jack shook his head.

'I'd have to clear it with Spider.' The boy swiped thick strands of hair out of his eyes.

'This ain't some kid's game, it's the real McCoy. Know who that was?' Jack closed his teeth over the smile. The boy stared. 'What's your name, kid?'

'Frank.' The boy put out his hand.

Jack kept his arms close to his body. 'Ever heard of Big Maddox or the Tooting Tiger? They were my fighters – won some big purses too. Southern Divisionals, Southwark Championships. But someone like you… These things don't happen overnight. Time and investment, son.'

Frank's hand dropped, but a smile crept up at the corner of his mouth. Jack had him hanging on for it now. Frank swayed on his feet.

'You could be my manager?'

'It'd be a big job.'

'I want to fight.'

'I can't help you if you just want to fight. You've got to want to win, and know that the only way you're going to do that is by listening to me.'

Jack tugged on his earlobe. The boy's eyes were wide as if they were glued open. He followed every wave of Jack's fingers.

'Well, Frank, you've talked me round. I'm Jack. You shake this hand I'm holding out here and it makes me your manager and you my fighter. That's like writing it in blood. You can't go back on it and you can't break the trust.'

Jack held his hand just out of reach from the boy. He glanced over his shoulder; he could hear voices and laughter: the fight was over. He didn't have much time before the poachers came out.

'Going to shake or what, boy?'

Frank grabbed for Jack's hand as if it would save him tumbling off a cliff. Jack snatched his fingers away, rubbed his nose.

'Dust in this place gets right up your Harry James… Trust, Frank. That's what we got to have or we ain't got nothing. Get that?' He looked into the boy's brown eyes, big as a horse's.

'I get it, Jack.' Frank's head bounced on his neck.

'Think on what I'm offering here. Spider'll understand. He wants you to do well, don't he? Make money.'

11

Jack smacked his lips around the last two words. Frank's hands seemed to swell in size as he made fists and took a fighting stance for Jack. A strong one.

'Come and find me when you're ready to shake this hand. Trust, that's what we got to have, Frank.'

He closed the door behind him. Jack Munday, he'd had a few names, but this one was finally going to bring him success. At the other side of the gym the bell for the next fight rang out. Jack knew the deal was sealed. He had his fighter, a partnership to last; this time he was sure of it.

The electric lamps behind the mirrored bar flickered day and night, but the old smoke-stained glass absorbed all the light. Jack blinked, adjusting to the darkness of the long room, ears still ringing with the sounds of his and Frank's first fight. Only two weeks of training and already landing knockout blows. An open competition over in Fulham; on the quiet, no brouhaha. The match was over in fifteen minutes, the same length of time Jack'd had to wait before Frank had come running out to sign the contract – that was a sign of some sort, surely? Jack jingled the prize money in his pocket. Picking a winner was hard work, and the hunger churning inside him threatened to spill over into sickness; the smell at the Man of the World wasn't helping. Beer was soaked into the wooden floor and panelled walls, slowly dripped into place over the years from the sweat of drinkers – no one was careless enough to spill a drop.

Pearl was up at the bar, her head buried in a comic. She spoke without looking up. 'Cousin Alf said I could wait here.'

He sat down next to her, prodded her bandaged finger. 'How's the factory?'

'Making blackcurrant pastilles, same as ever. I caught my fingertip on the belt. It's clean.'

'My new fighter won his first bout. Should have seen him going at it.'

She nodded, and turned a page.

'Could look a bit more interested. It'll keep you in Dan Dares.'

Sixteen, but she still wore those stupid pinafore dresses and long cardigans. All elbows and scuffed knees.

'It ain't a comic. Newton lets me borrow *Nature*. It's a science journal. King's have got plenty of copies. This one's about families, about their insides being the same, me and you – like twisted threads of spun sugar, they called it.'

'That what you making at the factory, is it? Innards. Tasty.'

'Newton works up at the hospital with all them scientists. He says – '

'Don't listen to his fairytales. Emptying bins for a living don't make you an expert. He told me once his uncle wrote a book about boxing. Newton can't even stand straight on his tin leg, let alone talk straight.'

Newton belonged with the group of dockers: caps still in place, spines fused to the curve of the wooden chairs. That wasn't going to be Jack's life, nursing warm stout until the next wage packet came in. He pushed Pearl off the stool. 'Exercise cures all ills.' That was what the trainers spouted down the gym, but nothing was going to fix Pearl.

'I'm fine, Jack. See.' She swung up one leg at a time, thin ankles and knees on display. 'Nothing twisted, nothing swollen up. Not today.'

He looked away from the white threaded scars and green shadows of fading bruises. The new barmaid was in, polishing glasses at the other end of the counter. He lit a cigarette, flicked a stray tobacco crumb off the tip of his tongue. She had flounces on her blouse but he calculated the weight of her breasts to be as heavy as eight-ounce gloves with hands inside.

Pearl was dragging him back. Telling him there was a reason their hair was the same colour, when he knew it was the rotten cheap soap his mum had used to wash their heads, brown as tar and not as sweet-smelling. When she died he still kept using the stuff until he and Pearl had hair the colour of winter drain-sludge. At least he used Brylcreem to blacken his down. He smelled the overripe fruitiness of blackcurrant trapped in her clothes.

'You should brush that mop.' Jack talked to the thin pink line on top of her head, the dark strands hanging over her ears.

'If you buy me a hair set I'll use it. This new fighter of yours going to make us rich, is he? That'll make a change.'

She ran her finger along the page. He studied her reflection in the bottles lined up behind the bar. Her face round and flat, not much of her mother about her, and the thinness of her neck carried straight down to her long fingers. She did have the look of a Munday, though. Maybe that was what those science magazines she read were on about – using the same soap when there was a shelf of new ones to choose from down at Simmonds' Grocers. They were both trapped in that mirror of the past. But they weren't the only ones; the pub was full of faces. They would all want to be his mate now he was on the up. The new barmaid was rolling his way too, swaying one pretty hip after the other. Her skin as creamy as the head on the pint of Courage she put in front of him.

'Evening.' Jack winked at her. 'First day?'

The barmaid made some reply but he couldn't hear her voice over the noise in the pub. He nodded anyway, hoped she didn't sound like a yapping puppy as the last girl had.

'Well, don't know if Cousin Alf told you, but he only marks down every other pint in the book for me. We're close.'

She flicked the cloth at him. 'He told me not to listen to nothing you lot said.'

That quick movement sent a buzz down Jack's spine. He reached across the bar, caught her wrist before she could snap the damp rag again. She let him stroke the sides of her fingers for a second. It really was her first day: hands soft, not cracked and dry from rinsing glasses; neatly filed nails, polished tin jewellery. The gold-coloured rings reminded Jack of Rosie but

14

he pushed the thought from his head. He concentrated on the pumping pulse in his neck.

The girl nodded in Pearl's direction. 'She with you?'

Jack nearly blew beer from his nostrils but swallowed it back in time. 'Christ, I ain't that hard up. She's my little sis.'

'She looks too young to be your sweetheart but I thought she might be your daughter.'

'Don't make me laugh. I ain't ready to be six feet under yet.'

The barmaid turned her head. Glasses were building up at the other end of the bar, but Jack didn't want her to leave yet. He gripped hold of Pearl's wrist, rolled up her sleeve. Small teardrop-shaped scars, white as milk, marked her arm.

'I'll show you a trick.' Jack kept his voice low, reeling the girl in.

He took the cigarette out of his mouth, sucked the dry-paper taste from his bottom lip. The end was damp with spit so he gripped it nearer the ember; as if he were holding a pen he dabbed a full stop on Pearl's forearm then whipped it away again. The barmaid let out a shriek – the best reaction yet. Pearl turned a page and the girl closed her mouth. They fell for it every time.

He re-lit the end with a fresh match, handed the cigarette to the girl. 'Go on, try it. She's been like that since a baby. Smack her across the face and she just ain't going to feel it.'

'I don't know.' The girl twisted the cigarette between her fingers. 'Sure it won't hurt none?'

'Did you hear her make a peep? Doctors got some name for it, can't for the life of me remember what.' Jack sat back on his stool. 'Tell her, Pearl.'

'Idiopathic neuropathy.' She stared at the girl. 'It wouldn't hurt if you cut me open with a knife.'

The girl picked up the cigarette, tapped it against Pearl's arm, and let out a small squeal. It filtered through the growing fog of beer inside his head. Pearl snapped her lips tight, snatched her arm away. Those grey irises, always staring at him. Sometimes a trick of the light or a fall of a shadow and it was like having Rosie back.

'Best leave it there.' He winked at the barmaid.

'At least she'll never get her heart broken.' The barmaid sucked down on the cigarette, drawing out the last spark. 'How can she, when she can't feel nothing? Lucky cow.'

'She's just a kid, not even interested in boys. Are you, Pearl?'

She shrugged. Too busy reading and dreaming; a lost cause, but still she was good around the house. Pearl rubbed antiseptic over the red bump; the pot of Clayton's she carried round stank of eucalyptus. The barmaid turned to serve one of the dockers. He gave Pearl a gentle push.

'Get supper on for me?'

'I waited here because you said you'd have money, Jack. I don't get paid until the end of the week.'

'Loan some grub from Mrs Bell.' He pressed her outstretched palm down before the girl saw.

'She'll make me stay for a chat.'

'Tell her I said you're to get dinner on quick.' He watched her roll up the comic, or whatever it was, and adjust the small bandage. 'It was a bit of fun. Not like you felt nothing, was it?'

'More than one way to feel things.' Pearl shrugged as she walked away.

They used to do the cigarette trick all the time. How was he supposed to keep up with her changes? Jack shook his head, turned back to find two big brown eyes in front of his. He smiled.

'Can't just call you "barmaid", now, can I? Tell me your name.'

'Georgie Smyth. Smyth with a Y.'

'Nice to meet you, Georgie. Call me Jack.'

He reached over, shook her hand. He thought he could see his own reflection in those eyes, light brown like the polished wood of the swing chairs at the summer fair. Higher and higher he and Rosie used to ride. Jack looked down. The bottom of the glass peered up through the cloudy mist that was left of his drink.

'You should come see my new fighter some time, Georgie.'

'Maybe I will, Jack.'

She took his empty pot and moved on to the queue at the pumps. He wiped the sweat from his eyes with his handkerchief, pushed it back into the depths of his waistcoat. Slowly he eased himself off the stool, but he couldn't help glancing at the pictures tucked behind the half-empty bottles at the back of the bar. The Bible Factory send-off; his dad at the front in his Great War uniform, proud and tall; his mum at the pub's VE Day celebration with a Union Jack poking from her hair. More photos waited for him back at the house. He couldn't leave that family behind; sepia eyes, sneaking up on him when his mind wandered: the boys in their East Surrey Regiment get-up; Winifred and Win lying on a fur rug, only ten months apart – the first was born sickly, never expected to make it, so their dad's mother's name was supposed to live on in the next girl. The Winnies at eleven and twelve, still side by side as if their dresses were sewn together, just before they left for good. And, half hidden: one of Jack, back when he was John. He'd had that photo taken after his first win, thirteen years old – hands up, hair slicked, shorts hanging low. He could list them all. But only one picture of Rosie survived; Jack kept it at the back of his bedside drawer. Sometimes it was as if she had never existed for anyone but him. The people on the front room mantel were from John's life. John James Munday – the name he was born with. He wasn't that runt any more, but he still couldn't get rid of their faces.

TWO

John recognises the house, all square windows and big red front door like something from Little Chums picture books. He heard the Winnies whispering to his mum about St John's Villa when his dad was out of the room. The gate is closed and John doesn't blame them. If he lived in a house like that he'd have a moat, a drawbridge, soldiers on guard, anything to keep the rest of London out. A copper walks along; any minute now he is going to wonder what a dirty canal rat like John is doing on that street.

He chews his nails and presses himself closer to the prickly hedge; the blue uniform crosses to the other side, goes into a house. John hasn't decided what to do yet, how to ask the question. So he waits some more. Leaving Camberwell, getting on the tram for Mitcham, coming all this way, it seemed so easy this morning.

Two ladies appear at the front door. Neat grey dresses and matching hats. John tucks in his shirt, swallows a squeak as his fingers graze the top of his buttocks; the strap marks are bleeding.

'What the bloody hell is he doing here?'

They turn back into his sisters as they reach the gate, hands on their hips. Same dresses, same hats, same scraped-back hair; got up like a music hall pair of old women even though they are only eighteen and nineteen. He isn't sure which sister is which.

'This is our place.' Winifred holds on to the metal latch. He recognises the sharpness in her voice. It is as if they are little again, the panic of having nowhere to hide, the seeker

18

counting down from a hundred: *coming, ready or not*. They aren't children now: long skirts and clean gloves, sharp bones stretching out their skin. But the staring dark eyes haven't changed, just like their dad's.

'You can't stay. We're going to work.' Win brushes invisible dust off her dress. 'Tell him he can't stay.'

Winifred puts a hand on her younger sister's arm. She is waiting for John to give himself away, to have an excuse to dob him in. The branches of the bush poke up against his bare legs but he doesn't step back. He doesn't want them to leave yet.

'Where d'you two work, then?'

'Book-keeping for the – '

'Don't tell him anything. If he knows where we're going the sneak'll follow us.' Winifred leans on the gate, her thin face pushing towards him. 'Won't you?'

John shakes his head, but he doesn't have anywhere else to go. When the Winnies came back at Christmas they had still seemed like girls, nudging each other and playing with their hankies, but here they are different. Taller and bigger, but maybe that's because there is more room out in the country. The windows up at the house are open wide, thick pink drapes and bright red cords looped around them, white flowers over the red brick, green grass, orange and yellows sprouting out of the earth beds in ordered rows.

'What have you gone and done this time?' Win hisses at him.

'Nothing. No law against coming to see you.' He tries not to chew his lip and give away the lie. 'Thought you might not know me otherwise – I've grown big.'

'Oh, we would recognise you anywhere. Wouldn't we, Win?'

'We would, sister. He looks…'

'… like *him*.'

'Fucking liars.' John kicks the gate. 'You two look more like Dad than I do.'

19

He didn't mean to do that; now they are never going to say yes. But it is true: their dark hair, transparent skin like a worm, and eyebrows sloping to meet in the middle.

'Let us come in.' He tries to smile, lips sticking together.

'Aunt's with visitors this morning.'

Winifred keeps a tight grip on her black bag. He isn't going to nick it, wouldn't give her the satisfaction. Win touches her sister's sleeve. 'What if she finds out he was here from one of the neighbours? Better to let him visit at lunch.'

'We'll be back at twelve-thirty. Stay out of sight, for heaven's sake. Go play in the stream or something.' Winifred, the oldest and in charge, nods at her sister.

'Have these then, if you must.' Win drops a bag of sweets in his hand but holds on for a second as if she doesn't want to let the bag go. He opens the crumpled paper. It is only liquorice, black and hard-edged; he prefers toffee.

'Stream's back there, and make sure you can't be seen from them houses.' Winifred's voice drops back into its south London lilt.

Win grabs his shoulders, turns him towards a long line of trees. Neither of the Winnies see the woman dressed in black come down the path, but John does.

'What is going on out here? I thought I said to send all beggars to the church, girls.'

They shuffle together to clear a spot on the path for her; the black folds of her skirt take up more room than she does. John tries to stand up tall, but the old postman's boots on his feet have rubbed blisters into his heels. The woman angles her beaked face towards him.

'They have assistance there on Thursday mornings, young man.'

'This is John, Aunt. Father's youngest.' Winifred bows her head a little.

'Oh, my, I forgot my cousin had this one left.'

John can't understand why they are all supposed to call her 'aunt' when she is only some sort of distant leftover-cousin; she even looks leftover, all grey and stretched thin like stale dough.

'I don't know what he is doing here, Aunt.'

'He certainly wasn't invited, Aunt.'

They fire off answers, so quick he doesn't know which Winnie said what. John rubs at the finger-shaped bruises under his shirt sleeve until it brings water to his eyes. The aunt neatly folds her hands in front of her.

'So, your elder brothers are off serving in the Army. Are you planning on joining up, young man?'

'Not likely.'

'Then the Bible Factory with your father?' Those hands nod together as if she is praying.

'I want to go places, get out of London. Barges maybe.'

'So, how can we help you, John? Come to see your sisters perhaps? We are all well in this sleepy place. Mitcham must seem like quite an adventure.' She keeps talking without leaving him room to answer.

'Aunt, the church warden's wife is at the window waiting for you.'

The Winnies look down at their feet. John wants to kick up the dirt around his boots just to make them see him. The aunt turns, gives a small wave and the face disappears behind draped curtains.

'Thought I'd stay here. I can work and I never eats much.' He hides the liquorice behind his back.

'It is very kind of you to offer your services but I think your mother needs you more. We trundle along quite well here, do we not, girls?' That watery smile still in place, wrinkling her skin. The Winnies smile too.

'But I'm nearly thirteen…' The words are lost in his mouth. The Winnies were around twelve when they left, his brothers have gone too – someone has to be coming for him; they have to. John wipes a hand across his mouth.

The aunt taps her fingers together as if she's playing a piano. 'It must be your birthday soon.'

He doesn't want to tell her he was only twelve last month; he hopes there is a penny in it. She smiles, but not at him.

'How would you like a present?'

It takes him a moment to realise she is waiting for a response this time. John nods. 'The gate looks a bit rusty. I could fix it up proper for you.' He scrubs a piece of paint away with his fingernail. 'There's lots of things I could do about the place.'

She stares out over the hedge. 'Now, what would be the best thing for a young man such as you?'

Winifred shakes her head. 'He won't look after it and it will just get broken.'

But the aunt heads up the trimmed path towards the house. John isn't sure if that is it, she isn't coming back.

She stands on the doorstep, calls into the house, 'Avis, my dear, a moment, please. I wish to ask your opinion on a most important matter.'

A woman inches forward; long dust-collecting skirt and pinched-in waist. The aunt beckons her to follow; they face John on the other side of the green gate. The two Winnies shoot sideways glances at him in case he makes a bolt to get inside the garden. John grinds his heel down on a pebble. He knows about people like his aunt and that woman with their smell of fresh laundry and sponge cakes: Sunday school fuckers. People like that are the reason his head hurts and his backside throbs; someone at the factory told his dad John hadn't been for two weeks. Summer is coming; how is anyone supposed to sit in that dusty hall for hours at a time?

The aunt is still talking. John is sure blood is running down the back of his knees, or maybe it's just sweat. The aunt brings them to attention with a small wave of her hand.

'Now, what would be a decent, suitable gift, for a young man turning thirteen?'

'Perhaps a puppy?' The small woman rubs the edge of a pale blue bow pinned to her throat, pushes her head towards

22

the aunt. John wouldn't mind a mutt, but he wouldn't be able to hide it from his dad.

'No, not in the city. Not at all suitable, Avis.' She gives a shake of her head. The Winnies smile politely but they keep one eye on John too, beady black eyes like the parrot at home which watches him from its cage at the back door.

The woman smiles as if she is about to win the prize. 'Perhaps a tin army?'

'Was the Great War not enough? Oh, no, that simply would not do at all.' Another shake of the aunt's head, but the curls are set firmly in place.

The woman speaks again, eyebrows arching. 'A book?'

'Look at the boy. Much as I would like to improve his mind, he does not look capable of sitting still at all.'

They all shake their heads this time. John hasn't moved, but he doesn't bother to remind them of that. The woman points at his feet.

'New shoes?'

They all laugh, in a high, glass-tinkling way. John sticks the toes of his ugly boots under the hedge. The thorns scratch his shins.

'Boxing lessons.'

The aunt looks him up and down as if she has just noticed there is someone standing in the boots. The woman nods vigorously. 'The vicar was only the other day extolling the virtues of the sport, keeping the young in line. Fit and healthy.'

'Lessons, Avis? They teach it?' The aunt angles her head towards the woman.

'Perhaps it will build the boy up a little? He is rather skinny. Put some colour in his cheeks?'

The aunt claps her hands. John wants to bite off her fingers; his teeth snap down on his tongue, and he holds back the yelp.

'Boxing. Yes, it will make a man out of him. A very splendid idea.'

They all smile as if it was the aunt's idea all along. The Winnies used to grab his ankles, threaten to hang him out of the upstairs window if he even looked at anything that belonged to them. He thinks he preferred them before they came to this big house and started wearing funny clothes.

'Win, collect my purse from the desk, there's a good girl.'

John expects Win to snarl something back at the aunt, or frown at least, but she just goes back to the house, resurfacing a few moments later. She hands over the crocheted purse. The aunt dips her fingers inside as if she expects it to be filled with cold water, brings up one thing, then clicks the clasp shut.

'One pound.' She holds it out. 'Winifred, secure it inside the boy's coat so it does not get lost.'

Winifred takes a pin out of her hat, pulls open his jacket and attaches the note inside. He feels like a tiny baby being dressed. The aunt smiles. 'I will be writing to your mother, so make sure you show the receipt for the lessons to her.'

And that is it, back off up the path; the woman trots to keep beside the aunt. The sun shining on them, glinting off their polished skin.

'Who was that?'

'Just a boy, Avis.'

'You are so very generous. I was only saying the other day to the vicar…'

Their voices disappear with the clunk of the front door.

'You're done, now clear off. This is our place. And you won't be needing them sweets.' Win snatches back the brown bag.

'You'll have to learn to look after yourself, John. *He* won't be around forever.' Winifred opens the gate then fastens it behind her and Win. 'The tram's back the way you came.'

They turn the corner and are gone. John kicks the gate, kicks a pebble, sets off after it towards the stop. The road slams back up into his feet as he stomps along: past flowery gardens, on to a high street of striped awnings and pyramid window displays. He will show them all, do something with that money, make it rich, then they will be sorry. They will all be begging to stay with him then, and he'll let them as well. Make them sleep in the outhouse with his dog, clean his library of books, and dust his tin army, all two miles of them when lined shoulder to shoulder. He'll have everything. John listens to the rustle of the paper against his shirt.

A tram is coming, heading away from the city. He could get on and go south, south, south, until he hits France and then keep going some. He could be anyone out there, not a Munday. No one to say, *Don't you look like your dad?* John can't breathe, can't look at the old woman in the fat hat at the stop in case she knows he is planning to run away. But he doesn't know where the tram is going. The ticket collector stares down at him. If he steps on, his mum wouldn't be there to make cups of milky tea, his dad wouldn't give him the second read of the newspaper or a borrow of the bike, and money never goes far, he's heard his dad say that a thousand times.

Another tram crosses in front, John jumps on. It is going back the way he came: home. He goes straight to the gym, pays membership up-front for the year.

THREE

He pushed the switch down. A circle of yellow light swung above the canvas, illuminating Frank's upturned face. The rest of gym slipped back into the shadows. Jack draped a towel over the ropes.

'Concentrate. You'll get seasick looking up at that thing.'

The gym was empty apart from the thick stale-cupboard smell. They were the first ones in, not that Frank had far to go. Jack had lined him up with a bed to sleep on in the store-room; he never asked where the boy had been before.

Frank sprang closer to the ropes. 'We've been going good for ages now. Are you going to stay my trainer, Jack?'

'Don't you worry about that. I've got feelers out. Need to get some money coming in first.'

They had to be quick. Frank was bouncing about as if he had springs for feet now, but a few years down the line he would be knocked flat. What did he have to smile about all the time? But Jack remembered what it was like to be that young, all the energy crackling around. Jack used to have Rosie, back then, but Frank seemed content with the ring. One sneaky left hook and *bang*, it could all be over for Frank too.

'I've got a couple of sparring partners lined up for you today, Frank. Some of the blokes from the gym can't wait to have a go. I've said I'll give a guinea to anyone can knock you down.'

'Right you are, Jack.'

Frank kept moving, feet shuffling up dust, shoulders dipping as he circled. Jack needed to make sure he could take some punishment. Only a real fighter could deal with pain and remember his moves. That had been Jack's best way to a win: thirteen years old and he could take anything they landed on him.

'Hold that guard up.' Jack pointed at the drop in Frank's left hand. 'Guaranteed, it's always the hit you don't see that'll knock you out.'

'It's just me... here.'

Jack threw the towel, it slapped Frank across the face. 'Didn't see that coming, did you?'

'Sorry... Jack.' Frank scooped up the towel between his heavy gloves and tossed it back.

'You'd be flat on your back now if there'd been someone in with you. Keep warming up.'

The echo of voices, the splashing of water, came up from the changing rooms. The old fighters were on their way: the ones with barges to unload, and a full day's work to get in. Jack usually liked to avoid these dropped pennies but they were the perfect sparring partners. The first of them were dragging their dislocated shoulders and cracked knees into the open hall. Jack always felt a rush of cold air slip down his shirt when the gym came awake. The sour smell of liniment tickled his nose. The eyes staring at his back made him tingle like the start of a muscle cramp. He became everything he was meant to be, everything they would never be, when those fighters were looking; not the flat-footed, snot-crusted kid he remembered when he was left on his own. A crowd of about ten fighters circled the edge of the light. Steel Bill, Black Bull, Putney Puncher – names as faded as their patched trousers.

'Hey, Champagne. Get over here,' Jack called out.

The man did the word *ugly* proud: head swollen from punches, muscles thickening into wood, and a two-day blackout had robbed him of a smile. Champagne hauled himself into the ring.

'Let me at him, Jack. Ready for this, boy?'

He stretched up his arms. It looked as though one of the iron girders holding up the roof had planted itself on the canvas. The other fighters muttered and clicked like disturbed cockroaches. Frank paced the ropes, eyes fixed on his opponent.

'Champagne… full of air… are you?'

Jack snuffed up a smile and shook his head. Something from those smart-mouthed friends of his had rubbed off after all.

'When your knackers drop, boy, maybe you'll get yourself a proper moniker too.' Champagne butted his gloves together. 'Let's see what you're really made of.'

'Is that him?' Pearl whispered in Jack's ear.

He hadn't noticed her sneak in. She normally left his morning tea at the door on her way to work, but he couldn't help feeling pleased that she was taking an interest at last. Jack pulled up one of the stools, sat with his knees pressed to the canvas. The other fighters were still as stone angels peering over a grave. Jack rang the bell.

Frank moved so fast the rest of the room seemed still frozen in the seconds before; even Champagne, with his heavy punch, only buzzed around him like a wasp caught in jam. Frank's footwork was so light he seemed to spend half his time in the air. But Champagne was getting wise, waiting to follow through with a cross. Frank danced straight into it, pulled up as if a door had slammed in his face. He glanced over. Jack didn't move. The boy had to learn what happened if he thought he was in there on his own. But Jack didn't need to worry too much.

'See that? He's changing rhythm, slowing down to calculate angles and projections.'

'What's he feeling?' Pearl came up behind him, rested against his back.

'Those Sunday punches would have most men on their knees, but not our Frank. He just clenches up.'

Now Jack was aware of her, her chest moving above his head, the sharp point of her elbows, he wanted to get free. He lifted his shoulders; she readjusted her tiny weight. She didn't notice how her touch burned right through him. He kicked the stool aside, moved up to the ropes.

'What he's feeling – is it scalding or freezing?'

'The blows he's taking from Champagne would be red as coal in the fire.'

She didn't understand *wrenching* or *stinging*; words like that had no meaning for her. Dragging Pearl to those hospital appointments, watching men in white coats stick pins in her feet, push straws up her nose and pinch her tendons; she had just sat and sucked the end of her plaits.

A short, straight punch landed against Frank's chest. The bright burn-mark of blood spread under his skin. Champagne was a swarmer, but he couldn't get near Frank's face, tiring himself out with windmill jabs in an attempt to smash that jaw. Frank's heart was fair beating out of his chest; he snorted air, nostrils flaring, but he wasn't slowing. Champagne's gloves began to drop. Frank could take him at any time now, but he didn't move in for the kill. *Oh, Jesus Christ, don't hand me a lame one.*

'Take him down, ya soft bastard,' a voice shouted from the other side of the ring.

Frank looked straight to Jack, waiting for instructions, alert as a dog. Jack nodded. Frank drew back his right; no twist, no hook. The blow impacted with the front of Champagne's face. The old fighter's knees locked, a real professional, but even his thick legs couldn't take that crashing weight. Frank dipped his shoulders, held the older man up, tipped him into his corner. Champagne clung to the ropes; losing was a disease and the other fighters left him to it. The faces collected around Frank's corner. They didn't need to applaud; the rush of voices were all talking about his fighter.

Jack held the ropes open as Frank jumped down. 'Meet my new middleweight champion of Great Britain. Well, he will be one day.'

Jack gripped the boy by the shoulder and squeezed. He wasn't really talking to Pearl. He was speaking to the rest of the men in the gym. Frank held his head on one side to let Jack's words drip down inside him better. His cheeks flushed red.

'Don't know… about that.'

'Put faith in me, Frank. I'm your manager. That's what I'm here for – to make you a winner.'

Other fighters were jostling against Jack, saying his name, trying to get his attention. They could wait. Pearl stood at the side of the ring, opening up the basket. 'I brought you tea. There's enough for both of you.'

'Give the boy a chance to get out of there. Go and wait by the doors.'

Jack made space for her between the men; they parted to let her through. Frank watched her go.

'Who… is that?'

'Don't worry about Pearl. We've got things to do.'

'I'd be up for sparring, if you're looking.' Steel Bill patted Jack on the elbow.

He couldn't imagine how it felt for them, at the end, when half-a-crown for a knockabout was as close to a good fight as they could get. Trembling hands and slurring words were all they had. 'Catch me later and I'll maybe put you down.'

Jack held an arm around the boy's shoulder, walked him away. The smell of hot skin seemed to burn up all the oxygen, sucking the men tight around him. Skill like Frank's didn't rub off, but boxers were a superstitious lot. Fingertips wiped up Frank's sweat as they slapped him on the back. The boy needed his edges sharpening, some work on his self-taught technique, but he didn't have any problems taking orders. Frank was one of the lost ones; probably been looking all his life for someone to show him the way. Jack's heels clacked on the tiles and soft-footed Frank slipped along noiselessly beside him.

'Cool down a bit, then I'll set you to some glove work.'

'Whatever… you say.' Frank rubbed a leather glove against his red chest. 'They call him… Champagne… because he's the best?'

'No, he used to half-inch bottles of the stuff and trade it for membership to the gym.' Jack held open the door.

'When do I get a name?' Frank ducked under his arm.

'Don't rush it. When the time's right, the name will find you.'

'I've told the boys. I can't go out with them no more… and I won't, not even if they call round. Fighting's more important. Ain't it?'

'That's something you've got to decide. But don't think about pissing me around.'

'I won't… What happened to your last fighter?'

'Glass jaw. Don't you go worrying about that, nothing wrong with your bones. Now stop chattering, get your breath back.'

Jack landed a soft slap on Frank's cheek. He wasn't about to tell the boy about his last investment running off with an East End manager: promises of plenty and his name in lights turning his head. Not much light where Frank was at the moment: a pile of dirty rags in one corner, boxes of something leaving a sticky black footprint where they leaned against the wall, a cot bed taking up the other side. Frank sat on the blanket, pulled his gloves off by trapping them under his arms. The place wasn't much more than a cupboard. Pearl hovered in the doorway; no room for the three of them in there.

'What's that god-awful stink?' She rubbed her nose. It wasn't like her to speak her mind, but the smell was sort of scratching his eyes too.

'I'll crack a window.' Frank clambered over the boxes; they sagged under his weight.

A scraping noise came from the wall, probably some dead rat being eaten behind the plasterboard. Jack hated rats.

'Frank? You back in there?' a voice called up from the street outside.

Frank stayed close to the boxes. Jack shook his head. The voice was getting louder.

31

'It's Spider. Open up. I know you wouldn't ignore me, Frank. Wouldn't want to do that. I'll be back later.' Footsteps marched over the cobbles.

'I didn't tell them I was here.' Frank sank down on to the bed.

Jack reached over and knocked the window shut; he needed to keep a better eye on the boy. 'How you feeling? You took some hard blows in there. Pearl can check you over, if you want? The girl can spot an injury at ten yards. She caught a sprained wrist this week.'

Pearl tucked her arm behind her back. Frank stared at his knees.

'I'm all right. Don't want to trouble anyone, Jack.'

'I've got to get to work or they'll dock me.' Pearl stepped back into the corridor. 'Jack, come here.'

'What?'

But she didn't answer, just pulled him out of the room. Jack shook himself free.

'He can't stay in there.' She hugged the basket.

'It's dry and it's free.'

'How's he going to keep well with that whiff? And it's so dark, Jack.' She shuddered. 'Who calls themselves Spider?'

'Frank's my fighter. He ain't one of your bloody stray mutts to smother.'

She used to collect injured animals, even snails with broken shells.

'I never took in a dog, and that cat with the snapped leg lasted for months.'

'Quite a casualty list it racked up, though. Birds, mice, rats.' He counted them off on his fingers. His mum had finally put her foot down when a fox Pearl was keeping safe under the sink died. The kitchen had filled up with bluebottles crashing against the windows and feasting on plates.

'I ain't ten no more. Said it yourself, didn't you – he's an investment.'

'Where do you expect I put him up? The Ritz?'

'Well, with his fights coming, I bet he could afford a little bit of rent for somewhere…'

She didn't need to say any more and perhaps she was right.

'We'll see after the next fight.' Jack sighed.

'Thank you.' She put her arms around his neck, half strangled him.

'I said maybe. We ain't keeping him forever, Pearl.'

'I know, I know. But I'll help out, I promise, and I'll make the money stretch.'

'Give me the grub, and get out of here.' He snatched the basket and went back into the room.

Frank wasn't going to sleep out his days in front of the fire; racehorses, greyhounds and boxers, they all got put out once they were used up.

'Suppose you heard all that – nothing wrong with the girl's lungs.'

'I promise to do me best. I won't get in the way none. You know how hard I can work. I'd do jobs around the place. Don't want no one thinking I'm a cadger.' Frank jumped up, but with no room to move he dropped back down again. The bedsprings jingled; his backside scraped the ground as the mattress caved in the middle. Jack supposed it was a bit like clipping a bird trying to keep Frank in that room. At least under his roof the kid wouldn't have the chance to start running with those mates again.

Frank started stuffing his clothes into the duffel.

'I'm looking forward to writing me ma on Sunday. She'll be happy to hear I'm doing good and might have found a good honest place to live. They only have little Sheila and Theresa left and they're relying on me. They'll be saying prayers for you when – '

'Nothing definite until after that fight. And we've got to have a few rules before then.'

'Anything you say, Jack.' He dropped his bag and stood to attention.

Jack held his hand straight, fingers sealed together. 'This means lie down and take the count.'

Frank stepped forward, glanced over at the bed.

'Not now, you fool. When you're in the ring.'

'Why would I want to do that, Jack?'

'When I start signalling, you stop thinking and start doing. Your trainer is going to have his own signs, but it's important you understand mine first.'

'Like secret messages?'

'This means get up.'

He placed his fist under his chin and banged it against the bone. Frank touched the base of his chin as he nodded.

'Finish it and get out quick smart.' Jack squeezed his hand around the base of his neck. 'I'm going to start throwing these signals out at you soon, so make sure you've got them.'

'A lot to learn, ain't there? But if you think I'm going to make it big then I believe you, Jack.'

'Rub yourself down. I'll see you out there in ten minutes.' Jack picked a towel off the pile, swung it over.

'Jack, can I – '

'Nine and counting.' Jack checked his watch.

He closed the store-room door on whatever question was lurking in the room. Champagne was up at the wall, replaying the bout: hook, upper cut, jab with the right; shadowboxing his demons. It was a dangerous practice: open an old wound and all that blood could stop a fight; Jack knew how easy it could happen. He rubbed the scarred pad of his right thumb where the nail used to be.

FOUR

Jack's reflection stared up at him from the polished black leather. It seemed a shame to scuff up the soles by walking over the pub's sticky floorboards. But Thursday night was Georgie's night off; Jack always did his research. What with the shoes and taking her up town it was going to leave him a little short this month, but there would be plenty more flowing in soon enough. If he was going to be the big manager he couldn't go around in old postman boots with cardboard filling in the holes and stitching hanging loose.

Heads bobbed up. *Get you a drink, Jack, got any tips for tonight, Jack, when's the next fight, Jack?* The words bounced off him. But he greeted each face with a smile and a nod. They couldn't help being the losers – well, they could, but it wasn't up to Jack to give them a helping hand. He stuffed his hands in his pockets.

Cousin Alf and Newton were the only ones at the bar. Cousin Alf was a man who had seen too many fights, ears puffed up, all the features misplaced slightly to the left, but it had bought him the pub. Jack had bigger ideas than a corner boozer. He nodded at Newton, head drooping over a half-empty pint.

'Evening, Jack. I was just telling Alf here about my boy Jimmy getting himself a new job up at Pentonville prison – '

'Georgie about?'

Cousin Alf rubbed a glass on the corner of his apron. 'Should still be out back with the delivery. I've just got myself a new Morris Oxford – she's parked out there too. Second-hand, mind, but she's got some go in her.'

His shattered nose shone with sweat, but the whole of his face was broken and scarred; the nose suited him. His car was probably clapped-out too; he should have saved for a new model. That was what Jack planned to do. But for tonight Georgie would have to settle for the bus.

'I'll pop and take a look, then.'

'I'll let you take a ride in her some time. But how about leaving the barmaid alone this time, Jack? She's a good worker. I don't want to have to replace her.'

'Won't be a minute, just want a quick word.'

Jack slipped under the counter and closed the door to the bar; propped behind it was a picture of Churchill, glass cracked, and in front beer-crates lined the wall leading straight to Georgie. Her buttocks strained against the seam of her skirt as she bent over and counted bottles. Jack tiptoed forward – one slap of the hand was all it would take. But her head was in bumping distance of the shelf, and she was humming softly under her breath. Jack hesitated; the floorboard creaked. She lifted another crate, placed it on top of the first.

'Peeping Tom.'

'You shouldn't look so good on your knees.' Jack wiped his shoes clean on the back of his trousers.

'I'll have you know I look good everywhere.'

Georgie smoothed a curl back into place; she turned to face him. His jaw dropped in mock surprise. 'Oh, Georgie, it's you. I thought it were someone else.'

'Think you're really something special, don't you, Jack?'

She seemed to slide down the passageway towards him; didn't quite reach his chin, even in her heels. But she stared into his face as if she thought they were the same height. He reached behind her for a bottle. She grabbed the neck.

'Put that back unless you've got money.'

'Ain't you heard the talk? I'll be rolling in it soon.'

The bottle clinked, settling back into place with the others. She folded her arms across her chest. 'No tabs.'

'You'd make a good boxer.' He couldn't help smiling.

'I've seen my fair share of fights. Five brothers.'

'Cleaned them up after a few scrapes, did you?'

'I spent years scrapping for my share.'

Her toes touched the barricade of crates and her shoulders rested up against the staircase.

'I don't want to brawl with you, Georgie. I came to take you out for that drink you promised me the other night.'

'I don't remember promising nothing and besides, I'm working.'

'You finish in…' Jack checked the clock by the door '… five minutes.' He didn't expect the excuses to last long; she only wanted him to think it was her idea.

'I don't know. My landlady expects me in early.'

'I'll have you back in time.'

'Hmm.' She leaned forward, twisted the neck of a bottle until the label faced the same way as all the others. 'Should have asked me before…'

'What's wrong with you? Most girls love a surprise, a bit of dashing *Gone with the Wind* stuff.'

'I don't expect fancy romance, Jack. But I've got rules. You're a sporting man, you'll understand that.' She sighed and pulled out a cigarette from somewhere in the folds of her blouse.

'Christ almighty, I ain't asking you to lay down on the train tracks. A bite to eat. A drink or two. Home by ten. What do you say?'

She took a deep breath but didn't answer, so he stepped around her and took a seat on the stairs. 'Well, Georgie. Seems to me you've got some sort of speech prepared, so spit it out.'

Georgie peered at him through the bars as she lit the cigarette. Her parted legs stretched her skirt wide, feet firmly planted in an upright stance. He heard her voice somewhere inside him, but he was thinking about that cigarette on her lips. No money left in his pocket for a packet of Woodbines. He should have walked out; it really wasn't worth the bother. Georgie smoothed the bottom line of lipstick into place with her thumb, not even pausing to let the smoke escape as she spoke. The banisters divided her up: brown eyes, red mouth, flushed cheeks. She wasn't really like a picture on the wall; if he reached through the bars to touch her skin it would burn his fingertips. But she would look good on his arm out on the circuit. He knew Frank was going to win his big fight next week, didn't need anybody there to hold his hand, only nothing smacked of lonely old codger as much as celebrating on your own.

She finally puffed up smoke. 'You listening, Jack?'

'Ain't no one else here chewing my ear off, is there?'

She was a bit like a Jack Russell Newton used to have; it sat under his stool at the bar, licking up the angel's share. Yapping and taking on anything that walked past. She was talking about promises or something, laying down her laws. Jack never could resist a battler. Maybe that was why he hadn't snuck up and slapped her on the buttocks; she would have bitten his bloody hand off. Georgie stabbed the cigarette through the banisters at him. 'What you laughing at?'

'I was thinking you'd make a good trainer for Frank. Come on, I'm taking you out.'

Georgie sniffed and tapped ash on to the floor. 'Hand me my coat, then.'

Jack snatched the cigarette and sucked down the last rush of tobacco. He took her hat and coat off the rack, drew her closer as she inserted her arms. He put his lips to her neck, she moved her hair aside, and he kissed her. There it was again, that small soft spot. No one had come close to finding his, not since Rosie: lips coated with sugared doughnuts and toffee apples. Georgie was none of those things, but the trace of talcum powder and lavender was warming.

'Do you bring all your girls up West, Jack?'

Georgie jumped off the bus, hopped forward as her heel caught in the grating. Jack bounced her up on to the pavement. 'South of the river can slump into the mud banks of the Thames for all I give a toss. I'm going places.'

'So I've heard, and more.'

She held on to her hat, gazed up at the purple sky snared between the buildings, pivoting, as if she had never set foot north of the river. People began to turn, peering back at her. Jack took her arm. 'Don't believe half the rubbish you hear at the Man of the World.'

'Apart from the chat about Jack Munday being on the up, I suppose.'

She let him lead her along, using the opportunity to check her lipstick in a gold compact mirror. They stepped out of one pool of lamplight into the next, weaving through the mass of swimming silhouettes. The sparkling glass circle lit up her face better than any star.

'What about you, Georgie Smyth with a y? I figured you as someone with plans.'

'Last year I shared a bed with two other girls – now I've got my own room with a sink in it. I'll get wherever I'm going in my own sweet time.' She snapped the mirror shut, slipped it away.

'You've got flaps and traps all over the place. Ever forget where you've put stuff?'

'A home for everything, and everything in its home.'

'When do I get to have a look around in there?'

He slid his hand inside her coat pocket: warm and woollen, neat darning holding the lining together. She extracted him by the wrist, linked her arm back through his. 'When I decide you won't mess up my order, and your hands are clean enough.'

'Don't you sometimes wish you could empty it all out and start again?' He thumbed the direction of the river over his shoulder. 'Money can buy you as many pockets as you want.'

'I wouldn't say no, but it's just as likely to run out as sugar is these days. I make what I make, and it's all mine. But seeing as you're so flush I presume the night's on you.'

'I'll see you right.'

Jack squeezed her arm as they ran between two buses and crossed Piccadilly Circus. The smoking traffic filled the air with clouds, haloed by the neon lights: Schweppes, Votrix Vermouth. Pulsing yellows and reds sparkled in the puddles. Past the theatres, acting out their stupid lives on the stage, thinking they were so grand and noble. City noise: loud as the gym on a Saturday morning. One day Jack would be driving through there in a flash new car, not some battered old Morris Oxford; he wouldn't even stop for the lights.

'Where we going, Jack?'

'The future.' He moved in close against her damp coat until her hair tickled his neck. 'Imagine it's a year, maybe two, from now. We've stepped out of that cab.' He pointed at one squealing away from the kerb. 'Fresh from Frank's middleweight title fight. I'm taking you – '

'Or some blonde like me – '

' – we're off to Soho, drink in any pub we want – '

'We want champagne.'

'Best make it the Ritz, then. Now we're walking off the pig of a hangover that's setting in. Oysters is just the thing.'

'I'll chuck up over your new brogues and suit.'

'I've got a wardrobe full of them. Wheeler's, that's where we're heading.'

'So, it's a promise, is it, this fancy night out some time?' Georgie wagged a finger under his nose.

'Cross my heart and hope to die.'

They turned off Shaftesbury Avenue, into the belly of Soho. Every narrow alley and black-painted door was some private club that would be begging Jack to join soon enough. Rosie would have loved that: candles in red jars and real cloth on the tables. The smell of brine seeped out of a restaurant, washing over the steps, high as a Thames springtide. He paused by the door. 'Put your iron gut into gear for me tonight, would you?'

'I promise not to get sick, Jack.' She tapped his cheek.

'Lovely – let's eat, then.'

They pushed their way into the restaurant. A man in a black suit and bow tie blocked the way. He held a menu in front of his chest as if he could drive them off with it.

'Excuse me, sir, but unfortunately we are somewhat busy this evening.'

'I see a table over there.' Jack pointed through the smoke, towards the corner.

'That one is reserved,' the Stiff answered without even turning to look.

'Maybe it's reserved for us, mate.'

'We are full this evening.' The Stiff stared over Jack's shoulder, pale stubble showing as he stuck out his chin.

'Jack, come on. He means it's full to people like us.'

'What about them lot?' Jack jerked his thumb at three tables pulled together against the wall. Diners glanced up from their white seafood sauces and shell collections to take in the scene. 'No offence, fella, but you look like you've just done a full day's graft down Spitalfields,' he called across the room.

The drunk nodded and sploshed wine on to the white cloth. It left a dark stain. Jack would never do that.

'Those are Mr Bacon's guests. Mr Bacon always books ahead.'

The Stiff held in his breath, blinked slowly. Jack wanted to tell him to go blow smoke up his arse, but a puffy-faced bloke rocked to his feet; his court of men turned to face him. He flicked a napkin against the table, the linen cracked like a whip.

'Find this gentleman and his fine lady a table, Johnson.'

'Yes, Mr Bacon.'

The Stiff gripped the menus tighter, spine so straight it was a wonder his ribs didn't crack as he moved. The man waved his hand and plopped down, dropping straight into conversation with the thin-black-tie-wearing bloke next to him. The Stiff seated them at a table near the back, behind a potted fern.

'This is nice.' Georgie leaned back in the chair. 'I thought you were going to knock that bloke's teeth down his throat.'

'I'm starving.'

Jack picked up a menu. These people, their smart suits and thin ties, made him itch around the collar. *You're good for nothing but a hiding.* Jack had heard those words often enough; they replayed in his head like a scratchy 78 record. But not tonight. He made himself stretch out in the low-backed chair.

'Have anything you want, anything at all. I'm good for it.'

They ordered and ate their way through oysters, cod, crusty rolls and sweet gin, until there was nothing left. He watched Georgie mop up with a hunk of bread.

'That were real butter, weren't it? I can't remember the last time I tasted it.'

'Keep your voice down, they'll think we're animals.' He loosened his tie.

'We're all animals, Jack. Pass us that bread roll if you ain't going to finish it.'

She licked her lips, ran a finger down the knife to wipe up the last of the butter. The pink willow pattern of the china shone through, only small bones left to decorate the plate. Jack downed the last of his drink, gasped like a fish as his throat blazed. He was going to need something to keep the chill off on the journey back south.

'Right, finish up. We're all done. '

'We've only just gone and ordered apple pie for afters, Jack.'

'Couldn't eat nothing more. Why don't you get yourself to the stop and I'll sort out here. Hold the bus for me when it turns up. I'm right behind you.'

'How fast are you going to make me run?' She pressed her elbows to the table.

'What you talking about?'

'Don't piss on my shoes and tell me it's raining, Jack Munday.'

'I always had you down as a sharp one.'

He glanced around at the permanent waves, and tight knots; he wanted everyone to know that he was with the smartest girl in the room. Rosie always used to make him glow like that – the best in any place she went. She'd been a fast runner too.

'You could have warned me, that's all I'm saying. I wouldn't have had that last bit of bread to slow me down. And just how are you going to get us past that guard dog in a suit, Jack?'

He winked at her, got up and reached out for her arm, guiding Georgie across the floor. 'I'm taking the lady outside. She needs a blast of fresh air.'

'Maybe them oysters weren't fresh, because I do feel queer.' She clutched her coat.

The Stiff barred the door with his arm. 'I am afraid I will – '

'It's all right, my coat and wallet's still on the chair. Ask them to keep the pies warm.'

The Stiff glanced over to the table; Jack's coat was there. He held open the door, but Jack could see he wanted to follow them out on to the pavement.

He whispered in Georgie's ear, 'I'm going to walk you up and down past the window. I'll take Old Compton, you head for Shaftesbury Avenue.'

'No, if we're doing this, we do it together.'

The Stiff peered over the checked curtain that cut off the lower half of the window.

'Have it your way.' Jack swung his arm about her waist. 'Three, two, run.'

They skidded around the corner. She was laughing so hard, he had trouble keeping hold of her. Jack slowed down as they reached the theatre crowds, melting into the fur coats and white silk scarf wearers. The spring air was shivering wet, but Jack didn't care. Georgie pressed closer. He remembered the last time he made someone laugh like that; it was a lifetime ago: his cold fingers nipping at Rosie's waist, their wriggling shaking the lamp on the bedside table.

Jack rubbed his missing thumbnail as they hustled down the street. Georgie reached around and buttoned his jacket. 'You'll have to get a new coat or you'll catch a chill.'

'I found that old thing on the bus the other day, been saving it for a special occasion.'

The number three was pulling away from the stop. Jack reached it first, looped his arm around the pole; leaned out, hand extended. 'Jump.' He only had to say it once. Georgie grabbed on tight, fingers pressed to his wrist. Sometimes life offered up things worth holding on to, for a while at least – warm like the smooth boiled stones his mum would put in their pockets on white frost mornings; things that made him want to keep fighting. He held Georgie's hand. Together they ran up to the cauliflower top, flopping on to the back bench; laughing as the bus rounded Eros.

FIVE

The ring is set in the middle of the church hall, marked out by lengths of thick brown rope; it keeps the fighters in but it doesn't keep the laughter out. John wants to throw another punch, puts all his life into it, but his limbs are soft. He takes a breath, moves forward, getting closer to the blond boy this time. Others wait their turn, scabby knees pressed up against the boundary: boys from the gym and St Chrysostom's over in Peckham. John shuffles after his opponent, feet dragging as if they're stuck to fly paper. A buzzing itches inside his ear, left over from the last clout. He slinks away from the dart of spring sun piercing the ring. He rubs a glove over his eyes – still cloudy. The blond boy is close; John smells the blackener on his plimsolls.

He takes a punch on the chin. Knocked spinning. Church-goers stare from the cracked-back Sunday school benches. Posters in pastel shades, reds and blacks, whirl across the wall behind them: *The Right and the Wrong Way, The Meek Shall Inherit and the Mighty Will Fall*. His legs shake; he will fall too if he doesn't find something to focus on. He spots a scrap of paper-chain pinned high up in the corner, left over from Christmas. The newspaper is too far away to read but he sees the headline: *John Munday, youngest ever flyweight champion of the world*. The boy doesn't follow through with another hook. John raises his guard. Head snapping back, he doesn't need to surface for air again: he can touch the muddy bottom of the canal with one lungful, keep his lips pressed tight for as long as his dad can bring a belt down on his backside. *You can't hurt me*. The words rattle in his head and harden as he takes a hit to the jaw. He lifts his arms, the gloves as padded as goose-feather pillows. He brings his fist up under the boy's pimply chin... hits nothing. The boy is quicker than a wasp.

Another sting – John doesn't know where it lands on him, and he hasn't got time to check. He follows the trail of the boy's white legs. One good punch is all he needs to put the spotty fucker down. Defend and attack, that's what they taught him at the gym. But he wants to rip the blond hair out of the boy's head, wants to kill him.

The boy twists, dancing John away from the corner. Hit again. They aren't laughing now. John will take them all on. He feels his vest stretching against his back. The boy is slowing, arms down. John comes at him again; the boy shoves him off. John digs his boots into the floor. But the rest of his body won't listen. He thumps a glove up against his own chest. *You can never hurt me.* A noise comes out of him, vibrating against his teeth. It isn't a cry – too loud and deep for that. The blond boy lowers his gloves, presses them against his grey vest. The room gawps, all those dusty Sunday smirks. But John is only worried about one of those faces. His dad stands up. A bell rings, only it must be in his head: John isn't done yet. He bangs a glove against his ear. The sound stops.

His dad pushes through the neatly ordered rows, kicks the rope, turning the square into a triangle as he gets into the ring. John is in for it now. He sinks his neck down into his shoulders, waiting for the slap. It doesn't come. His dad sticks one cold hand up under John's armpit, taking his weight. John's scuffed boots drag all shape out of the rope; he is guided like a stick through mud. His dad's suit, taken out early from the pawn shop for the Saturday afternoon fight, rubs against the skin under John's arm. They are laughing again. The door slams against the back of John's heels, making him skip forward into the daylight. After the dimness of the hall it is like falling into fire: *all those who stray from the righteous path will burn for all eternity*. His dad wants to take him somewhere they won't be seen – even the All Seeing Eye must need to blink.

John shivers as sweat drips through his cut-off trousers, rolling down into his socks. The ground settles under his feet; his dad is slowing. He hasn't any energy to lift his arm and block the sun; red runs behind his closed eyelids.

'I'm sorry, Dad. Let me back in, I'll knock him down good.'

His dad steers him round to the bike shed, John's bare shoulder scraping along the wall, the vest strap hanging down. He opens his eyes when they reach the shaded side of the building. His dad places his hands to the bricks behind John, holding him up under the armpits, pressing hard enough to make red dust.

'No second places in boxing. I won't be there to save you again, boy.'

'No, Dad.'

But John could have lasted against that streak of piss, lasted as long as it took. He sucks up sticky snot; it catches at the back of his dry throat. His dad lifts up John's chin with his fist, tapping higher, until their eyes are level.

'Tell me, how long were you in there, son?'

John pauses, but can't think what the right answer might be. 'Five minutes maybe.'

'A week, felt like a week, didn't it? Those fools in there don't know nothing. Laughing like that bloody parrot we got stuck with.' His palm slaps the wall beside John's ear. 'Know why I go to church every week?'

John shakes his head then has to close his eyes to stop the world wobbling; nothing is making sense.

'It's because I staked my hand on this life, son, and I lost. Your mother is the only thing I ever won. I can't be parted from her for all eternity. I pay my dues so there'll be something better waiting for me up there. But you've still got a chance.' He flicks John's earlobe. 'Don't get sick on my shoes, boy.'

John twists his face to the wall and a thin liquid, grey as turning milk, dribbles down the bricks. He pulls back his lips, tongue stinging as if dipped in vinegar.

'Don't pay no attention to them cowards in there. Listen to me.'

John lifts his head again, nods, skull weighing as much as a sack of coal.

'They ain't good enough to lick my laces, especially not the vicar and his nose-stuck-up-her-own-arse wife. Our lot used to own half the streets round about, but your aunt and her side robbed us Mundays of it. All we've got left is one stinking house and one mangy bird.'

A face appears around the corner, glasses catching the light. 'Is your boy all right, Munday?'

'He just needs a little fresh air, thank you, Vicar. Kind of you to ask. He'll be right as rain.' He rubs the rim of his cap as he speaks. 'I'll make sure he beats those St Chrysostom's boys for you, next time.' He elbows John in the ribs. 'Apologise to the vicar.'

'Sorry, Vicar.'

'Good, good. Well, I am sure you wish to get the boy home. No need for him to wait for the prizegiving.'

The vicar pushes his spectacles up, nose twitching, then he is gone. His dad spits; it hits the foamy vomit seeping towards John's boots.

'Anyone would think his shit don't stink neither. You worked hard in there, son.'

John sees his chance to win something. 'Bet my brothers wouldn't never get in the ring.'

'They got your mother's soft looks and quiet ways. They do what they're told, shoot where they're told. But they'll never be their own man…'

John smiles, even though his face aches like it is numb with cold; he nods as his dad talks. There isn't even anyone else around to overhear – his dad must be speaking the truth.

'… and your sisters, they got my dark looks – never marry well. Your aunt's got my money – why shouldn't she have my debts too? Let her see my face staring back through those girls every morning at breakfast.'

His dad talks to the corner, but there's no one there. John doesn't want him to stop; he watches the way his dad's eyebrows rise and drop as he speaks. But he has to move, shifting and loosening the old postman boots digging into his ankles.

'But you! That was quite a show. Never even came close to getting knocked down or giving up. Never be a great fighter, mind, not with them plank feet. You've got no grace, no swift footwork. Thin as a canal-weed, and all. But you can take it.' A hand slaps John on the shoulder. 'When's your next match?'

'Junior Southwark Championship qualifiers are July.'

He holds still as his dad unlaces the gloves, yanking them free, releasing a muggy stink like a ripe fart; tying the strings together and slinging them over his suited shoulder.

'What will you do in your next fight?'

John studies his sweaty hands, but they aren't floating up past his face as it feels they should be.

'Win?'

'I wouldn't hold out much hope, boy. But you'll lose better.'

His dad snorts, steps away from the wall; John's knees sink but he stays upright. The bike squeaks as it is wheeled out of the rack. His dad pumps the pedal with one foot, swings his other leg over the saddle, turning a wide circle in the yard. 'Jump, if you want a ride home.'

John staggers towards him, but the bike rolls past too quickly. His dad manoeuvres into a tighter circle.

'Jump, I say.'

John doesn't have the strength to make it back to the house on his own and he can't return to the hall. A cheer goes up inside; someone must have hit the floor. A hand stretches out towards him, sweeping round like the minute arm of a clock.

'Jump.'

John grabs the wrist, sticks the toe of his boot on the wheel nut, feels himself hauled up on to the back. The bike swerves but keeps moving: across the dusty bricks, out through the rusted gates, on to the road. Air hits John's face; he squeezes his eyes against the sun and the grit. He locks his knees, resting up against his dad's spine.

'Will you come to my next fight, Dad?'

'I seen you – don't need me there again. Time to decide what sort of man you want to be. Any old fool can swing a few punches when he's got an audience. But can you stand on your own and take the punishment?'

'I can take it.'

'You're a lucky boy. I never had a man to teach me nothing. My dad, now, he'd give anyone anything, do anything for anyone. Much good his kindness did me and my mum. Old Winifred worked herself into an early grave holding on to that house of ours.' His dad pokes a finger into John's hip. 'Only free dog is one who hates the hand that feeds it, you'd do well to remember that. Make something of yourself. They'll be laughing on the other side of their faces then.'

His dad sticks out his arm, signalling a right turn. John rests for a moment, chin on the top of his dad's head. He blinks down at the long forehead and bony tip of nose, the empty imprint of that pointed finger scalding his skin. He rocks backwards as his dad puffs his lungs out, building up speed to cross the junction of Camberwell Road; zigzagging past the number three bus waiting at the stop – a blur of red metal and pink skin out of the corner of his eye. John wants to hate: feels it like a fist lodged deep and dark in his windpipe, he wants it so badly. A boxing glove bounces against his thigh. He is going to win his next fight, and the next, and the next.

His dad pushes the swinging leather aside. 'Howl again like you did in the ring and I'll pick us up some batter bits from the chippie.'

John thrusts out his chest, hands gripping his dad's shoulders. His mouth is parched but he opens it wide; his jaw clicks: it rumbles out as a low, animal bellow. His dad joins in with a roar as a tram overtakes. The sound shakes their ribs, rattles on down to the spokes of the bike: round and round.

SIX

Fight night had arrived. Jack's cheeks burned as the cold wind pinched at him. He crossed at the fish and chip shop, turning on to Camberwell Road. He always took the long way round to the gym. He couldn't risk catching a glimpse of Albany Basin through the arches; its smell of washed-out bonfires, and the last sulphur tang of a match, was enough to make his breath run short and the back of his knees sweat.

Pearl trotted behind, wrapped up in his mum's old rabbit fur. He should be making sure she didn't twist an ankle on the wet cobbles; she already had a burn on the palm of her hand from filling the tin bath last night. But Pearl would be all right. She never asked about the long-cuts he took, but it wasn't as if she could remember back to that night. His footsteps echoed around the deserted street like applause ringing in his ears. The only light in the road was from the top inch of the gym windows that weren't painted out; the shadows ran like deep scars across the bombed-out warehouses on the other side of the alley.

He beat out a victory drum on the wall as he went in. He parked Pearl in the corner. The noise pounded his ears as if he had tumbled into the public baths on Tanner Street. Men everywhere: in the ring, lounging on the benches, darting between hanging punchbags. Long trousers frayed at the hem and braces stretched tight. The energy made Jack's step bounce; chalk dust stirred in the air. He licked his lips, swallowed the taste. Eyes watching him; Jack straightened his arms to hide the lumpy darn on the elbows of his jacket. He passed a fight at the first bag, twisting in and out of its swinging arch. The two men sparring in the ring were bundled up in sweaters and scarves, wearing more clothes than Pearl. He wondered if they even noticed the landed punches; that must be how she felt, as if blankets had been swaddled around her and she was hidden somewhere inside. Voices called out to him but he didn't have time tonight. All the colours and faces bobbed around in front of him but Jack's eyes were drawn to the only thing that wasn't moving: Frank, dressed in a thick turtleneck and baggy slacks.

'Hello, Jack. I'm all ready.' Frank pulled at the top of his sweater.

Jack stood and took him in: still in the middle range, about a hundred and fifty pounds; on weight for the night, and easily two inches taller than the opponent lined up.

'You look more than ready. You look like a winner.'

Jack pressed his hand down on Frank's neck; his muscles poked through the woollen knit. They were the same height but the boy was thickset, the length of his shoulders straining against the knitted seams, standing to attention like George Sanders. They walked towards Pearl. She twisted a strand of hair around her finger, tried to press it into a curl but it didn't work.

'Hello, Frank.'

Frank nodded and shuffled his feet. Jack pointed at the old duffel beside Frank and Pearl bent down to get it. Frank clung to the bag, the shadow of his eyebrows hiding his eyes. 'Jack said you'd burnt your hand. Does it still hurt?'

'Don't worry about Pearl. She's stronger than she looks. But we can't have you straining something before the big fight.'

'No need for Pearl to carry it. I want to take it. It'll help keep me warm on the journey over.' Frank looked at Pearl and smiled. It was a lopsided smile, as if he had never seen himself in the mirror and wasn't sure of the muscles to pull. Strange that such a boy could be such a man in the ring. Frank lifted the bag into a clinch against his chest. Jack gave it a prod.

'Looks full to me. Remember we said we'd wait to see about you moving in until after the fight.'

Frank kept smiling, not at Jack but at her. Pearl grinned back. What a pair.

'Get a move on, you two.' He ushered them outside.

Open liniment bottles singed the air, the smell of Royston Hall changing rooms powerful as a jab to the face.

'Let's get you sorted, it'll be us up soon.'

Jack laid out Frank's shorts and gloves, unwrapped the new boots from their cardboard box. Jack had spent the last of his money on those black boots, but they would be coming out of Frank's share tonight. The leather smelt fresh but Frank had taken his advice and broken them in during training: chalk dust settled in the stitching and the soles scuffed.

'They're the best boots, Jack.' Frank watched everything Jack touched, ready to give thanks or soak up advice. He thought Jack was bloody Father Christmas.

'You've got to be the part. Can't have you looking like a second-rate fighter – got to look like what you are.'

'Who am I tonight?'

'Frank Bull – good English ring to it. Don't worry, once you're more established you can pick a name and we'll stick with that one. '

'My own?' Frank's voice rose in excitement.

'Well, no. There's a time and place for Irish names but they don't always go down too good. It's like having a stage name, ain't it?'

'But Pat O'Connor is up tonight.'

'Don't worry about what other folks are up to. Trust me. You ain't Irish enough to play that part.'

Jack took out the powder, dusted his hands; it was just like acting only he knew the pain was real enough. He couldn't even remember what the boy's surname was, O'Kearney or O'Keefe, but it didn't really matter. Frank laced up, fresh black socks rolled over the top; he squatted and jumped. The creak of leather could be heard in the room but soon the noises from the hall would wipe out all sound. It always surprised him, the quiet preparations – as if the fighters, with their constant rituals, were praying to something Jack would never understand. Frank wasn't in double figures for proper fights but his routine was set already. It was the same deliberate habit that he performed before every sparring bout and Jack took this as a good sign. It was one of the main reasons he'd picked the boy up. He might not be able to read a newspaper all the way through but he knew his own body; knew the reach of his arm, knew how to perfectly balance his weight while springing from foot to foot.

Frank went to get his bandages signed off. Jack sat on the bench and waited. The boxers with trainers started to arrive. He envied their managers sat out in the best seats of the house, bookies' runners swarming around them. Too much money to be seen backstage where tailored suits and soft leather could catch dirt. Frank's opponent for the night was the last one in. Jack gave a nod as he went past, wrapped in three jumpers, scarf and woolly hat. Ernie was a pro: in and out, no hanging around. He took himself off to the furthest corner. Frank came back in and Jack tested his gloves: sweaty as skin. He didn't want a punch slipping straight off Ernie's chin. He wiped up some grit from the floor, worked it into the tough hide.

'Just get on with what you got to do. Never fight your opponent's battle. Make him fight your way.'

He laid a towel over Frank's shoulders like a cape. But all the time his eyes fluttered over the other fighters, taking in weights and measurements. Pat O'Connor, touching six foot, and Johnny Hall, shorter but solid as a wall, were doing the Grand Ten-Round Contest, on after Frank. Pat was still a concussive puncher but Johnny was on his way out, hands shaking so much that his trainer had to tie up his shorts.

Frank punched out his arms next, sizing up the distance from his fist to the coat pegs, then slowly retracted them –

measuring out his muscles like knots on a piece of string. He didn't notice anyone else in there.

'Stretch those tendons out proper, or your opponent will snap them for you.'

Frank nodded and slowly started hopping on the spot, hands firmly swaddled in his gloves. They were hauling in the remains of the first match. One of the men was bleeding from a gash on his cheek. The other was being dragged in, his boots squeaking behind him on the polished boards. Jack didn't know which one was the winner.

It was their turn at last. Jack pulled away the towel; the boy was warm underneath, not sweating but slowly simmering in the chill air. They marched out into the hall. They had to smash through this fight and they would be on their way up. Bodies were packed on to the benches, lining every wall, zigzagging in front of his eyes. They were there to see Frank fight Ernie. Usually seats stayed empty before the main contest, but tonight word had got around, he'd made sure of that; everyone would see what type of manager Jack Munday was. The empty canvas of the ring was the only space left. Red bruises marked the surface where blood had been worked into the grain. Everybody pushed for a better look at Frank. Jack didn't care if they squeezed so tight that he jumped clean out of his own skin. He tested the spring of the ropes – just enough give. Frank swung himself into the ring. Jack paced the sides, measuring with his steps. Satisfied, he sat down in the front row; Pearl had saved him a spot. Frank searched the crowd for something, turning to look across to the benches. Jack felt as if someone was clutching his lungs, squeezing and releasing out of rhythm. Frank had to win; that grasping need was like falling in love. He tried to steady his breath. Frank stood in his corner. Jack waved and a raised glove saluted him.

The fight began. Frank came out fast, landing blows before Ernie had even left his corner. The peppering shots were to test Ernie. Frank circled, driving Ernie around the ring. But

Ernie was a battler, came back with a left Frank couldn't step out of. He rolled his shoulders into it, landing a punch on Ernie's beezer; it was just for show but the crowd cheered.

Ernie's legs were thickened with age and overwork; he couldn't twist and jump out of the way of Frank's oncoming blows. Now wasn't the time to knock out his opponent in the first round, and Frank held back enough to leave Ernie standing. The first bell went and Jack leapt up to Frank's corner. His skin glistened like a basted joint and a small red welt was forming on his upper left arm, a shadow of the only punch that had made hard contact.

'Keep dodging around him and they're going to think you're yellow. Let him get up close, keep your head covered, take a couple. It ain't enough to beat him. Got to play him, let him think he's getting somewhere then take him out. That's what they've paid to see.'

Jack crouched in front of Frank's stool, wiped sweat from the boy's face with the white towel. The voices and shouts in the hall, the laughter and clapping around him, and all Jack heard was Frank's breathing. Regular and strong, like listening to a baby in a crib. The bell for the second round was going to ring any second but Frank's eyes were already focused, his sweating beginning to slow. It was Jack who felt as if a train was thundering inside his veins.

'Your folks wouldn't half be proud.'

Jack stood up and took himself out of the ring. But he caught the look in Frank's eyes – those words did the trick every time. It was part of their routine. He sat down next to Pearl.

'What do you think?'

'They love him, Jack.'

Jack saw it as they stamped their feet and shouted out, some of the men around him on the benches already leaning over each other, trying to get his attention, calling out encouragement. But Jack didn't care; the bell went, he was lost in the next round. Frank caught a couple of good hits in

57

the second: one to the ribs, one to the back. A small cut opened up under his left eye; that would need seeing to.

Frank managed to control himself until the fourth; the longest he'd been out there on his own, and every minute must have felt like an hour. With a right upper cut he stunned Ernie. Jack saw the old fighter's eyes as they flickered white. Frank glanced over. Jack squeezed his hand around the base of his neck. Frank pressed closer, forcing Ernie's curling spine up against the ropes. *Bang. Bang. Bang.* A burst of hooks so fast that Jack wasn't sure if he counted three or four. He landed one last blow to the right temple. Frank stepped back as his opponent spun in a half- circle then crashed down on to the canvas: KO. No need for the referee to count to ten.

For one moment Jack tasted the frozen silence of the hall; it fizzed and crackled on his tongue. Then the place exploded, louder than the feeble clapping of the other fight. Some even began to throw coins into the ring. It was just as Jack had imagined it would be.

'Frank. Frank!' He fought his way through. Hands tugged at his clothes, slapped at his back, but he had to get to the ring. The smart managers, the shine of silk thread in their jackets, hair slicked into place, began to circle his fighter. Jack made it to the ropes and up to Frank's side. He breathed in the coppery smack of blood, the taste of success. Frank was his fighter.

'We... did it... Jack.'

Sweat ran into the boy's eyes; he tried to flick at it with his gloves. Jack held his head back and wiped his face dry with the greying towel. He dabbed at the small cut, but it was going to need Pearl's attention; she could stop bleeding as good as any cornerman. Together they climbed down and into the crowd.

A thin man in a dark blue suit stood next to Jack. 'That's quite a fighter you've got there. But we all know where good gets you – too much to handle, that's what. My boss might be interested in helping you out.'

All the others with their pushing and shoving but no one banged up against the Thin Suit, a space around his body like someone had taken a lathe to him, sharpened up all the edges. The Thin Suit stretched his arm through the mass and slipped a small bottle of Cutty Sark whisky into Jack's pocket; he did it as smoothly as if he were paying the clipper. Jack was too caught up in the throb to care about having to return the favour some day.

'Pick up the nobbins,' Jack shouted across to Pearl.

He held the rope for her as she climbed in to scoop up the coins, and he and Frank made their way back to the changing rooms. Cards were slipping all over the place, falling like soot from the chimney. Some asking for tips, plans for the next fight, promoter's details, but others were brazen poachers. Jack guided Frank through them all. By the time they made it to the changing room, it was empty. The Grand Ten-Round Contest had started.

'That'll be you out there soon, headlining the big comps.'

'I did… all right?' Frank panted and propped himself on a bench.

Pearl came in behind them. 'The best.'

'See him… take those hits? I landed some good… but he didn't want to go down. I weren't… expecting that.'

Frank tried to lift his hands to demonstrate but they sagged straight back on to his knees. Blood from the cut under his eye dripped down his cheek.

'Stay still, get your breath back.' Pearl stood in front of him.

'I could see… everyone cheering… standing up… but I didn't want to believe… until the ref lifted my arm.'

Jack paced the narrow space between the benches. 'Make yourself useful, Pearl. Clean up that cut and check him over.'

Pearl hung up the fur coat and stacked the coins next to Frank. 'You could've got a fractured rib or muscle sprain when you were fighting. Probably not a dislocated shoulder or your arm would be hanging strangely. Don't worry, I've had them before, I know what I'm looking for. Stand up.'

He did as she said. Pearl was taller than Jack remembered; still growing, probably. Her chin level with Frank's neck. She tapped her fingertips along his collarbones, and patted the palm of her hand down his calves. Jack pulled at his collar. Georgie had said she was coming, but no sign of her yet. Frank didn't move, obedient as ever, his face turned down to stare at the top of Pearl's head. The sounds of cheering, high-pitched whistles, the scraping of benches and fading bursts of laughter were muted behind the wooden swing-doors.

'Get a shift on, Pearl. The boy's dying of boredom standing around.'

'All done.' She snatched her hands away. 'But hands and feet are the most likely places for damage.'

She twisted the end of the bandage covering her palm. Frank prodded under his eye with his glove. 'You couldn't sort out… this cut, could you?'

'Course she can, she carries a whole kit around. Never know when you're going to come undone, do you, Pearl?'

Jack opened the bottle of whisky and took a long draught; the fiery taste grounded him in his body again. Pearl didn't answer but she pulled the small Altoids tin out of her cardigan and set to work.

'Any of that left for me?' Georgie's voice echoed against the tiles as she closed the back door.

'I knew you'd show up.' Jack offered her the bottle.

'I missed your fight.' She took a swig and coughed.

'We won, that's all that matters.' Jack took back the bottle. 'Can't you smell it?'

Pearl tilted Frank's head as she swabbed the cut with iodine. Jack saw Georgie pushing her gloves into her pocket, itching to touch the sweat running down Frank's back. Pearl interrupted him again.

'I'll use the money I collected up to get some more food in, shall I, Jack?'

'What?'

'Frank can move in now, can't he?'

'Just help him get packed up here. Get some beer and I'll see you back at the house. I want to show Georgie around the place first. We've got some celebrating to do.'

He swiped the damp towel off his shoulder and threw it at Pearl, shook his head as she missed the catch; it hit her face before slipping to the floor. With the bottle in one hand, Georgie's wrist tightly gripped in the other, Jack left them to it.

He took her through the changing rooms, giving her a grand tour of the place. The warm feel of the wooden lockers, the crisp lines of the tiles, and the long shadows washing across the floor: familiar smells and sights. But he didn't tell Georgie that, just kept her close and let her see how tall he stood, how easily his dark hair and skin blended into the place. Georgie's fingers sought out his and soon they were firmly latched together. He pulled her around another corner; the door slammed behind them; they were on their own at last.

'Ain't you in a hurry. Anyone'd think you're the one been prancing around in that ring.'

'Last contest will be over soon. But I leave the fighting to Frank. I like to get rid of my energy other ways.'

'I'm glad your fighter won.' Georgie's breath was sticky like the whisky.

Jack stopped to take another drink. 'I said we would.'

'That's quite a talent you've got, predicting the future.'

She draped herself against the wall. Jack moved a finger to push back a curl resting on her forehead. 'Shall I tell you what's coming up next, Georgie?'

'So, now you want to tell me things. Go ahead if you like, tell me.'

'Maybe you ain't ready for it. Have another drink and I'll think about it. I wouldn't want to scare you away with my rare gift.'

She held back a laugh. 'Rare gift?'

'Telling the future. Have another?' Jack waved the bottle in front of her face.

'People have been telling me a lot about you and your sparkly eyes.'

'All the good stuff's true. Stay around and I'll show you. Look, my hands are clean.' He held them up for inspection.

'What happened to your thumbnail – does it hurt much?'

'Been gone for years.' He shrugged. 'One less to scrub.'

She smiled as he touched the neck of the bottle to her shoulder. She took it. She had to stop talking now. He wanted to hear that ringing in his ears again, the heat of skin. She took a snifter then pushed the bottle into his pocket. He dropped his shoulder against her chest and wrapped his arms around her – an underhand move in the ring, but she laughed as he manoeuvred her into the bath area. The tiles were scratched, greased yellow with use, and the copper piping was mottled green in patches. Her high heels skidded beneath her but without them she was too small to reach. Jack steadied her against the wall, pressed closer. He bit the edge of her pink coral necklace: salty as a turning tide. He wanted to breathe her in, to have her smell rub off until he didn't recognise himself. He pushed his fingers into her hair and prised apart the tightly set curls. She pulled his hand away.

'Mind. It took me an age to do that.'

But Jack didn't mind. Her hair was loose enough to nuzzle his face into, searching for the scent of grass and toffee apples. All he found was the chemical smell of permanent wave lotion and the flowery sweetness of Georgie's perfume. But she ran her hands down to the small of his back, tugged him towards her, and it didn't matter any more that she was only Georgie. He just wanted someone. Jack's ribs slotted up against her breasts. He had to bend his knees to get his hand up under her skirt. The material rucked in his fist and his nails caught on the string holding up her stockings. He heard her laugh and slipped his tongue into her mouth to keep her quiet. His fingers eased apart the simmering folds of her camiknickers.

'Rosie…' His voice smothered by her hair.

'What?' Her breath was beating against his chest.

'I said you're rosy.' Jack kissed her again to cover the lie. 'Say my name.'

'Jack.' She jutted out her hipbones, harder against him.

'Jackie. Call me Jackie,' he breathed into her ear.

She murmured the name back to him as she jerked at the buttons on his trousers. He could close his eyes, remember how it should have been. She opened up for him, planting her legs a little wider. He pushed deeper, sucked at the skin around her neck. But that name was still beating in his ears as the blood thudded through him. Felt his back tighten, his legs go stiff. He wanted to return to the first day that his life began: warm blue-sky hours, lying on the hard grass, young enough to think summer lasted forever. *Please, please.* He begged himself not to come before he pictured Rosie's face again.

SEVEN

Someone thumps on the door; John's shins hit the wooden toilet. His trousers drop to his knees. The parrot squawks, woken from sleep, battering its wings against the bars. He bites his lip, flexes his left hand against the back wall. The door is locked; he hopes it is Tommy, that he will get bored and walk away.

'What you doing in there?' His dad thumps the cracked wood.

'I'm done.' John's voice sounds high and tight. He tries to reach his belt, lying across his foot, without making a sound. A grey feather floats in under the gap between the door and the cobbles. His dad paces. John stuffs himself back inside his trousers, gym sub money jingling in his pocket. He rubs his hand down the back of his shirt as he scans the toilet: nothing to give him away. He opens the door.

'Disgusting.' His dad shoves past him. 'You'll go blind, boy.'

John stares at the red bricks of the outhouse but his cheeks smoulder from the inside, heat flushing down his neck. *Look out, look out*, the parrot cries from the cage by the back door. It extends a claw through the bars, but John doesn't have any scraps for it this morning.

'Think I don't know why you get up early before work? No point practising. Who'd ever want you?' His dad stretches his arms against the doorframe, leans out towards John.

The boys' bedroom window creaks open, the scrape of wood echoing in the yard. Tommy, his eldest brother, home on leave, is probably hanging out, trying to eavesdrop for ammunition to use against him.

'God landed me with three boys and not one of them can catch a girl. What a waste of Munday blood. At least Bill doesn't bother turning up here for his leave, getting under our feet,' his dad calls up to the window; the sash drops shut again.

John is glad the morning sun never reaches the yard: it would burn him right up. His dad doesn't bother to close the door, just coughs and shuffles his feet.

'Wait till I tell the men down the factory what I caught you doing.' His dad's laugh is drowned out by a rush of piss hitting the bowl.

John tastes last night's smoked kippers hitting the back of his teeth. He doesn't want to face those eyes down the line of the Bible Factory – fingers pointing, mouths flapping. With the money in his pocket he could just keep riding the tram until he reached a place where no one knew who he was – further than Mitcham this time. His dad keeps talking as he shakes off the final drops. John wants to be somewhere that no one knows his business, no one listening outside doors waiting to pounce. He is fifteen now, as much of a man as he'll ever be. John grasps the coins in his pocket and lifts his feet so as not to make a sound, shrinking backwards into the dark alleyway beside the house. The black eyes of the parrot watch him.

He makes it to the end of Lomond Grove; no one is following. The early morning air is thick as bath steam, a hats-tilted-against-the-sun kind of a day. It presses down on John, making him itchy in his skin. When his dad gets to the factory he will find out John has gone, then they'll all be sorry. He stands in the shade under the trees and waits for a tram. He sticks an arm then a leg into the sun, testing the burning sensation on his skin. It is the kind of heat that boils up a storm. A tram pulls up, he climbs on board and the rush of air as it goes along lifts the sticky sweat from his neck. He even manages to read some of the paper the man in front is holding. Something about that German bloke they are always ranting about, but John doesn't really pay attention until the sports pages. Seemed as if Germany had something to celebrate: Louis versus Schmeling, knockout in round twelve – Joe Louis' first defeat. He wants to read the rest of the fight reports, but doesn't get the chance before the man folds up the pages and gets off at the next stop.

John kicks his feet up against the pole in front and settles on the view outside the window. He doesn't care where he is going, as long as it's away from Lomond Grove, and Waterloo Market, and Watkins Bible Factory: the whole stinking place. The only thing he will miss is the canal.

Brick and tarmac blend to green as they near the Common. The tram slows to round the corner at Peckham Rye, and that is when he sees her. A girl making her way along the path, arms full with boxes and kicking another one in front. Dark hair knotted around her head. She shouts something, craning her neck down towards the boxes; behind her on the Common, a red striped circus tent, a big wheel. The tram begins to pick up speed again. She is getting smaller. John hops over to the doors. If he gets off now it means there will be more days in that factory, smell of ink and burning grease, and his dad's face at the end of the Bible line. Why can't the print machine ram his dad's head on to those blank pages, make him someone else's story? But now he feels as if he could take the house and the factory as his life, because that girl is out there on the wilting grass. He will be docked a day's wages but John doesn't care about any of that; he wants to help her with the boxes. A fair is just sitting there on the Common; he wants to have some fun. John jumps off, the momentum sending him running towards the girl.

'Need a hand with them?'

Her dark hair seems paler next to her dark skin, ripened like the apples she carries. She stares as if he has just sprouted up from the ground. He picks up the box by her feet.

'You'll need more than one hand.' She tips the top box into his arms.

John braces the wooden slats against his chest, tries to pretend they aren't heavy. 'What you got all these apples for? They'll give you gut rot, won't they?'

'You ask a lot of questions. Like a copper or something. No, you're not old enough for that.' She laughs.

John likes the way she does it, head thrown back and mouth wide open.

'I work over at Watkins & Co. Bible Factory. Just thought you needed some help.'

'They might give you the elbow, wasting time out here.'

Her hands are full; John wants to sway forward and kiss her plump on the lips before she has the chance to slap him away. But he doesn't.

'I'll get another job – don't like the factory anyhow. I'm going to be a boxer.'

If he can keep her talking, maybe she won't notice that the top button on her dress is undone, that a piece of white lace nestles on her breast. She has to be sixteen at least: every bit of her pushing out against the sunlight. He smiles at her, walking backwards along the path.

'I can sort you out all the fruit you need. Free. There's farm buildings over Dulwich way store them up all year.'

'That's where I've come from. How do you think I tore my dress?'

'I can jump that orchard wall, easy.'

'Maybe I'll take you with me some time, then.'

She peers over his head to the trees behind. His dad will know John is late by now; the foreman will have crossed out his name for the day.

'We could go now. What about it?'

'These apples will see us for a while, boy. Anyway, ain't you already offered to help me carry this lot back?'

'I can carry them far as you need. My boxing training makes me – '

'I know all about you wanting to box, and being happy to carry a box, and we only just met. Your mum never tell you not to play with gypsies in the wood?' She steps up close, making him step backwards.

'Maybe I want to run away and join the circus.'

'It's a fair, and I'm not a gypsy anyway.' She turns off to the left and walks away. 'Hope you find your circus.'

The grey eyes, the black hair, blue dress squeezing her hips. She is beautiful, like those pictures of ladies on biscuit tins at Woolworth's. But those painted faces never grinned and showed their teeth the way she does.

'I only said maybe. What's the fair like, then?'

She looks back over her shoulder. 'Ever had a toffee apple before?'

She balances the box on her hip, rubs a red apple on her front and bites into it. John shrugs again as if he is some sort of idiot that can't do anything else.

'Cat got your tongue? Where've all the questions gone? I liked the questions.'

He sees flashes of white apple flesh on her tongue as she speaks. He wants to hook a finger inside her mouth, fish out those chunks of sweet apple; teeth aching for it. Just one bite, that's all he wants.

'Come on, then, keep up. If you want to be a fighter you got to be quick on your feet.'

John sticks beside her, apples jiggling and pressing into his bladder.

'What's your name?'

'John Munday.'

'No one call you Jack?'

He shrugs again; he has to stop doing that. She comes up in front of him, so close he smells apple juice.

'Jackie, that's what I'll call you, suits you better.'

He holds his breath, and this time he doesn't back away. But she is off again. Sunshine splits between her legs and he can see her thighs through the papery thinness of the dress. He trots to catch up with her.

'You know my name now. So, what's yours, then?'

'Rosie.' She keeps the apple clamped between her small teeth.

'That's a pretty name.' The words pop out before he can stop them. What a real pillock he is; his dad is right.

'For a pretty girl?' She grins at him, lips knocking up against the apple.

He gives one last shrug. Now they are both laughing. The trees are getting thicker, twisting shadows around them. He smells the sharp dryness of sap. The trams, and the people on their way to work, press around the edges of the Common. But he and Rosie are alone on the grass.

'You're the type my mum warns me to steer clear of.'

'Your mum sounds like she's got some sense, not like her son, offering to carry stuff for any old person.' She shakes her head. But she is still smiling as their elbows brush together with each stride. She gnaws on the apple as she watches him. 'I could have carried them on my own, you know.'

'I know, and I could have stayed on the tram.' He feels sick saying it out loud.

But it feels good, her looking at him. He doesn't care about the loose threads on his shirt or the ink stains darkening the cuffs; doesn't care that his boots are at least one size too big.

'Bet you couldn't carry all the boxes, Jackie. I'll let you have a toffee apple – one of the broken ones but you won't be able to taste no difference – if you can do it.'

'Easy, Rosie.'

The boxing training is finally going to be of some use. He places his feet apart, locks his arms. She dumps the last box on top. He stands tall as the London plane trees, stronger even. Then her finger comes towards him. She wipes it under his nose: smell of apples, something musty like mud. But he holds strong. The finger moves under his arm, wriggling against the worn material of his jacket. He can withstand it all. That house taught him how to hold back a laugh, a cry, even a sneeze. But he doesn't want to any more. She runs her finger down to his waist. This time he laughs, his tongue rolling backwards with the force of it, and he doesn't want to stop.

She stands back with her fists on her hips. 'Knew you couldn't do it, Jackie.'

'Cheater.' He lunges forward.

The boxes fall in a stack on the grass, apples flying and rolling to escape. She is off, shouting out insults; he screams back until his voice cracks. They run in and out of the trees. He chases her up to an oak; she stands behind its huge trunk catching her breath. Round and round they go until he is dizzy with it.

'Jackie boy, Jackie boy.'

She chants his name until he can't remember ever being called anything else. Her special name for him. He makes a grab for her, grazes his arm on the bark. John is still on that tram, at the printing press, stuck in that house. Jackie is free. She breaks away, legs pumping as she sprints across the grass. The sun roasting her cheeks to a bright red, a bird darting past her head, a horn blaring on the road and that is it: the moment. Clear and framed as a photograph on the wall. He knows he can keep running forever. Far, far away from the factory, the house. He is so hot he might explode like an overflowing boiler, but he doesn't care. She is up ahead, circling back towards the boxes and the pool of red apples; he nearly has her. If he keeps going then he knows he'll have the courage to spread his arms around her waist and squeeze her tight. He'll be able to catch her at last. Rosie.

EIGHT

The armchairs were pushed back to their usual positions and Frank's bedding lay rolled up in the corner beside the sideboard. A red apple balanced, dead centre, on the blanket; Jack gave it a quick punch and it disappeared down into the folds. He opened the sideboard drawer: the bright white paper of Frank's contract sat on top of his dad's souvenir Luger and his mum's wedding ring; the house was overflowing with dead husks. Even his pyjama bottoms were old as a relic: wearing thin, the blue stripes as faded as the veins beneath his skin, and a cold draught ate away at his ankles. But none of that mattered as long as he had that contract. Jack carefully closed the drawer.

'Shut that door,' he yelled out to Pearl.

The back door slammed as he stopped to pick his mac off the coat-stand. It was supposed to be May but the house hadn't caught up, it still held the damp of constant April rain. The house was bloated, doors didn't close and windows were swollen shut. Jack used to think if he pulled up the carpet runner that started at the front door, reached along the hall, up the stairs and touched the threshold of every room, then he could yank out the spine of that place.

He propped himself against the kitchen door. 'Where's Frank?'

'Out running. He told me yesterday some boys followed him and threw mud.'

'He'll have to handle a lot more than roadwork if he wants to be a fighter. It's all part of the training. What you doing?'

'Porridge and golden syrup.'

She kept stirring and clouds of steam rose up around her; the walls were stained yellow from years of cooking.

'I never eat that muck.'

'You ain't in training. This is for Frank.'

He and Frank were due at the gym soon but he still had time to sit and get warmed through by the fire, drive out the lingering sickness of last night's beer. Georgie had kept him drinking in the pub all night, celebrating his winning bet on Bruce Wells getting gold against Max Resch in the European Amateur Championships – one in the eye to Germany again. Jack had lost some on young Cooper getting knocked out, but it didn't matter; he was still quids in. He reached for the bread bin. His tongue felt raw and furry as if he'd been licking the rug in the front room – the dirty patch under the table that Pearl thought he never noticed. He tore off a chunk of bread; with Frank's weekly money coming in now they could even afford Robertson's Golden Shred, not the old stuff that ran off his knife like water. Pearl made sure that most of the money went into feeding up the boy: like breeding dogs, fighters had to be taken care of to get the best out of them. She was finally realising that they had to be together on this. They were a team.

Jack put the jar down on the cracked dresser, ran his finger down the break in the wood and smiled. Pearl paused with the dripping spoon in her hand.

'Tell me where you're off to – you've got that funny look. What you thinking?'

'Can't I even eat in peace?'

He hated the way she dug for information: what are you doing, what are you thinking, what was it like when Mum and Dad were both here? Always full of questions, always searching for stories. Well, some things were his alone.

'Careful with that flame. I bet you've burned yourself now. Check it.'

'It's just another scar.'

Pearl dunked her hand in the sink. The old stone was fractured in places; teardrops of water swelled on its side.

Nothing much had survived in that house without being damaged, and that was true long before Hitler dropped his bombs.

'What do you think about doing this place up once the money starts rolling in, Pearl? We could start again: fresh paint, bright colours. A new kitchen like the ones in Georgie's American magazines. White walls and wire furniture, a new white cooker.'

'A white cooker? I like the place as it is, just like it used to be when Mum was here. She said Dad picked out all the paper. It'd be like getting rid of them.' She checked her palm for blisters.

Every time he heard Pearl talking about his mum and dad, Jack felt Rosie's small hand tapping him on the shoulder, pulling at the hairs on his neck. *What about me, Jackie?* He had to concentrate on Pearl, she was still talking – if he could just make out the words, the walls of the room would come back into focus.

'... some new clothes maybe. My frocks don't fit and I ain't much good at taking in Mum's stuff, even though Georgie said she'd help me.' She held up her sleeves for a closer inspection.

'Don't listen to everything those girls in tight tops and fake pearls tell you.'

'Georgie says everyone's got permanent waves these days. Do you think I should get it done?' She pulled at a loose strand of hair.

'No, I bloody don't.'

Rosie's curls sprang so tight when they were wet that they seemed to be climbing back into her head. He swore he still found her hairs sometimes, draped over the back of the chairs, in his sheets. Pearl didn't need curls.

'But Georgie – '

'No.'

The back gate closed with a bang and Pearl jumped up. 'Frank's back. I ain't finished his breakfast yet.'

Footfall echoed through the alley; he almost felt the vibrations in the bricks. No one had run through that passageway for years.

Pearl called out to him, 'Frank, come and sit by the stove.'

'I just... need... to cool... first.' He clutched his sides, woollen jumper and serge trousers splattered with black mud.

'I'll leave the door open for you.' Pearl went back to the porridge.

'I can close... it if you're... cold, Jack.' Frank's breath raced away from him; forehead beaded with sweat, dark patches staining his old sweater.

'You're all right, mate. I've got the beer chills – nothing's going to warm me up but another pint.' Jack shivered.

'If... you're sure.'

Frank dragged a chair into the doorway, sat half in, half out of the room; he hesitated as Pearl handed him a mug of tea and the bag of sugar. He rubbed the pink scar under his left eye with his thumb. The boy couldn't even make his mind up about which way to stir his spoon, as if he'd given himself up to fighting and everything else was only a confusion. Pearl perched on the edge of the table. Frank leaned over, pressed the back of his hand to her mug.

'Bit hot... for you.'

'Thanks, Frank.'

'How far did you get this morning?' The manager in Jack was waking up.

'To the warehouses... the canal. Back up the green. I didn't stop... once.'

'Good, about another half-mile on last week. But stay away from the canal. Those paths are slippery.' Jack stood up. 'We're seeing that new coach of yours later, so save something for him. I'm off to get dressed then we'll head to the gym.'

It wasn't so bad having Frank at the house all the time. He stayed out of the way, worked hard at his training. It was nice to know that on the evenings when Jack made it home there would be someone else sitting in the front room. Another body sprawled in the armchair, someone to cover the hours of quiet when he and Pearl had nothing to say to each other.

Jack could hear them downstairs, chatting in the kitchen: Pearl's small voice, the odd low response from Frank. He smiled and felt sorry for Frank. Pearl had a habit of talking at people, blathering away like one of those birds that learned to repeat sentences. *Who loves you, who loves you?* The parrot used to cry the words over and over, banging its beak against the cage outside the back door. It had belonged to his dad's uncle, left to them in the will instead of the money his dad had always thought they were owed. Feathers grey as a stormy day and a crown of red perched on its head. The bird had lasted a good few years, longer than most things in that house ever did.

Jack slid off his pyjama bottoms, sat on the bed to get changed. He hated the room, and Pearl was always asking him to swap, she liked the blue flowered paper and the twisted brass of the bedstead, but he wouldn't let her have it; the room had a bad feel to it, a sulphur smell in the air. His dad used to sneak them aside, whisper lies in there. *You're my favourite. The others are no better than a pack of worms. But don't tell them, they'll only be jealous.* Even now Jack heard that voice inside his head; the screeching of the damn bird had drowned it out for a few seconds, but it was Jack who silenced it for good.

NINE

'Someone close that door, or am I going to have to get up and do it myself?'

The kinds of questions his dad asks never have answers that John wants to wait around to hear. But it will only be worse if he doesn't show his face. John goes into the front room, closes the door behind him. His dad sits at the newspaper-covered table, making two piles of coins. John rubs at a grass stain on his sleeve.

'Better keep those paws to yourself, boy. I know how much is on the table.'

John stands up straight, wedges his hands deep inside his pockets. His dad fingers each coin in turn, nails tap-tapping as he tallies up the count. All John's sub money is spent. He crosses his fingers, hoping his dad won't ask him for change. His thumb gets caught in a hole in the left side of his trousers; something his two brothers must have left behind during the time they had spent in that hand-me-down woollen pair. But neither of them has ever had the day he just did, his cheeks burning from the sun and the taste of sugar on his lips – worth every penny. Being with Rosie is worth whatever is coming. She sent him back to the house but she wouldn't have if she knew.

His dad opens his mouth but he just swallows down air and doesn't speak. John frees his thumb; he'll need his balance if his dad makes any sudden move. His dad stacks a handful of coins, patting the top with his palm.

'This pile's for your mother. It's short because of your slacking today. Think work grows on trees, do you?'

'No, Dad.' John keeps his eyes on his dad's hands.

'Well, printing on paper all day, now that does grow on trees, don't it?'

John raises his eyes to his dad's chest. 'Yes, Dad.'

'Look at me, boy. All the way now.'

John does as he's told; his dad's eyes narrow as he grins. John may only be fifteen but he knows that however much is on the table it won't be enough to get them through the week without eating porridge for every meal. The door opens and Tommy is standing there, arms and legs poking out of a suit long past ready for the rag-and-bone man. And the other dad is back, the one that gives him pennies and ruffles his hair; the dad who only appears when other people are in the room.

'A little bird told me you were out with some girl today. Well, I can understand that, even if your mother wouldn't. But us men have got to stick together. This is for you, son – go and buy your girl something nice.'

His dad slips him a coin. Maybe today will stay a good day after all. But that smile is tightly sewn into place, pulling the lips back to reveal sharp pointed teeth. Those dark eyes and that spiked mouth catch hold of Tommy.

'What you doing skulking around? When I was in the Great War…' His dad is pointing above the fire.

Tommy obediently looks at the picture but John catches him sneaking sly glances at the grubby hand holding the coin. John creeps from the room then darts out the front door when he knows they can't see him any more. He is nearly as big as Tommy now, but he still needs to get to the shop before anyone tries to take the money away from him; Simmonds' Grocers is closest, but Potter's has nicer things. He runs along the street without stopping.

On the way back, the yellow pocket mirror he has bought Rosie sits, cool and smooth as an apple, in his hand. The taste of toffee hangs on his tongue; he sucks out a last fragment caught in his teeth and remembers the warmth of the day. It is getting late but he doesn't even care that there will be

77

porridge for dinner. He needs to hide the mirror under his bed before anyone sees it. He is going to scratch *from Jackie* on the back. He makes his way through the alley before the darkness can pull him down into the muddy ground. But he isn't a boy now; thoughts like that only belong in nightmares. He stands by the parrot cage at the back door; the feathers glow like a ghost hovering inside. John presses his face to the wire – the bird blinks then goes back to staring at its reflection in the saucer of water. He only looks away when he sees his mum through the kitchen window.

'John. Any later and you'd have missed dinner, then what would we do?'

She beckons him with her finger, lifts up a steaming spoon of porridge, her cupped hand ready to catch any drips. He is too old for things like that, what he feels for Rosie proves it, but he lets his mum have her little boy stuff one more time at least; he sucks a burning lump into his mouth. He sniffs soap and the sweet charcoal smell of fire on her fingers. She winks.

'I put some butter in, just for you. You'll be big as your father soon.'

'Can't come soon enough.'

The parrot chatters in its cage, his mum stirs the bubbling porridge, and no one hears Jackie's voice. He slips the mirror away. Strands of hair escape from the bun at the back of her head and lie like straight threads of black cotton over her shoulders. He turns to watch the flames. But someone else comes into the kitchen.

'There you are.'

His dad has him by the arm. The face pushes closer, nose pressed to John's forehead. Wet breath hits his eyelashes and John stares at his boots.

'Where's the money, boy? I'll give you one chance to give it back.'

Rarely is there shouting in the house but the constant drip of lies eats away at John like rain weathering the doorstep.

78

His dad's grip tightens. 'The little thief skived off today and stole your housekeeping money too.'

'Why do you do these things, John?' His mum shakes her head; the spoon plops down into the copper pan.

He is losing sensation in his arm, hand hanging limp; he wants the numbness to spread through his body. His dad grabs hold of his shoulder, nails digging through material into skin, jarring the bones together. 'I'll get the truth out of him, Ada.'

But his dad can't lift him high into the air, can't make him feel as if he is dangling above a big hole – not any more. He is shoved towards the stove instead. The back of John's calf catches the edge of the grate; the scream is molten in his throat.

'It's no good crying now, boy. Lying, thieving little bastard. I bet he spent all the money on sweets. Show me.'

John tries to keep his jaw locked but his dad prises his lips apart. A finger is inside his mouth, the blackened nail scraping at his teeth, trawling for evidence. John swallows down the bitter taste of Bible Factory ink that has soaked into that skin over the years. Another finger reaches into his pocket and starts up a search.

'Maybe he's hidden the money.' His mum turns to him. 'John, tell us where it is.'

Tommy walks into the kitchen, attracted by the sound of a row. He stands in the corner by the dresser, smiling, and waits his turn. John tries to cough up the taste of ink.

'Tommy, son, you were there. What did you see?'

'I saw him do it, Dad.' He chews his nail and passes the lie without blinking.

John knows every debt has to be paid, knows this will be over quicker if he keeps his mouth shut, but Rosie's smiling face, her grey eyes glow in the embers of the fire beside him. He can be what she thinks he is. He can be strong. He can try.

'I never done it,' John whispers.

'Are you calling me a liar?' His dad's voice is cold and low. 'Are you calling your brother a liar?'

He slides the yellow mirror out of John's back pocket; lifts it up for the room to see. Light catches the glass; it winks. His mum reaches out for it, holds it up to her face.

'My birthday's next week. Maybe it's for me.'

'No, Ada. It's for some tart, ain't it, boy?' His dad shakes John's arms until the tremor spreads up his neck.

'Turning against your own mother like that.' His mum bends down, pushes the mirror between the bars of the grate. 'It's only bad luck if I smash it.'

The fire licks and consumes it, cracking and snapping. The grip on his arm slackens; John drops to the floor. His mum keeps her back to him, warming her hands by the stove. He has let them both down, Rosie and his mum. He doesn't blame her for not wanting to look at him. He blames his dad.

'Get out, I need a word with the boy.' His dad speaks and everyone leaves.

John waits but the belt doesn't come. The parrot is talking to itself, loud enough to be heard down the corridor. His dad opens the back door, throws the porridge spoon at the cage. The parrot is shouting now.

'Damn bird. You better shut that bloody creature up or I'll whip you in front of that girl. Won't be such a cock of the walk then, will you?'

John pulls himself up; he could run for it but his dad is still fast; he'd have John by the neck before he made it to the street.

'I mean it, boy. Now.'

John tries to hush the bird, puts his fingers inside the bars. But it pecks and scratches. The parrot plummets from its chewed wooden perch to the newspaper-covered floor of the iron cage. It bangs its beak into the bowl, trying to join its reflection. Water spills; shredded paper and dust swirl in a dark cloud around the bird's wings. Alone, it begins to scream.

'I can still hear it,' the voice rings out. 'Bring that bloody thing here.'

John unhooks the cage, but he knows that isn't going to make the bird quiet.

'I'm going to teach you a lesson, son. You might think you're the big *I am*, going round with girls, but you've got responsibilities, debts you owe me and your mother. It's about time you learned to be a real man, ain't it?'

'Yes.' John stands with the cage in his hands. The bird screeches, its cries getting raspy.

'How you going to shut that creature up?'

'I could feed it something.'

It is the wrong answer; his dad's eyebrows are still hunched together.

'I could cover its cage up.'

A blast of wet air explodes from his dad's nostrils. Still wrong. John has to be a man. He puts the cage on the dresser, opens it up. The metal door gives a loud cry of its own as he reaches inside. His dad peers closer.

'That bird's never been nothing but bad luck – take, take, take all the time. Never gives us nothing but shit and hot air.'

The parrot screams and screams. John doesn't feel the clawing, but the feathers stick like needles. 'Shut up, shut up,' he hisses. But the parrot won't listen. John squeezes his hands around the thin body, traps its wings. The battering of its heart is faster than the spin on a motorcar wheel.

'That's it, boy. Show it you won't take no more. Stand up to it.'

Shut up, shut up. He sees the nod of his dad's head and the rustle of newspaper as he settles back in the chair by the stove. *Lying, thieving little bastard*. John tightens his grip; the parrot fights against him. *Shut up. Shut up*. The parrot's black eyes blink. He has to make it stop. He squeezes until his knuckles crack, until bones crack.

'What have you done?'

His mum is behind him; he can't make himself turn around. The parrot won't stay still, rolling, but it is his hands shaking not the bird waking up, rustling its feathers, plucking at itself as it did in the mornings.

She pokes his shoulder.

'John. Show me.'

John the son, not John the father. She has it all wrong. *He* did this. John turns, offers up the lifeless little body. Something cold and sharp as the bird's beak about the look his mum gives him. She takes the parrot, holds it gently against her cheek, its claws curled up like snapped fingers; listening for something: a heartbeat, a whisper? *Who loves you, who loves you?* The broken neck swivels back but the dead eyes are still on him.

'I told you we never should've taken that thing in, Ada.' The voice is angry again. 'You haven't got time to take care of all of us.'

The paper drops down, sheets drifting across the room, a finger points at his mum and John steps in front of her. The porridge steams and pops behind them. She knocks against John to get to the stove; pushing the bird back into his hands as if it is scalding, but he won't touch it, not again. Grey feathers flutter; the body bounces once as it hits the floor.

'That parrot never lied and cheated me out of what was mine, not like my own son.' She lifts the pan and sniffs for burning.

His dad laughs. 'You better get that cage cleaned out. I can sell it down the pub, seeing as we can't ask for money back on the mirror. Every debt has to be paid…' The voice trails out of the room.

The bird lies by the empty chair. John pokes a wing with his boot; it fans out like the pages of a freshly printed book. 'I'm going to kill *him* one day.' The chair shakes as he grips it tight.

'Don't speak about your father like that. *He'd* never give my birthday gift to someone else. I thought you were different

82

from your brothers and the Winnies. Thought I was enough for you.' She bangs the pan in the sink.

'I've been saving up for your present, honest I have.' He wipes his sleeve under his nose. His mum points at the floor.

'Stop snivelling. It's your mess. Clear it up.'

John gets down on his knees, scoops up the paper and covers the bird. He sees her brown leather boots leave the room: no hand to tap his cheek, no soft brush of her apron. She is gone. And he is gone.

Footsteps thump around upstairs, trampling him. He runs out of the house into the alley. He shudders, watching the shadows from the bedroom as they slither across the muddy yard. Nothing left for him here. John Munday is dead. Hot sick hits his boots and brown lumps lie in his hand. The remains of that sweet toffee apple sink into the dirt under his feet.

TEN

Jack pulled on his shirt and waistcoat, the arms threaded through from the night before. Pearl and Frank were talking in the kitchen. It was good to hear voices in the house; it drowned out the whispering echoes that had never left. He smoothed his thick hair into place with Brylcreem until it was black as pitch, pushed his chin out a little further. He swung the jacket over his shoulder as he went downstairs. 'Get a move on. We've got work to do.'

Frank came out of the kitchen. Jack had a surprise for him; he couldn't let his fighter look like a tramp. He undid the parcel on the coat-stand, brown paper and string drifting to the floor; he tossed the new jumper to Frank. Pearl stood in the doorway to watch, her fingers tugging and curling at a strand of dark hair. Jack knew the importance of warm, quality clothes even if she didn't, but then she'd never really gone without.

Frank held up the pullover; the bright white wool glowed in the dim hallway. 'It'll fit perfect, Jack. Better than anything I've ever had.'

'Make you stand out at the gym, won't it? Put it on – you'll get a chill in that old rag you've got on. I got you one too.' Jack dropped another sweater into Pearl's arms. 'Man down the market was selling off his old winter stock cheap. I got a better price for two.'

'Thanks, Jack.' She smiled and came towards him. 'Yellow's my favourite.'

'Enough fuss. Let's get going.' He sidestepped her, rapped his knuckle against the door to speed Frank up.

It was warmer outside than in the house; a buttery daylight covered the pavements and buildings. They headed up Lomond Grove past Mrs Bell's, smell of mangy cat and flyblown bread; the hardware shop on the corner, sticky tar and chalky carbolic. Jack could find his way around by his nose alone. Bombs had stomped out the northeast corner of Addington Square, the top end of Medlar Street, and most of Hillingdon Street was flattened. But when Jack turned down Cowan Street flashes of light from broken glass and weathered rubble made it seem as though the old Watkins Bible Factory had risen again; hot ink and a dampened paper smell hung in the dusty air. *Wot no bibles* daubed with red paint on a heap of bleached bricks. The past always found a way of squirming back into your life like that, smacking you in the face. But there was Frank now, trotting beside him: something to work for.

'Hey, Frank,' someone called from the other side of the street.

'Keep walking, Frank.' Jack gave his shoulder a prod.

'We not good enough for you, that it?' Spider crossed the road.

'Course you are. We're late, that's all.'

Frank shook hands with him. Spider was followed over by others, all dressed in slick suits, greased, sprouting hair at the sides of their faces – cosh boys. Too young for the war to have knocked any sense into them; too busy humping and snarling like a pack of dogs. They sprang from foot to foot, jostling each other; now seeming like four, then, with a shuffle and punching of arms, like six. He couldn't keep track of them all. But the mouthy one was Spider and Jack thought he recognised the others, except the two girls hanging from Spider's thick arms.

'Good – thought what with your big win we heard about, you might have got yourself airs and graces. Looking after him, are you, Jack?'

'Like he said, we're late.'

Jack coughed and spat on to the street as he lit a cigarette.

A web of fine scars was etched on to Spider's square face, the kinds of markings a boy got from having his head smashed through a window. Jack had heard talk about the kid, but most of it probably got spread around by Spider himself; he thought he was something big but the little rat didn't have connections, didn't even have a family. He always stuck his chin out as if he was proud of his face somehow. Jack just thought it was ugly.

Spider draped his arm around Frank. 'Come on now, Frank. You forgot to tell us where you were moving to. How we supposed to keep tight if we don't know where you're at?'

'I was going to tell you. I've been busy.' Frank rubbed his head.

They carried on talking but Jack watched the two thin girls, arms tightly linked through Spider's. They puckered their lips, pointed their hips towards him and then at Frank. But Frank smiled and his eyes slid on without even noticing the push of their breasts under tight woollen cardigans. Jack blew smoke at the one with narrow ankles and red knees; she didn't even have the decency to blush. One of the other boys stepped up.

'We got you something, Frank.'

He handed Frank a large heavy rectangle wrapped in a dust-sheet. The boy wiped his hand through his nest of brown hair, and the sheet was covered in greasy fingerprints. Frank lifted a corner and peeked at the package. 'Chocolate!'

'We done a delivery lorry at Blackfriars. Can get you stockings and smokes too if you need anything, Jack?'

Spider pulled out a small blue notepad, flicked it open with his stubby fingers, his knuckles grazing Jack's wrist. Jack stepped out of reach of those white hands, blue veins running under the surface, cold as marble despite the warmth of the day. He patted Frank on the shoulder as he turned away. 'Put the chocolate in your bag, Frank. A bloke could get lynched with that much sugar. Don't flash it around at the gym, neither.'

Spider called after him, 'We're not doing no harm, are we? I meant what I said, Jack. I can get you anything you want. Not kids' stuff like chocolate. Any friend of Frank's is a friend of ours.' He kept his arm around Frank's neck, elbowing, laughing, swatting the girls away from the chocolate, but not loosening his grip.

Jack lit another cigarette, shaking his head as he walked away. 'I need you at training, Frank. Catch me up when you're done.'

He didn't need to get dragged down by that lot, and a banged-up boxer was no use to him. But it'd be a crime to let good chocolate go to waste. They were just boys really, all teeth and ears, nipping at ankles like pups. It was a good job Frank was living with Jack: it meant he could keep a tighter leash on him. Spider was always foraging for something, he'd be fat given enough time; but he wasn't likely to make it through to comfortable old age. His sort never lasted long; they always ended up picking a bad fight, one they could never win.

Jack waited in a patch of sun that slithered across the bomb site between the factory rubble and the church. In the distance, wrecking balls hovered over Peckham like bluebottles. Jack could almost smell summer in the air, the Thames tide carrying it up from the coast: fish and chips in newspaper, sweet melting ice cream.

'Sorry, Jack.' Frank was back at his side.

'Thought you said you were going to stay away from them lot.' He stubbed out the cigarette on his sole, pocketed it for later.

'They just wanted me to have this.' He held up his prize.

'Don't go sharing it around with girls, Frank.' Jack shook his head; those cheap pieces of skirt would drain Frank of energy.

'Pearl likes chocolate, don't she?'

Frank's fingers were agile; he worked quickly, pulling and yanking the bag to make it fit. Another few years in the ring and Frank wouldn't even be able to uncurl his fists. Jack helped him squeeze the slab away.

'No distractions from training before a fight, remember that.'

'No chocolate?'

Jack laughed. Frank slung the bag over his shoulder. 'So we can eat some after tea tonight when we get home, can't we?'

'Just stay out of trouble.'

Frank would have to be out on his own one day. Jack couldn't afford to keep waifs and strays the way Pearl used to. He picked up the pace and they were at the gym in no time. They were the first there, the front doors propped open, but only the lights over the ring were on. Jack rested his arms on top of the canvas.

'Warm up. Bert'll be here soon.'

He watched Frank put on his boots and climb over the ropes. Somewhere in the store room Newton was working his second caretaker job: moving boxes, shifting mats around, familiar noises and comforting. Newton banged through the door, heading for the washroom. His tin leg swung too far forward with each step, his body shuffling to catch it up.

'Hello there, Jack.'

'Your boy Jimmy not earning enough up at Pentonville to let you quit one of these jobs yet?'

'He's a good son, Jack. Chaplains earn a fair bit but I don't want the boy's money. Work keeps me out of trouble.' He straightened his brown caretaker's coat and kept going.

Jack turned his attention back to the ring, the vibration of the canvas throbbing through his arms. 'That's it, hold your guard up, feint with your right and follow up with a jab to the left.'

'Coaching him yourself, are you?' Bert came up beside him.

Jack had to stop himself from grinning like an idiot and pumping the little egg-shaped man's hand; slam him down and he would bounce right back. Bert taught his fighters to do the same; that was why he was a name on the scene.

'Just breaking him in for you. Got a couple of local fights coming up, but next real money-maker's set for September.'

'Better find out if he's going to be ready, hadn't we?' Bert fitted his glasses into place.

Frank leaped and jumped. Energy buzzed through him. He was faster than the dust that he stirred up, moving through the light. Scouring shapes into the canvas with the pattern of his footwork: triangles, squares, circles. Jack always liked the order of boxing. He used to wish life were more like that, when a fighter was quick enough to second-guess his opponent's next move. Bert leaned in closer.

'Push off with your left toe when moving right. Push with the right to move left. Step into the pain. Everything in fighting is backwards. That's the first thing you've to remember.'

He didn't say anything more, but he did keep licking the end of a pencil and making notes in a brown book. Jack couldn't make out what the scribbles meant.

'I don't need to tell you he's good, Bert. I know people who'd kill to have a hand in training my boy. But I'm offering it to you first, out of respect.'

'No one's got proper respect for their elders these days, so says my wife. He's got a good right hand, though, I'll give you that.' Bert rolled up his sleeves. 'I like him enough to take half the money now, half when he wins.' He slapped Jack on the back. 'We're on to something all right.'

Jack sat back on the bench to watch the rest of the session but he couldn't get those words out of his head – a static pulse like the air before lightning. Good times were coming: Jack Munday the great boxing manager.

'It's not just the way he moves, is it?' Bert tucked his pen and paper away.

'No, he's one of the few I've seen with *it*.'

Bert nodded. Most betters looked at the form, past defeats and glories; the scouts looked at technique and style. But Jack studied the eyes. Anyone could learn the tricks of the trade but no one could be taught to want to win; they had to need it more than breath itself. Jack could never tell the reasons why, and some of the most hard-done-by and toughest souls he had ever seen didn't have it in them. It was just that one look, and sometimes it only appeared for a single fight, once in a life. But it was always the same: a glassy blackness like that strangled parrot's eyes.

It was drizzling when they left the house. Pearl had been carrying on for days, baking and washing, but it was only the Coronation, another backside on the throne. The homes with television boxes were easy to spot: front doors thrown open to let in air, front windows full of bobbing heads. Other families sat huddled round radios ready to catch every description relayed to them. More good suits were scrunched up in those rooms than Jack had ever seen in one place before. All dark browns and greys, hats and headscarves perched on laps like paper flowers; it reminded him of funerals.

He turned up his collar and kept moving. The rain made his hair into a mass of wire and his socks soaked up puddle water until even his shins felt damp. Frank and Pearl were squashed under an umbrella like gnats above a puddle, never once colliding or jumping out of the way: hovering. Poor Frank, she must have woken him at the crack of dawn with her pacing and banging: ironing her dress twice, scraping fish paste on to bread, polishing shoes.

'Why ain't you wearing your support shoes? I paid good money for those.'

'I don't need them all the time, Jack. I can wear sandals.'

'Won't be saying that when you get toe curl or break an ankle. You know what the doctors said…'

Frank held up his elbow.

'Here, take my arm. I'll make sure you don't trip.'

The closer they got to the Man of the World, the more people blocked up the street, joining the rainwater flooding through the gutters. Pearl and Frank trailed behind him. It would serve them right if they got lost in the push; so many people that the pavement disappeared under a stomping army of feet. The pub was closed but the lights were on in the flat above. Jack banged on the door; Cousin Alf came down to let them in. He wasn't really family but that was what they'd all called him since they were kids hanging round the tap to collect their dad's beer. Pearl pulled Frank into the hallway; Cousin Alf made room to let them through.

'We're staked out like garden fencing up there. So you'll have to take the windowsill seats. But that shouldn't matter to young things like yourselves.'

It would be as full as those front rooms they passed: no air to breathe. Jack stared at the narrow stairway, the peeling paint, the wet black footprints on the boards. 'Think I'll leave you to it, Pearl. The food'll last longer. You've already moaned about me eating the last of the chocolate. Frank, you want to join me at the pub? I'm off to catch Georgie.'

'Thanks, but I'm looking forward to them fish slices Pearl's made.'

Cousin Alf shrugged. 'You'll miss the fireworks, Jack. Old Eli's got some for later. He's setting them up on the bridge over the Basin.'

'No, I'm going to get off. And Pearl – '

'I know, I know. Don't go near the Basin or I'll get hurt. We'll see you later, then.' She waved as she trotted up the stairs; Frank close behind.

'Come and find me at the Anchor when it's all over.'

Jack set off on his own. He kicked at a leg that swung too close to him. Shouts and cries slapped against the wet bricks as he turned on to Camberwell Road. The crowd became one heaving mass and Jack found it hard to tell which arms were his, which two feet he had to keep marching. It was like drowning. Rosie's dress had billowed around her head, turning black in a creeping line from the hem to the waistband, before she went under; that was long before January's North Sea floods burst the banks of the Thames. All around Jack, summer dresses and Sunday suits were soaked through but no one seemed to notice. Everything darkened when the air was full of water. It had been raining that night at Albany Basin; the black muck had stung his eyes as he grasped for Rosie's blue flowered dress. But he wouldn't think about that; he tapped the bed of his missing thumbnail. The Anchor was up ahead, wedged between two thin warehouses, set back from the scrabbling of the street.

A wet wall of noise hit him as he pushed open the heavy wooden door. Throaty choruses of some old song, the sort his mum used to like, rolled over the flagstone floor; someone banged their fists on the piano. The notes got lost in the cry. Jack almost toppled over against the weight of it but shoved his shoulders forward to the bar and shouted out his order. He would feel better when he had a beer in his hand, more part of the mass, and the prods and jolts of elbows and knees wouldn't feel like hands trying to hold him down. That was what they had done on that wet evening years ago. The rusty hook slicing through the black water; trying to swim after the hem of Rosie's dress, but they had him: landed like a newborn, dragged up on to the mossy cobbles. The bargemen steaming as one sat on his frozen chest, the other pinned his legs: a tangle of limbs like being caught in the bedsheets by a nightmare. And all that time Pearl screamed and screamed until all she had left in her was a high squeak like the swimming rats. Jack was glad she wasn't with him in the pub. Sometimes he needed not to be near Pearl. He half drained the pint when it came, one swift mouthful, and even joined in a chorus of 'All By Yourself in the Moonlight' before he went looking for Georgie.

He found the three of them in an alcove at the back of the pub. She was with a friend, all tightly curled hair clamped to their heads, clothes that looked ready to slip to the floor at any moment. The boy with them looked as though he was about to slump too: tie yanked down, collar dirtied, and cheap blue suit.

'Started already, I see.' Jack sat next to Georgie.

The bench felt warm, tucked away from the door and its draught. The still air was so thick with gin and port he felt drunk just from taking a breath; his limbs sinking and his face tingling. The boy topped up Jack's pint with gin, drops splashing on the table as his hand shook. Jack took a slug; the vapours kicked inside his chest.

'Back early from that family do, ain't you?' Georgie slurred, dragging out the last word.

Her curled hair unravelled around her neck, her blouse drooping open. Jack wanted to run his finger along the full length of her throat. He inched up against her, felt the rise and fall of her chest.

'I left them to it. Ain't really my thing.'

'Celebrations? Or families?' But she held her fingers up to his lips, pressing back any answer he was about to give, and snorted down more gin. There had only been him and his mum and Pearl for so long. Pearl was lucky, Jack thought. But she had heard from his mum so many tales of the good days, when all the Mundays had lived under one roof, that sometimes for seconds at a time Jack had even believed the lies himself.

Georgie rubbed at the skin under his sleeve, gold rings tugging at the roots of his hair. 'You staying out for the night, then?'

He nodded.

'About time that girl had some fun on her own.' Her eyes rolled slightly from the drink as she spoke.

'Expect she'll turn up soon.'

Jack looked up as the door opened; it wasn't Pearl. A round girl was sandwiched between two soldiers, spilling out of her dress, turning to whisper behind her hand to each of them. Georgie squeezed his arm, her breasts squashing up against him. 'Sure you can trust Pearl to find her way.'

'Frank's with her, so she'll be all right.' His eyes rested on the next button working loose on her blouse.

'Frank? He the one you were telling us all about, Georgie?' The girl stuck her head across the table.

'Maybe he'll teach her how to have a good time.' Georgie winked.

'Don't be disgusting – they're more like brother and sister, just kids really.'

'I've seen that fighter of yours. Bit ginger for my tastes but you don't have to look at their faces when you've got a sportsman like that, does you, Georgie?'

'I think it's sweet. They're both a bit lost, ain't they?' Georgie cooed.

The other couple went back to clinking glasses, wet lips and heavy-lidded eyes sagging from the booze. Georgie's tongue darted to check the lipstick at the corner of her mouth. But he didn't care about that smudge of red.

'Not all girls need it regular like you do,' Jack whispered against her ear.

'I'm not complaining, just said it'd be nice for her.'

'She's got her head stuck in some comic most of the time. She's a good kid really.'

'You saying I'm bad?' She ran a finger along the ridge of his thigh.

'Right down to your marrow – that's why I'm here sat next to you.' He pressed his lips to her neck.

'Cheeky bastard.'

'Not interrupting anything, am I?'

A thin bloke stood next to the table. Jack was just about to tell him exactly what he was doing; but there was something familiar about the shiny suit and peaked features.

'How did you enjoy the whisky, Jack?'

The burning peat taste in his mouth, the cool shadows of the changing rooms, the silky feel of Georgie on his fingertips.

It all came back to Jack as if someone had sucked him right out of the pub and dumped him on the cold cobbles. The Thin Suit blocked off the rest of the room with his coathanger shoulders.

'The whisky,' Jack repeated the words like a stuck gramophone.

'My boss likes quality.'

The Thin Suit didn't seem to be moving at all, not even breathing. But his big pale eyes protruded further from his head with each blink.

'Your boss...' Georgie's friend started to laugh. Her bloke had enough sense to shut her up, gave her arm a yank; the Thin Suit blinked again as she popped free of the table. Those narrow-set eyes watched the couple push their way up to the bar. He sat down in their place, smoothed a wrinkle from his dark suit, his head rising above the back of the booth. Jack wished the pub would go silent to make sure he caught every word the man had to say.

'That was a nice snifter.' Jack tried to keep the excitement out of his voice, but under the table his leg started twitching. Georgie laid a steadying hand on his knee.

'That's why my boss likes your fighter. Quality.' The Thin Suit opened his mouth wide to pronounce the last word.

'Frank's going to be the best...'

He didn't bother to finish the sentence; the man knew all about that or he wouldn't be sitting opposite Jack.

'My boss has been keeping an eye out for a boy like yours. Both of you are getting quite a name for yourselves round here. Didn't take me long to find you.'

The Thin Suit lit a cigarette, fingers long and unbending like sticks. He offered the packet to Jack, who shook his head, but Georgie grabbed at it. That was another mark on Jack's slate.

'Who's your boss, then?' She blew smoke across the table.

'Why don't you go and help with the drinks.' Jack stood up to let her out.

95

He was pushing his luck, he knew that. She clucked deep in her throat but went up to the bar anyway. Jack watched her leave and sat down so fast he nearly slid clear across the bench.

'Thank the boss for the whisky.' He raised his voice as the piano kicked to life again. He wanted to lean across the table, shake the man's hand, grasp at any offer with both fists. But he leaned back, folded his hands away behind his neck, pretending to hold back a yawn. Every game had its rules.

'My boss would like to be friends with you and your fighter.'

Jack shrugged. 'We've got friends.'

'My boss understands that there's only so far you can go on your own. He thinks you could make some special progress together. I'm acting on his instructions. To you, right here and now, I am the boss.'

Jack slapped his hands on the table, leaning forward. 'I don't deal with middle men.'

He couldn't help himself; he felt that tightening hand around him, wanted to kick free. The Thin Suit nodded his head slowly, running his hand down the back of his neck as if he was counting the bumps on his spine.

'But let me get you a drink, a thanks for the whisky.' Jack took out his wallet.

The Thin Suit smiled, the front teeth off-centre, and rose out from the alcove. 'It was just a bottle, nothing more than that. I'll talk to my boss.'

He gave a nod and snaked his way out of the pub. Let the *boss* come to him, Jack was someone now. He stuffed his empty wallet back into his trousers, and made his way into the crowd. Georgie popped out from the mass around the piano, grabbing his elbow. She squeezed him into the space between the wall and the upright mahogany. Jack let himself become one of them again, but he was on the up. Before long the Thin Suit's boss, and, who knew, maybe a hundred others, would be after making deals. He wedged himself close behind Georgie, warm and solid, her buttocks grazing against the front of his trousers. Jack was thirsty for it: for her, the money, the deals. He grabbed her breasts from behind. 'Where's that drink?'

The squeal of her laughter melted into the next song. Jack was in there, shouting himself hoarse with the best of them, 'God Save the Queen', his hand sliding down to Georgie's waist. Frank already had five fights and five clear wins to his name – not big purses, granted, but people were taking notice. Jack bobbed to the surface every time; nothing could keep him down.

Bunting and flags hung sodden from the trees and littered the ground: a dawn without sun. The house tilted out into the street as if it wanted to slump face-first into the gutter. But it hadn't fallen yet. Nothing moved, not a twitching curtain or stray mog. Jack made himself go down the alley. It wasn't anything but a stinking dark place, no different from half the passages in London. Gin coated his mouth and he spat the taste of it into the mud. Pearl never showed up at the pub but that wasn't what had kept him awake at Georgie's; it wasn't even the threat of the landlady coming back early from her sister's in Eastbourne. He couldn't sleep anywhere else but that rotten house. When he stayed there, at least he had those few brief seconds, before fully waking, when he felt Rosie's shape patted into the mattress next to him. There didn't seem much point in sleep without it.

Jack stood at the back door. Mrs Bell's ginger tom waited on the step; it was always trying to get into the house. Jack raised his foot, and its slit green eyes widened, but a noise drew his attention.

Frank was running up from the far end of the road, his footsteps a thudding heartbeat in the empty street. But Jack wasn't the only one watching. Someone stepped out from the bomb site on the other side. Frank came to a halt then slowly started to run again, only this time on the spot. Too far away to hear what they were saying, too long just to be passing the time; Jack knew who the lurking figure was. Who else but Spider would be squatting in dark spots? The stooped shoulders and thick neck, hat pulled down tight. Jack wanted to call Frank back, bring him quickly into the house, but Pearl was sleeping upstairs. No point the whole street waking early.

The house was dark, no decorations hanging from the windows or doors. It was as if yesterday had never happened. But he still felt himself walking tall after that visit from the Thin Suit – despite all the gin, he remembered that clearly. The rest, he had about drunk enough to forget.

Frank turned towards the house, ran across the road. Jack stepped out from the overhang of the front step. 'Morning.'

Frank pulled up sharp. 'Hello… Jack. Didn't… see you there.' He was out of breath; been wasting it all on that fool Spider.

'Good run?' Jack smiled at him.

'Not bad.'

'That chat at the end must have put some seconds on your time, though.'

Frank glanced over his shoulder to the spot he had just come from and then down at his feet, his face puffy as the clouds tumbling overhead.

'I know… I said I wouldn't… go round with Spider no more but he came to see me. Just… hello… check how I'm getting on.'

'You're on the up, Frank, can't afford for old connections like that to drag you down again.'

'I know, Jack. I said so to Spider… After telling me about this department store – '

'I don't want to hear what it was.' Jack snapped his teeth down on the words.

'I told him I couldn't… told him it's all about the fighting now.' He did a couple of jabs at the shadows.

98

Jack put a hand on Frank's neck, guided him through the front door. Just enough light to see by in the hall. Jack hung up his jacket.

'Where did you and Pearl get to last night?'

Frank paused long enough to get his breath back. 'Nowhere. I mean, it was so busy Pearl didn't want to get pushed around in some crowd, so we came back here. I got an early night for training this morning. Pearl went straight to bed. I don't know what else she did.'

The words came out in a rush of steam. Frank hugged his arms around his damp jumper, shivering like a soaked cat.

'Get those clothes off. Get some breakfast down you. I'm going to get a couple of hours' kip then I'll see you at the gym.'

'Right you are, Jack.'

The floorboards groaned as Jack made his way along the upstairs landing. He knew every crack, every loose nail of that house, but there was light on the landing that morning. Pearl's door was ajar as if someone had just left the room. Jack crept to the edge of the carpet-runner. A fingerprint of blood marked the crumpled sheet, and he wondered how she had damaged herself this time. Pearl wasn't moving, just a bundled-up lump lying under the blankets. He used to watch her sleeping as a baby, plump legs and arms protruding from hand-knitted woollen suits. His mum liked to keep herself between him and Pearl. No one to stop him now. Pearl's breathing, the slow rush of air, was like a draught from the window. He didn't cross over from the rough carpet-runner to the warm boards, but he didn't shut the door either.

Pearl was the only thing he hadn't ruined in his life, and even that wasn't quite true. She came out of that night at Albany Basin all wrong: no feeling of pain, no cries to warn them when the food was scalding or the shoes too tight, just the web of scars and bruises on her numb skin. Watching her sleeping, he couldn't help wondering if it all could have been different. It was easier to imagine the way things should have been when she was still and quiet. But Georgie was right, she wasn't a kid any more, and now there was Frank to look out for too. Frank was down in the kitchen – the soft padding footsteps. It was a relief to hear something other than the sound of Pearl breathing. All those years she had been on the other side of the wall, that snuffling breath all he heard until he thought he might go mad from it, wanted to hold the pillow down on her round face just to get some peace.

Jack pressed his hands to his ears but it only made the sound louder and he let his arms drop. *The forces at work*. Jack heard his mum's voice of disapproval trapped in the grainy surface of the floorboards. The forces his mum always complained of, the things that made people do bad things. The forces that finally took her away: fear of falling under a bus, fear of leaving the house, fear of eating bad food, until there was nothing left to do but curl up and die. Fuck that; Jack could fight them all. But some nights, when he was younger, he used to wake up, shivering-cold, worried that he would do something to Pearl, hurt her somehow. A bit of his dad left on him like a sweat stain. Then there were other times, stranger times, when Jack saw her, when they weren't squabbling or rubbing each other up the wrong way, and he knew he'd rather suffer anything, rather die than see her cry. What was that? It didn't matter if he was a *fucking waste of Munday blood*; he had heard that all before. He was there to make sure Pearl made it through to the very end. Jack crossed the hall to his room and lay down fully clothed on the covers. Arms and legs spread wide, knocked out for the count.

II

★ PERSONAL ERROR ★

'Roughly described, "personal error" is the time which elapses between the mind deciding on an action and the body getting to work to execute it.'

Boxing, A.J. Newton

PROGRAMME

Saturday, September 12th 1953

Ireland v England

Grand 10 Rounds National Contest

FRANK BULL
Camberwell

vs

BILLY JONES
Ireland

6 Round Contest

Rory Murphy
Ireland

versus

Jerry Brown
Notting Hill

Special Notice
Free Seats For Patrons.

Seats for this Hall will be given away at each show to holders
of lucky programmes. All programmes are numbered;
please check your number with those called from the ring.

ONE

A new arse on the throne for well over two months now and another two wins for Frank; Jack felt stupid even thinking it but things did seem different. A brighter tint to the sun outside; people let their smiles linger a little longer. He shifted on the stool at the bar. Only just after six-thirty; most fools hadn't found their way in yet, just Jack and a couple of old timers in the pub nursing bottles of stout. Georgie was due in soon; Jack ordered his first drink of the day as he waited for her. Over breakfast he had decided that she was going to be his lucky rabbit's foot for the night. It was time to do more business, and he had some promoters coming to Manor Place Baths off the Walworth Road. The Thin Suit's boss would be there. Jack knew there was nothing to worry about, but he didn't want to tempt fate. The first hit of beer soothed his mouth. Still, he couldn't shift the congealing taste of worry that lodged in his throat.

Newton sat down next to him. 'Seems like it might be a nice one this evening. Don't you think, Jack?'

Jack took another swig.

'Got any plans? My wife made me get one of those television sets for the big occasion. Thought we might keep it. Come over if you want, bring Pearl. My Jimmy was outside the Abbey – they filmed him at the celebrations, you know? My boy inside that box. Ain't that funny, Jack, about Jimmy?'

Jack lit a cigarette. Newton might have lost a leg before the war but he talked so much that sometimes Jack would have willingly given him his own leg just to get away. That tin peg of his didn't even creak enough to act as a warning signal, and now Jack was stuck with him until Georgie arrived. He scanned the room for somewhere else to take his pint, but in the end he didn't even need to move from his seat. Jack reached behind the bar and scooped up a copy of the *Daily Express*. Christie's face plastered across the front page again, his dark eyes peering out into the pub – a face to make a child cry. Jack read the pages and ignored the ramblings of Newton. But bits of Newton's life filtered down into Jack's head and he lost his place on the page. Jimmy doing well now he was a fully signed-up member of the cloth; Jimmy doing the Lord's work with all those sinners up at Pentonville; Jimmy thinking of buying a car; Jimmy looking to move up in the church ranks. Newton did a good job of selling his chaplain son. If the tarts in the paper had had such a good salesman behind them, maybe they wouldn't have ended up in Christie's downstairs pantry. Jack licked his finger, turned the page.

The newspaper called them *young ladies* but everyone knew what they were. Jack didn't have a problem with them: worse ways to earn a living, like down the docks or at the meat market, chained up in a factory. Jack didn't know how Pearl stood it every day at that pastille place, coming home reeking of blackcurrant, but he supposed she had nothing better to do. Jack pitied people who didn't have plans. All Newton did was drink and spout rubbish about his blessed son. He pointed over Jack's shoulder at the picture of Christie.

'Jimmy hears some stories up at the prison. The war damaged a lot of those men.'

'Maybe it did. But we don't all go around strangling women, much as some might deserve it.'

Jack gave up on the newspaper, left it open on the bar. But he wanted to ask Newton if the rumours were true, if Christie really did those things to the women when they were lying warm but dead, the things they wouldn't report in the paper. Newton's son must know; he worked at the prison, after all. Jack felt the weight of change in his pocket, enough for another pint for himself and one for Newton. If he just topped

Newton up with another drink the information would come flowing out. That would be a tale to tell down the gym.

But it was something his dad always did: offering up treats when he wanted something, throwing out punches when it suited him, and driving apart his family until each stayed in their own corner of the ring. Jack let the coins slip between his fingers. Newton could buy his own drink, and his son could go to hell. Jack, son of John: two separate lines on the census that never had to meet again. He flicked ash to the floor. The old timers rambled on. One of the men raised his glass at Jack.

'What regiment were you in, son?'

They were talking about the war again, and Jack didn't know what people had ever had to speak about before Germany had set its sights on running the world.

'I did my bit.'

Newton wiped the beer from his lips. 'Your brothers were with the East Surrey lot. But you were in the ARP, weren't you, Jack?'

'A fit young man like you should have been off fighting somewhere.' The bloke next to Newton wrinkled his face up into a frown. They couldn't have been much more than forty years old but Jack did look like a young man next to them. Their faces were bleached as the paving slabs outside the pub and just as cracked.

'Well, I weren't. I were here, saving your home from burning to the ground.' Jack took another mouthful of beer.

'Still…' Newton's voice trailed away.

Always that doubt hanging in the air. He'd been nineteen when he'd signed up; the war was meant to be his way out of it all. Collapsed arches, the medical slip said. Jack had hoped they wouldn't notice like the trainers down at the gym hadn't, but one doctor with a vicious streak wide as London Bridge got him discharged on to civilian duties. Jack got stuck in the ARP along with the schoolboys and grandads. Hanging round the bases organising fights wasn't enough to earn respect, and sometimes Jack would wait hours at his post so he could leave after blackout. With the collar of his coat turned up and the helmet under his arm he could almost pass for wearing a uniform as he slipped through the dark streets.

'Been waiting long for me?' Georgie held on to the pump; he hadn't noticed her come in. 'What can I get you, Jack?'

More questions, always questions. The men gave him sly glances, nodding at each other. He pushed his empty pint away.

'This one's dead. I'm done with it.'

'Suit yourself.'

Georgie's mouth shut tight as she snatched the glass away; she would sink into a sour sulk if he wasn't careful. Her eye-teeth had a sharp little way of cutting into her bottom lip when a mood came on her, and he'd seen her snarl at men on the other side of the counter. Jack didn't want her ruining his luck for the night. He followed her down to the other end of the bar, reaching across to take her arm.

'It's a big night for me. Got to be ready to duck and weave. In my head I'm already there, if you know what I mean. But I did want to see you.'

'A punchbag you want, is it? Well, I ain't swinging your way.'

'Not even this Friday? Come up the house. Pearl's doing pie and mash.'

Jack touched the cuff of her blouse; his fingers slipped inside and rubbed the small round bone on her wrist.

'All right, then, I'll get off early, Jack. But I like gravy not liquor on my pie.'

He held on to her sleeve, a white cotton blouse with silver buttons worn to a silky finish with age, and beneath it Jack almost thought he could see the rippling of her skin. He wanted to breathe her in.

'Better get off now before you lose some of that edge.' She slowly untangled herself, heading to the pumps. A ladder threaded its way up her left stocking and he wanted to put his finger inside to feel her warm skin. Stockings were safe, something he never saw before the war, something that wouldn't spark to life the memories of before: summer evenings lying under the trees on the Common, Rosie's white socks and lace-up boots threaded between his legs. Jack followed the line of Georgie's stockings up to the hem of her dark green skirt. He tried to concentrate, imagining her thighs spilling over the tight string garters. He felt a tingling at the tip of his fingers just as if he had been stroking a rabbit's foot; but he couldn't hold Georgie, couldn't drag her out from behind the bar. The sweat was building up beneath the wool of his suit, nipping at his skin. He liked to do business that way, the thing he wanted just out of reach, and it made him run faster than a dog at the track.

Manor Place Baths felt as if it was on fire, and Jack had stood near some giant blazes in his time. The exposed bricks of the walls and the wooden floors pumped out more heat than they ever did on washday when the coppers boiled and spewed. Bert was there already. Jack leaned against the pillar beside him. 'How you doing?'

Bert nodded in reply, small and round as a ball, securely tucked into a starched shirt. Rolls of fat threatened to spill over his trousers, and Jack could count the wisps of hair on his head. Even his glasses were little circles of silver metal, but there was nothing soft about him.

'Full programme tonight – doubt there'll be any surprises. I've warned Frank to take it easy. We've got a proper fight next week.' Bert folded his arms, one on top of the other.

'My boy needs to be seen by the right people.'

Jack strained his neck, trying to spot other faces in the crowd. The bell for the first fight sounded. He stood up straight as the crowd began to push around him. The names were called out: Big Roberts from out west in the left corner, and someone or other over in the right. Bert rocked on his heels to get a better view of the ring. Jack turned away, tilting his head back to take in the baths. The Thin Suit was easy to spot in the mass of Burton's tailoring – the same long legs and arms but the cloth looked different, a chocolatey brown this time: made to measure. A big bulk of a man walked behind, the Thin Suit sweeping people aside. Jack wanted to know what it felt like to lead your life at the head of the procession. He nudged Bert. 'Hope they're coming our way.'

'Be careful what you wish for. I've got to see a man about a dog.' Bert ducked his head and was gone.

Jack willed them closer: step to the left; don't talk to that bloke, he's nobody; keep coming; this way. The Thin Suit stopped, indicated the man next to him. 'Jack, this is Mr Metzger. He takes a great interest in new fighters.'

Jack wanted to stamp his feet and tell the world he was right – they had come for him. Heads turned: Jack had arrived.

'Only the taxman calls me Mr Metzger. The name's Vincent.' He didn't try to raise his voice above the thud of fists and whistles from the crowd.

'Good to meet you. So you've heard about my new signing?' Jack held out his hand.

Vincent gripped it with a firmness that didn't match his velvet voice. Gold watch, cufflinks, and two rings; Jack had never seen so much metal even in the pawnshop window. It gave Vincent's skin a yellow tinge; with the black suit and black hair, it made him look like a wasp. But somehow, staring into those green eyes, Jack didn't find the picture funny.

Vincent lit a cigar.

'My Frank's the best you'll see here tonight, best you'll see anywhere – '

'Slow down, boy. We don't talk business in public. But I do need a drink.'

A cloud of dusty smoke filled Jack's nostrils, dry as burning leaves; he tasted money. He looked at the Thin Suit, wanted to tell him to hold the ice, but he didn't seem the type to take backchat. The Thin Suit clenched and released something in his outside pocket; it made the muscles on one side of his neck tremble like piano wires.

'Get yourself one too, Jack. I never trust a man that don't drink.' Vincent patted his arm.

He wasn't anyone's skivvy but a drink would hit the spot. It was probably one of those test things. Vincent wanted to see what drink he came back with. Jack nodded and walked off. The hall was thick with smoke and the scent of whisky slipping off the cracked white tiles. Jack knew most of the men in there hadn't suffered under rationing, he could see it in the strain of their seams and the brightness of their skin. But those blokes were old, their turn nearly up. Jack lit a cigarette. Even in his cheap suit he was better turned-out than those overfed lumps. The other promoters were easy to spot: people moved around them thick as flies, but they kept to their own corners. Hands waving, arms locked, shifting footwork. Let them step out of his way. No one noticed the knocked elbows and spilt drinks; they had other fights going on. Jack was sharp as the clink of glasses and the scratch of fountain pens.

The tray of drinks sat in front of him: bottles of dark beers, sediment settled in the bottom, a clear liquid perfumed like gin. Off to his left the bell for the next fight went. Frank stood in the blue shorts, Champagne in the red. It wasn't a real match, just a bit of display: some good technique, swift footing. Champagne kept to his role as journeyman – moving Frank around, showing his best side. The seats in front of the low ring were taken, ice cubes melting from the heat off the fighters, the sweetness of booze replaced by liniment and sweat. Spider stepped up to the table, pressing his palms down beside the bottles; his shadow seeped into the wall.

'Evening, Jack. Frank's doing good. Bet you're glad I let you sign him up.'

'Don't even think about lifting any wallets here.' Jack blew smoke into the space between them.

Spider waved his hand. 'Nah, I'm not into that no more. That Vincent Metzger you were talking to?'

111

He scratched a fingernail along the deepest scar on his cheek.

'Course it was.'

Spider stuck out his chin and nodded. 'What you talking about?'

'That's man business, son.'

'You're a funny bloke, Jack. But I seem to recall I did you a favour by letting you take Frank on. How about paying me back?'

Jack handed a bottle of beer to Spider. 'Take this, son. Now walk away before it all ends in tears.' Some day someone would teach the boy a lesson, but Jack didn't have time to get distracted tonight. He picked up two glasses of whisky from the tray and carried them back to Vincent. He wanted to feel the golden liquid, smooth as Milandu toffees, slip down his throat. He stubbed out the cigarette on a pillar as he passed, stretched the cuffs of his shirt.

'Here you go.'

'Bottoms up.' Vincent sipped his drink. 'Good choice.'

Another suit had appeared next to Vincent, and they were staring at Jack like a couple of magpies: one for sorrow, two for joy. Vincent waved at the suit with his hand.

'This is Harry Starr. He runs some business out on the Mile End Road.'

Harry sniffed in Jack's direction but kept his hands firmly clasped around his walking stick; a bronze dog's head reared up from under his palm. Jack had seen him on the scene before. He dressed to match his name: sparkling. Vincent put his hand on Jack's shoulder.

'What do you say we all have a chat some time?' He smiled. 'Harry's got a few interesting stories, Jack. I think you'd like to hear them. Not here, though, the noise gives me a headache.'

'My boy's in the ring now. Fighting fit.' Jack glanced over: Frank's head ducking and swaying, his body hidden by the crowd.

'Showboating, Jack. I don't take any notice of it. I'm here for a pleasant evening with old pals. Come to the club and I'll introduce you.'

The Thin Suit flicked out a bright white card, scissored between his fingers. He raised an eyebrow at Jack. But Jack didn't need any encouragement; he grabbed it. He couldn't have done much better if Solomon himself had been there – promoter of champions. Vincent downed the drink and handed back the glass. Jack watched them leave as Bert sidled up next to him. He wouldn't have to wear old-style jackets and darned socks for much longer.

'We're in the big time now, Bert.'

'Don't give up more than you have to, don't let them get one over on you, and don't ever cheat them.' Bert squeezed his folded arms over his chest, forcing out the words in one long breath.

'I know how to take care of my interests.' Jack laughed at the lines on the old man's face. 'You only have to keep your eye on bringing Frank's left hook back faster.' He pointed at the ring. Champagne had the power, muscles thick as brick walls, but he was slow; he got an uppercut in but Frank spun off and came back with a jab from the right. Champagne went down. A roar went up.

'Knockout in the first round. Hope Vincent caught that on his way out. Frank don't know how to go easy.'

'It won't just be about Frank no more. Sign up with that lot and it's about you too, Jack.'

The waiting fighters helped Champagne out of the ring, and threw a towel over Frank's shoulders. The next pair was up on the canvas before the blood had hit the ground.

'If I get in with Vincent we'll all be rich. Money's my business. You want to see him be a middleweight champion, don't you? Well, we can't do that without them backing us.'

Bert put his arm around Jack's shoulders, hauled him closer until all Jack could hear was Bert's voice in his ear; he still had quite a pinch on him.

'Remember what I said to you. Vincent's only about the money.'

Bert let him go. Jack watched him take a seat at the side of the ring; he didn't know when to relax. Jack could outsmart any of those old cocks. He dropped the glasses on to a trestle table by the door. Bert spent all day and night fretting about his fighters – the cuts and strains. But Jack had it bang up to the Elephant; nobody stood a chance of getting one over on him. Laughter and shouts of encouragement filled up the hall to the high glass ceiling. None of them knew what Jack could do. He had missed opportunities in the past, taken the knockback, but this time he would beat the lot of them to the punch.

TWO

Another win for Frank; he beat down Jimmy Flash in a four-round walkover. Jack rubbed the white card in his pocket. Vincent had been waiting a week now, and Jack would make him wait some more; it didn't do to look too keen. A bottle of Courage clinked against his knuckles. Frank would be back at the house already, but Pearl would see he was all right; they deserved a drink. Two boys thundered past him, towels flapping over shoulders, boots kicking up the dust of Addington Square, straight over the brown mound of earth, no railings to keep them out. Pink clouds leaked across the sky above them like streaks of blood tingeing a water bucket. Jack checked the card again to make sure it hadn't slipped through a rip in the lining. The warm evening made the streets sweaty with children: chasing tyres and pushing prams, high fluttering voices rolling out from alleyways.

Mrs Bell was balanced on a chair outside her house, a broom handle shaking above her head, trying to knock down the framed picture of the Queen above the door. Her cat cried as it zigzagged between the wooden legs.

'Evening, Mrs Bell. '

'Oh, dearie. Get this down for us, would you?'

Jack nudged the ginger tom out of the way. The rickety seat creaked as she got down and he stepped on. The bedroom curtains trembled and a hand disappeared. Jack didn't care if Mr Bell never got out of his pit again. He pulled at the nail sticking from the brickwork. Mr Bell used to be friends with his dad, as short and fat as his dad was tall and thin. They were always chatting over the side fence or walking to the pub, deep in conversation. Jack never understood how no one else saw his dad for what he really was: the way he swished side to side faster than a cat's tail and you never knew which side of the whip you were going to be on. One final yank, and the picture came free.

'There you go, Mrs Bell.' Jack jumped from the chair and handed her the frame.

The name suited her too: pinhead then flaring out to a round body and trunk legs. The cat clawed at the grey socks around her ankles. She rubbed the glass against the fat roll of her breasts.

'Agile, even with your flat feet, aren't you, dear? Coming in for a cuppa?'

'I'm due back, sorry. '

The cat followed him, slip-sliding between his feet, trying to trip him up.

'I haven't seen much of Pearl lately. I've noticed a boy hanging about, though. Had a letter from the Winnies, they were asking after her. She keeping all right?'

'Fine, fine.'

Georgie was walking down from the other end of the road. She waved, her tight jacket and blouse lifting up as she raised her arm.

'I didn't know that you'd thank me for telling you about…' Mrs Bell lowered her voice, elbow against the bricks for support '…the boy.'

'Nothing to worry about.'

None of your bloody business was what he should have said. He saw her out of the corner of his eye, clutching the frame, edging closer. But those neighbours still had something over him: memories that stretched back past the bombs and the skeletal remains of Camberwell. Jack waited by the front door for Georgie, so he could have someone to go in with.

Mrs Bell picked up the cat, placed it on the windowsill between them. 'Your mother was such a good woman. I was only saying so yesterday to Mr Bell.'

Jack had never brought girls back to the house, not since Rosie. The cat sprang down and trotted towards him. It wasn't anybody's business what he did inside his own home. The cat clawed at the doorframe by his leg. Georgie bent down to rub it behind the ears. 'Hello, Jack. Who's your ginger friend?'

'Come in, neighbours are on patrol.' Jack ushered Georgie through the front door. She looked out of place on the street with its aprons, hairnets and parade of dirty children. He didn't want anything dulling her edges.

Mrs Bell peered over from her doorstep, the framed face of the Queen staring at him from under her arm.

'That mog gets in my house again, I'll snap its mangy neck.' Jack aimed his foot but the cat was too quick.

He slammed the door, blinking as his eyes adjusted to the darkness of the hallway. Georgie took off her hat. 'Ashamed of me or something?'

'Course not, but it's none of her beeswax what we get up to.' Jack slid his hand down the back of her blouse. 'You know – the sort of thing that means you're too tired to go home after.'

She was breathless from striding down the road, a pulse beating in her throat; that heat surprised him every time, so raw, as if life itself was draining from her skin. He let her surface for air. Her hands went into his pockets, took hold of the bottles.

'I'm guessing this means you won your fight.'

He nodded, and landed a couple of play punches to her shoulder. She moaned in mock agony. 'My landlady will kick up a right stink if she thinks I've been up to no good.' Georgie handed back the bottles and shrugged off her coat. 'Long as I'm back before morning, suppose it'll be all right.'

She rocked forward in her heels and kissed him on the chin. That was when he wanted her most – in the mornings, when he stretched out his arm, and he could pretend, for a moment, that he'd dragged Rosie out of those dark dreams and into the daylight with him.

'Only about fifteen hours until morning, Georgie. Let's get started, then.'

He grabbed her arm, waltzing her towards the front room, the bottles tinkling percussion. He pushed through the door with his shoulder; Pearl and Frank were dim shapes in the corner.

'What you two up to? Playing statues in the dark?'

He plopped down in the armchair, toppling Georgie on to his lap. Her blouse was untucked; the draught they stirred up flapped the buttons against his chest. Pearl drifted over to the wall and turned the gas. The lights hissed and ballooned to life.

'It was such a nice evening, didn't think we needed lamps on, Jack.'

'My head's a bit sore from that right hook.' Frank swivelled a loose thread from his shirt around his finger.

'Pearl cleaned you up good, has she?'

Jack stretched out his arm and let the bottles sink to the floor. Pearl rolled up two strips of cotton and handed them to Frank; he plugged up each nostril.

'There's some swelling over Frank's ribs, and that cut under his eye has opened up again – '

'What?' Frank rubbed his head.

' – and his right ear's blocked.'

'What?' Jack mimicked Frank.

'It ain't funny, Jack.'

Frank paced in front of the fireplace, distracted as he was in the days before a fight; but that was over for now. Or maybe Pearl with her chattering and fussing was unsettling him, as if the rose tendrils on the wallpaper weren't enough.

'Frank, don't you go putting up with her strange ways. Put the lamps on when you want to, mate.'

'Will do, Jack.'

Frank scooted past Pearl as if her dress was on fire and took a seat. He tapped his fingertips around the edge of the cut under his eye. Pearl frowned and shook her head at him;

118

his hands slipped under his backside. Sometimes the girl didn't know when to stop.

'I've got news will put a smile back on your face, Frank.' Jack shifted Georgie in his lap.

He put the card on the table; it shone so bright it made the white starched cloth look dingy. Frank picked it up, held it closer to his left eye, and turned his good ear towards Jack.

'You've got me another fight?'

'Better than that – we're going to have one arranged for us. Vincent and Harry will handpick you an opponent. I've decided to go and see them next week.' Jack tasted the salty bite of excitement.

'What if they pick the wrong fighter?' Frank slid the card back.

'Don't fret over that. I'll sort it. Anyway, you're ready to be pushed.' He nestled the card into his pocket.

'He needs longer between fights, Jack. That scar will rip open. And what about his ribs? He'll have marks all over him like mine.'

Jack rolled his eyes. 'That's different. This is boxing, Pearl, not pillow-fighting.'

Frank ducked his head and rubbed the back of his ear, avoiding the swollen side of his face.

'Don't even think about sulking. This is a celebration.' Jack opened the bottles. 'Get us something to drink out of, Pearl.'

'These are pretty.' Georgie held up the engraved glass Pearl handed her; leaves and petals caught the light.

'They were Mum's favourite. Dad won them at a fair.' Pearl beamed and straightened the ends of hair that fell over her shoulder.

'Is that them up there?' Georgie nodded towards the photographs above the fire. 'Lose them in the war, did you?'

'No, our dad fell down the pub cellar, broke his neck in the fall. That was before I was born. He would have been off fighting otherwise.'

'If he weren't six feet under.' Jack spoke into his beer but they weren't looking at him.

'He worked at the Bible Factory. They printed up ration books during the war.' Pearl took a card out of her pocket. 'Funny really, to think this might have come from the same place he worked all those years.' She turned the paper over in her hands. 'Our mum only passed four years and five – '

'We've all got to go some time. Pass me the bottle.' Jack didn't wait for a response; he snatched up the Courage.

'Thought it felt cold when I was collecting crates down the cellar. Cold strange, I mean.' Georgie rubbed her arms.

'That'll be Dad.' Jack emptied the beer into his glass; Georgie stretched her arm around him and they sank deeper into the cushions.

'Is your hand all right, Pearl? There's blood.' Frank passed her a tea cloth; she wrapped her palm in it.

'I must have nicked it cutting up those bandage strips. It'll be fine.' She smiled.

'Best put some cream on that, to be sure. Didn't go and use it all up on the cut under my eye, did you?'

'She's tougher than you, Frank. Pearl's stronger than any fighter. Do your trick for him.' Georgie nudged Jack in the ribs.

Frank's large eyes swallowed light from the room. Jack shrugged; he was too full of beer to move.

Pearl rubbed the pattern of white scars on her arms. 'I ain't got time to mess around here. I'm going to fill the bath for Frank to have a soak.'

'Think a woman can't take some pain.' Georgie sat forward and took hold of Pearl's wrist as she went past. 'Who's got a cigarette?'

'What's she going to do with the ciggie, Pearl?'

'It ain't going to hurt her, Frank.' Jack sighed and wanted it to be over.

'Come on, Pearl. Show these men what you're made off.' Georgie laughed.

Pearl sank against the arm of the chair.

'I promised I'd meet some mates for a drink.' Frank rubbed his ribs as he stood up, stuffed the bloodied nose plugs into his pocket. The front door banged behind him, the loose flaps of rose wallpaper slithered lower. Georgie pressed her other hand to Pearl's waist.

'I didn't mean nothing by it. I just wanted to show him it's only – '

Pearl pulled free; Georgie twisted in the chair, neck straining to watch, as Pearl rushed from the room.

'If you wanted to send the children out to play, you could have just asked them, Georgie.'

'When was the last time you saw her messing with dolls?'

'She's all long socks and comic books.' Jack yawned. 'Frank, granted, might look like a man, but he's got the mind of a child.' He tapped his head.

'Maybe you see what you want to. I'm going up to speak to her. Me and my big mouth.'

He unhooked her top button, ran his tongue along the base of her throat. 'Well, I'm building up to my second wind. So, make it quick.'

Jack jumped up from the chair, only just caught Georgie in time before she slid to the floor. Pearl was pacing upstairs; the ceiling squeaked every time she reached the floorboard by her bedroom door. When his mum first got ill, he and Pearl used to practise all the time by rolling a cigarette on her arm.

'And one more thing, Georgie. About that ciggie thing – '

'Trust me. I ain't even going to mention it again.'

Jack went out to the toilet at the back. It was cool in there, untouched by the sun. He left the door ajar so he could see the houses opposite. One was missing like a pulled tooth from a rotten row; the frozen ghost of a staircase shone on the exposed brickwork. When he was a boy he used to hide in the bog after a beating (forty-eight seconds of crying – the time it took the cistern to gush and fill up). He used to wish that he belonged behind one of those windows opposite: no tear-streaked faces pressed to the glass. He ran his fingers under the lip of the bench: *kiss my hairy arse*. Jack scratched that with a pin when he was fifteen, the last time his dad ever caught hold of him. Jack had let a friend store a sack of potash in the yard; it must have been one of Mrs Bell's cats that ripped it open. *Look out for yourself in life, son, because no one else gives a fuck*. That was what his dad had said as he kept his hand squeezed around the back of Jack's neck, made Jack scrub the yard clean with a flannel until his nails cracked. Later that night, when Jack soaked his hands in soapy water, his broken thumbnail had floated up to the surface. As he'd rubbed the raw nail-bed, he'd made a wish: *let me wake up with a new nail and let him be dead, let him be stone dead*. The nail never did grow back.

His dad was wrong again: there was a houseful of people who gave a damn about Jack now. He separated leaves of paper from the Izal Germicide box, shiny and sharp as glass; he preferred newspaper. But soon it wouldn't matter if Pearl wanted to waste money on stuff that sounded like some foreigner's name. A few more fights, then they would be eating chocolate every day and driving giant gleaming cars like the Americans. Georgie would be with him, wearing the best fur from Oxford Street. But he had to have a minute before he went back inside: his body needed longer to recover these days, time to remember he was still young. Up through the cracked tiles of the roof, a swift somersaulted and dived at insects humming in the evening air. When he was younger, stamina had never been a problem; he smiled and closed his eyes.

THREE

Jackie rolls over in the grass and plucks a tall blade. He places it between his hands, as if he is ready to say a prayer, and blows hard. A screech breaks through the whistle of swifts, high up in the sky, and the distant thump of the funfair. The tree above him and Rosie branches into an umbrella of green, protecting them from the sun. Another beautiful day; he needs to call to it again, let the birds and the humming flies know he is here.

'You'll wake the devil.'

Rosie snatches the grass from him, shredding it until her fingers are mossy. She wipes the green stain off on his white shirt.

'Rosie! My mum's going to have me. Look at the state of it.'

'Put your jacket on. No one'll notice.'

'She does the washing – she'll notice all right.' He tucks in the loose tails.

'You're old enough to do your own laundry.' She tugs the shirt free again.

'Never seen you do none. That's the same frock you've been wearing all summer.'

Polka-dots of shade mark the blue flowered dress. Jackie lets his arm flop across her body, and it nestles against the cushion of her belly. She puffs and pushes his arm aside.

'You seem to like my dress well enough. Can't keep your hands off it.'

'I love it.'

His arm doesn't meet any resistance this time. Jackie loves the worn-thin feel of the cotton as if it is just another layer of skin under his hand. He loves the tear in the hem at the back, the specks of mud on the sleeves from the day they nearly got caught raiding the apple stores in Dulwich and Rosie fell from the wall. She'd bounced, but the dress wasn't so lucky. That evening they woke up under a tree and light rain had crystallised them as they were sleeping. The blue dress is love, for him, and he can't remember any summer before this one. Jackie rolls closer towards her and stares into those grey eyes as she watches the birds in the sky; battleship grey, she calls them. He has never seen a battleship, but she lived some of last winter in Portsmouth so he trusts her. She grips his hand to her ribs.

'We'll be packing up the fair come the end of summer.'

'Are you hungry? I could get some doughnuts?'

He sits up, draws his knees to his chest, one hand still attached to her. She tugs on his fingers.

'I'll be leaving London for the winter.'

'Or fish and chips, if you fancy?'

'Always was one for questions. Well, here's another for you, Jackie. You ever been to Portsmouth?'

Her voice pinches him; bringing him back to the bald baked mud, the burnt bark of the tree that runs straight up and down behind them. Remains of a tramp's fire and blackened tin cans lie scattered around: a place where people come and go and summers don't last forever. He rubs a hand across his mouth.

'Mitcham is the farthest I've been.'

'I used to like the docks, but now it's different. The navy's taken over, there's nothing else in the harbour, no coal or food to collect. They're planning for something all right, my uncle says it.'

'I know people can get you anything you want, just ask.'

He studies the clouds: a giant boot and a squat elephant float above him. She yawns as she stretches, folding her arms behind her head.

'Fetch me a doughnut, then, Jackie.'

His released hand hangs limply in the dirt next to her body. He doesn't want to think about anything but licking sugar from her fingers. He gets up and heads towards the fair. The laughing faces on the swing chairs and shouting mouths at the coconut shy don't care about some war in Spain. How could something like that ever happen here?

Music dances over the Common: a tooting steam organ, lolloping laughter, and the squeal of wooden brakes. He turns for one more look at Rosie under the tree. Her body stands out like a flowerbed, skin darkened by summer and blended with the earth. To anyone else she is just a patch of shade under the branches. But all other eyes are trained on the fair. She is plump as a doughnut and Jackie likes to hold handfuls of her at a time. All the girls he knows, down his street, are thin and brittle with greasy plaits. But Rosie is different: sixteen already and her body fits her like a freshly made bed, smoothed and piled high. Long dark curls falling down her back that Jackie could lose his fingers in for hours. And he doesn't want to leave yet. What if she is gone by the time he gets back, upped and disappeared like the white trailing clouds whizzing over his head, nothing left but an empty expanse of blue? He runs back to the trees and drops down on his knees beside her.

'That wasn't half quick.' She shields her eyes.

He blocks out the sun as he kisses her. They have kissed before, every day since they met, but not like this. His tongue pushes deeper into her mouth, rubbing itself against the sharp points of her teeth, sliding over the ledge of her tongue. He wants to go so deep they can't ever be pulled apart. The cotton of her dress catches against his legs; the underskirt wrinkles around her waist. And still they kiss. His legs either side of hers as she lies on the grass and wriggles up against him. It feels as if heated coals have been thrown down his back – nothing will cool it, not even if he stands with arms and legs wide and lets the breeze carry him away. She kicks off her boots. He rests on one arm as he slips his other hand to her thigh. She breaks away for air, comes up panting like the first day they met.

He grips her socks and she grins at him, rolling them down under the palms of his hand until they pop off the end of her toes. He has never touched the smooth soles of someone else's feet. His hands are hot, her skin cool. Then he tickles her, slowly tracing his fingers up and down the pink toes. Working faster, moving up to her exposed shins, he squeezes her kneecaps until she can't hold back. Laughter cascades out of her. Biting his bottom lip, he concentrates on her feet, wants her to keep laughing, keep wanting him to touch her. Jackie nips at her waist as she twists in his hands. But he is afraid to stop for a second; like riding high up on the swings he wants to keep going, and the fear that he might fly over the top drives him harder. He smells the soap from last night in her hair and the fresh sweetness of peppermint on her breath.

Jackie joins in her laughter. His hands rub at the skin under her dress that is stuck to her like brown paper soaked in vinegar now; he wants to peel back the layers. The buttons above her waist pop open between his finger and his thumb with a twist, like shelling peas. A chicken pox scar sits next to her belly button, a small mirrored dent as if she was born twice. He presses his hand to his middle and thinks he must have one too. He blows warm air on her; she raises her head up off the ground to watch him. Soft pale hair runs in a line down under her dress; he traces it. His nails rub against the top of her thigh. Birds fall silent, insects hang in the air: his fingers are inside her.

She pushes herself up on to her elbows and tugs at the front of his trousers. She finds the buttons, rips through them; she has him in her fist. He is going to burst, loud and messy as an over-baked potato. *Breathe, breathe.* Together they push him into the hollow his fingers have just left. His hands are around her face but he is still moving in her. She wants to keep him there; her legs hook and pin him. He can't keep his eyes open. Mumbles and moans as loud as shouting in

126

his ears. Her tongue squeezes itself past his lips. He wants to burrow inside her. It seems to last longer than six rounds but they aren't fighting; they are struggling to find a balance, floating upwards towards the top of the trees. But he can't hold on any longer. No pain, but he lies there KO.

'Jackie, you're a ton weight. Roll off.'

Rosie presses her knees together and touches the top of her thighs. He sinks down on to the grass next to her, slowly threads his buttons closed again.

'Did I hurt you?'

She laughs, reaches across and brushes an eyelash from his cheek. Her chest moves slightly as she breathes. He feels the same: he isn't asleep but he isn't awake; he is made of heavy lead – malleable and rolled. He can share that feeling with Rosie as he never shared anything before.

'You're more beautiful than anything I've seen...'

'Better stop looking at anything else but me now.' She smiles as she sits up and presses her legs together. 'I'm starving.'

He heaves himself up. He would get her anything she wanted. On his way he turns once more – she is a blue speck in the distance. Jackie has to stop himself from running back to check that she is still there.

The fair squats at one end of the Common, brightly painted wooden horses and swing chairs flying past him. Steam clogs up the sky. People everywhere but none of them knows that he is different now. Every time the sunshine comes out from behind a cloud the screams and shouts grow louder, but they can't be as happy as him. Paper flags, curling doilies and brown bags flutter along the grass, twisting and bouncing in the breeze as if they are trying to pick up the trail of a procession. Just walking into the fair is like watching the world spin around him. The colours bleed into one another until there is only a white heat; the smell of toffee apples, doughnuts and cockles is so syrupy-thick that it makes his tongue quiver. Jackie loves the fair; he can forget the Bible

Factory, the stink of old-man sweat and burning paper. Rosie tastes of peppermints and spun sugar; he won't ever forget that taste.

Jackie puts his penny for the doughnuts on the counter. They sit in a scrunched-up piece of yesterday's newspaper, in a dark circle of grease. He takes the wrapped package and dodges through the crowds. He touches the dimpled skin and licks specks of sugar from his fingertips. He won't eat any until he gets back to Rosie. She will be where he left her under the shelter of the tree, arms and legs waiting to hold him. Everything has changed between them, but then nothing is ever going to change again.

He runs all the way. She waits, standing up with her face tilted towards the sun, following it like a daisy. For a moment he thinks he has vanished because she doesn't move; Jackie doesn't exist if she isn't looking. But she smiles; her eyelashes flutter and filter out the sunlight. The doughnuts roll free as she grabs his hand, leading him back under the tree. He lies on his back as she sits on his belly. High up in the branches, gnats bob and glint in the green light, but they don't come any closer. A lifetime of summer before them.

FOUR

Frank was late for training. Jack sat on the benches, scratching an insect bite on his hand. He checked the time again: ten minutes overdue. It was a scorching afternoon outside, the tarmac sticky in places, and pigeons clustered in the shade. But Frank wasn't supposed to be out running, so that couldn't have held him up; he was resting.

Two other fighters sparred at the back wall by the bags, taking advantage of their extra time. The boy with the cropped blond hair couldn't have been much more than sixteen; wearing a loose sweater but his muscles were planed into shape under the thin cloth. The boy's feet skipped over the mat as he dodged blow after blow. His partner was older, bigger, which didn't always mean much in a fight. But each time the boy came back with swift rabbit punches of two and four, and six. The older one finally caught on, threw out his fist and the blond boy hit leather. He clutched his chest, bent over and sucking at air; the boy needed to learn a few more tricks.

'Jack… Jack.'

Frank dropped his kit to the floor in front of the benches, nodding like an excited dog. Jack stepped over the bag and went up to the ring.

'Come past the pastille factory, did you? You stink of blackcurrants.'

'The bus broke down. I'm here now.' Frank pointed across the gym. 'I've sparred with that boy before – he ain't so good. Right hit, right hit. Same every time.'

'A manager now, are you?'

'No, course not, Jack. Just saying.' Frank lifted off his shirt, tossed it on the bench.

'Well, don't jabber, get warmed up.' Jack gave him a shove as he passed.

It was gooey as custard in the gym, too thick to move, and Jack sank back down on the bench. The punchbag took a beating as Frank set to work. Bert came out of the changing rooms to take the other side. Frank circled and bobbed, but something wasn't right. Jack prodded the crumpled shirt with his foot. Frank always left his clothes in a neat pile; tidiness was part of his thing. Jack folded it into a square, slid it out of sight. But the white cotton flickered at the edge of his vision. The two boys sat on the floor to watch, soaking up any drops of training sweat that spun their way.

Bert rammed forward with his shoulders, bracing himself against the bag. Frank landed hits. Deep punches, hitting the same spot each time; enough force to break a rib or smash yesterday's dinner down to the knees. Left, right, hit after hit as if he were ploughing his way through a brick wall. Frank punched with the confidence of a man who could lift his own weight in coal then crush the lot to dust. Bert grimaced against the impact, spectacles sliding down his nose, and the heavy bag quivered. Frank kept going, not even breaking to rest for the length of the round bell as he usually did. It wasn't the fighting that Jack had expected. Excitable, that was what he was, and maybe Jack shouldn't have told him about going to see Vincent. Sweat radiated out from Frank in a growing circle of splashes on the floorboards like rings on a tree. He looked older than those watching boys: his right ear blossoming into a cauliflower, a scar high on his cheek, fluid puffing up his eye sockets. Fighters didn't need tattoos – they had their life drawn over their body. The boys got up to leave, rubbing at cramping calf muscles, and still Frank didn't stop. The gym was theirs again, his and Frank's.

Frank snapped his head up for a second. The bag caught him a glance on the forehead before he got back to it, and Bert followed it up with a slap across the neck for his mistake. Jack checked to see what had distracted him; he hoped it was a fire, a ghost, anything to justify the break in concentration. But it was only Pearl, hair tied up in a scarf, as if she had turned into Mrs Bell.

She placed the heavy wicker basket next to Jack. 'I'm too excited to wait. Tell me where we're going this afternoon. I won't ruin the surprise for Georgie, I promise.'

'You'll find out when we get there.' Jack helped himself to bread and margarine from the paper; he wrinkled his nose as he bent over to eat. 'Jesus, what you been up to, burning bacon?'

'Georgie helped me do my hair.'

'Do what to it? Cremate it?'

She unwrapped the red cloth from around her head. 'Permanent wave. Look, I've got curls now.'

Pearl slipped her finger inside one and held it up. The bread crumbled in his fist. His eyes flickered and widened: it wasn't Pearl standing there. The bread scratched his throat, swelled in his mouth. She shook out the new waves around her face, long, thick tendrils that looked darker and shinier than they ever had before. Jack felt sick at the sight of those curls, sick that he wanted to reach out and stroke them. He coughed.

'What's wrong?' Pearl stepped closer.

He grabbed his throat, couldn't breathe. Pearl slapped him on the back, banging her fist against his spine. He spat the chewed up muck on to the floor. She poured him some tea from the flask. 'Better?'

'It's not you.' The only words he could force out.

He rinsed the sting of bile from his mouth; tea dribbled over his chin and he swiped it away with the back of his hand. Pearl caught her reflection in the metallic flask. 'I think it looks something. Georgie said it suited me.'

Jack held on to the cold edge of the bench. It was as if all those years hadn't happened: Rosie was standing there. Jack wanted to put his arms around her neck, bite down on the tight skin across her shoulders. He turned away, coughed up the last of the tea into his hand. He dropped the tin mug into the basket; it rattled against the sides. He kept his back to Pearl, stared straight ahead at Frank and Bert. Frank kept trying to step around the bag to face the benches; Bert pushed him away each time.

'I like it. Anyway, what's wrong with it? Georgie's got her hair curled,' Pearl defended herself with a high-pitched whine.

'You're not her.'

'Jack, you all right?'

'That chemical stink reminds me of the war.'

'Sorry, I didn't think.' Pearl tied up her hair with the scarf.

Those thin arms and legs, so small, so breakable. She stood next to him, watching the training. Jack took up her hands and turned them over.

'Didn't get any of that muck on your skin, did you? Some chemicals can burn through bone. Check yourself, before we go out.'

No red marks, no broken cracks, just the threaded lacework of scars from other times.

'You've taught me to be careful.'

He placed his elbows on his knees, shrank his limbs together as she moved around. He tried to concentrate on the hiss of the flask, the crackle of paper covering the sandwiches.

'What should I wear? Will this do?' Pearl held forward the edge of her blue skirt. 'It's too nice for these support shoes, they're all clumpy. I've got them sandals…'

'Stop prancing, men are trying to work here.' He pushed her hand back. 'Be ready for three.'

She stepped down, but turned to glance at Frank working at the bag before she reached the doors. The gym windows couldn't keep out summer; rays pierced their way in straight lines along the scuffed floor and directly on to her round face.

132

Her eyelashes squeezed against the light and Jack held his breath until her footsteps faded away. No one reached out to take his hand and lead him into the shade.

Two buses, an hour later, and they were at Ackroydon Estate. Jack felt giddy from the ride but he couldn't stop smiling. The sun tugged at the corners of his mouth, the smell of grass filled his lungs. Southfields was everything he'd expected: parade of shops, a pub, and trees, lots of trees. It didn't matter that the journey took so long; it was like travelling to another land. Jack gripped Georgie's hand in his.

She shook her head. 'We're out in the bloody country.'

'Look at all this green.' Frank reached up into the branches and gave them a shake.

Leaves pattered down on to their heads, sounding like rain. A tangy smell of sap hung in the air, vinegary as mint sauce, the sun baking everything and wafting scents like drying washing on the line.

'It's close to Wimbledon, not Everest.' Jack hugged Georgie closer.

'That building looks as high.' Pearl pointed up between the branches.

'I read about this new place in the paper. Thought we'd all come see what the fuss was about.'

Georgie fitted snugly beneath his shoulder, as if he were the paper-chain and she were the missing cut-out. Newly planted saplings lined the path, white buds forming as if the confusion of being uprooted made the branches believe it was spring again.

'I'll race you, Frank.' Pearl darted off.

'Don't trip and break anything, either of you,' Jack shouted to the corkscrew of dust they left behind.

'What are we doing out here, Jack?' Georgie picked her way along the dry bits of the path. Evaporating puddles sat at the edges of the grass.

He kicked a stone and watched it skid into a pile of leaves. 'Taking some air.'

Frank and Pearl were too far ahead to see, their voices floating back on the breeze. No one else was on the straight path, and the street was nothing more than a fading buzz of traffic; just him and Georgie.

'Feels like a family outing to me.' She let out a small click with her tongue.

'I only wanted to show you where I was heading. I'm not hanging round that dump of a pub and those rotten streets forever, no chance.'

Above the foaming line of blossom on the slope, the estate began to appear from the top down. White concrete gleamed and reflected the sun, still as a pond. Everything looked new, just unwrapped and placed on the shelf fresh. Pearl and Frank waited at the end of the path, cheeks red. The grass was trimmed flush to the building, the black-painted doors shone, windows sparkled, and electric street lamps hummed. Jack only ever imagined places like this existed, but now here he was standing on the edge of it. He looked up at the flats and it gave him vertigo; he counted eight storeys, and a flat roof that looked like a platform to the skies.

Frank shifted from foot to foot. 'We can lend them bikes over there! Let's have a ride around, Pearl.'

'I suppose, as long as we return them. But you'll have to teach me how first.'

'You can't ride?' Frank laughed. 'Everyone can ride.'

'I suppose our mum thought there were plenty of ways I could break my bones without falling off a bike.'

'The point is you're not supposed to fall off.' Frank tapped her forehead. 'I'll teach you. Don't you want to take that off? It's hotting up.'

She held on to her sleeves. 'No.'

'Can't even tell they're scars – bet they'll fade in the sun. We'll see you back at the bus stop, Jack.' Frank touched her arm before he strode off towards the bikes. Pearl trotted beside him, knotting her cardigan around her waist. They followed the angles of the path down the side of the estate. Jack crossed the grass towards the double doors.

'Think this would be a good place to live?' He wasn't sure who he was asking.

Georgie followed him and put her hand on his shoulder, shaking mud from her heel. Vincent's business card was good as any banker's draft; he rubbed the softening corners under his thumb. He wanted to open those glass doors, go up in a lift, put a key in a lock, sit down in a chair: for that place to be home. Every room planned out in his head like the pictures he had seen in an advert for Courts Furniture Exhibition. A walnut dining room set for thirty-six guineas or only thirty-three shillings every month. A cosy three-piece, a settee and two easy chairs covered with hardwearing tapestry for nineteen and a half guineas. Everything would be new, not a smudge or scratch on it.

'We're having fun, ain't we? Don't go and get all sentimental on me, Jack.'

'Don't make me laugh. This is business. I'm thinking about opening a gym and it'd be cheaper and easier to take care of somewhere around here.'

His sagging trousers picked up pollen and blades of grass as they walked along. He tried not to think about all the potholes that Pearl could crash into; laughter and the squeak of wheels faded into the distance. The shadows from the trees created a patchwork of dark hollows around them.

Georgie took his arm. 'Last place I worked, this girl said she got chased by a pack of stray dogs once. Are there animals in these woods?'

'Doubt there are dogs in there – the wolves keep them away.' He eased her along with a press of his hand.

'Wolves? Shut up.' She slapped him away.

'I'll see them off,' he growled, and sucked his lips from his teeth.

'You're the worst beast of the lot.'

They stumbled backwards until he caught his balance against a thin trunk; it swayed and bounced him upright again. They stood like giants among the small budding trees. He sat down on the grass, pulled her with him. Dried leaves crackled under them and released the coming smell of autumn: deep puddles and damp wool. She nestled against his shoulder, staring up through the thin straggling branches. A song drifted over from the estate. Frankie Laine's 'I Believe'. And he wanted it to be true: the flat, the pushbikes, the furniture... some day it would be his. He had wished for lots of things in his life, and they rarely happened. But it worked once, a long time ago: *let him be dead, let him be stone dead*. No reason it couldn't work again, one day.

The purple bruised edges of evening were creeping along Camberwell by the time they got back. Pearl and Frank had gone ahead to pick up some whelks from the barrel man.

'Where are you going, Jack? I'm late. We'll cut through the alley.'

Georgie steered him towards the Man of the World. The click-click of her heels on the cobbles made the hair on the back of his neck twitch. Damp licked his face, the warmth from Georgie's body diluted in the darkness. The streaked pub windows barely let the yellow lamp-glow reach the pavement but the noise was loud enough to trouble hell. On top of that there was a tapping coming out of the shadows, a shuffling of feet. Jack's grip tightened; he had to stop himself from breaking into a run. The footsteps were nearly on them.

'Evening there, Jack. Georgie.' Newton came alongside. 'I just popped in for a swift half.' He lurched off the pavement.

'Can't stop, Newton.' Jack tried to step around but the open cellar stopped him, black as inky canal water. The propped doors trembled in the growing wind, a chain rattled and the ropes swayed. Newton staggered backwards to the mouth of the delivery hatch, clutching Jack's arm for balance.

He let the wall take the weight off his tin leg, his foot touching the edge of the hole.

'Coming this way always makes me remember your poor old dad and his snapped neck at the bottom of them steps. I used to raise a glass with him on his way back from the factory. The Lord takes the good ones young. John Munday was no exception.'

'He should have outlived us all, then.'

But Jack couldn't stop himself from glancing down again. After all those years he still expected to see that small brass cup glinting up at him; perhaps it was down there, hidden behind an old oak barrel, blocking up the drains.

Newton shook his head. 'Crying shame it was, too. Religion, science, they all say the same – everything happens for a reason, even if we can't understand the pattern. The book my uncle wrote talks about the patterns in boxing, you know. I ever tell you about that book, Jack?' He let go of Jack's arm and tried to straighten the lapels of his janitor's jacket. 'Well, I'm off to fetch a couple of fish suppers. Jimmy's popping round.'

Newton tipped his cap at them and stumbled towards the orange glow of the street, the drag of his tin foot echoing across the flagstones. The trip out to the new flats seemed like a lifetime ago, not hours. Somehow Jack always ended up back in that pit. He glanced over at Camberwell Road, a trailing line of headlights and shop fronts; he caught the salty whiff of chips. He took hold of Georgie's arm, stepping away from the edge: nothing but the deep blackness of the cellar down there.

FIVE

Rosie wraps her arm around his, their hands slipping together. Jackie smells the fusty sweat of Brixton Boys' Club trapped on his skin and in the wool of her cardigan. He isn't sure when the evenings started to need another layer, summer short sleeves not enough. Rosie knocks his elbow.

'Jackie, let's get fish and chips.'

'We had Chelsea buns after the fight.'

'But I've been worrying about your poorly thumb. Worrying makes me hungry.'

'I've been in the ring and you're only worried about my thumb?'

'That other boy never landed a proper hit because you were too quick. The winner's cup proves it.' She pats the brass base peeking from his pocket.

'If it'll stop you from fretting, I suppose I could let you kiss it better.'

He holds up his missing thumbnail; the raw bed still throbs but what stings more is the lie he told her: an accident at the Bible Factory. She kisses it, gently nudging her nose against his palm. 'I'm still starved though, unless you want me to eat what's left of your thumb?'

'Let's just get back to the fair.'

He smiles and can't understand why she is always hungry lately, always something sweet and sticky between her fingers. She walks next to him but drags her feet, the clumpy boots thumping up dust. It is too dark on the street to see her frown but he feels it like a tightening hatband around his head. Jackie wants to lift her up again.

'There's a chippie up on the road.'

Her pace quickens, and he is glad. The alley is alongside the Man of the World, too close to the house; his breath catches at the thought. The summer will be over soon and the fair moving on; he could go with Rosie, up and disappear. She hasn't asked him yet but he knows she'd want to. The pub creeps up on his right; Jackie grips Rosie's hand as the doors swing open and suck shut again. But he doesn't recognise the woman or the tap of high heels. Jackie breathes in the smell of malt and sawdust. It is dark in the alley but he doesn't care; he knows his way through these streets and he will keep Rosie from stumbling. The only light comes from the open cellar doors: a pale yellow triangle like a scraping of butter. Their steps have an echo, but they are nearly out on the road.

'What's wrong?' Rosie's lips trace the shape of the words on his neck.

The mortar between the bricks glows white like exposed bones, but corners and kerbstones are absorbed in the gloom.

'Sound made me jump, that's all.'

Nearly there, the rumble of a bus, he can almost smell smoking batter. But now footsteps are coming up too quickly. Jackie recognises the long stride, a delay between each firmly planted step. If those footsteps catch up with them she will realise what he really is. Nothing but John: *stupid... sneaky... thieving... scheming... shitting... waste of Munday blood.* His balls squeeze tight up against his leg. He is running now and she lurches to keep up, the darkness towing him under. Her broken soles flap against the stone slabs.

'Boy, come here. I saw you walk by. Show us what you've got there. *Boy!*' The last word screamed out.

'Don't look back, Rosie.'

They keep running, feet smacking the pavement. Out on to the street: blinking against the lamps, flying headlights, shop fronts splashed in yellows and whites. They collide up against the arch of the railway bridge. Jackie grips the bricks, red dust crumbling beneath his nails.

'Who was that?' Rosie pants.

'Some old drunk.'

'We didn't need to run. You're a boxing champion, the cup says so.'

He shrugs. Jackie won't ever let his dad near Rosie; how can he even let those two things live in the same world? Rosie is right: he doesn't need to run. He is a boxing champion. He squeezes some coins into her hand. 'Get the chips for us, won't you?'

'Where you off to?'

'Just remembered, I promised to let them know at the gym how I got on.' Jackie focuses on his boots to avoid this second lie.

Her face tightens into an angry point. 'But we're set for the swings tonight. My sister fixed it with the lad running it and everything.'

'I'll wave the cup around then come and find you. Won't take me long.'

'Don't expect me to be waiting.'

She bounces the ha'pennies in her hand, crosses the road to the chippie. Jackie knows she will be standing at the gates looking out for him and he watches her stomp away, the silky swaying of her dress familiar as the feel of his own clothes. Her dark hair absorbs the sparks from the trams. A train rattles overhead; the bricks tremble against his back. Jackie levers himself away from the solid safety of the archway; he slinks back around the corner.

The drunk is weaving along the road, silhouetted against the light from the open cellar. No one else around: only him and his dad. Jackie goes towards him, fists clenched in his pockets; the brass cup knocks against his knuckles. His dad isn't a happy drunk, isn't even an angry drunk – he is as much himself as ever. Shirt neatly buttoned, cuffs starched, hair slicked. Appearance is everything: *Church and state never fingered a clean collar*, that's what he says. He lurches forward and the words topple out.

'I knew you'd come back to me, boy. Where's that little titbit you had with you?'

'None of your stinking business.'

His dad laughs. The smell of beer leaches into the cool night, fermenting the air around them. And even half-cut his dad is still taller and straighter, eyes focused, not even a touch of grey to his hair, as if he isn't ever going to get old.

'Ain't we the big man? Be signing up for the Army like your brothers, will you? Don't make me laugh. She's leading you like a donkey. What a surprise – tarts like that are no good for you.' A pointed finger jabs at each word.

'What do you care?'

Jackie scratches his thumb, and it starts to bleed again. The open cellar grins between them, lighting his dad under the chin and making his face a mask. His dad presses a hand on the upright flap, fingers gripping the wood.

'Make a fool of yourself and you make a fool of all of us with tat like that. People will talk. Notice you haven't brought her over to the house, like any respectable son.'

'I'm not having you anywhere near her.' Jackie says it slowly, wants to make sure his dad hears him right.

'I can smell cheap scent a mile off. She'd probably be helping herself to the silver soon as she stepped in the door.'

His dad's shadow wobbles and disappears inside the cellar before he rights himself again. There is nothing of value in that house, probably never will be.

'Bring her back to the house, boy. Do things proper for your old mum's sake, be a good son.' The soft lisp of the *s* as he tries to drag up a smile.

Jackie almost believes him, the wheedling, the sweet lies; it is worse than any fist in the face. He bends his knees slightly, ready to bounce forward on the balls of his feet just as they taught him at the gym.

'Go to hell.'

141

It comes out louder than he expects, rumbling over the bricks and the stone.

'I'll have you for that, boy.'

His dad reaches across the gap, snatches at the front of Jackie's shirt. The top buttons spin and rattle down the steps. He wants those hands off him, wants those fingers never to grab anything again. Thin yellow light from the cellar doors makes his shadow tower over Jackie. His dad yanks the hand back, high into the air. Jackie sees the palm coming but he can't duck out of the way; his body sets hard. The open slap knocks him off balance. He drops to his knees, bites down on his tongue. Tastes blood. He sees laced boots in front of him. For a moment he is back at the gym: he can get up off the ropes; he can stand tall and land a punch to finish the fight. But something else is in front of him; it catches the light. Jackie grips the metal cup in his clammy hand.

'What you going to do with that, boy? You haven't got the spine to make a fist at me, couldn't even fix that damn parrot right. Weak little bastard – you'll never be a Nipper Pat Daly or Tommy Farr. Looks like they didn't even bother to engrave that thing. Go put it with your collection of second-place certificates.'

His dad grins, opens his black mouth wide to let out the laughter. He pats Jackie twice on the cheek, soft and flat. And he is right: one day even Rosie will find out. The cup falls from Jackie's hand. *Bang*, *bang*, *bang* as it jumps down the cellar steps. His dad watches it, then those pin eyes are back on him. Jackie holds his breath. He won't cry no matter how much it hurts. He can't close his fist, gripped into a claw where it held the cup. His dad's face hovers above the hatch doors.

'If you want to finish me, boy, here I am. Fetch up that scrap metal and do it.' Whispery sour breath. 'But, so you know, I always thought it'd be one of your brothers, Tommy or Bill, coming after me. They're real men now, trained to kill.' He winks. 'No? Ain't got enough hair on your balls to finish me? Then think back on this night. The night you had your chance to be a big man but you were too much of a coward to take it. Run, boy. That's all you'll ever be able to do.'

Laughing so hard those eyes flip back into his head. His dad's hands rattle the cellar door; one side drops flat on the cobbles with a smack. The laughter stops; his dad reaches out. Jackie takes a step back. Nothing for his dad to hold on to: he goes head-first. His dad falling through the light of the steps, disappearing into the blackness beneath; feet follow, twisting in mid-air. The crack is more of a vibration than a sound, but it makes Jackie's knees shake. The other hatch bangs down – the light slammed out.

The alley is black. The sound of scraping chairs and raised voices pulses through the walls of the pub. Jackie presses his hands and forehead to the warm wood.

'Dad?'

Nothing. But Jackie can't bring himself to open the cellar. Whatever is down there will drag him under too; he feels it tugging on his bottom lip like a snagged fishing line. The doors of the pub swing open; the clattering of shoes spills over the cobbles.

Jackie runs. A salty taste fills his throat, and the welt on his cheek throbs. If they find out what Jackie has done they will hang him for it. The cup is down there too; maybe they will believe it didn't happen that way. But it is his fault, he wished it into being: *let him be dead, let him be stone dead*. He runs all the way to the fairground, throws up beside a lamp-post and dries his mouth on his sleeve before he goes through the gates; dredges up a smile as Rosie jumps out from behind the rose bushes – boo. His stomach slithers down into his boots; he feels it sloshing. The press of Rosie's body against him doesn't feel the same; she leads him through a pulsing stream of crowds. Why are they all staring at him? Doesn't she pull away just a little too quickly? Doesn't she look at the swing-man just a little too long? What if she already knows what he is?

143

Jackie squeezes her hand tight as they get on to the chairs and she kisses his sore thumb again. She asks to hold his winning cup but he tells her they put it on display at the gym. They ride higher and higher. He shouts, not words, not anything but noise, until his jaw feels as if it has been pummelled by a thousand fists. Rosie laughs beside him. He wants to scream until his lungs explode but every time the swing dips back to earth he feels his innards dropping out of his body. For all the things his dad has done, Jackie hates him for this hollowed-out sickness the most. He has no right to make Jackie feel this way: empty as the cellar before the doors banged shut. He yanks on the rope until it scorches his palms; he wants them to fly above the Common, over the whole of London. Rosie screams with laughter as the swing travels up, up, up. The wind whips around him. Eyes dry and filled with grit, he won't cry. He won't. The world disappears beneath Jackie's feet, a puddle of coloured dots: purple, silver, melting into black.

The body is buried: mourners gone, cloths taken down from pictures and mirrors. The Winnies are back in Mitcham, but the brothers' black-edged telegram of condolence still perches on the mantel (must have saved at least a thrupenny bit by sending one together). Jackie sits in his dad's chair. No one to tip him out of the seat and make him crouch on the rug now; no one to laugh with as Mrs Bell's fat rolls out of her dress when she tries to reach the washing line each Monday. Jackie sniffs and stretches his legs. It really is the best spot at the table: he can see the street outside, and is close enough to smell ashes in the grate. He hears his mum in the kitchen, banging cupboard doors, rattling cups. Rosie sits opposite him, tracing the grain of the table with her fingernail.

'What's your mum up to out there?'

'Letting us know she's none too pleased.'

Jackie let Rosie in the front door and his mum is making a point of staying in the kitchen. He picks up his cold mug of tea and searches the greasy film of milk for a way to start the conversation. Rosie is kicking his ankles under the table, but he doesn't look at her; he needs to think. The summer is over and the day is cold enough for a fire but the coal bucket is empty. The framed picture of his dad stares down from the mantel. Jackie thinks he hears the old man cackling like a magpie.

His mum comes into the room with the tea tray in her hands. She looks older than he remembers, another woman returning from the kitchen. A streak of grey runs from her brow down the back of her head and twists itself into her bun. She closes the door quietly, pressing it with her hip; his dad hated banging doors, and it is as if she still thinks he is in the house. Sometimes when he is alone Jackie tries to imagine what it would have felt like to hold those thin bits of shattered skull together – to bring him back. But today isn't about that.

He helps his mum with the tray; it delays having to speak for another few seconds. He knows there is bread and jam in the larder but none has found its way on to the table. Rosie releases a scent of fresh air and grass as she tilts across. He wants it to be over as soon as possible so they can get back to the Common. She reaches out, squeezes his hand, and for the first time Jackie sees new walls being built in that house: it is him and Rosie together now. She is wearing the same blue flowered dress but there is a bright red ribbon in her hair and a large silver brooch at her chest. Her curls are brushed into one thick wave. Jackie runs his fingers through his hair and puts his jacket back on. His mum picks up the pot to pour more tea, and the rattling of the lid breaks the stillness.

'Mum, this is Rosie.'

His mum sits down on the other side of him. She looks washed-out with Rosie in the room, shabby and drab like the house. Rosie shines, a red gloss to the tips of her black hair and skin brighter than milk. Jackie's lungs throb inside him whenever he looks at her.

145

'So, you're the one who's kept my son out of the house all these months.'

His mum picks up her mug. Rosie doesn't bother to be offended and helps herself to tea, loading sugar on to the spoon. 'That's me. Jackie likes the park and the fair, don't you?'

He grins at her and nods.

'Jackie, that's an Irish name. Are you Irish?'

His mum's brown eyes are unblinking. Rosie doesn't notice the question isn't for her; she slurps up the sweet tea.

'My ma's Irish. He looks like a Jackie.' She glances back at him through the milky steam.

'Funny, John always used to be good enough for him. Sugar, John?'

His mum has put a bowl out, but it is only for show and he knows she is counting every grain. He takes another spoonful. They drink in silence. Rosie makes soft blowing noises as she cools her tea, and that animal sound makes him smile as he remembers the shade of the trees again. She sees his smile and blows louder. Jackie straightens his face. He wonders if his mum can tell – whether there is a smell or a look that women detect, the way Mrs Bell's cat always finds eel spines at the bottom of a bin. But his mum is drinking tea and rolling the loose gold wedding ring around her finger; she doesn't know. Rosie winks and puts down her mug. With that one little movement, which is meant just for him, he falls in love over again.

Rosie clears her throat with a loud cough.

'I'm expecting.'

She grins, moves forward in the chair, bending around him so that his mum can see the smile better and the gentle push of her stomach against the blue dress, the flower pattern in bloom around her. His mum's face turns greyer, like fish scales.

'No, John. Don't tell me it's yours?'

'Mum...'

'I said I don't want to hear it.' She stands up. 'Your father would know what to do,' she mutters, pacing around the small room and its big furniture.

His dad lingers in the house, worse than the smell of fried kippers. Jackie sees his face in the thorns of the rose-pattern wallpaper. He won't have it any more, won't have it ruining his new life. 'Don't mention his name to me again, Mum.'

'This is his house – my house now. And don't you forget that.'

'I'm glad he ain't here. I wouldn't want him around Rosie or my son.'

'Your son?'

His mum clutches her hands together, looming over the table, and for a moment she seems as sturdy as he remembers when he was small, when he thought she could protect him.

Rosie laces her hands over her belly. 'It's a boy, I feel it.'

'Well, we'll see.' His mum grabs her by the elbow.

'Mum?'

He doesn't know what she will do first, slap them or throw them out of the house. Since his dad died she has been moping around the place, but now she is awake, moving with purpose as if it is wash-day. She marches Rosie to the rug in front of the fireplace, pushes on her shoulder until she is flat on the floor. 'Stay down.'

His eyes dart from Rosie to his mum, but Rosie is smiling so he kneels next to her, that thick hair curling across his lap. His mum takes off her wedding ring and fetches a length of string from the dresser drawer. She ties the ring on to the end, drops it from her hand and lets it settle above Rosie's belly. They wait, and slowly the gold begins to move in a tight circle.

'It ain't a boy.' His mum wedges the ring back on her finger.

'It feels like one. There've been enough boys in my family.'

Rosie eases herself up against the armchair. Jackie helps her settle into the cushions, but he doesn't know who to

147

believe. His mum goes back to the table; he wants Rosie to be right.

'We'll see.' His mum picks up the pot. 'I'll put more tea on.' But she turns before leaving the room. 'Mark my words, it'll be a girl.'

SIX

A kettle whistled, and a door clicked shut; it was enough to wake Jack. He rubbed his eyes and rolled towards Georgie. Evening's dirty fingers crept in through every crack. The white wool of Georgie's hair lay knotted across the pillowcase. Jack lowered his head on to the same pillow. The movement tilted her forward, so close that her damp breath settled on his nose. She was stirring now, eyelids moving. Her lashes, thick with mascara, tickled his cheek. He gently touched her shoulder. He didn't want to get up alone.

'Where am I?' Georgie opened one eye.

'Don't even know what bed you fell asleep in – what a disgrace,' Jack whispered in her ear.

She chuckled, burying her face down into the bedding. She was wearing his shirt and he tweaked the back of it.

'I would've warmed you up if you were getting cold.'

He pressed his fingers to her spine. He liked her roundness, the way angles and lines tripped and curled away from her body; it made him want to slide his fingers from her neck to the heel of her foot.

'Suppose you're hungry, that's why you've woken me.' She flipped over, trapping Jack's hand against the mattress.

He checked the clock on the bedside cabinet. 'It's teatime. I think Pearl's back. She'll have something.'

He hopped into his trousers. Stepping over her upended dress and underclothes slumped in a pile by the bed, he reached into the bedside drawer and felt the curled edges of Rosie's photograph; he couldn't leave the room without doing it. No smell of summer grass and peppermints, just war dirt and unwashed cotton. But Georgie was there now. She threw the warm shirt at him.

'I'll see you down there, Jack.'

The house was dead, all doors closed against dust, and no light touched the landing. He used his fingertips to balance against the wall as he went downstairs. A lightning-struck tree lurked at the end of the hallway; it only turned back into a coat-stand when Jack took his mac from one of its branches. The floorboards creaked. But there were other noises, a soft rustling and the bumping of furniture. Mrs Bell's damn cat had got into the front room again; Pearl must have left a window open. The tomcat liked to scratch its claws down the table legs and piss in the cupboard under the stairs. Well, it wasn't going to get away this time; that cat had escaped drowning once too often. Jack carefully turned the handle, holding back until the click told him it was open. He swung the door wide, slammed it shut behind him. The animal was trapped now.

'Jack.' Frank's voice leapt out from the depths of the room.

Frank and Pearl were squashed together in the chair, his armchair. Her yellow jumper lay discarded on the floor at his feet. Jack stepped over it. Frank's left hand slipped down from her face, his other hand buried somewhere deeper in the cushions. Released from the touch of Frank's fingers, Pearl shuddered, the curls on her head snapping into place. She was up, buttoning the blouse and tugging her skirt into shape before Jack crossed the room, twisting her stockings round as she bent in front of the fire, blocking the fading heat. The static crackling of a storm was building up. Jack couldn't understand why blue sparks, bright as coal flames, weren't leaping from his skin. But now he was in front of them, toes touching the chair, he couldn't move. Frank stood up; his shirt and waistcoat rumpled, greasy smudges splattered around the buttons.

'Jack, I know this don't look too good, me with Pearl. But it definitely ain't what you're thinking. I mean, it is what it looks like but it ain't like that…'

'We love each other.' Pearl reached for Frank's hand.

Jack strained to hear her above the cracking of his lungs inside his chest. She didn't even turn to Frank. This was all her doing. Pearl stood in front of him, toes curling inwards and grasping at the thin rug; no support shoes to keep her straight. Sweat sat on her upper lip; the trail of a wet kiss lingered on her neck. No grazed shins and running nose. Jack tightened the belt of the mac.

'Frank wanted to tell you. It was me, Jack. I'm the one told him we should wait until we had it all sorted...'

Jack felt the words coming at last, rising and bubbling up out of his chest. 'Sorted? Christ almighty, you're knocked up.'

He sank on to the threadbare arm of the chair. The door opened. Georgie swayed her hips across the room towards the table, touching the pot and pouring herself tea.

'It's all out, then. Did you tell Jack or did Jack catch you? I'm hoping you told him.'

'You knew about this?' Jack's head snapped up.

'It weren't hard to guess. But I didn't think it was none of my business.' She shrugged and perched against the table, searched for a spoon.

She was just like the others, trying to break him.

'Please listen, Jack.' Pearl shook her head.

'You knew Pearl was up the duff and never said nothing.'

'Well, no. I didn't know that. But there're things you can have done. I know a woman who can sort it.' Georgie tried to smile.

'Pearl will need to see – '

'I ain't expecting.' Pearl clutched the front of her skirt.

'Then why all the shouting?' Georgie pulled her lips into a straight line and went back to pinning a strand of hair in place. Jack ripped off the mac, held it balled up in his lap.

'That's something to be bloody thankful for. Frank'll move back to the gym. We can forget about this happening, because it won't happen again.'

'It ain't up to you, Jack. You ain't listening properly.' Pearl picked up the spoon from the floor and placed it on the table. 'We love each other.'

'I'll be all right at the gym, Pearl.' Frank held on to her hand. 'Jack's got a right to have his home the way he wants it. We got to respect that.'

'Ain't it my home too, Frank?' She pulled him closer.

They formed a wall in front of the fire, and all Jack had left before him was the dent of the seat, a long dark hair caught across the back. He studied the threads of the armchair, unravelling after years of wear; draped his coat over to cover it up. Georgie clinked the teaspoon as she stirred; it sounded like an iron hook scraping against his head. Not enough air to breathe. Jack planted his fists on his knees, swallowing down air before he could speak.

'You two will do as I say, that's what I understand. Home and gym ain't for mixing.'

'Tell him, Frank...'

'I've got responsibilities now, Jack. It's not just me – there's Pearl, and when we do have kids... well, I need to stop fighting soon. I have to think about our future. Look at me, Jack. This eye's scarred, I don't hear none too clearly – '

'You're only a kid yourself. No point thinking like an old pro with hundreds of fights to your name.' Jack shook his head. 'That's fear talking.'

'Pearl can't protect herself, all the damage she takes. All them scars. But I've got a choice, Jack. One of us has to stay strong. It's not right for Pearl to be putting me back together too. I need to be taking care of her.'

'Poor you.' Jack's fist clasped the arm of the chair. 'We signed a contract, Frank. I paid out good money.'

'We'll see you're not out of pocket. Pearl wants to be a nurse and I need to support her, get a job, regular money coming in.'

'A job? Labouring, the steel works? Think that kind of life's going to keep you pretty? You won't be able to stick it.'

'We got it all decided, me and Frank. I'm going to go do nursing, it pays same as the factory to begin with but we can save.'

Shut up, shut up. Jack stood up and the chair slid backwards with the thrust of his calves. 'What a load of cock and bull. Next you'll be saying you're off to buy them ten-pound fares to Australia. I'll bloody well take you to the ticket office myself. See how you do on your own out there, shall we?'

'We want to stay here. Please…'

Jack swatted Pearl's words away with the back of his hand. 'That contract binds us, Frank. I've got deals lined up. I'll never get another booking, another fighter, if I cancel it all now. Vincent and his friends ain't the type to take no for an answer.'

Jack grabbed for Frank then stopped, frozen in the dusty evening light just like the first time at the gym. The leather bag had swirled around but this time it was Pearl getting between them. She held Frank's hand behind her back, eyes fixed on Jack. It was always her, always making him choose. He didn't move any closer.

Georgie stood up. 'Come on, Jack. We can go to the Electric for a cuppa. Let things settle a bit.'

'I've got years' worth of tea slopping inside me, and you want to keep pouring it down my throat.' Jack grabbed the pot. 'I'm choking on fucking tea.'

The blue ceramic sides burned into his palms. Pearl blinked back at him. 'We need you to understand, Jack…'

Understand. She had torn it all into shreds, stamped on every hope he ever had. Jack hurled the pot at the picture frames on the mantel. Glass and pottery cracked open on the brick hearth; a brown stain like blood soaked into the wallpaper. Frank might as well be lying out for the count on the floor, no hope of ever getting up. Pearl scrambled on her knees and Frank helped her pick up the bent photographs, their heads touching. Georgie gripped the edge of the table. When Frank and Pearl were crushed together, sneaking around, they had made a fool of him. Jack strode towards them. Laughing behind his back, setting him up and waiting to snatch it all away – just like the rest of them: his brothers pushing him around; the Winnies smiling and spreading poison; his mum's boiling jealousy; his dad standing back and admiring his work as they ripped each other apart. He reached up for the framed picture.

'Don't. Leave him alone.' Pearl tried to cuff his hand aside.

The walls of the house slammed up against Jack. He pushed back. His palms thumped into contact with Pearl's shoulders. She stumbled against the fireplace, the side of her head knocking against the heavy-framed picture with its funeral wreath engraving. Frank side-stepped to catch her. The picture hung askew. His dad stared down at them from behind the splintered glass.

'Pearl, you all right?' Frank tried to hold on to her arms but she shook herself free. 'No more, Jack.'

'He ain't done yet. Are you, Jack? Admit it. You've been waiting years for me to do something wrong. Ain't you? Show me what you really think of me. Do it, Jack.'

Shut up. Shut up. He wasn't Jack, he was John Munday, son of John. He slapped Pearl, knuckles hitting bone.

'Enough.' Georgie got down on her knees, picking up pieces of glass and splinters of wood.

'What you all looking at me for? She didn't feel a thing, not even a bloody twinge.'

That flat round face was still as a mirror, the red shape of his fingers reflected back at him. Everything she made him do: grabbing her from Rosie's arms, yellow bundle of wool, screams fading to a squeak like the rats; the black water had plugged his ears until he was deaf to Pearl. Now she was ruining everything again. She held the fading photographs. He raised his hand, wanted to break his fists against the metal fireplace. Frank seized his wrists, thrust him against the wall: fingers burning into his skin, feet lifted into the air, dangling like a child.

Pearl touched Frank's arm. 'No, you'll hurt him.'

Frank placed him back in the chair, gently as a snow-flake settles. Jack swallowed down air and melted into the cushions. Georgie dropped the debris on to the tray. Frank helped Pearl set the broken pictures on the mantel; she shook the glass from the paper and straightened the bowed frames, carefully settling them in their original places. All carrying on without him: Jack, head of that rotten family.

'Think on this, Frank – I gave you a chance. Without me you've got nothing – you *are* nothing. Now fuck off out of my house!' Jack's voice crashed over into a scream. 'And you.' He pushed his face towards Pearl. 'Get out of my sight.'

Spit landed on her chin. As she moved he smelt Frank on her skin. Jack looked away but he could taste them: the lies. It was everywhere, in the heavy wallpaper and the worn rug, dripping from every surface in that house. He couldn't trust any of them.

Pearl and Frank stood side by side in the doorway.

'I love him. Even you can see that, Jack.'

The first time Jack heard that word, 'love', he'd been so happy; it had meant that at last he would have something of his own. Someone to spend his life with, and the baby was supposed to bring him all that. He knew better this time. Jack snatched up Frank's bag from beside the chair, threw it at his feet. 'He was *my* business. *My* future. Not yours, Pearl.'

'I wouldn't play her around. We want to get married.' Frank picked up his bag.

'Fighting's all you had, Frank. There ain't nothing else for you.' Jack let out a sharp laugh and the push of air tightened his throat.

Frank rubbed at a scar on his cheek. 'It ain't like that.'

'It's exactly like that.' Jack gripped his hands around the base of his neck, their signal to finish and get out. 'Just make sure you turn up to our next fight, or I'll come looking for you. That contract binds us more than anything you've said to her.'

'I'll fight our next fight. I'll win it for you, you know I can.' Frank hauled the bag up on to his back. 'But I can't keep at it.'

'A fighter that don't want to fight. Fucking big fat joke on me.'

Georgie circled behind them, looking for an in; they were all coming at him.

'I'll see you at training, Jack. We'll be mates again, I know we will.'

'It's only business to me.'

'Don't worry, Frank. I'll see you later.' Pearl stepped back into her shoes as she kissed him on the cheek.

Frank left the room, the front door clicking shut behind him.

'I won't stop seeing him, Jack.'

'None of you even know what's broken here, do you? A bloody fighter that won't fight – that's our ticket out of this hole flushed right away.'

'There'll be other fighters.' Georgie twisted her eyebrows into an arch.

'Why don't you shut up and fix your hair or whatever it is you got to do.'

The sharp nagging of her voice was like a set of nails scraping down his face, her fat shoulders rolling forward and her head pushed out towards him as she spoke.

'I'm just saying, no need to be narked. It ain't my fault – '

'Nothing's ever no one's fault.'

She was only an arm's reach away, her chest rising and falling with short, shallow breaths. Being with Georgie was no good; she could never fix anything: she could never be Rosie.

'You're nothing but an ugly sow.'

Jack pushed himself out of the chair and across the room; he opened his hand. Georgie's head turned to deflect the coming blow, but she didn't pull away; she didn't flinch because she was expecting it. Jack's hand fixed in mid-air; it was as if someone held a flame to each of his remaining nails, making his hand curl, the joints crack. Georgie righted her head until it was squarely on her shoulders, and with the back of her hand she smoothed her eyebrow into place.

'Why don't you piss off?' Jack took out a cigarette.

He had to use both hands to strike the match; the orange flame flickered and nearly died, but he couldn't keep his fingers steady.

'It's the shock. She's not a baby no more. That's what you'll tell me when you come grovelling, anyhow.' Georgie turned to Pearl slumped in the chair. 'He'll come round, don't you worry. I'm giving you a week to make this right, Jack.'

Her brown eyes were sharper now; he almost thought they were watering slightly but she didn't wipe back any tears. Georgie touched Pearl's shoulder as she left. She was gone: no blood, no contract, to make her stay.

'Go after her, Jack.'

He wanted to dig his nails into Pearl's skin, scratch down until he found a layer of her that had to be able to feel something. But she would never understand what it felt like to have burning pain pierce her skin, to feel herself flayed open and pinned out by the memory of a kiss. That was what love did, in that house anyway. Always that house. The greens and browns of the room spread towards him like flowing mud. And he would be soaked up by the rotting furniture and moth-eaten fabrics, trapped forever as nothing but a shadow in that house.

The chair creaked as Pearl stood up.

'You're wrong if you think I can't feel. I know what the pain is doing to Frank. You're breaking him down piece by piece. It's what you always do. You might as well stub cigarettes out on him too.' She sounded distant and small, as if she was in another room. 'If you don't let him go, you'll lose me.'

'Stupid cow.' Jack kicked a broken square of blue pottery across the room. 'Some things can't never be put back together.'

She closed the door on his words. Frank was never going to be part of their lives; outliving his usefulness. Jack stared at the blackout curtains as they flapped in a draught. He went over to the window and bit the edge of his thumb, peeling back the skin with his teeth. It made him laugh to think of taking Georgie up town to Bobbie Black's; she was a south-of-the-river piece of skirt. Good enough for a bit of jolly, but the fun couldn't last. He didn't need her burrowing any deeper into his life. The clop-clop of her heels had echoed in the room as she walked away, but it was only a trick of the rising smog. His teeth chewed skin until he tasted blood. He didn't care, was getting bored anyway, waking up next to her fat body, keeping his hands out of the way. *Don't mess up me hair, don't smudge me make-up*. He didn't care: plenty of better things to do with his time. He didn't care: they all left him in the end anyway.

SEVEN

'Hurry it up.' Rosie draws him closer.

Jackie's thighs bang against the dresser and the row of enamel mugs clink against each other; the good plates and glasses are shut up inside the cupboard – his mum thinks it will keep them safe if no one uses them. Rosie works at the buttons on his shirt, smiles as the Bible Factory ink smudges off on her fingers. Jackie feels the breath of the factory men still on him.

'Maybe I should wash first.'

'No, stay here.' Rosie glances at the door. 'I miss you.'

He can't help holding still, swallowing his breath in case he hears footsteps in the alleyway. He slides her dress up. The whiteness surprises him for a moment, soft and pallid as a block of soap. The baby is six weeks old but his mum still makes them keep separate beds. Rosie's smell is unfamiliar: sour milk and something musky like the stink of fight-swaddling.

'What?' She puts her hand on his shoulder. 'I told you your mum's gone down the butcher's, won't be back for ages.'

He glances up at the ceiling.

'She's sleeping like a baby, that's what she does. If you don't want to, you could've just said.'

Rosie shifts along the top of the dresser. Jackie puts out his hands and stops her. 'I always want to. Only I've been thinking. I have to go and register the birth soon. Wondered if you'd decided on a name for her?'

'I've already said what I want.'

'But Mum's been talking about the name Joyce.'

159

'She's our daughter, Jackie. What do *you* want to call her?'

'I want what you want. Pearl it is. Had to stop calling her "the baby" some time.'

Their faces are level: a bridge of freckles crosses her nose and runs under her eyes – the only sign left of summer sun.

'Come here.'

She holds him to her chest, rubs her cheek along the side of his face. She kisses and cradles him as if he is the child, not the tiny pink bundle of Pearl upstairs. He feels protected in Rosie's thin arms.

'I'll get you anything you want, I promise.' His voice softened by the folds of her cardigan.

'I've lost my ribbon down the back of the dresser. You can start by getting me some more tomorrow.' She taps his head.

'Easy. Anything else?'

'Promise me we'll get out of this house, Jackie.'

She squashes his face in her hands, noses touching. He nods and pushes his lips against hers. She keeps talking but he doesn't hear the words; he swallows them inside himself, feels buoyed up with the air she exhales. The dresser top creaks under their weight but they can't stop; a splinter lodges into the soft skin at the top of his thigh but they can't stop. She keeps her hand pressed to the back of his neck; they stare into each other until he feels that he is seeing with her eyes, facing his own reflection.

Rosie stands at the stove, clouds collecting about her. Jackie imagines her in only the steam, no brown cardigan, no faded blue skirt. He leans back in the chair to get a better view. His mum points a knitting needle at him; Pearl is draped on her shoulder and the yellow wool trails over her on to the table.

'What have you got to smile about?'

'I'm saving up for us to move out.' He rocks on the back legs.

'Break that, you pay for it. Perfectly good home here for you and Joyce.'

Jackie bangs the chair down on all fours. 'Her name is Pearl, you know that. This is my family, Mum. You don't want us getting in the way, having to share your bed with Rosie.'

He winds the end of the wool around his finger. It rubs against Pearl's hand and she flinches, eyes screwing up as if she is about to cry.

'There's not enough houses out there for those that really need them, let alone ones who'll rent to children. You're not like the Winnies moving to the country, out Guildford way. Not like Tommy and Bill off serving King and Country. No, you belong here, John, with me.'

'I'm sixteen now.' He puts his hands behind his head, stretches out.

'What about my Joyce? Better for everyone to think she's mine, and the council would have something to say about an unmarried – '

Rosie clangs the spoon against the side of the pot.

'Who'd believe you? You can't even get her name right. It says in black and white she's Pearl. Jackie filled in the papers today.'

'Want to watch that mouth of yours, girl? Before someone watches it for you.' His mum points the needle across the table at Rosie.

'There'll be nothing for dinner if I let the tongue boil dry.' She pokes the pink lump with the back of the spoon.

Pearl's head wobbles to the side as she yawns. Everyone stops to watch; his mum rubs her hand over the baby's spine. Rosie pours more water into the pot; it hisses angrily.

'John, fetch up J… Pearl's blanket from the front room.'

But he only goes as far as the stairs in the hallway; he has taken to lingering in doorways whenever his mum sends him on an errand. Jackie likes to know what lies she is dropping in Rosie's ear. He sandwiches himself between the door and the wall, the rose pattern scratching his hands.

'I know my son. He's all big plans and grand ideas now. How do you expect him to find time for his fighting, with you and the baby always needing something? He was going to be a name, make it big. But he don't stick to things, that's his problem. Now his brothers, they're in the Army, my brave boys. There might even be another war.' She shakes her head. 'Just wait until it gets difficult, wait until money gets tight. And it will. He won't mean to but he'll turn on you. Family, rent, food to get? Ain't you all better off here, where I can help?'

He clenches his fists, bites down on his bottom lip.

'I'm grateful you've taken us in, but you ain't getting us for keeps. Jackie will...' The rest of Rosie's words are lost in the sizzle of water hitting the stove ring.

'He's only a boy, I say, and don't think you're taking my Pearl – '

Jackie strides into the kitchen, cuts her off. 'We're getting married. We'll be a proper family. Understand me?' He leans over the table, hopes his mum feels small sat on the chair.

'John, son. You can't do this without me.' She smiles and strokes her hand over his. 'Who's looked out for you all these years?'

'Rosie is my family now.'

Rosie hugs an arm around herself, half turns to smile at him.

'You can wipe that smirk off your face. My Pearl will be married before you are, young girl. Your sort don't marry.'

'Mum...'

Pearl moans and his mum's hands shoot up to pat her back. 'Shh, you'll wake the baby shouting like that. I was right about her being a girl. I'm right about lots of things.'

'Not this. When Jackie asks me to marry him, I'm going to say yes. Then you, the council, the Church, the whole city can piss off.' Rosie waves the spoon in the air.

His mum pretends she can't hear, shushing and cooing over the baby. He can't stand the hurt look in his mum's eyes, the one she uses each time now when she feels betrayed: if he raises his voice, if he disagrees with her, that wet-paper look. She holds up her white apron, covering the baby.

'I'm going for a lie-down. I probably won't be able to get up for supper. Tell *her* not to wake me when she comes to bed.'

'Maybe *you'll* get out the right side tomorrow.' Rosie watches her leave.

Jackie closes the door behind his mum. Saturday night, and smog is bumping against the panes. He pulls Rosie away from the stove and on to his lap as he sits at the table. She stares into the yard.

'Summer's late in coming but it's not far off. The family'll already be set up for the first fairs of the season.'

'We could go and see them.' He gathers her hair into a bunch.

'We need to save the money.'

She sucks down on the end of a curl. He shifts in the chair and she drops a little deeper into his lap.

'Can't hurt to check the trains. We'll do it tomorrow.'

'I'm not sure they'd take too kindly to Pearl.' She indicates the ceiling with her thumb.

He listens to the footsteps, the closing of doors and banging of drawers. It goes quiet at last.

'Next year, I promise. I'm doing good at the factory – it'll be enough to get by for now, but things will look up when I can get some real fights.' He can't help whispering.

'She was right about Pearl being a girl, that's all.' Rosie sighs.

'Well, you said it yourself, she's wrong about the rest.' He wraps his arms around her waist.

'Then let's get married now.'

Rosie clutches his sleeve in her fist. The shirt stretches tight across his shoulders; none of his clothes fit any more. Upstairs in the wardrobe hang a suit and two good shirts but they don't belong to Jackie and he is never going to wear them, not even if he bursts at the seams: dead man's clothes. The pot rocks; peeling tongue rises and bursts on the surface.

'I want to do it proper, Rosie. Make it nice for you. Can you let me do that? Give me a few more months.'

Rosie stands up to face him. She nods and her breasts wobble; she sees him looking and loosens the woollen cardigan a little. What they did earlier, it wasn't like lying in the grass and feeling the sun tickle his back. The baby has sucked some share of life away from Rosie – her eyes, her soft curls, her skin – but everything that is left is his: a family.

He walks down Lomond Grove; the rain can't dislodge his smile but it has washed the smog away, leaving a stale bonfire smell, and by the time Jackie gets home the stench is lodged deep inside the folds of his clothes. He is late but Rosie will forgive him when he shows her what he has been to collect. It took nearly a year but he has finally saved enough, more than enough. He rubs the little green box in his pocket: something to make Rosie laugh and clap her hands. He opens the back door and steps into the light of the kitchen. His mum and Pearl are there; they always are. It smells of coal and stewed tea but there isn't any sign of food. He pays his own way now but it all goes on that house: the baby, Rosie. They didn't even have the money to visit her family; she misses them in a way he can't understand. But he knows how to make it up to her.

'Evening, Mum.'

She looks up then goes back to wiping the corners of Pearl's mouth with the edge of her apron, leaning against the heavy wooden draining board. Her wiry hair is slicked back against her head from the steam rolling out of the boiling nappy pan. Jackie holds his breath as he crosses the kitchen and goes into the hallway.

'Rosie, I'm home. Where are you?'

He can't wait any longer, wants to show her the jewellery box, what's bedded inside. He has been planning it since

Christmas. It doesn't matter who else sees; the whole street can witness it for all he cares. He taps his fingers on the door-frame.

'Shh, or you'll wake Pearl.' His mum stokes the fire.

Jackie never understands how she manages to do something else when Pearl always occupies one arm. Every time he is allowed near her, it takes up every hand and thought, struggling to stop her from falling into the grate or rolling away across the floor. He moves into the hallway.

'Rosie?'

He has worked hard, and now they can do as they please. No more lying about Pearl; get a home of their own, he can afford it with his new apprenticeship at the Bible Factory. Jackie rubs the hard cover of the jewellery box in his pocket; that gold-plated ring will make everything right. He grips the banisters and sings her name up the stairs. 'Rosie.'

Jackie holds on to the poles and leans backwards so he can see into the kitchen. 'I had to call in somewhere after work. Is she angry because I said I'd take her out?'

'There's no point asking me what the girl thinks. She inherited that face from her people. They're not called bare-faced liars for nothing.' His mum smacks her lips.

'Leave Rosie alone.' He goes back in to the kitchen.

'You don't see what she's like every day, that nasty tongue. Barely even looks at the little one.' She kisses Pearl's head. 'And I know she caused that crack in the dresser. I told her to dry it proper after washing it down.'

'Is Rosie in the lav?' The anger is rising, his throat constricts around the words.

The plates rattle on the dresser beside him, and he runs his finger along the crack in the surface.

'She ain't out there.' His mum smoothes Pearl's wisps of hair.

'Where is she?' He plants himself in front of her, one hand on the sink.

'She's gone.'

'Gone where?' He holds back the stone growing in his throat. Scum from the soaking baby clothes in the basin collects around the sides, crawling towards his fingers.

'I gave her the train fare. And told her the truth – there ain't going to be any marriage. You haven't even asked me for your grandmother's ring. I only said what she already knows. We don't need her.' His mum tightens the ties of her apron, her body spilling over the sides.

'I won't let you drive her off like you have everyone else. I'll fetch her back.'

He wants to get out of the house, away from that street just to find some air. The cold of the rain has worked its way down to his bones, and he will never be able to get warm in that kitchen.

'She took all her things.' His mum blocks his way to the door.

'Pearl's here.'

Jackie wants to grab his mum and shake the words out of her, push his hand over the baby's snuffling face to stop it from taking all her attention. And perhaps it was his mum who had driven his dad for all those years, sharpening him to a point until he had no choice but to run them all through.

'She's not coming back, John.' She shifts the baby to her other hip. 'We're better off without that slovenly tart. Pearl's better off.'

Jackie doesn't hear her; he is riding high on the swing chairs again, so high that he can see his mum and Pearl like a distant pinprick. The kitchen is miles beneath his feet. His whole body shakes with the effort of tugging on the ropes. He holds his breath. He waits for the sickening plummet, knows if he doesn't leave now he will never be able to find the strength to drag himself up and make that rope tight again. He scoops up Pearl, slams the door behind them. He runs down the alley, the yellow blanket slapping against his shoulder, splashing into the darkness of the street.

EIGHT

Jack surfaced from the Underground at Leicester Square, the clattering voices of Pearl, Frank and Georgie still stuck in his head, not even the din of the Northern Line having dislodged them. He entered Soho, street-light shrivelled away from unlit doorways; the smell of beer and scalding tea, gas heaters and rainy pavements. He took long, heavy strides as if he spent every night walking that side of the river. Jack flicked up his jacket lapels; he'd got all the way to Kennington before he realised he had forgotten his coat but he hadn't been about to go back for it. Unaccompanied women stood in groups of two or three on the corner of Dean Street. He kept moving. He found himself on Wardour Street three times before he spotted the club. Nothing but a small brass nameplate tucked beside a doorway: Bobbie Black's.

Jack stepped into the thin alleyway, avoiding the oily puddles. A man in a woollen suit stood on the step.

'This here's a private place.'

The leaded lamp by the door turned him into a patchwork of green and black lines. Jack knew the bloke was eyeing his cheap shoes from the market and his pre-war suit.

'I'm a private man.'

He slid the card out from his pocket: *Vincent Metzger* printed in gold across the middle of the white square. The steel-plated door opened. Jack went down a narrow flight of steps and was eaten up by the club. Heavy red carpet covered the floor, right up to the edges of the room. The walls were navy blue, tinged with purple, the colour of London's night sky. Jack stood and squinted at the bottom of the stairs; music pulsated against his ribcage. Circles of white light pierced down like moon rays scattered across the room. But between those pools of brightness the place was murky as a coalhole. Jack skirted the edge of the tables, made his way towards the strip of bulbs illuminating the bar.

He stuck with the whisky. It came on a small, shiny metal mat. Jack hoped it was real silver, as he'd blown the best part of a week's money on that one glass. Ever since he'd got the card, Jack had been planning this trip to Vincent's. It was supposed to be a big night, one of the best; make Vincent wait a week until he was ready to bite Jack's hand off. And now here Jack was, sooner than he wanted, much sooner. The drink didn't touch his mouth, just hit the back of his throat; he blinked away the water that stung the corner of his eyes. It was good stuff, fiery and cold, with a dryness that made his tongue shrink. Jack let the drink burn inside as he leaned against the bar. Frank had turned all those plans to ash.

Small groups sat around the white tablecloths, legs hidden under folds of material, features sheared off by the light drilling down from the ceiling. A woman sang on the stage at the front, all tight blonde curls and snugger silk gown; the dress reflected the club. Her whole body shone, rippling and bouncing to the murmur of voices that lay just beneath the level of the music, as though mercury had leaked from a thermometer. Jack couldn't make out a word, he couldn't even hear the two suits near him at the bar, but he didn't suppose it was the type of conversation he wanted to overhear.

He tuned back in as the music changed: slowed-down and breathless, the trumpet barely peeping, the singer's voice thick as malt syrup off the back of a teaspoon. The tap of the drum disrupted his heartbeat: he recognised the song. Rosie had soothed the baby to the opening lines, soft as a lullaby. *Say a prayer for me, but not farewell.* His mum out of the room, and they'd pretended for minutes at a time that it was their home. He had rested his chin on her head; Rosie kept rocking but lifted one hand up to stroke his cheek. *The lights will soon be out.* Jack bit into the ice cube, a deep marrow-ache spreading through his jaw like taking an upper cut. *Darkness might cast its spell, But dawn will see us together again, don't doubt.*

He ordered another drink; it went the way of the first. A deadness crept into his arms and legs; he couldn't leave even if he wanted to. He had to make the best of a bad fighter. Tonight, Pearl and Frank had left him with no choice. The Thin Suit appeared at the side of the stage. He held back a red curtain and Vincent came into the room; hands and faces tilted in greeting as they passed the tables. Of course Jack could sneak and he could lie, as good as Pearl and Frank – it was the stock he came from. If that science journal Newton gave Pearl said his dad was spun around them, twisted up in their insides, then who was Jack to argue? Scrimping on the morning run, the lateness to training, it all made sense now.

Vincent stepped off the carpet and on to the black bricks surrounding the bar. Frank was willing to throw away all they had worked for, and for what, for what? He was going places, and didn't need Frank to get him there. He was Lucky Jack after all, thinking on his feet as usual. He scooped the last cube from his glass, splintered it between his teeth again just to feel something.

Vincent stood in front of him, blocking the stage.

'Evening, Jack. I was starting to think you'd got cold feet.' His voice was low, as if it came from deep down inside his chest.

Jack raised his empty glass in greeting, his tongue numb from the ice. The Thin Suit ordered more drinks by tapping his finger like a pointed bird's beak; the barman came running.

'You all right? Seems to me you look a bit off.' The Thin Suit held the drink, just out of Jack's reach.

Vincent rested one arm on the bar and his knuckles rapped the polished wood in time to the music; a gold watch was draped around his wrist and silver cufflinks sparkled.

'Ain't nothing wrong with me.' Jack stuffed his hands in his jacket.

'No, there's something. Touch of fever maybe, bad news…' The Thin Suit wagged his finger.

'You must be thinking of someone else, mate.'

'No, I'd have to disagree and say that's not a happy face. What could it be?' The Thin Suit tapped his chin as if he was thinking it over.

'It's a fucking top-of-the-world face.' Jack grinned, his molars grinding.

Vincent patted the Thin Suit on the elbow and indicated his drink. The Thin Suit took a slow gulp of whisky, his Adam's apple bobbing like ice.

'Top of the evening to you too, Jack. Your fighter's Irish, ain't he?' Vincent smiled.

'South London, born and bred.'

Jack coughed as the last shard of ice scraped down the lining of his throat. The Thin Suit slapped him on the back, so hard he felt his ribs shudder.

'Pity. Everyone likes to see the Irish take a beating.' Vincent pulled up a stool.

'He's got Irish blood.'

Vincent laughed. The woman stopped singing and the band changed their music, but no one turned to look at Vincent: thrown back head and open mouth. The music started again, the Stargazers' 'Broken Wings'. Jack had always thought it was a stupid song until then. Vincent spread his hands on the bar.

'I'm glad you've come to see me. I wondered how long my card would burn a hole in your pocket.'

The Thin Suit angled his head and whispered something into Vincent's ear. Vincent nodded. 'But right now I've got some business needs my attention. Make yourself at home.'

Jack's eyes were glued to the singer on the stage, every curve and stretch of fabric. She stopped singing and focused on him, lips apart, chest rising.

'I'll be back.' Vincent winked. 'She probably thinks you're a young Tyrone Power.'

'She's got good taste, then.' Jack pulled out his packet of cigarettes.

'It's dark in here.' The Thin Suit straightened his razor-slim tie.

Vincent thumped Jack on the shoulder. 'Well, don't leave without seeing me.'

Jack watched them move off to a table at the edge of the room; the Thin Suit pulled the seat out from under one of the men, offered it to Vincent. The man had to crouch, gripping the tablecloth for support. Jack slipped two cigarettes out of the packet, lit one and swallowed the dusty taste of tobacco. He licked the tip of the other, sucked down harder as he drew a flame from the glowing end of the first. The music still played but the singer glided through the tables as if her feet weren't touching the ground, dress swelling against the white foam of the tablecloths. Georgie never bothered to dress fancy like that. Jack held out the cigarette. The singer took it as she positioned herself against the bar, elbow down and bent as she rearranged the set of her hair. Smoke slipped out as she smiled. He summoned the barman with a click of his fingers.

'Two whiskies.'

'It's medicinal, for the voice.' She draped her other wrist over the curved lip of the bar.

'I don't think you need any help.'

'Stella's the name, like the stars.' She held up her hand, fingers dripping down.

Jack didn't know any film stars, they were more Pearl's thing, but he took the hand and held it in his without letting go. She didn't pull away.

'Haven't seen you here before. How do you know Vincent?' With her free hand she raised the glass of whisky off the bar. Jack downed his drink in one mouthful, cigarette dangling dangerously between his fingers.

'Business.'

171

'I know, none of mine.' She revealed a tightly packed row of teeth.

Her smile broke the firmly lacquered layer of her hair and face; teeth that could bite. Georgie was the one who'd walked out; probably found herself some other bloke before she reached the end of the road. Stella's pupils swallowed up most of the whites of her eyes, and Jack couldn't help remembering that parrot. She had the same stretched veiny neck, but it was too late to leave now.

'Vincent likes my voice. He's setting me up with some recording time. I only sing here for the practice.'

Away from the hazy lights of the stage he saw that the hem of her dress was wrinkled from constant washing and a loose thread hung from the scooped neckline.

'Sounded pitch-perfect to me.' Jack dropped the dead cigarette into his glass; his fingers reached out for the stray thread and plucked it free. 'Dust.'

He looked into those kohl-smudged eyes. His fingers laced their way under the satiny material, hooked themselves into the hollow of her collarbone. He let go when he noticed Vincent coming back from a table in the middle of the room. The Thin Suit slid down into Vincent's seat, moving it around so he faced Jack. The last curls of smoke drifted up from Stella's cigarette.

'So, you like the place, then.' Vincent put his arm around Jack's shoulder and the other around Stella's waist. 'My sweet young things.' He pulled them against his silky suit.

'It's classier than my local.' Jack breathed out as he was released from Vincent's grip. 'But that's not why I came.'

'Why don't you tell Vincent why you're here?' He smiled, then held up a finger to Jack as he turned to the girl, pushing a curl from her face. 'What use is there in a singer that don't sing?'

'I was just on my way back to the stage, Vincent.'

Jack watched her go, but, pretty as she was, much as he wanted to bury his face against that pillow chest, he was there to see Vincent. Plenty of girls out there ready to lie back just like Georgie. And there were plenty of fighters too. He straightened his shoulders.

'I'm here to talk business.'

'Do you know how I do business, Jack?'

'I've heard things. But I ain't interested in rumours.' Jack pushed his empty glass away. 'Things are changing with my fighter.'

Let Vincent plan and scheme all he wanted, Jack wasn't going to fight against him; he would save something from the mess Frank had left behind.

'Don't dismiss rumours, Jack. Just make sure you're the one making them for yourself. Rumours, alibis, threats. I didn't get to be partners with Bobbie Black by keeping my nose clean.'

'London's always been a dirty city.' Jack kept his focus locked on Vincent: dark hairs sprouted at the inner corner of his eyes where tears came from.

'And long may she stay so. I'll salute that.' Vincent raised his glass. 'But you've finished your drink. Let's top you up.'

He held Jack's empty glass in the air. Another whisky arrived on a silver tray in seconds. The groomed barman placed it down, his white shirt pleated and starched, a black bow-tie strangling his neck. Jack took the drink and the man disappeared back behind the lights of the bar. The Thin Suit sat and stared from across the room, rubbing his knuckles under his bony chin. Vincent edged closer. 'Work is all about money and dues, but boxing, that's something different. It's an art. Don't get me wrong, I'm not going to hang up some watercolour my old nan did. I want Van Gogh, I want Turner. Art's about value, about money.'

'Like I said, things are changing.'

'Really? I'll be honest, I thought the boy was a keeper, but you are the expert, Jack. If there's something I don't know…'

'He's better than any I've ever had, but they all get broken down in the end.'

'But are you looking for a handout or are you looking to sell, Jack?'

Jack rubbed his arm. Frank was like bomb shrapnel embedded in the skin: cut it out before the flesh grew around it, sucked it into the body where it could do more harm, rip things up, leak its poison – ARP training had taught him that much. He licked the last of the whisky from his lips.

'Maybe I'm ready to sell… for the right price.'

Vincent took his empty glass and raised his hand again; and again; and again; and again. Jack lost count of the drinks, and the conversation slipped away from him. He blinked hard as he tried to bring the room around him into focus. But the floor jumped beneath his feet and he couldn't keep still, lurching and listing like a man on the ropes. Vincent was still talking. Jack clung to those words and dragged himself back.

'… you can be the manager everybody wants. I can see to it. A telephone call here, the odd telegram, and all of England will know what sort of man Jack Munday is.' Vincent lit a thin cigar and added to the smoke that swirled around their heads. 'The best bloody manager there is, Jack. That's what you want, don't tell me it ain't.'

'What do I have to do for it?' Jack tried to clip each word but they ran together in a stream. Stella and the musicians on the stage swayed to the rhythm of their song; either that or Jack was spinning now too.

Vincent puffed on his cigar. 'Don't be coy with me. Your fighter's on top form. You're an unmarked man, new to the big scene. We're not talking amateur now, you know.'

The milky fog swamped Jack's head, stinging his eyes until the edges of the room began to seep away. The painted stars on the night-sky ceiling twisted and shook above him; the dark purple walls drifted like clouds towards him. Jack clutched the bar to steady himself.

'I heard odds on your boy's last opponent winning were twenty to one. Those are profitable numbers, Jack. And I bet his next fight will be even higher. The world and his dog think he can't lose.' Vincent smiled. 'Maybe I'll even come down and have a butcher's for myself, make sure he hasn't turned lame.'

A gust of cold air hit Jack's legs as somebody left the club. The chill wind clung to him, he shook himself free with a judder. 'He's fighting better than ever. But he takes a fall and where's that leave me?'

Jack shielded his eyes against the white lights. He wanted to ask the barman why he had turned the lamps higher, why the music from the drum and Stella's voice on the stage were raised to a glass-cracking level. Jack held back a burp. Vincent kept smiling. And only hours before Jack would have thrown back that offer, laughed in Vincent's face... probably would have – probably, but not now.

'Don't be in such a rush, Jack. We'll break bread soon enough. I've got a bright future lined up for you. It won't be bookings for town halls and public baths. We're talking York Hall, Empire Pool at Wembley. Imagine the percentage of that purse money. Need Pickford's to take it home each night. I like to hand-pick my people. I've got the fighting future, even better than your boy, and he's all yours, if...' Vincent showed his teeth.

'I deserve this.'

Jack shook the brightness out of his eyes. His head felt as if it was attached by rope, and it cracked back into place as he tried to stop the rest of his body going limp.

'Course you do, Jack.' Vincent held out his hand.

The cigar smouldered in the ashtray; the tip rocked and hung in the balance. It was all in the handshake. Frank broke their deal and Jack was free to take any offer he could get. He reached out his hand and Vincent clasped it in his. He shook it until Jack thought he would fall forward; the skin was cold, smooth like gripping the rim of a marble sink. Vincent released him. Jack slipped his fingers around the base of his neck to get some warmth back into them.

'That's a gentleman's agreement, boy.'

It was familiar: *boy*. The way the *y* exploded from Vincent's lips with a puff of air, Jack had heard that a thousand times before. But not here, not in this place; somewhere darker.

'I'll be at his next bout. We'll see how your fighter's getting on. Then there's someone I want you to meet, depending on how it goes, course. Go get some air, Jack. You're looking a bit green.'

The Thin Suit followed Vincent back behind the curtain. Jack held on to the bar, polished as liquorice; he smudged away his face with the flat of his thumb. All of life was in that print somewhere. The air was too thin underground. The thick carpet caught at his feet like waterweeds. He clung to the banister, hauled himself up the Everest steps. The doorman's hand reached for him. Jack tugged away, elbow crashing against the leaded lamp. The exposed bulb yellow as a baby blanket; flapping against his neck, running all the way to Albany Basin. Glass shattered on the flagstones. Blood on Jack's hand, dripping down his wrist. He staggered to the bins, the movement spreading like a wave: knees, thighs, chest. The whisky reignited inside him, started to lap against the back of his tongue. Rats squeaked behind the snapped fruit boxes and soiled papers. He spat.

In the puddle-rings at his feet something was rising: a memory, half-formed, silted-over like objects caught in mud at low tide. The water settled and in reflection he saw young Jackie peering over the cobbled edge of Albany Basin. The door to Bobbie Black's slammed behind Jack, the pool of purple light, and sulphurous smoke, yanked back into the sealed-up club. His balance evaporated in the dark tunnel of the alley. Falling. Everything black…

… Jackie tries to move his legs but something weighs down on him; he parts his lips but no water surges in. His cock is hard, straining the worn cotton of his pyjamas. He opens one eye:

176

plaster cracks zigzag the ceiling; a dark wooden headboard looms over him like a casket lid. Still in bed – every time he wakes he loses Rosie again. He is shrivelling. But something wriggles in the space between his knees. Small fingers grasp at the blanket pinning him. He snaps his legs up to his chest, cradles his shins.

'Mum. Come and fetch her away.'

No noise but the baby's chattering. If his mum is in then she isn't answering. The baby claws at the blanket; he inches away. She chuckles. But he won't look at Pearl. Jackie squeezes the blanket against his eyeballs. It feels as if he can see inside his head: under the black water with Rosie, surfacing, fingers sliding in her blood as he tries to grab the iron mooring ring on the bank. But he can't hold on to any of it: she slips away. He needs the doctor to come back with his cold needle and leather straps, tap Jackie's thin blue veins, let his body die again (for a few hours at least). Breath condenses on the rough wool. The baby snuffles, struggling through the churned-up bedding. He blocks her with the soles of his feet.

Jackie keeps his head under the covers, but dusty daylight still reaches him. He scratches at his missing fingernail, black and burned from that bloody match. He wants to make it bleed, needs something to show what a weak, useless cunt he is: a real man wouldn't have dropped the match on to her dress; a real man wouldn't have let the blanket unravel and the baby hit the cobbles; a real man would have had the strength to drag Rosie out. He puts his teeth to the rough skin, bites down until he hits a buried nub of nail; he tastes iron. It doesn't hurt. Nothing can replace that last touch: Rosie's forearm, heavy and cold as a marble effigy; the mud and silt swarming like blackfly around them, swallowing up the sparkle of the gold ring. He tried to save Rosie from the Basin, almost had her, but the hook was forged steel, those bargemen too strong to fight against. *We're saving your life here*, that was what one of them had shouted as Jackie punched out. What a fucking joke…

'What?'

He sits up. But Pearl goes silent, squeezes her empty fist in the air: again and again.

'She ain't coming back, you stupid lump.'

He kicks away the blankets, goes over to the window. Maybe his mum is scrubbing the doorstep, chatting with Mrs Bell. He presses his bare toes to the wall. The street is empty except for a horse spread dead in the gutter, skin hanging off its spine like brown sacking. He saw them making extra glue for the Bible pages at the factory once: horse bones boiled down into a golden colour like toffee. The back of his mouth stretches elastic but there is nothing left inside him to sick up. Someone will come to drag that carcass away soon, but Jackie isn't going anywhere. He tightens the cord of his pyjamas, pinching his skin. Not that he deserves release – too many debts to pay: his dad, Rosie. And he knows he has more bad things in him, buried deep like the black canal gunk he was still coughing up all last week.

Jackie thumps his forehead to the damp glass; it sucks at him like a wet kiss, and he presses harder. He searches in his top pocket for a packet of Capstan. His fingers fumble, no spit in his mouth to seal the paper, but he lights it anyway. Ash falls, settling on his fingers. His mum is coming down the road, a swinging shopping basket propelling her into the wind. He bangs on the window as she gets closer, signalling with his hand for her to make it quick. Ash and a drop of blood from his thumb falls on to the floorboards. The kitchen door opens; footsteps thud up the stairs. She rushes to the bed, bringing with her a chill blast of outdoor air, dropping the basket to the floor.

'Is Pearl all right? Are you all right?'

'Why didn't you take her with you? She's making noises.'

'It's nearly time for her dinner.' She groans as she scoops Pearl up, struggling to hold her to the light as if she is looking for cracks. 'I thought something was wrong – you gave me a fright.'

178

She sits down on the bed, Pearl plopping into her lap. He keeps his eyes on the street outside, hunching his shoulders against the noise of his mum's breathing and the baby's chuntering.

'How am I supposed to sleep with that din?'

'Sleep? That's all you've done since it happened. Time to wake up now, John.'

He drums the tip of the cigarette against the glass; a black smudge grows in front of him. He sucks down; the ember glows, barely alive.

'I'm so tired, Mum.'

'You're tired? How do you think I feel? With Pearl to look after too. You haven't done a day's work for nearly three weeks. What'll happen if you lose your job?'

'No one asked you to do nothing.'

'You're my family, you and Pearl. But who told you your life would be any different from the rest of ours? I lost my husband but you got to – '

'I don't even know where Rosie's family went and buried her.' His breath condenses on the pane, flickering silver threads like a spreading frost.

'Someone had to tell them, John. She was their daughter. But I never told them none about Pearl. She's ours.'

He glances over his shoulder. 'It shouldn't have been Rosie.'

His mum sits Pearl in the middle of the bed, nesting the blankets around those fat limbs, and strides up to the window. His mum's lips move but she doesn't speak; the bristles of her coat scratch against him. He blows smoke to cover up her reflection. But she snatches the cigarette, stabs it down into the web of skin between his thumb and finger.

'What the hell you doing?'

'Hurt, did it? Long as you keep feeling means you keep living. Put them pyjamas in the wash basket – dinner will be ready in an hour. I want you dressed decent at the table, John.' She hands back the cigarette; squeezes her lips around the red

179

mark on his flesh then rubs it dry with her elbow. 'I picked you up some second-hand shoes down the market while I were out. No one's going back into Albany Basin to dredge up them lost ones.'

His mum drops each shoe, thump thump to the floor, gathers up Pearl and leaves the room. Burning tears swell and burst, turning everything outside the window into a distorted Hall of Mirrors likeness. He won't ever wear some other man's shoes again; he's done with that; he's done with it all. He finishes the cigarette, one breath at a time, until like smoke Jackie dissolves and slips away.

NINE

Jack stayed long enough to get Frank's gloves signed off by the official and then he left him to it. The light from the changing rooms didn't reach the tunnel but the steam wrapped around him like smoke. He kept away from the slimy wall, heading towards the yellow glow that was the door into the hall. Footsteps echoed around the tiles. Cheam Baths dripped through the flaking paint; he left a trail of water behind. Somehow, after leaving Bobbie Black's, a few nights ago, a crack had grown in the bottom of his left shoe. His damp sock swelled inside; the hole needed seeing to. Make do and mend, that was most fights too these days: stuffed into local halls, covered pools, above pubs – towns where the Tube hit the buffers and buses went to bed. Jack wasn't going to miss those places, not when he was filling arenas with a new fighter.

He kicked a lost button; it pinged from wall to wall. He didn't survive one drowning just to disappear down the plughole of south London. Jack scratched the dry scab on his palm. Pearl had cleaned it up, not that he remembered. He stuffed his hands into his pocket and Frank's letter was in there waiting for him. Pearl had warned him it was coming; probably took the boy days to scrawl the apology. Jack ran his fingers through his slicked-back hair. Safer to keep his hands where he could see them. He was nearly at the doors, but other shapes swam there too.

A shadow spoke, 'Watch it, old timer. Oh, hello, Jack. Wouldn't have said "old timer" if I'd known it was you. You recognise me, don't you?'

'Spider.'

The boys surrounded Jack, fencing him in. The double doors stood only feet away but the noise up there was deadened and hollow like the banging inside a pipe.

'It's the new suit, ain't it? I told you I was on the up, Jack. I'm doing well for myself. Tailor-made.'

Spider stood so close that Jack saw the yellow teeth, pointed as matchsticks. He held up his arms, doing a slow turn to show them all the cut of the cloth.

Jack smiled. 'Tailor-made for who?'

'Didn't I say he was funny, boys? I'll tell Frank we've been having a laugh. That's where we're off to now. Popping in to see Frank before the fight. He's been with us since you kicked him out. No hard feelings, like. Got caught with his spoon in the jam jar. Man's got to take what's coming to him. Ain't you bothered why we want to see him?'

'No.'

Spider loosened the fat tie cutting into his neck; the shirt puckered his red scars. The smile was gone. 'Knocked us all back for a piece of skirt, didn't he? But mates are mates.' Spider stepped closer. 'I hear you're thick with Vincent Metzger now?'

'No.' Jack scrunched his fist around the letter in his pocket.

'Couldn't put a good word in for me, could you? I'm looking to expand my trade.' Spider fell into step beside him; the cluster of boys dropped back.

'No.'

'I've got other deals, of course. Just thought Vincent must be looking for new men too. What the war didn't finish off, time will. I could make Vincent some money, all right. Like I made money for you with Frank. We need to have a word about that, about debts. Don't we, Jack?'

Jack opened his mouth as if he was about to speak then pushed through the doors; they swung shut on his silence. If he didn't have other places to be he would have laughed in the kid's face – just who did he think he was? Jack took a seat in the front benches. The grease off Frank's skin stuck to his hands and he wiped himself clean on the sleeve of his jacket. Vincent was in the expensive seats at the side: no benches for him, but a chair with a padded back. His grey suit glowed, and a thick brown woollen tie rested on his chest; he looked bloated next to the sharp angles of the Thin Suit beside him. No visible scars marked him like Spider; no features loomed out of proportion to the rest of his face, no stoop, no withered limbs. Nothing about him stood out at all – a blank. Jack woke from nightmares like that, sweat-soaked sheets and steamed-up breath, knowing what he had seen was real, but no amount of dragging and poking in dark corners would make the memory show itself. Vincent was a man to have on your side, and that all depended on this fight. Frank was top of the bill – a Grand Ten-Round International Contest, the posters said. Jack dug his knuckles into the stiff centre of his spine; he hadn't been sleeping right since that night at the club. When he lay in bed he couldn't get comfortable, all his bones knocked out of joint, and no matter how much he rubbed he couldn't get them to fit into place again; like an old worn nub of a man.

The double doors parted: Frank came through followed by Bert. The old wooden steps up to the ring creaked, and the dirty bandage holding one side of the ropes together flapped in Frank's face as he climbed through. He stood in his corner, eyes measuring his opponent: the length of his reach, the power in his arms. The other fighter was an old hand, been round the circuits more than once, and it showed.

Billy Jones had a face to cut glass, sharp and fiercely pointed as his fists. He always wore a red stripe down the side of his shorts, and it looked as if someone had sliced him open; many had tried but no one had succeeded. Frank's forehead was pulled into a frown, easy to mistake for anger, and for the first time Jack imagined whose face Frank saw when that black look came into his eyes – maybe it was his. Frank's boots weren't new any more, but the silk shorts had been fashioned and mended by Pearl. Two thick white blocks down the leg, a red pocket, and the initial 'F' carefully embroidered at the bottom of the right leg. Jack was a fool not to have seen it before, the attention they gave to each other. The way she talked to him, even talked about him, that quiet voice rising and dropping like a wave.

The bell went. Frank eased himself out of his corner. Slowly circling his opponent, and his left arm hit out at nothing, finding his range. It was like watching two dogs, looking for any in: an old wound, a drop in attention. And then Frank lunged. He had Billy Jones on the ropes. Frank pressed his head against Billy's chest, rose, and swung his arms to land hits. No punching room for Billy and his arms were trapped at his side like broken wings. The white-shirted referee stepped in and dragged them apart, but the damage was done. Billy sweated, blinking against the sting as it ran into his eyes, swiping at his face with his gloves.

Jack wanted the fight to be over, for it to be decided one way or the other. He scratched at his collar; the longer he waited, the tighter it felt. Frank ploughed on, moving into the shelter of his opponent's chest. Both men were cut and bloodied – not enough to stop the fight, but enough to bring out shouts for more from the crowd as they followed every blow. The bell would be sounding soon, and Jack checked his watch again. Frank peppered Billy's head and shoulders with blows, leading with the right. Jack needed Frank to take Billy out. It wasn't enough to win on points.

Jack gripped his hands around the base of his neck. Frank saw the signal and threw a left hook deep under Billy's chin, crunching his jaw together. The air rushed from his body, silencing the room as everyone held their breath. Jack didn't want him to just be winded. Billy's legs began to shake from the ankles up. He disappeared inside himself, thighs raised to his chest, head thudding on to the canvas. The longest count of Jack's life: Billy raised his head on seven, but his knees wouldn't hold on eight, and he didn't try again. The referee held Frank's arm high into the air. Vincent stood on the other side of the ring, smiling at his investment. Jack ignored Frank's calls, climbed out of the benches and pushed his way towards Vincent.

'Jack. Your fighter did well. He's on good form.' He sucked down on his cigar and released a mouthful of sweet smoke into Jack's face; moving away into the crowd as he spoke, 'Looks like we're all on to a winner. I'll be in touch.'

But a shadow followed behind Vincent and the Thin Suit. Spider. Jack lost sight of them all as the bodies pressed and shoved their way towards the doors. The promise to give up those mates was just another one of Frank's lies. Arms and shoulders knocked up against Jack. No one knew who he was this far from Camberwell – no slaps on his back, no offers of a drink.

Bert prodded Jack in the ribs. 'Why didn't you come straight to the ring? Frank's waiting up there. Have you two had a falling out?'

'He's played us all. He's been lying since day one.' Jack stepped away from the raised platform.

'Lying's what all good fighters do. Feint, trick. He's just a boy. It's up to us to teach him right and wrong,' Bert shouted above the shuffling of feet and the scraping of chairs.

'I ain't his bleeding dad. See to him, will you? I'm needed elsewhere.'

The main doors were wide open; rain bounced into the hall. Jack pulled a cap out of his pocket and Frank's letter came with it. He held on to the paper and jammed the hat on to his head; checking Vincent wasn't around to see. Soon he wouldn't be swimming off with those other saps, bedraggled as a wet cat; he would be hailing cabs, or sliding into the leather seat of his own motor. He opened the letter and folded it back; only a few lines visible in the middle. The thick curling letters melting away in the rain, but Jack couldn't help reading them: … *my best pal and the best manager I ever wanted. I feel lucky you took me on, and I know I have done wrong. Pearl never meant to hurt you. That was my fault as I knew you wouldn't want me to be with your sister. Be lucky…*

Frank's letter floated down on to the marble tiles. Jack's muddy footprint stained the cream paper. Be lucky – that was what everyone used to say in the war when what they couldn't bring themselves to say was *let's hope it's not your turn to die.* Jack was caught on the top step, too many people clogging up the way in front of him. He waited with the rain running down his neck. He hadn't seen much of Pearl since that night. She disappeared into the darkness of the upstairs landing when he came into the house. She rushed to use the lav first thing every morning before he was up. A seagull screamed, circling for dropped batter bits. He heard Pearl crying at night, but he didn't know what she had to be upset about.

The mass of men began to thin out, separating back into coats and hats, legs splashing through the puddles; Jack turned around and went back into the hall. The letter was still there, kicked and trapped against the door. He bent down, picked it up, smoothed it flat. He slipped off his shoe and wedged the paper inside; it would keep the water out on his journey to the pub.

The bar was nearly empty; only a bundle of old blokes sat wheezing in their usual corner; Newton playing chess by himself, his tin leg sticking out into the aisle; and Pearl at the bar, a half-finished glass of cloudy Robinson's in front of her. Jack dragged up a stool.

'Come out of hiding, have you?'

'I thought you might be feeling sorry for yourself by now.' She flicked through a magazine, finger reading the lines.

'Tell you the truth. I've enjoyed the peace and quiet. Oh, wait, you ain't well acquainted with the truth.'

'I'm not here to spar with you, Jack.'

He eased himself out of the sopping overcoat, draped it over the rail. Drip drip, coughing from Newton, a muffled whispering from the huddled men. Jack's mouth twitched to say something else; he sucked on his bottom lip. She finally looked up. 'Frank all right?'

'He won.' Jack scooped some coppers out of his pocket and felt her pinch his sleeve. 'He's fine. You?'

'Got a blister on my left heel, walking up and down the line, sorting those pastilles at the factory. But I caught it in time.' She tried to brush some of the water from his jacket but the cloth was soaked through. 'Frank ain't got a raincoat.'

'It's only a shower.'

Jack slapped his hat against the side of the bar; puddles were breeding on the floor. She rolled the magazine and stuffed it, upright, into her cardigan pocket.

'How many fights has he got left now?'

'Let's just leave it for the night, Pearl. I'm done in.' Jack propped his head up with his hand.

'I better check Frank over, see what needs fixing. Have you read his letter? He didn't tell me what was in it…'

Jack shifted his feet, the edges of the paper sticking through his sock and into his sole. 'Don't matter how many fights Frank wins, he's one of life's losers – '

'Mum and Dad would be ashamed of you.' Her bottom lip shook.

'That's what bloody well keeps me going.' Jack laughed, then swallowed it down into a grunt. How could Pearl ever understand how the mum who had washed her hair in rainwater, softened her crusts in milk, kissed and stroked her head, had a son like Jack? She ran her finger along the curled edge of the magazine; she was going to cut herself. Jack fished in his pocket for a smoke, crushed the empty packet.

'Don't suppose you've taken up baccy when I wasn't looking.'

'I've got better things to spend my wages on.'

He blew his nose. It was full of black streaks and lumpy snot; he didn't want to think about all the filth and dirt lodged deep down inside him. But he didn't like being in that house alone, having Pearl drifting around the edges of his vision like a ghost too. She took another sip of orange, swivelling sideways on the stool to watch Newton move a queen.

'Don't let me keep you. I should be celebrating but – '

'No need to worry, I didn't put nothing on your tab, Jack.'

'Small mercies.'

Jack waved to Cousin Alf at the other end of the bar, trying to get his attention. He caught Pearl's reflection in the speckled mirror; she didn't look like those old photographs. She was red around the eyes; it would lead to an infection if she kept rubbing. She just needed to keep busy to help her forget about Frank.

'Them potatoes you left out for me last night were rock-hard, Pearl.'

'I only par-boiled them.'

'I'll probably get sick from eating them.' He already felt himself starting to steam, swelling with heat from the gas fire in the corner.

'With you in a tick, Jack.' Cousin Alf waved but carried on with his work.

'Is that why you're waiting for me here, to see if I'm OK?'

'I've been chatting with Georgie.' Pearl raised her eyebrows. He recognised that half-smile; she knew she had him hooked now.

'Where's she been all this time, then?' He made a show of looking over at Newton's chessboard.

'Ask her yourself.'

Georgie carried a brown crate in from the corridor. Cousin Alf struggled to fit the Courage brass back into place on the tap. She squeezed around him, put down the bottles and carried the waiting pint to Jack.

'Back, then, I see.'

'My landlady kicked me out. I've been staying with my sister.' She twisted the copper bangles around her wrist.

188

Pearl spun back to face the bar, took a deep breath. 'Georgie needs a place to rent. I said she could share my room.'

Jack blew beer across the bar.

'I think that's a no, Pearl.' Georgie slapped a cloth down in front of him.

He wasn't sure why he did it; since the night at the club he'd felt as though he had been trapped in one of those ice cubes. Now here Georgie was: the sweetness of her perfume, the way it grew stronger as her breasts moved; the curl that always bounced out from behind her ear. Jack tried to concentrate on the brown cloth. 'What do you want me to do with that stinking thing?' He couldn't bring himself to look up and show them the smile tingling at his lips.

'Clear up your own mess.' She prodded it closer, then shook her head at Pearl. 'He ain't going to say sorry.'

'He won't, but he is.' She touched Georgie's fingers.

'I am here, ladies.'

'If he won't say it... well, I've got work to do.' Georgie straightened up, fitted her skirt into place and walked away. Jack picked up the cloth, weighed it in his hand. In one swift move he wiped the bar clean, mopping up the spilled beer, even polishing the rail.

'You'll have to pay your way. I'm not a bloody doss house.' He threw the cloth; she caught it and tucked it behind the pumps.

'Meet me at the Elephant tomorrow and help me with my bags. Oh, and Jack, if you keep me waiting like that again you won't be so lucky.'

Georgie turned to take Newton's empty glass. But Jack saw her glancing his way, eyes narrowing and measuring him up. She didn't need to worry: he'd be there tomorrow. Another body to fill up that cold house, something to keep Pearl occupied. Someone to come home to. He finished his pint and banged the glass down. 'What about another drink?'

Pearl met his eyes in the mirror. He tugged on his earlobe and wondered how long she would make him wait.

'This squash tastes like licking a penny.'

It was enough of an invitation for Jack and he thumped his hand on the counter.

'A bloke could die of thirst here,' he called to Georgie.

She twisted sideways as she moved past the waiting stack of bottles. The outline of her breasts filled the narrow space. Jack wanted to dry his damp skin by slipping his hands under those layers of cotton and wool. She brushed down her apron. 'What can I get you, *sir*?'

'Two pints of Courage, and one for yourself. I really am celebrating tonight.'

'Courage,' Pearl said the word as if she was practising the sound.

Georgie smiled. 'Now, both those pints would be for you, Jack, ain't that right?'

'Course. I'm one of Her Majesty's most law-abiding subjects.'

Pearl squirmed on the stool, the magazine in her pocket pulling the cardigan from her left shoulder to uncover one white, goosepimpled arm. Jack remembered the first time he'd realised she wasn't small enough to lift high up into the air any more.

'Drink it all up. It'll do you good.' And he meant it. 'One more fight, that's all I need, Pearl.'

Jack reached down, straightened her cardigan, and waited for his pint. Pearl always came back. After his mum's funeral the Winnies had whisked Pearl off to Guildford, but the very next day she was on the doorstep waiting for him, suitcase by her feet. The Winnies sent telegrams that he didn't bother to answer, and when they finally got hold of him, on the phone at the pub, he'd told them it would be his funeral before he'd let Pearl go again. She had bobbed up, like Jack that way.

The door opened and Newton shuffled out. The rain fell in vast sheets, razing the street; scrubbing everything into silvery blackness.

190

TEN

Jackie doesn't notice the blackouts any more; he hasn't the energy to look up. He drops off the kerb and crosses the road, turning the corner to the pub – too dark to see down the cellar. But it is there. A voice sings inside: Newton raising another glass to dull the pain. Jackie knows how he feels. Newton lost his toe, then the sickness ate up his whole leg and it was lopped off above the knee. Nobody knows what is missing from Jackie, but without Rosie there is no balance. The slit headlamps of a car stop suddenly as he steps out in front of it. Jackie had spent months clinging to walls, to lamp-posts, or he would crash to the ground. He presses his hand to the hot bonnet, pushes himself on. Sometimes he still feels that black water sloshing inside him. He makes it out on to Camberwell Road, past the darkened fish and chip shop, steam clouds stockpiled around the doorway.

He turns off Wyndham Road into the yards. Nineteen years old, and he is still stuck in stinking Camberwell. The doctors sent him back to the factory so he signed up for ARP – they don't care about his flat feet. He has come straight from work, no point going back to the house. Pearl keeps him awake with her chattering, and he doesn't have any use for daylight now. The metal gates glint, mirroring the moon. The building supplier's yard is closed, planks of wood and bricks piled up as if it has already taken a direct hit. The shed off to one side is Control Point. Jackie lifts the horsehair blanket to get inside. An old bloke stares at him through watery eyes; lined face and white hair. Jackie shouldn't be here: he should be lying sunk in the mud at the bottom of Albany Basin, or rotting under some foreign soil. He kicks a stone; it skids across the floor and ricochets off a tin bucket of sand.

The red-faced bloke checks his list. 'What's your name, son?'

'Jackie.' He lines up another stone under his toe.

'We had an old timer here by name of Jackie. He got burned up last week. You'll have to be Jack. Good, solid name for a young bloke like yourself.' The man sits hunched like a toad.

'Jack it is, then.' He gives a shrug and sits down on a stool: there is no Rosie and no Jackie. He is just glad the man didn't question his surname. Jack isn't sure he could put up with the old git saying he remembered his dad and what a good sort he was, how sorry he was his brothers bought it in France.

'Name's Eric. Kettle's on, so make yourself useful. The others'll be back shortly.'

'I ain't come here to make tea every night.'

Jack warms his hands on the thin flame coming from the primus stove. Eric uses a stick to knock a jar from the shelf into his lap.

'Just as well. We ran out of leaves last week. How did you get yourself assigned?'

'Flat feet. Bloody doctor wouldn't keep his mouth shut, marked my slip.'

The walls run wet with condensation, tilting towards the flame as if they might collapse at any moment. Eric rocks forward on his stool and mixes up the Camp coffee, wraps his hands around the battered red enamel.

'Don't suppose you brought your own mug with you? Well, you can use mine after I'm done.'

'Don't worry, I ain't going to be here long. I don't need no mug.'

'Got plans, have you? Think the Army'll be begging you to hit the front?' He lets out a low laugh and rubs his balding head. 'I was out there, back in the Great War. Give me a warm hut any day.'

'I'll likely be under a pile of bricks by week's end, my insides burned up by smoke.'

'Be lucky, Jack. Maybe you'll be pulling someone else out the rubble, or saving some poor sod's house. Here.' He thrusts a tin hat and armband at Jack. 'What you've got on will serve as uniform. Keep it clean and tidy. You're with me now. And, so you know, smoke don't burn. It chokes like some fat fucker kneeling on your windpipe.'

His white wisps of hair wilt under the steam from the mug. Jack licks his lips; his mouth is dry and cold. Eric buffs the mug clean on his trousers then pours more for Jack.

'Drink up. It's going to be brass monkeys.'

'Cheers.'

Lumps bob on the surface but Jack doesn't care. He places one finger at a time around the sides. The bed of his missing thumbnail turns from ice-white to live pink; feeling spreads slowly up his arms and back into his hands. He has been numb since the night at the Basin. He still can't bear to look at Pearl, but the weight of her is drowning him all over again. His mum is all smiles and sloppy kisses for the girl – even hung a bigger picture of his dad over the mantel and held her up to see him. Jackie didn't care enough to make it stop, but Jack is different. He isn't a boy in short trousers any more. Heat slides down his throat, smooth and heavy as a pebble. He finishes it without looking up then puts the mug down on the floor. Eric is watching him, scratching at the fat purple veins on his nose.

'I've seen you at some fights, I'm sure I have done. Used to belong to the gym over by the canal, didn't you? You were quick on your feet.'

'I ain't been for a while.' He can't keep enough weight on, no matter how much sugary tea and powdered milk he drinks.

'Not much chance of making it professional now, mind. No men left to fight. They've all gone and signed up.' Eric scrapes out the dead skin from under his fingernails with his front teeth. 'But you had a sharp eye. That's worth something.'

'That's worth nothing. Since I was twelve I've wanted to be a fighter.'

Jack sits up a little taller. But even as he says it he knows it isn't true. He is never going to be great, not like those big names in *The Ring*: Nipper Pat Daly, Joe Louis, Alf Mancini. Eric relights a pipe, breathes in.

'There are shit-shovellers and there are those who know where to find shit. Money's in finding it, not shovelling it. Think on that.'

'What you on about?'

'Christ, you young ones today haven't got the brains you were born with.' Eric shakes his head. 'Let some other chump wear the gloves – you keep the book.'

Eric is right about one thing: Jack does have a keen eye. He isn't going to sit out the rest of his life in this shed at the forgotten end of nowhere. Jack could be a good manager. He glances up as something smacks against the corrugated iron roof.

'Only rain. Sounds like rats running over, don't it? We've got those too. But tonight it's the rain.' Eric licks his tongue along the tip of the pipe.

The rain jumps and leaps, rattling above Jack's head. But there will never be enough water to wash him back to Rosie.

Pearl is crying again. Jack dumps his helmet and gas mask in the hall, follows the sound into the front room. His jacket and trousers are damp with rain; it was a cold walk back but better that than the jumping flames reddening his skin: six houses and a pub gone. He wants to smell something clean, feel something soft in his arms. Pearl stands against the wooden bars, her mouth open in some red rage. Jack sits down beside the pen, pushes his hand through the gap. She thrusts out her bottom lip, sounding some word he doesn't understand, but her fingers slide through the bars. She grabs him tight. It surprises him how strong she is, the way her fist makes his finger throb as if with sheer will alone she can break him. Jack sits cross-legged in front of her and curls out his bottom lip too. For every house he is going to see burned to the ground, every heap of blackened bricks and shrapnel-carved street, there will be Pearl waiting for him when he comes home. Plump legs and arms protruding from a hand-knitted woollen dress that his mum never had time to make for the others; the shades of yellow and pink make her look like a joint of ham. Jack shakes his finger and her arm wobbles as she hangs on.

He reaches down to scoop Pearl free. She gets heavier every time. The wooden bars won't hold her for long; he has seen her trying to climb over then dropping back on to her backside. But she is all right. Not a scratch on her; with all that surrounds her, Pearl seems to bounce through the days untouched. Even the cut from a midnight trip to the Andersen shelter has healed, and she didn't snivel once. Jack lifts her up, high above his head, and a tuft of dark hair grazes the ceiling. A laugh rumbles up from inside the layers of wool, and he lets his arms drop suddenly until Pearl is level with his face. He hopes for her sake she is going to look like Rosie, but she is three now and still no sign. The face staring back is his: same thin tilt upwards of the eyes, thick lips and high rounded cheeks. She is a Munday. He rubs his cheek against her thin hair, remembering the small soft spot that used to move as she breathed. She smells of cold cream and soft-boiled carrots. Jack studies those pale eyes. But he can't find what he is searching for.

'Put her down.' His mum's voice stops the laughter.

She stands in the doorway, apron dusted with flour, arms tightly folded. She beckons for Pearl with her finger. 'You don't need to be picking her up like that.'

'She's my daughter.' Jack holds on to her.

'That's the first time you've laid claim to it since that night. What happened out there? Saw some tragic scene, someone died?'

'But Mum…'

He feels small next to her solid frame. Pearl hiccups and thrusts out her free hand towards his mum.

'You should know better. Don't you see what I suffer? I've lost my own brave sons now. Never even got their bodies back. Makes me weep to think of them buried where they fell. And it ain't safe for the Winnies to be taking trains to come and see me. Pearl's all I've got left.'

'What about me?'

'You know what I mean. Give me back my Pearl.' Her lips press tight, brown eyes almost black. 'Careful, you'll hurt her playing around like that.'

'I'm not *him*.' He breathes out the words so quietly he isn't sure his mum hears.

Pearl gives another hiccup and wobbles in his arms. But he can't ever be sure that he isn't like that face staring down at them from the picture above the fire: maybe Jack will throw his dinner against the wall because someone chews too loudly; maybe he will give gifts then smash them up when the thanks don't sound grateful enough.

'I don't know what you're talking about, son. She's big enough to walk on her own now.'

He pushes Pearl outwards at arm's length. Her body slippery in his hands like cooked tripe. 'Take her, then, see if you can't keep her quiet. I need some kip.'

She disappears into the folds of his mum's housecoat, lost against the rolls of her body. His mum winces slightly as she takes the full weight of a toddler. Five children, three left, have made her limbs thick with age, and she creaks like an old bed when she moves too quickly.

'There's some of last night's supper on the stove if you want.'

'I ain't hungry.' Jack moves to the doorway.

His mum's hand is firmly placed on Pearl's back, holding on with her big open palm as if she can keep away everything that has happened before.

'Let's button you up, Pearl, keep the cold out. She's not as quiet as you were.'

'We weren't allowed to cry.' Jack picks at a graze on his knuckle.

'She's got a set of lungs on her.'

'Too right she has – that kid is all I bloody hear.'

'It's the tone of your voice. You've got a man's voice now.'

Pearl isn't used to a man's voice because there aren't any men left: his dad is long dead and his brothers are buried in French sand. He is the only one left to look after the damp, rotting house. Last night, as he sat at his post, watching the sky and the passing dark aircraft-shaped clouds, he considered if the weight that crushed his chest would be lifted if he came back to find the house was nothing but a black pit of rubble and ashes.

'I'm done for.'

Jack climbs the stairs. He drops his jacket to the floor, gets into bed with his shirt and trousers still on; too tired and too cold to change. Getting between the chilled sheets is like slipping underwater – icy and slimy. But he can't sleep, not yet. He takes out Rosie's picture from its hiding place at the back of the drawer; his mum has got rid of everything else. Jack brings it closer to his face until it is pressed to the skin between his eyes. But the air raid siren starts to scream. Who will carry Pearl down the shelter? Who will dig her out if they take a hit? He buries his head, photograph wedged in place, drags the clumpy sides of the pillow over his ears to block out the screeching world. He shuts his eyes, concentrates on the moving darkness and the cold paper. Nothing. He holds his breath and tries again. It isn't working: he can't see Rosie's face. What if she isn't waiting for him? What if he can never picture her again? *You had your chance to be a man and you were too much of a coward to take it.* His dad's voice cuts through the siren.

Jack throws back the blankets, slides the photograph into his top pocket and skids down the stairs, swinging into the

197

hallway from the bottom newel post. He catches up with his mum at the back door and snatches Pearl out of her arms. He herds them both into the yard, cracking his big toe against the piled-up earth as they descend into the shelter. Pearl clings to the front of his shirt, squeezes it up around his neck, and even when he sinks down on the bench she doesn't let go. She wheezes against his ear. He turns on the torch: two benches, and one large patchwork lump at the back of the shelter; Mr and Mrs Bell sleep down there most nights.

He focuses the light on Pearl. 'She's breathing funny.' Jack tilts back her head with his thumb. 'You've buttoned her up too tight.'

He loosens the lace around her neck, wide enough for his finger to fit between her skin and the white material. His mum pulls a cardigan tight across her chest and spreads a blanket over her knees. 'She'd soon let me know if something was up. She can speak, you know. Keep your voice down and hand her over.' She pats her lap.

Pearl's face is luminous in the torchlight. A bright white line stands out against her pink skin like a rope-burn around her neck. Her fist is clenched about his shirt but her head begins to nod, her eyes fluttering closed. Snoring comes from the back of the shelter; one of the Bells' farts gurgles up through the thick blankets. Jack doesn't answer his mum. He folds his arms under Pearl's backside, supports her weight as he leans against the corrugated iron. He closes his eyes, feels the hem of that blue flowered dress rippling between his fingers, hears the rumble of Rosie's laughter: the sparkle of the gold ring brightened by the flame of the match, warm yellow baby blanket tucked under her arm. The all-clear siren rings out, another false alarm; and Rosie is gone again.

III

★ THE CLINCH ★

'A boxer to avoid punishment steps in right up to his opponent, so that their bodies are as close up to each other as in a wrestle, and he manages, without actually holding, if possible to entangle his arms with those of his opponent, or round his opponent's body, as to prevent any blow being struck on either side till one of them breaks away.'

Boxing, A.J. Newton

– PROGRAMME –

Friday, December 11th 1953

6 Round Contest

KID SULLIVAN
Cardiff

versus

TOM WADE
Marylebone

6 Round Contest

Freddie Hope
Manchester

versus

Jerry Manning
Blackfriars

Important 10 Round Contest

RICH ELLERY
vs.
FRANK BULL

Birmingham   Camberwell

Referee: George SMALL.   M.C.: Tony PARTON.
Timekeeper: Charlie STONE.
Seconds: Jim HOUSE & John MALONE.

Matchmaker: D. Bunter.   Promoter: Harry Starr.

ONE

Jack didn't get lost in Soho any more. The puddles were alive with sparkling reds and greens, gold-edged; it was just a matter of being careful where to tread. He saluted Newcastle Pete and stepped into the basement light. The door closed behind him, a metallic clang, but he was used to it now. He went down the narrow stairs, sidestepping the loose board on the left, and pushed through the thick red drapes; first-timers trying to pull them ended up getting caught in the velvet layers. The tables were lined with brilliant white cloths, gold lamps, gold watches, gold bracelets. He strode through them all, straight up to the bar.

'Jack. Good to see you. Have a drink with us.' Vincent raised his glass. 'Why haven't you brought that girl of yours?'

The Thin Suit and Vincent both had starched handkerchiefs poking out from their top pockets.

'A bloke's got to keep something for himself.'

Jack pulled out his clean handkerchief and rearranged it, disturbing the smell of peppery stews and fluffed sponges. He was getting fat with all the food being made in that house. Jack reached for the whisky and sniffed, bringing himself back into the world of the club.

'Really smart, aren't you?' The Thin Suit nodded at Jack. 'Know your whiskies too, do you?'

'I know if it's been watered down.'

'There's no rationing at Bobbie's.' Vincent rocked the ice against the sides.

The band were setting up: adjusting drums, rubbing a shine into their instruments. But the room was so full of low, rumbling voices, high-pitched laughing and the clinking of glass against teeth that Jack didn't know how anyone would be able to hear the music. Vincent hooked his index finger in the air and Stella crossed the room as if she were attached by a silver thread; he put a hand on her shoulder, pressed his mouth to her ear. Her pale eyes looked cloudier than the ice in Jack's glass, and under the coats of white face-powder blue bruises were imprinted around her eyes like a willow pattern plate; small scratches along her arm as if a cat had been toying with her. She readjusted her sleeves. Vincent obviously enjoyed driving himself home on that puffy face. It seemed a waste to Jack; he stuck his finger inside the glass, licking it clean. Georgie had a purple outfit like the one Stella wore – cheaper, thinner, but she filled every inch of the nylon material. Stella seemed to be shrinking into pockets of air under her dress, every curve dispersing with the lightest touch. Vincent kept a grip around her wrist. She probably wasn't much older than Pearl, thin-limbed, and the new short cut gave her a boyish look.

Vincent touched his palm against Jack's elbow.

'Jack, come and join us. You stay here.' He pointed at the Thin Suit, whose slightly too close-together eyes narrowed even further.

Jack grinned at him, and followed Vincent as he led Stella into the centre of the room. Men in tight-fitting suits, women with shoulders showing, the back of their necks shining with hair lacquer. Black gloves clutched at sparkling purses; cigarette smoke spiralled up from fingers locked around glasses. They stopped what they were doing to watch Vincent, and walking just behind him they would see Jack – he was somebody. They moved towards the band, leaving the marooned tables behind.

'Hit the notes tonight, sweetpea. Consider it fair warning.' Vincent patted Stella's cheek.

She nodded, putting a hand down to steady herself as she wobbled up the steps to the stage. Vincent shook his head as he held aside the red velvet curtain. Jack passed under his arm, his first time backstage.

The wall lights dimmed; the electricity seemed to thin and make the bulbs flicker. They went deeper, the corridor sloping down; ahead of them another door, he could just make it out around the sides of Vincent's Savile Row pinstripe. Pipes and wires snaked their way above Jack. Somewhere a tap dripped. But every inch of the corridor had been swept and bleached; the dry-cleanness of the place tickled inside his nose.

Vincent opened a door. A cloud hung below the ceiling, like steam, as if the Chinese laundry next door were leaking through the bricks. Jack held up his hand, fending off the bright light. Someone angled the lamp downwards. Two men were already seated: the black man with his back to them didn't turn around, but Jack recognised the other one from the exhibition night at Manor Place Baths: hair so oiled that the skin around his scalp looked like a thick drawn-on line, a dog's head walking stick leaning against his leg.

'Evening, Harry.' Vincent pulled up a seat beside him.

The large desk seemed to be growing out into the small space, pushing the chairs back against the walls, leaving no room to stand.

'Take a seat, Jack.' Vincent indicated the chair in front of the desk. 'You remember Harry?'

Jack raised an eyebrow, but Harry didn't offer his hand; he lit a cigarette and blew out more smoke. If Georgie had been there they would have laughed at the heavy-set, loose-skinned old man. Jack sat in the empty chair; the coloured bloke tipped his rabbit-felt trilby, and he gave a nod in return.

'Thought we should get some of the details of the fight set down.' Vincent smiled. 'See if we can't spread some early Christmas cheer for the punters.'

'Venue's set. The Rose and Crown on Mile End Road, and I've got old Danny Bunter acting as matchmaker.' Harry let the ash from his cigarette drop to the floor.

'I thought we had this sorted. I don't want to be giving any of my cut to a matchmaker.' Jack tilted forward in the chair.

The coloured bloke next to him laughed, removed his hat, and rubbed a thumb along his off-centre razor parting.

'It's just for show. Muddies the link between us. We don't need people putting two and two together when we want them to come up with five.' Vincent tapped a metal ashtray against the desktop. 'There'll be plenty to go round.'

'People getting greedy could cause all sorts of problems here, Vincent. I need to know his fighter is set. I need to know none of this is coming back on me. I've got big bets in already.' Harry turned to Jack, smoke spiralling from his nose. He jabbed his cigarette. 'You need to know what you're fucking – '

'Harry, keep it clean, there's ash going everywhere. This ain't the East End here.' Vincent banged the ashtray on the desk. 'I said I vouched for Jack. Since when was my say not enough?' He signalled the final word by slicing his hand through the air.

Jack felt the room shrink a little tighter. Harry held his cigarette vertical, stack of ash wobbling, as he reached for the metal dish. The man next to Jack tapped a cigarette packet on the chair, shaking out a fag.

'He might be dark but he don't exactly blend in with the furniture. Who is this bloke?' Jack pointed with his thumb. 'Does he speak the Queen's or is he fresh off the boat?'

'What's it sound like, fella? I'm from Fulham – born there, weren't I?' The man's eyes popped a little wider as he screwed up his nose.

'Never liked that lot.' Jack straightened his cuff.

The bloke squashed the packet in his hand, cigarettes spewing out. 'Got a problem with blacks?'

'That West London lot. Wouldn't trust them far as I could throw them.' Jack picked up a cigarette balanced on the arm of the chair.

'It's as well no one's asking you to throw me anywhere, sunshine. Vincent, I don't think I can work with this fella.' He waved his hand under his chin.

'Vincent, I can't do this. Vincent, I can't hit the notes, can't pay you back, can't take the pain.' Vincent lowered his voice, raised his eyes to the ceiling. 'Do I look like a nursemaid? Do I?'

They shook their heads.

Vincent took a deep breath. 'I see the issue's that you've not been formally introduced. Rich, this is your new manager. Jack, your new fighter.'

Jack lit the cigarette; eyeing the fighter as he shook out the match: neck knotted, knuckles protruding; hands that had landed some blows. Jack offered him a loose cigarette off the floor; the bloke punched his hand away. Jack smiled as a tingling sensation spread up his arm: a real slugger.

'My manager? Hold on a minute, Vincent. I didn't agree – '

'Maybe you didn't hear me, Rich. This is your new manager and you're his new fighter.'

Jack held out his hand. Rich sniffed, rubbed a knuckle under his nose. They shook. Jack inhaled dampness and furniture polish with the smoke.

'I'll need to see Rich train, tell my fighter how to make it look good.'

'It better look bloody magnificent.' Harry stubbed out his cigarette, carefully sweeping up the ash.

'He thinks I'm a walkover. I'd wipe the floor with your boy any day, sonny.' Rich shrugged. 'I know a trick or two.'

Jack nodded. 'That's why we're fixing this fight, is it – because you're a sure bet?'

'Jack, we've been keeping Rich quiet for a reason. This is going to be his breakthrough. He's lost five, drawn two, so far… on my instructions. It's a little like the club, all about stage management. But don't doubt he can deliver on the goods. I only have to say the word.'

He saw Rich's eye twitch at Vincent's words, his fist clench, and Jack liked him a little more for that sign of irritation.

Harry stroked the top of the bronze-handled walking stick. 'My numbers say that your fighter goes down against Rich in the fifth. I want to make sure he knows it's your word on this, Vincent.'

'Jack knows.' Vincent turned to him. 'We've decided. First three rounds your fighter does what he likes, long as he doesn't dole out too many hits. The fourth round he starts to slip. Then out in the fifth. We're talking straight out here, no getting up, no hitting back. He stays down.' He was all teeth but no smile now.

'Out in the fifth. I'll make sure he keeps count.' Jack wanted to run his fingers through his hair to clear the slack strands from his eyes but he didn't move.

The lamp boiled up the air in the room, the varnish on the desk cracking. Vincent pushed back his chair. 'Why don't you boys get a drink in? Me and Harry got housekeeping to sort.'

Jack had to stand up to let Rich out. At the bottom of his grey suit, Rich was sporting training pumps, scraped and tattered around the toe. Jack took a deep breath of cool air as the office door swung shut behind them. Rich kept beside him, taking quick, short, shuffling steps as if he were practising for the ring.

'Can't stay, the wife's waiting up.' Rich held open the thick curtain.

Stella was hanging on to the edge of a table as she sang, the words out of time to the music like a badly loaded film reel.

'I've got places to be myself. But Vincent said we should get a drink.'

'Quick snifter, then. I need a good manager, Jack, but I'm not so sure you're it. I've had a rotten run of luck in the past… Everyone's got a sob story, suppose.'

Jack ordered the drinks by raising two fingers. It sent a little shiver down his neck when the barman got straight to his order, ignoring a couple perched on the stools. Jack shook his head as Stella tripped and staggered to another table.

'If you're as good as you think you are then I'll take you all the way as my fighter.'

'That what you said to your last fighter, was it?' Rich propped himself against the bar. 'Don't worry, I'm not looking to cause trouble. I've got mouths need feeding. Only the ring puts enough food in their bellies. Come by my training, I'll show you something good.'

Jack raised his glass towards Rich. The woman at the bar tutted and clutched her gold bag to her ribs. 'I would have thought that they would be more select about members.' She made herself heard above the music, accent sharpened for effect.

The man with her coughed into his hand and tried to draw her away. She swayed slightly on the stool, heels clicking against the metal rung, but didn't get down. The man hovered at her elbow, eyes fixed on his wristwatch.

'We're wearing ties.' Jack flicked the end out from under his belt.

'I think she means this dress code.' Rich pinched the skin on his cheek.

'Well, would you believe it, it don't come off, Rich.'

The man knocked his hip against the stool and the woman dropped to her feet, her head half-twisting off her neck, but he prodded her towards a table at the edge of the room, close to the draught from the door: cheap seats. Rich crunched an ice cube between his teeth. 'Can tell a lot about someone from the company they keep... Know that fella, Jack?' The Thin Suit was getting up from a centre table.

'I've had the misfortune.'

'He's a walking cock, one-eyed and dangerous. Only sees half of what's going on and no brain controlling it.' Rich spat shards of ice into the glass. 'Leaves a bad taste.'

Jack laughed. The Thin Suit stared at them, head swaying to get a better look as he crossed the room.

'Be seeing you, Jack.'

Rich fitted his hat into place, nodded at the Thin Suit, and went up the stairs.

'Suppose it is pretty funny, seeing a darkie in a place like this.' The Thin Suit put his empty glass down next to Jack's elbow.

'Blow your nose some time, see how much black comes out.'

'What you saying? There's nothing fucking black about me.' The Thin Suit fingered the handkerchief in his top pocket.

'I'm off. Got to see a man about some paint.' Jack buttoned up his jacket.

'Got a deal going down? Vincent gets a cut of the action, *all* action, now you're working for him.' The Thin Suit tapped the glass against his off-centre front teeth. 'Or has the wife got you painting the house up?'

Jack called over his shoulder as he walked out, 'I ain't the marrying type.'

TWO

Georgie and Pearl looked as if they had walked off a shift at an ammo factory: hair tied up in scarves, dungarees with belts pulled tight. Jack pointed at them from the kitchen doorway.

'All I need is a headscarf too and you wouldn't be able to tell us apart.'

'Easy fixed, Jack.' Pearl snatched up a tea towel.

Georgie grabbed his arms, dragging him into the room. Pearl pressed on his back, holding him down as the laughter wobbled through him. She fitted the towel into place, his ears squeezed back. Jack straightened up, put one hand on his hip and placed the other behind his head. He shoved out his groin and waggled across to the sink. Georgie wolf-whistled but it spluttered into a laugh.

'Jealousy is an ugly thing.' Jack shook his head and climbed the ladder.

The paint was thick as porridge, but Frank had been stirring the pots with a stick most of the morning and it was nearly smooth. A dollop ran down Jack's wrist as he reached up to the ceiling. Pearl stood at the window.

'Let him in, Jack.'

Frank crouched over another pot in the yard, leaning on one knee as he took it in turns to whisk with each hand. Mrs Bell's cat squatted on the wall, flicking its head from side to side, mesmerised by the snap and twirl of the stick.

'It weren't me invited him. Newton sent him round with the paint. Couldn't ask his Jimmy for a hand, could he? No, not now he's a respectable man of the cloth.'

Jack brushed more paint on to the ceiling, covering a hairline crack spreading out from the corner of the room. The ladder rocked as he stretched across.

'What do they call this shade?' Georgie held up a brush and sniffed as if the colour could be revealed that way.

'Cheap and cheerful's the name.'

Jack extended his arm. His view of the yard, and Frank, disappeared behind his sleeve. Pearl worked the paintbrush into the rotting indoor sill below the ladder, splits widened by the tremors from bombs. Her mouth moved; any minute she was going to ask again, and again and again, not paying attention to anything else until all the new-painted surfaces were ruined. Jack swiped the cloth off his head, leaned over and banged on the window.

'Frank, come and make yourself useful. You can paint the other bit of the ceiling.'

Frank came to the doorway, overalls flecked with paint; blobs of it ran down the stick splashing on to his Woolworth's pumps. He stuck his head inside. 'What's that?'

'Jack said he needs your help with the ceiling. Stand on the table.' Pearl took his arm, led him into the middle of the room.

He didn't need Frank's help for anything but Georgie raised a finger in warning. Jack shook his head. 'Make yourself useful, then. Brushes are in the sink. Be quick about it or the paint'll be dry.'

He tutted as he splashed more paint into the crack, but it kept soaking it up. Frank climbed on to the table behind him. Pearl touched the base of Frank's leg as she moved past to start work on the back door.

'Thanks, Frank. We'll get this place done in no time with all of us helping.'

'It'll look better than it did before, even with this funny colour.' Georgie smoothed the paintbrush along the skirting board. The tatty blue dungarees were stretched at the seams as she worked around the edge of the room, sliding along on

212

her knees. Wasn't space for things to lurk in corners, or stick to furniture, when she was moving through the old place. Jack got down from the ladder to help her shift the dresser. Georgie stuck her arm behind it, shoulder catching on the corner of the wood. 'I'm not going to be able to paint all the way behind it, Jack.'

'Don't worry, it ain't going far. That dresser's probably grown roots.'

Jack rested against it, his fingertips automatically feeling for the split across the top. He glanced up at the ceiling, muscles remembering, straining to catch the sound of a stirring baby. But Pearl was working on the back step, chatting about something to Frank as he nodded, chewing his lip in concentration.

'Memories?' Georgie reached up to touch his fingertips. 'Good or bad?'

'Only trying to work out what colour this really is.'

'Hang on, I've got something here.'

Georgie extracted a length of ribbon from behind the dresser, mossy with grey dust. It coiled like a snake into the palm of Jack's outstretched hand; he ran it between his fingers, bringing out a red sheen.

'Pearl, there's some ribbon here. You can add it to your collection box.' Georgie went back to painting.

Rose-red was the colour of the ribbon. Funny, when he'd thought about freshening up the kitchen, he hadn't stopped to think about what they might unearth. Rosie would have liked to paint the place up when she first moved in. She'd made him spend a whole evening sticking pictures from magazines, and sweet wrappers, to the wall on her side of his mum's bed: cottage gardens, dogs and kittens; there was even a picture of Grand National winner Reynoldstown – a near-black gelding. The headline had read *Father trained, Mother owned, Son rode*, but Rosie folded the words back. How had he forgotten that? They'd laughed when his mum pencilled out the bit dangling between the animal's legs.

He crouched next to Georgie.

'I've got a question for you.'

'I couldn't even guess at what it is – bluey green, yellowy grey?' She swept the brush back and forwards over the wood.

'No, not that. Ever feel like you're more than one person? I mean looking back on things. Like it were someone else?' He wrapped the ribbon around his wrist, polishing the colour back to life.

'Sometimes, and sometimes it seems like years ago was only yesterday. Memory plays tricks like that, Jack.'

'You're right.' He put a hand on her shoulder as he stood up. 'I don't even think this colour's got a name.' He studied the half-covered skirting.

'Not worried I'm going to see through you, Jack? That tough old hit-first-ask-questions-later routine.' She smiled. 'I've got news for you. I already see far more.'

Jack felt as if that sticky paint had him rooted to the spot. Pearl tapped her brush on the doorframe. 'What are you two whispering about? We're running out over here.'

'Georgie was going all fortune-teller on me.' Jack rubbed the stiffness from his knees.

'Can you read tea leaves and palms? I didn't know that.' Frank righted his head.

'He's pulling your leg, Frank. If I were a mystic I'd be off predicting the Grand National winner, living the life of luxury.'

It was just a coincidence, but Jack couldn't help feeling that somehow Georgie had poked at the edges of his thoughts. And, stranger than that, he didn't mind. He dropped the curled ribbon into Pearl's front pocket. 'Take the steps, Frank. You'll strain your neck looking up like that.' Jack walked around the ladder. 'I'll put a brew on. Now get back to it, workers. It ain't clocking off time yet.'

'Thanks, Jack.' Pearl caught him around the middle before he could get to the sink.

'Can't breathe... she's trying to kill me...' He made a show of gasping for breath.

For three whole seconds at least, he let Pearl grip him tight. But slowly, his hands settled on her back. He squeezed once then pushed her away to reach the kettle. 'Leave off. Tea won't make itself.'

Frank stood on the ladder behind him: clink of brushes against the tin, rustling of overalls. 'I'm glad I could help out today, Jack. I was wondering if there was any news about – '

'One more fight, Frank. Only one more. We'll talk about it Monday, at the gym. It'll be a good one, see you off with some money in your pocket. You'd like that, wouldn't you?'

Pearl glanced up, paint dripping off the brush and on to the floor. Jack reached for the whistling kettle, shaking above the flame.

'It'd certainly come in handy.' Frank nodded.

'None of us can afford to turn down money these days.' Jack warmed the old blue pot, weeping tea from the zigzag fractures the glue hadn't quite healed.

They sat together on the back step, Pearl and Georgie squashed in the middle: mugs steaming, extra milk in Pearl's to cool it down. The close-pressed warmth was insulation against the nipping November wind. Three stray gnats bobbed in the back yard as though they were suspended from the sky by separate pieces of string: bobbing and weaving, but never meeting. Jack took a good lungful of London air; it cleared the sharp sting of the paint fumes.

Frank drained his tea. 'I better get back to the ceiling.'

'I'll help.' Pearl jumped up beside him.

'Best put some gloves on or you'll get blisters.' Frank took her mug, and they went into the kitchen together.

'My God, you're going to let those two be alone in a room? Feeling all right?' Georgie pressed the back of her hand to Jack's forehead.

'Laugh all you want. I wouldn't trust any bloke. They can't shut themselves off, remember.' He knocked the open

215

door next to him. 'Damage is done anyway. Frank's walking out of the ring. I can't make him stay.'

'You've got something planned, ain't that right?' Georgie tugged at the hair above his ear.

'I'm just looking out for me and mine.' He patted her backside.

'Cheeky sod.'

A banging sound echoed around the yard. Jack leaned backwards, calling into the room, 'What you doing in there?'

The banging came again.

'Someone's at the door,' Pearl shouted back.

He knew why she hesitated, why she didn't want anything to interrupt the afternoon; the gnats bobbed and disappeared into the fading light. Evening was coming, tomorrow was coming.

'Well, go and see who it is, Pearl.'

'I better get ready for my shift.' Georgie stood up, stretched her arms.

The step was cold without her; the tea was cold. Jack hurled the last dregs across the yard, aiming for the ginger tom. The cat skidded off the wall. Frank was halfway through the ceiling, edging from the middle into the far corner of the room, balancing himself above the sink. But there was no sign of Pearl. Jack went into the hallway. Noises came from the front room – not Pearl's voice but something deeper, talking without waiting for an answer. He didn't want to find out if it was Mrs Bell, or Newton come to check on the paint. Pearl opened the door. He had his foot on the first step.

'Jack.'

'I'm in a hurry, need to get changed.' He made it to the second step.

'Win and Winifred are here.'

Jack wanted the loose threads of the carpet runner to twist around his legs and pull him into the dark cupboard beneath the stairs. He hadn't seen the Winnies since his mum's funeral. He made it to the third step. 'I've got places to be, Pearl.'

'They want to talk to you.' She left the door open.

Jack pictured their faces – Pearl's get-up, her paint-splattered face. He rubbed the grin from his face with the palm of his hand, walking backwards down the stairs. The Winnies occupied an armchair each: dark suit jackets buttoned up, coats on their laps. The room felt bone-achingly cold; no sunlight reached it. Pearl sat at the table, hands hanging limply at her side, scarf tucked neatly in her belt. A sharp whiff of paint followed him in; the creak of the ladder in the kitchen, footsteps walking above them. He closed the door.

'Who died?'

'No one, I hope.' Winifred shook her head as she answered.

'We are all of us here in this room, aren't we?'

Win patted the coat in her lap as if it were a cat. Her hair was greying around the line of her temples – too proud to dye it. Winifred's dark hair was faded as the colour of the old rug; the older they got, the more they became the same.

Jack picked at dots of paint caught in the hair on his hands. 'We're the ones just won't die.'

'I'm sorry?' Win tilted her head.

'Apology accepted – remember to send a telegram warning next time.' Jack yawned.

She shook her head, and Winifred blinked. Like black beetles clicking in the armchairs, predicting heavy downpours with their shiny hard shells; he'd only bring a torrent if he stamped on them now. Better to let them run out on their own.

'So, it's been a while, then, ain't it?' Pearl smiled.

'I simply don't know where the time goes.' Win nodded.

But nothing had changed between them, it never would; the wedges were driven deep. Jack scratched his nostril, working his finger up inside. He wanted to make them look away, tut at least. But, despite all their lace handkerchiefs, scented drawer bags and crustless sandwiches, he couldn't get a reaction.

Winifred's gaze passed over Pearl then swung back to Jack. She was trying to start things again, take control, fingers tapping the coat in her lap.

'We thought it had been too long. I said that only last week to you, Win, and you said…'

'Too long.'

Win tucked her arms over her ribs. The bones in her hands were like the spines of an old umbrella thrusting up through black cloth. Winifred flicked dust from her skirt. 'How are you, John?'

They didn't seem to notice that he didn't give an answer, didn't even bother to correct his name; they settled themselves deeper into his chairs. Pearl was positioned at the point of the triangle beside him. He was glad she didn't look like the other women in the family. Jack wondered what they had been telling her, their lies scraping back the curling wallpaper.

'Ain't nothing wrong with us. If that's all you wanted to know then you can head off again. We've got work to get back to.'

'We came to talk about the future.' Winifred straightened a jet brooch pinned to her throat.

'Perhaps it's time for a fresh start. Have you thought about moving out of London?' Win tried a smile but it sank away unfinished.

'Pearl's got a job at the factory. I work out of the gym.'

'Yes, your work. It really seems a most unsuitable profession. It could bring you into contact with all sorts of people.' Winifred clipped each word.

'What dirty little gossip have you been listening to?'

'Do you want tea? I could have made a cake if I'd known you were coming, but there's digestives in the cupboard.' Pearl twisted her hands around the seat of the chair.

'Now, how can it be gossip if it's true, John?' Winifred smiled up at him.

He wouldn't meet her smile; he let his eyes search the grey street on the other side of the nets. Win clicked her heels together. 'There's been talk of people coming and going. Men and women. Winifred and I don't want that to be true.'

'How is Mrs Bell?'

'You live next door to her, John.'

Winifred touched a handkerchief to her nose with one hand, clutched the brooch in the other. He wanted to ram the white rag down her throat. No wonder she'd never cried when their dad's inky hands slapped out: too afraid the neighbours might hear. Jack wouldn't get the truth out of the Winnies even if he held the back of their legs to the burning stove. He saw them looking around the room, heads tilting, lips pressed tight; but if they noticed the soot outlines above the fireplace, square as the picture frames which had hung there for years, they never said a word.

He knew why they were there. 'They don't think it's right you still living here with me, Pearl.'

'Making money from Mother's house – that's not right either,' Win piped up.

He was surprised he couldn't hear the flap of their wings as they hovered inside the small room. 'Never seemed so interested before.'

'We tried after Mother's funeral.' Winifred laced her fingers together. 'We offered Pearl a place to stay. We wanted to get her out of London.'

'I had to come back home. Jack needed me.'

Pearl rubbed her palm on the table. A splinter poked from the side of her hand; he touched her shoulder to get her attention. Pearl sucked it out between her teeth.

'But fighters in the house. And women – '

'Not "women" – one lady. Pearl likes her.'

'Please, don't try to get the girl to defend you.' Winifred tucked away the hanky with a sharp shake of her head. 'Pearl isn't old enough to understand the true implications of your actions. But understand our concern, John. The agreement, informal as it was, was that you and Pearl could stay here until such time as she was ready to move on.'

'We've never pressed you on that. But it has been several years now. And to be making money behind our back, it simply isn't fair.' Win shook her head.

'I don't think it's right for the child to hear all this, sister.' Winifred's feet sat firmly together.

'Go and make that tea, there's a dear.' Win smiled and waved Pearl away. 'Can she make tea with her condition?'

Jack didn't want her to go; somehow her being in the room held them all in their place, and he was afraid of what they would do to each other if she wasn't there to hear.

'We're out of tea.'

'I can use the leaves left in the pot – they'll do for another brew, Jack.'

'They ain't staying.'

He tightened the belt around his waist. There wasn't a fighter Jack ever met who could cut him up and shred him into pieces the way his own family could. But he wasn't a small boy any more; let them beg this time.

Winifred fixed her brown eyes on him. 'We simply think it would be better for Pearl to move from here. Don't you want her to have a chance?'

'We ain't ready to go yet.' Jack inspected his fingers; he bit away the layer of dirt from the top of his missing thumbnail. 'I've got deals coming off, but not quite yet.'

'She isn't a child any more. We have to plan for her future.' Win patted her gloves and smoothed them into place on her knee. 'With her affliction it may not be a very long future.'

'I've got some numbness in my arms and legs. That don't make me a cripple.'

Pearl, with her baby-fine hair and grey eyes… she was better than anything they could ever have to offer. They wanted to rush her out of that house in a flap of winter coats and fur-lined gloves. Jack would lose everything – no fight, no Frank without Pearl.

Winifred sat forward. 'Pearl, wouldn't you like to leave this place?'

'It's for the best, Pearl. A new start.' Win smiled.

'But we live here,' she whispered to Jack.

'Don't worry about John. He doesn't need another person getting under his feet. He said it himself – he's a working man.'

Winifred held out her hand. But she couldn't reach Pearl without falling off the chair. Jack was closer; he took hold of her belt.

'Pearl belongs here.'

'What about what I want?' She brushed his hand away but stayed next to him in the doorway.

'Of course, what is it the girl wants?' Winifred nodded.

Jack opened his mouth but Pearl put a hand on his sleeve. 'I want to stay. I'm happy here, and now there's Frank…'

'It's happening all over again, sister.' Win stretched out to grasp Winifred's hand. 'She wouldn't stay if she knew.'

'No, not if she knew.'

'Knew what?' Pearl braced herself against the doorframe.

'The lies, John. Did you really think you could keep them all to yourself?' Winifred twisted the brooch at her neck.

Jack scratched at his collar. He wanted her to stop fiddling with that black brooch; the more she twisted it, the more it felt like hands squeezing his own throat.

'You heard her. She ain't going back to Guildford with you.'

'Of course not. We haven't got the room in our small home. Times are hard for everyone.' Win shook her head.

'But we do have a share of this house too, John.'

He opened his fingers into a V, pointing at them both, as he lowered his voice, 'Are you coming after me?'

He should have guessed – all they wanted was money. They would never be able to say it, not in that house when every creak of the floorboards and rattle of the windows could be *him* coming back from the Bible Factory.

Pearl turned towards him. 'We're staying here, ain't we, Jack?'

221

'The girl is poisoned against us already, sister.'

'The vicar said we have to do what we think is right. It's not too late for Pearl to have a life away from here.' Winifred unfolded her coat.

'I ain't a baby.'

'We should have kept her then, saved all this. Mother would be so disappointed in you, John. She was always too soft, covering for your lies.' Win's voice cracked a little. 'We want our share of this house. Our mother provided for us.'

Our mother. They knew. All these years and they'd just been waiting to throw a knockout blow. He lunged forward and grabbed the coats from their laps. 'Get out. I'll send you a bloody postal order.'

'What about Mum? What they talking about?' Pearl touched his elbow, but he couldn't look at her.

Win rose out of the chair. 'We tried to be pleasant.'

Winifred brushed down her skirt as she stood beside her sister. 'We're going to sell the house, John. Slum clearances are starting up all around here. We have to do it now before it's too late. We want our two-thirds of the money.'

'Why thirds? If there are two of us and two of them, they can't make us go. Can they, Jack?' Pearl was tugging on his sleeve now.

'Don't say it.' Jack shook his head, offered up their coats with an open hand. 'Don't.'

'It's not your house, child.' Winifred snatched the coats back from him.

'The deeds still say Mum on them…'

The Winnies stared as Pearl tipped out the top drawer of the sideboard: wedding ring, papers, Dad's souvenir Luger. *Pick a sister and fire*, that was what his dad said when Jack was nearly seven years old. But their dad was the only one laughing at the joke after Jack had clicked the trigger. He couldn't remember which Winnie he chose.

He heard them suck in their breath, but Pearl only came towards them with a folded bunch of paper; she tapped at the signature. 'Look, her name. That means we all have a share, don't it?'

'Just get out of here.' He pushed the Winnies towards the door. 'I'll be wanting to get rid of this stinking place soon anyway. You'll both get your dues. Go on, get.'

He never should have touched that parrot, but them two – he wished that bloody gun had been loaded back then.

Winifred turned as she reached the front step, keeping herself inside the threshold. 'She told us, John. Mum couldn't take the lies to her grave.'

'Why not? The rest of us fucking will.' Jack lowered his face, pressed it close to hers.

'What's going on?' Georgie stood at the top of the stairs, peering over the banister.

'Don't come down,' Jack called back.

The Winnies shook their heads, clucking like birds, but he saw them trying to sneak a look at Georgie's stockinged feet.

'Tell me what you're talking about!' Pearl slapped the rolled-up deeds against the wall; Frank appeared behind her in the kitchen.

Jack wanted to press his hands over her ears, cover her eyes, but she was too big to pick up and carry away. The Winnies pulled their skirts straight, buttoned themselves up, pinned their hats in place, and stepped outside.

Winifred glanced behind her, checking the street before she spoke. 'Only the three surviving children were named in Mother's will…'

'Legally a share of the house would only go to a grandchild after the death of their parent. Jack is still very much alive.' Win nodded her head.

'It's most regrettable that you made us say these things, John.'

Jack turned and snatched the yellowing pages from Pearl's hand. He still remembered them standing outside the aunt's garden gate, smirking. He ripped the black brooch from Winifred's throat, stabbed the pin through the paper and into the green lining of her coat. The Winnies never even flinched.

'Piss off. This is our place.' His breath steamed.

'It's not the way we wanted things, John.' Win sighed.

'His bleeding name is Jack.' Pearl reached forward and slammed the door, grabbed the banister and ran up the stairs. Frank darted after her, feet thumping against the steps.

'Jack? Jack!' Georgie kept calling his name.

It felt as if he'd been landed with a bolo punch to the gut: swallowing sharp gasps but no air getting in. He should have denied it, called them liars, but his dad had him too well trained: *fighting only makes it hurt worse, boy.* Jack pressed his palm to the wall, made his way through to the kitchen. He had kept Pearl with him for all those years but all that time he made her stay on the outside, the same as the Winnies did to him as a boy, keeping that garden gate closed between them; it must be rusted shut by now. Georgie followed him, stood by the dresser, blouse untucked and her slip on but no skirt.

'I overheard it all, you know. Every word your sisters said.'

'The ceiling ain't finished yet.'

He picked his brush up from the pot, paint dribbled on to his hand. The colour reminded him of all those hospital rooms: listening to doctors rabbit on, watching nurses take blood, waiting to find out if he had broken Pearl the night he dropped that yellow bundle of wool at Albany Basin: the mud, the mossy cobbles, it had marked her too. He sank down on the back step.

'Well, penny to the pound there's never a good time to let out a secret like that.' Georgie came up behind him, her shins pressed against his spine. 'I should be angry, only I'd do better to think you would've told me some day. But I ain't the big problem at the moment. What you going to say to Pearl?'

A bedroom door slammed, shaking the glass in the windows.

'Later, after I've done out here…'

The breath ran out of him, whistling between his teeth. He felt light as if he could float up after those gnats. Jack leaned his head against the doorframe, hair sticking in the paint. The walls inside were drying lighter than he thought, brightening up to the same grey as Pearl's eyes.

THREE

The scar on Pearl's leg has shrunk to a pink, gathered line; the weeks have passed but they are back at the hospital. The doctor is talking at Jack but there is a crack in the left side of his glasses: why can't the doctor see it, and what else might he have missed? The doctor pauses, folds his hands on the leather-covered desk; he is waiting for some answer. Jack nods his head as if he understands. The room is full of dust, thick sheets of it cover the high window, and the doctor's pale hair looks as if it is coated in it; blackout curtains, tape across the glass, left in place even though the war is over now.

The doctor beckons Pearl. She doesn't move, and Jack has to roll his shoulder to shift her upright; it leaves a cold patch at his side as Pearl goes behind the desk.

The doctor takes hold of Pearl's arm, hauls her closer as if he is drawing the curtains. Jack sits up in the chair, grips his knees. The doctor picks up a paper straw and cuts it in half; he holds Pearl's small chin in place with his thumb and sticks the straw up her nose. One test has led to another and another, Jack can't even remember how many. But this is the worst. It doesn't hurt, he knows that much, but Jack recognises the look on her face: the same red shame burned him up after each run-in with his dad. The doctor moves the straw, talking all the time. Pearl stands perfectly still; he wishes now he hadn't promised her a comic if she behaved. Why doesn't she pull away, make a noise at least? The doctor drones on, all nasally as if he has a cold; maybe someone should stick a straw up *his* nose.

226

'As you see, as all our tests have shown, there is nothing demonstrably wrong with the nervous system, Mr Munday. The nerves appear to be conducting signals normally but the body is not interpreting this as pain.'

Jack wishes the doctor would stop calling her *the body*; she was right next to him a minute ago, tugging on the ends of the plaits either side of her head. His mum has dressed her in her best green pinafore and matching green cardigan. Jack shifts on the hard wooden chair and stares at the hanging skeleton in the corner. Funny that underneath they are all the same: him, that doctor in the knitted waistcoat and thick-rimmed spectacles, all of them. Pearl glances up and blinks heavily and the straw drops out a little lower; it is her signal that she wants to leave. She is only eight, but Jack wonders how much she understands.

'She is of normal intelligence. The body has good muscle strength but numbness to the skin, especially the arms.' The doctor sits back in his chair. 'If, as you say, there is no family connection, then we could suppose it was as a result of a trauma to the head, or an infection. Are you sure there has been no such incident?'

Pearl presses a finger to her nostril, blows the straw out of her nose. Jack shakes his head. His mum made him promise that he wouldn't tell the doctors about Pearl's *little accident* – how she refers to that night at Albany Basin. Jack taps his foot against the desk, click click, in time to the clock over the bookcase.

'So what you're saying is, you don't know nothing?'

'No, on the contrary. We know what it is. As I told you there is even a name for it, if you remember. Idiopathic neuropathy.'

'Idiopathic neuropathy,' Pearl parrots as she chews on the straw.

Jack nods. Fucking doctors. That's what he gets for pawning everything he owned, and selling off his only fighter too: a name. He can't very well admit he hasn't been listening

227

now, and the old fool is looking at him, eyebrows drawn together, nostrils flared, as if Jack is the one with the problem.

'It is not so rare as one might suppose. It could strike any of us at any time, given the correct correlation of events. She is more fortunate than some. She has limited sensations at least. Support shoes to prevent curling of the toes will need to be made. Careful monitoring for blisters on the hands and feet will need to take place. But I am afraid, as yet, there is no definitive treatment.' He wipes the glasses on the edge of his tie; they are covered with dust now too.

'No tablets, nothing you can give her?'

Jack glances at Pearl: her cardigan buttons are fastened wrong, one ribbon hangs undone. She studies a pair of pigeons on the windowsill, shuffling closer together as buses rumble past, pecking at the moss-covered stone.

'Of the cases reported, not all make it into adulthood, but those are the acute cases. I would advise a watchful eye when caring for this one. Breaks can become infected, as can blisters, grazes. Boiling water can burn internally – '

'She'll outlive us all.' Jack shakes his head, blocks the doctor out. His mum is already looking at Pearl strange, making her bath scalding to see if she notices – *shock her into feeling*, is what his mum says. She refuses to go to the hospital, thinks Jack is making a big fuss about nothing, that the doctors have got it wrong: only she knows how to take care of Pearl.

'There are a lot of things to be aware of.' The doctor unclips his fountain pen and goes back to the chart in front of him. 'Bring her back for a yearly check-up. My first case of this kind. I will be interested to monitor any deterioration.'

He disappears behind the paper, holding it close to his face. He wants them gone by the time he looks up. Jack has been through this before: so many waiting rooms with tightly packed chairs, so many doctors with short trimmed hair and round glasses. Maybe his mum is right about the doctors. Pearl is already waiting by the door, clicking her heels and holding out her hand.

'What are you going to tell Mum?' She walks in front of him down the corridor. 'What about school?'

Heavy raindrops impact against the skylights like a fist. They are going to get soaked.

'Didn't you hear the doctor? Ain't nothing wrong with you.' He wipes away the thin little plait that brushes his hand. 'Doctors don't know nothing. Life might have been easier if I hadn't felt a few things.'

'So, I'm all better.' She pivots and smiles.

'There are things you're going to have to do. I want you to promise me you'll check yourself every day. I'm going to get you a first aid tin and I want you to carry it round.' He puts a hand on her shoulder.

'Why? You or Mum can do that.' She slips away, skipping ahead, raising her knees to her chest.

'You have to look out for yourself in life, Pearl.' His voice echoes around the half-tiled walls.

'Why?'

She skips back to him. She never stops moving, it makes Jack dizzy spending too long with her.

'Because no one else gives a fu...' He swallows down those words. 'No one else can do it as well as you. You're good at taking care of things, ain't you?'

She nods, and tugs on his sleeve. 'I'm going to tell you a secret.'

He lowers his head. She cups her hands around his ear, blocking out the thump of the rain above them.

'I told the nurse with the red hair that you're my dad.'

She laughs and runs on, the bar-strap of her brown leather shoes flapping free. It's just a word she has heard, repeated in the classroom, shouted across the street: *wait until your dad gets home*. But he finds it hard to straighten his back, feels as if he is carrying her on his shoulders. The cartilage in his knees creaks as he stands upright. She holds out her arms and tries to walk along the grouting lines around the tiles; she travels in a square, in a rectangle until she is pressed against a

229

wall. She waves. That word will bubble up again one day. She might think back on this moment in the corridor and wonder – *did he do something to give it away, did he want to wrap his arms around me and claim me even just a small bit?* But he doesn't have any right to think that way; he's never done anything to deserve the word 'dad'.

Pearl disappears into another corridor. Jack runs after her, gripping the wall as he takes the corner. 'Get off there.' He lifts her from the banister. 'If you don't see no one else doing it, don't do it yourself.'

She hops quietly beside him as they go down the stairs. But he is glad there are some things that will never make her sob, never make her hug her arms around herself and rock. He won't tell his mum everything the doctor said; no point worrying her. Pearl is never ill – small and thin maybe but she always heals, always bounces back: the dog bite, the twisted ankle, burned hands, grazes, cuts, bruises. *Indestructible* is what Jack calls her.

The red-haired nurse comes out of the door at the bottom of the stairs. Pearl slips out of reach, laughing as she sprints past.

'Wait inside, Pearl.'

The nurse is pretty in a young sort of way, padded around the face and small hands. Her fingers rub against the edge of a paper file, squashed up against her chest. 'She's a lively one, your daughter.'

Those words make Jack's neck itch. His nails dig in; the sound vibrates in his ear. The rain has stopped, through the double doors just ahead, sunlight pokes between the patterned glass.

'She's my sister.'

'Oh, I thought she said…'

He doesn't want to be here any more: the echo, the stink of carbolic. He keeps walking. The nurse follows beside him, marching quickly as if she has places to be. The grey paint in the corridor isn't thick enough to cover the cracks in the wall.

'Dad's dead. I help out.'

He holds open the door; a bus huffs and puffs, pigeons coo around an old man with a brown bag of breadcrumbs. Pearl waves from the bottom of the steps, kicking up puddles. The nurse smiles, her blue eyes going soft around the edges as if she might cry.

'So, like a father, then.'

'No, nothing like that.' Jack lets the doors swing shut behind him.

FOUR

The smog swallowed up Jack's hand, but he reached the lamp-post with his fingertips then two steps further and he was at the kerb. It wasn't so much pea-soup as mustard, and it burned the back of his tongue as if someone had left the top off the smelling salts. No sound, not even the echo of his footsteps. If he got lost he could end up anywhere: the railway tracks, the canal. Someone brushed against his elbow but they weren't close enough to see. Jack kept the kerb on his right side, walking towards the junction. All he had to do was cross over and go straight down to reach the Man of the World.

An orange circle of light hovered in front of him; as it grew closer the colour leaked out like melted margarine. A conductor marched slowly, torch flare burning, the bus right behind. Jack doubled back twice before he found the pub. The fog seeped in with him, grey shapes like hanging bags at the gym positioned around the tables. It took him a second to see them: pushed up close together on a bench away from the door, waiting as Georgie had promised him they would be. They didn't look the same – older somehow, Pearl's forehead lined as she spoke to Frank, leaning in against him. The pub was busy: staying at home with smog bumping against the windows was like being suffocated.

Jack's knees banged against the table as he sat down opposite them; the glasses of squash, orange as the fog, rippled.

'You're sat here waiting for an apology, suppose.'

'Is that all you've got to say to me?' Pearl straightened up.

It wasn't going the way he'd thought it would, the way he had played it in his head. Jack took his hat off and dropped it on to his leg.

'What do you want me to say, Pearl?'

'What do I want you to say?'

She unbuttoned her coat, shrinking out of it. Jack rubbed his head; it was going to take some time.

'Can I get you a drink, Jack?' Frank stood up.

Pearl took hold of his wrist. 'No, stay here.'

'This is family stuff, Pearl.' Frank twitched his nose, glancing at the bar.

'Frank's right.' Jack nodded. 'I'll have a pint.'

'Stay. You're part of my family.' Pearl pulled Frank back down. 'Seems we're allowed to call people whatever we like now. How about we call him a cousin, Jack? That suit you?'

But she wasn't looking at Jack; her face was turned aside. Frank stroked her hand. They sat in silence for a minute that felt like a full thirteen rounds. Jack watched her chewing on her lip, trying to form words. If he didn't speak now she would walk out of the pub, maybe for good, and take Frank with her. No fight, no big future for Jack then: nothing. He ran the rim of the hat between his fingers, spinning it on his knee.

'I was just a kid. Mum sort of took over. You seemed happy together.'

'We were.' Pearl kept her eyes focused on Newton at the bar.

'Then it was for the best, weren't it?'

'All Newton ever talks about is his Jimmy, his son the chaplain.' She nodded in his direction. 'When I was small she used to say *my Pearl*. I won't let you blame Mum for this.'

'We can't all lead a charmed life like his son.'

Newton kept his hands wrapped around his pint, sinking mouthful after mouthful – drinking his way through Jack's paint money. Frank kept still, like a referee in the corner.

'Where is she, Jack? Why didn't she take me with her?'

The cold air crawled around him; he pulled his arms against his sides, held himself still.

'She died. Never would have left you otherwise.'

Pearl tilted her head back, taking him in. 'Supposed to be grateful for that, am I?'

Jack had let Pearl have his mum, and he had seen for himself how happy they were: the way Pearl would sit so close, her knees on his mum's lap; the chatting that would stop when he walked into a room, and the laughing that would start when he left again. And towards the end, when his mum was ill, he'd stopped her from ruining it for Pearl then. He smeared a speck of soot across the back of his hand. Pearl stared at him, waiting. He was the only one left who could give her any answers.

Pearl squeezed the coat on her lap; trapped fog seemed to trickle out of it. 'So, she died and you forgot to mention it? Or maybe she never meant that much to you in the first place?'

Frank stood up. 'I know you're hurting, Pearl. But you can't expect Jack to tell me these things too.' He walked over to the bar.

Jack gripped his hat tighter; it smelt like damp fur. The ginger tom must have been sleeping under the stairs again. He settled the hat on the empty seat next to him, taking a moment to sweep the dust and dirt from its rim. He took a deep breath.

'She was the best thing ever happened to me.'

The lights in the pub seemed to burn a little brighter now that he had said those words out loud.

Pearl pointed at him. 'It's always about you, Jack. Always.'

'Me? I could have given you up, could have passed you on after Mum died.' He loosened the tie around his neck before it strangled him. 'You had the picture of the old man, worshipped that enough. None of it was what I wanted.'

Pearl dug her elbows into the table, clenched her teeth. 'I chose you every time, Jack. Stood up for you when people talked bad about you. Came back from the Winnies' after the funeral. Mum kept us together, then like an idiot I thought I had to do the same.'

'I'm sorry, ain't I? I don't know how many times I can say it, Pearl.'

'You ain't ever said it me. It didn't matter before because I knew… I knew you didn't really want me around. I thought it was just a petty brother-sister thing. But now – I think, maybe, you wished I'd died too.'

'That ain't true.' Jack hung his head lower; even when he'd thought those things, even when he'd hissed them at the sleeping baby – *I wish it'd been you* – he'd never really meant it. 'I'm sorry, Pearl.'

'You must have really hated me all those years to keep this from me…'

'No, I never.'

'… to let me feel sad at only having a picture of my dad, to let me think I was an orphan when our mum died… *Our mum* – I always called her that. Well, you must have been laughing at me all this time.'

'Christ, Pearl. Nothing about it ever made me want to laugh.'

Jack tapped her arm, pointing at her mouth. She forced herself to loosen her teeth before she bit clean through her lip. He shifted in his seat. 'Bet Frank's loving it, having something to drive a wedge between me and you. Give him the excuse he wants just to walk away from our deal.'

'He's my family now, Jack. The only reason I'm sat here is because he begged me to see you. Whatever happened back then, you shouldn't have lied to me, not about this.'

'I never let you go without.' Jack spread his hands out on the sticky table, covering the ghost prints of a hundred other drinkers. 'I thought it was for the best.'

Frank came back, handed her the glass of squash; she gulped it down, wiping her lips clean with her thumb.

'I see you're both not done yet…'

'Stay, Frank. Jack had his moment of privacy and he wasted it again. Sit down. There ain't nothing to be embarrassed by, is there, Jack? No tears. No feeling.'

Frank sat down, took her hand in his. Jack wanted a drink, his throat scratchy and dry – all those answers stuck inside him. He licked his bottom lip. No one else in the pub even glanced over at them, not Newton at the bar, not the group playing dominoes, not the couple ordering Guinness; the fog kept them all cut off.

'… and she was my mother.' Pearl started speaking half-way through whatever conversation she was having in her head, her voice rising higher. 'Why do you get to keep her to yourself?'

'Because she's *mine*!'

Heads finally turned in the pub, but there wasn't enough money to waste on letting beer go flat, and they soon picked up their glasses again.

'You said she were dead.'

'Don't mean I don't carry her around with me.'

His hand rose up to his top pocket as if she really was in there. He took out his packet of cigarettes but left them on the table; no point raising his guard, it was a fixed fight – he wasn't going to win this one. Jack glanced over to the bar, and would have done anything for a drop of what Newton was drinking.

'She died, you washed your hands and Mum worked herself to the bone raising me. Tell me that ain't the truth of it?'

He'd expected there to be tears, shouting – something, at least. But Pearl inspected him across the table like a cut that needed cleaning. Frank gently placed his hand on her back; she blinked twice, breaking her stare.

'Pearl, it's Jack. He's looked out for me, and if he says he's tried…'

She brushed Frank's words away with a wave of her hand.

'I did try, Pearl.' Jack scratched his nail across the grain of the wood. 'I kept a roof over your head. Fed you. Clothed you. It might not have been much but I'm coming into money now. Things are starting to look up for us.'

He smiled for a moment as she reached across to take his hand. She held on tight, tighter, digging her nails deep into his skin, but he wouldn't make a sound.

'You're selfish, Jack. Keeping her all to yourself. It's all been lies. Don't suppose I should expect no different now. There can't be nothing left between us.'

She threw his hands back. Frank pressed an arm around her shoulder. And Jack knew now why she had chosen the pub: not because she was afraid of him, but to control herself. He rubbed his chin, pointed at the end just like Pearl's.

'There's Munday in you all right.'

'Are you sure about that? Sure that there weren't others?' Her lip curled up into a one-sided smile.

'You ain't got the right to judge her. Call me what you like, but I ain't going to hear nothing against her.'

'I don't even know *her* name. What could I say about *her*?' She turned to Frank, expecting him to step in.

'You've got to tell Pearl something, Jack.'

Rosie took salt in her porridge, always put her left boot on first, and made a clicking sound deep in her throat when she had a cold – none of those things was what Pearl wanted to hear. And the rest: the tiny dent above Rosie's belly button, the way he liked to press his little finger against it and the way Rosie kept her eyes open when he did that and when he kissed her, when he was inside her, even when she panted, squeezed him closer, as if she never wanted to miss a thing he did and that perhaps it meant he really was worth looking at, worth something – none of *those* things could he ever share with Pearl. The spit dried in his mouth, but the facts wouldn't take much breath; they would fit on the back of a boxing programme.

237

'Her name was Rosie. She was the one wanted to call you Pearl. She said you glowed when you came out, all pink and white like a mother-of-pearl button. She was born in '20 and died in '38.'

It didn't feel right reducing Rosie to those figures, as if somehow he was losing part of her, her face fading like newspaper left out in the rain.

'Why don't I remember?' Pearl directed the question at Frank.

'You must only have been a baby.' Frank stroked the side of her face.

But it was the question Jack always wanted answered: how could Rosie have been in Pearl's life and yet she didn't remember?

'What do you want me to say, Pearl?'

But this time he really meant it. She shrugged, and picked up her coat; she was going to leave him too.

'I want to put this right, I do, honest. I can tell you more, I really can. Just give me a little bit of time, Pearl.'

Maybe he should let them both up and disappear, but he couldn't imagine not seeing those grey eyes staring back at him. Jack knew what sort of world was out there perhaps that was why he never just opened the cage doors and let the parrot fly free. She didn't want to listen to him but Frank just might.

Pearl buttoned herself up. 'You've had more than your fair share of the count, Jack. There's nothing you can do to prove to me you ain't just a selfish – '

'I read the letter Frank wrote me.' Jack shifted his feet under the table; the paper padding was still there.

'I told you he would.' Frank grinned at Pearl.

'I understand now. Frank needs a new start and I know you want one too, Pearl. But you'll never have that unless you get some money together. This last fight means you can forget about Spider and that lot. Frank can come and work for me when he's done in the ring.'

238

'Doing what?' Pearl stared at him.

Jack turned to face Frank. 'I'm going to have backers this time, real money. Maybe even set up my own gym soon. I'll need people I trust for that.'

'Don't listen, Frank. No one should trust no one like him.'

'It's not me walking away from a legally binding contract, Pearl.'

'What do you call having a daughter? Lies are like breathing for you, ain't they, Jack? Come on, Frank. Let's go.'

'I'll tell you both something for nothing. Show how much I trust you.' Jack reached up, hooked an arm around Frank's neck. 'It's a fixed fight. All you got to do is go down in the right place, we'll cash in big,' he whispered.

'That's cheating.' Frank reared away, dropping back into his chair, taking Pearl with him. Jack held up his hand for hush.

'I didn't have to tell you, Frank. I could've tipped the other fighter how to put you down and you'd never have known. But I want you to believe me, both of you. I'm doing this for us. So you two don't make the mistakes I did.'

'And you're not making nothing out of it, course you're not.' Pearl puffed up a sharp little laugh.

'I had plans before – me and Frank making it big. But if he don't want to fight no more then I had to find another way. Don't you want to get your own place, do things proper? Let me make it up to you.'

'Frank don't need that sort of help – we'll do fine without you.'

'Come home. I'll tell you more about Rosie. I will.'

He sat back. Georgie came out from behind the bar with a tray of glasses, not a drop spilled as she swayed towards them. 'I thought you might need top-ups.' She put the drinks down. 'Things not sorted out yet? Well, maybe I'll come back later.'

'It's all going to work out fine. Ain't it, Pearl?' Jack took a mouthful of bitter.

'It's up to Frank if he wants to throw the fight.' She turned his hand over in hers, running her finger across the bruised knuckles.

'Jack wants this for us, Pearl. We need money.' Frank's eyes reflected the light from the lamps. 'I'll do it.'

Pearl shook her head. 'He'll mess it up, Frank. He always does.'

'If Jack says it's sorted, then it is.' Georgie sat down next to him.

'Happens all the time. Why shouldn't we have some of the payoff from that?' He shrugged.

'What if it goes wrong? You could get hurt, Frank.'

'If he plays it right, and you all keep your mouths shut, nothing goes wrong.'

'Is that what you said to Mum? Don't worry, no one'll ever find out…'

Georgie reached over the table and put a hand on Pearl's shoulder. 'Things were different during the war, Pearl. No one knew if they were going to make it through. Jack and his mum must've thought they was doing the right thing.'

'Jack thinks whatever he decides is the right thing.'

'Frank wants to do it, he said so. Come home when you've finished those drinks. I've got to get to a meeting but I'll bring us back some pie and mash. You set for money?' He didn't wait for an answer, emptied the coins out of his pocket. 'Frank, you look like a mushy peas type to me. Pearl, you'll have yours without the liquor and a ginger beer to go with it, won't you?'

She nodded.

'See, I got that right. I can put this all right. Give me this last chance.'

Frank raised his eyebrows at Pearl. 'We ain't going to get a better offer. We need this, don't we?'

She nodded again. 'I'll eat the food. I'll even hear you out, Jack. But you don't deserve no promises from me about last chances.'

'That's sorted, then. I'll see you all back at the house.'

Jack got up; Georgie went with him. They stood outside the pub, his hands jumping as he tried to light her cigarette. She cupped her palms around the match.

'Is this fight really the best thing?'

'What's that supposed to mean?' He stuffed the cigarette between his lips.

'It's just a question...' The fog swallowed up the rest of her words.

'The money'll give them a start in life.' Jack watched shapes shifting in the gloom, re-forming into cars or people as they went past the lights of the pub. 'She might not think it, but she still needs looking after.'

'Why you? Why not Frank? You give him a job, enough to support them both.' She took the cigarette and inhaled. 'Think keeping her around's going to keep part of her mother in that house too?'

'Jealous, are you?'

'Maybe I am, though I'm not stupid enough to try and compete with a ghost. But we had an agreement, rules of fair play, Jack. Sure there's nothing else you're not telling me?'

'I had two brothers meant less than nothing to me. They're dead too, as it happens.'

'Come up with something better. It's dark out and no one else can hear you. Say something truthful. I dare you.'

Breath and fog and smoke – all blended together. He couldn't tell where one ended and the other began; he used to feel like that lying with Rosie. He closed his eyes, took a step towards Georgie until her blouse brushed his wrist. He wanted to feel blended again.

'She drowned in Albany Basin. You can smell the canal from here. I reached for her but grabbed Pearl instead, then I dropped her too.' His hands shook and the cigarette fell, he ground it out under his foot. 'I've got to make it up to her.'

'Sounds to me like you saved Pearl's life.'

'I never got Rosie out. Two bargemen dragged me up. Why didn't they save her? After it happened, Pearl never woke in the nights, never even made a noise if she cut herself. That's down to me too. Sooner or later every debt's got to be paid.'

Georgie reached around his neck, put her lips to his ear. 'Didn't you learn nothing in six years of war? There's no higher being, no fate, no grand plan. Guilt's the only thing will burn you up, Jack.' She slid another cigarette from the packet in his pocket and fitted it between his fingers. 'Pearl's your daughter. I don't need to hear it, but you're going to have to say it to her soon. Tell her you love her.'

Her heels snapped back down on to the paving stones. She struck a match and lit his cigarette. He wanted the smog to cover him up.

'I'm late.'

Jack reached the corner but couldn't help glancing back. His heart stumbled a step when he saw the outline of Georgie watching him. He tipped his hat, turned and walked away.

Rich moved around the ring, driving his sparring partner back on to the single rope. The boy was good – couldn't really call him a boy, though. The walls of the basement sweated, salty streaks staining the exposed bricks. Jack sat on the stool. Rich's trainer stood behind, coughing with his mouth shut each time Rich ducked a blow. Jack wasn't sure how the trainer hadn't passed out through lack of air. Rich dodged another, drove up under the other bloke's guard with one to the chin. But it wasn't the hit Jack was expecting. He stood up, holding on to the corner pole to get a better look.

'He switched. Which is he? Left or right?'

Rich led with right jabs again, following through with a left cross before stepping off and throwing a right hook. His trainer grinned, lifting up his long chin.

'Yanks call it southpaw. You wouldn't know it, though. Neither do his opponents usually until it's too late.'

Rich held up his arms and stepped back.

'Why don't he follow that shot up?'

'He's only got one spar partner, Big Roberts here. Can't keep any others. They don't like to get knocked around by his sort, and I'm not talking about him being a leftie.'

He blinked twice when he finished speaking, sniffing like a rabbit. Rich picked up a tattered towel from his corner. His skin didn't have the red, blotched look of other fighters, didn't show up the marks the same. He looked untouched, indestructible, to a punter anyway. Jack bet his eyes and lips would swell up same as white fighters, though. Rich held the rope up as Big Roberts toppled under and the trainer helped him to a stool.

Jack held out a clean towel to Rich. 'Who you going to knock around with now?'

'He'll come round in a minute. I didn't even hit him hard. Think he just likes the buzz from the salts.' Rich's words were smothered as he scrubbed his face.

The trainer opened up a bottle of smelling salts, waved it under the balloon red nose.

'I told you I'd show you something special. The southpaw.' Rich jumped his arms up in the air, towel waving like a flag. 'States is where it's at, Jack. That's where we're heading one day.'

His trainer nodded. Jack stepped away from the dry taste of the chemical fumes.

'What do you fight under?'

'Here it comes, telling me to change my name. Some rubbish like Jungle Johnny. That was Vincent's idea.'

Rich loosened up his arms, holding each under the elbow and drawing it across his chest, steam rising off him.

'He don't know what the punters want. Surname?'

'Ellery.'

'Rich Ellery. Well, I never thought the day would come, but we should stick with that.' Jack slapped him on the back.

'Got a certain ring to it, don't it?'

'Who don't want to be Rich?' Jack turned to the trainer who was still knelt by Big Roberts, flapping a damp flannel in front of his face. 'So, why no manager?'

'Had a spot of bother with the last one, got a bit loose-lipped and odds for Rich's fights went down. That were three months past.'

'I'm ready for it.' Rich held out his hand. 'Been waiting long enough. Well, seems to me we've got to make this arrangement work. Treat me right and you won't get no trouble from me.'

'I've plenty riding on this too. Seems to me that makes us a perfect arrangement.' Jack shook with him.

He let go and paced around to the other side of the room, taking in the crumbling ceiling, beetles scuttling back under the boards. He prodded the blown plaster on the back wall; his finger left an imprint, sucking against his skin, pulling him down into that place. The river was rising up beneath the floor, the Central Line eating away at the walls.

Rich dipped his hands into a bucket of water by the ring. 'Penny for them, Jack? Better not be thinking about how to scam me.'

'I'm thinking business.' He extracted his finger, wiping it clean on his sleeve.

'I've got business. Twins need taking care of. And a wife who won't speak to me for a week every time I got to lose a fight.'

'Ever think you'd be better off without them?'

'Every time someone needs a new pair of shoes, or they wake me on my morning off from the railway yard.' He laughed but shook his head. 'Lucky they stick by me, Jack.'

Rich moved about the small space, keeping warm, waiting for his partner to sober up. Jack scooped some of the water out of the bucket and scrubbed it across the back of his neck; he shivered. Rich pulled the towel from under his armpit and flicked it outwards.

'Someone walk over your grave?'

Jack ducked and sidestepped on the balls of his feet. 'They'll never hustle me into a churchyard. I'm too fast. But I've seen nicer-looking cemeteries than this place. We need to think about setting you up somewhere better.'

The lights dimmed as a Tube train vibrated on the other side of the wall. The room slipped into darkness for a moment before the yellow electric bulb surged back to life.

FIVE

'Turn the lamp higher, son. It's dark in here.'

Jack puts the mug down on the bedside table, walks towards the glowing light around the thick drapes. He peers out of the crack; the sun is low, snagging on the roofs opposite, sickly-looking.

'Let me open the curtains, Mum.'

'No, son. They're spying on us.'

A black dog runs after the rag-and-bone cart. Jack wipes sweat from his forehead. He only manages to get the windows open for a few hours a day, after his mum has drifted off. He sits back on the edge of the bed and shivers as a trickle runs down his spine. She pats the woollen cover, asking him to move nearer. 'They should be walking over my grave, not yours.'

The gas lamp only touches light on one side of her face, the left eaten up by shadows.

'Just a bit close in here, Mum, ain't it?'

She is disappearing under the heavy mound of blankets; hasn't left the room for three weeks. He empties her pans, Pearl washes her down, and they both try to make her eat.

'The doctor says it'll make you feel better if you get up.'

He blows air across the Bovril, touching the side to make sure it is cool enough to drink. She clasps the sheets to her chest, left hand clawing at the crocheted blanket on top.

'They don't know nothing. The forces are everywhere. Doctors can't control things like that.'

'Nothing can get you while I'm around.'

He boxes the shadows, one hand still around the mug. The brown liquid sloshes against the sides; the salty heat makes his eyes smart.

'Some things even you aren't strong enough to hold back, son. I know you think you can stop this, but my time's coming.'

Her skin is wrinkled as thrown-away paper. Jack can't look into those watery eyes; he feels as if he might topple too. For all these years he has been fighting against her, watching from the corner as she raised Pearl.

'I've brought you something light. Broth and a slice.' He looks at the jug of water. 'You ain't even had a glass. They'll make you go to hospital soon. I won't be able to stop them.'

'This is my home. They can't make me leave.' Her fists bounce on the covers.

'We want you to get better, Mum. Pearl needs you – she's only twelve.' He tries to soothe her with his voice. 'Why don't you let her sit with you this afternoon?' *Don't make me do this on my own*, is what he doesn't say.

'Is she keeping the place clean? Dusting the family photographs?'

He nods. She flicks her tongue across her flaking top lip. 'That's something Pearl got from me, because that girl never did no housework.'

His arms tense and squeeze tight against his ribs. Since she took to her bed, time hasn't just stopped, it is running backwards.

'She's still here, you know. That girl. I see her standing in doorways, watching me from corners.'

She leans forward, and her nightgown sags open; Jack turns his face away from the deflated body visible underneath. The whiff of sour sweat is strong as at the gym.

'Pearl just wants to see you, Mum.'

'Not her, the other one. Rosie.'

He catches sight of something over his shoulder but it is just a shadow from the chair, draped in worn underclothes –

nothing there. It isn't fair that his mum sees Rosie when that is all Jack has wanted for years.

'I wish your father was here. I never imagined I'd live so long without him.'

'Be thankful he didn't outlive us all.'

'He was a good husband.' Her head tilts with the weight of the words.

'If you say so.'

He presses her shoulder to get her to lean back on the pillows. Her scalp shows through the thinning hair on top of her head. She grasps his arm.

'Don't speak like that, not about the dead.'

Her fingers burn into him. For someone who has given up, she clings on tight; his pulse beats against her fingertips. Jack prises her hand away. It floats back on to the bedclothes. She is smiling again, staring at the ceiling as if it opens on to another world.

'Remember the night Colonial Wharf burned? He woke me and he had two bikes. We cycled all the way. He slowed at each junction for me to catch up. Calling me on all the time. *Come on, Ada, pretend we're sixteen again*, that's what he kept saying.' She smiles and makes a gurgling noise low down in her throat.

'I don't remember that.'

'You slept through it, son. We were back by the time you got up next morning, only just.' She smiles and rubs her thumb down her throat as if she is easing up the words. 'The most beautiful thing I ever seen. Fire like water, kept rolling in waves. John held my hand, kept the bikes upright with his other hand. He was so strong.'

'All those flames, all that noise. He must have been in his element.'

'Wait until you raise children, John. They change things, bring a responsibility even a good man can drown under.'

He listens for the sound of Pearl down in the kitchen; nothing.

248

'Don't you remember when you had 'flu that time? No, you were probably only about four. He stayed up all week with you, washed you with a cloth, mushed up your food.'

'I do remember playing horses, climbing over his back. He just didn't like it once we started having thoughts of our own. He could play all day, long as we never said a word.'

What does he care if his mum chooses to wash down all those memories, clean them up with sweet-smelling lies? She reaches for her wedding band on the bedside table; it doesn't fit any more.

'He was my husband too, not just your father.'

'If you get up today, Mum, I'll take the ring to a jeweller's. Get it made smaller for you.' He holds out his hand but she doesn't give it up.

'No need, John. We're tied by something greater than that piece of metal.' Her false teeth don't fit either, clopping inside her mouth. 'I don't know why you want me to get up. I could fall down them stairs. One of them new buses could run me down. Normal folk feel pain, don't forget that. It's safer up here.'

Jack puts his arms under her shoulders to haul her into a sitting position. She must weigh less than a flyweight but she makes his muscles ache: leaden. She keeps the ring gripped in her hand.

'Have some Bovril at least, Mum. Pearl made it for you.'

She spits, and spots of brown stain the front of her nightgown. 'It tastes funny – maybe it's poisoned.'

'No one's trying to poison you. Look.' He takes a sip of the dark drink. 'Lovely.'

'Always was a good liar.' She smiles, but shakes her head when he holds up the mug to her mouth. 'I won't do it.'

'Mum, you got to get your strength back. Think about Pearl.'

'That's all I've ever done. Thought if I raised her, loved her, then that Rosie wouldn't have no claim.' She holds the ruffled front of her brown spotted nightdress. 'Pearl don't want me no more. I've seen the way she follows you about like a dog. Heard her calling you Jack too. My time's done. No one needs me here now.'

'It ain't true. Sit and let her have a chat with you. I can't keep making excuses.'

'You can't bring Pearl in here. I don't want those eyes to be the last thing I see before I pass over. Rosie's eyes. Judging me and what we done. '

'There's nothing wrong with you, the doctor's said so.'

'Feel my heart, son. There's not much left in it. I want you to bury me next to my husband.'

She makes a grab for his hand but he is too quick. Jack moves away an inch, and the springs jangle.

'I ain't going to talk about it.'

'You're the only one stayed with me, John. I always knew you were different from the others, so like your father.' She reaches out. 'John?' She topples against him. 'John, my love, I've always been your Ada. I love the children because they are part of you, not that they replace you.'

Jack jumps away, his ears burning up. His mum folds forward, hands keeping her face from sinking into the covers. Pearl knocks at the door. 'Mum, let me in, won't you?'

'All the lies, son. I can't face them no more.' She rolls back against the headboard. 'Promise me something. There's money in the dresser drawer for the funeral. I don't want much, but lay me with him.'

He stands on the rug, caught between the bed and the door. 'You got to see her.'

'No. When are my Winnies coming? I need to say goodbye to my girls.'

Jack goes to the door, opens it a crack. Pearl stands there with her socks falling around her ankles. 'Please, let us in, Jack.'

'Just give Mum a minute to finish her drink.'

'Good, she's taking something.' Pearl's smile bounces into place.

Jack closes the door again. He downs the Bovril, swallows back the acid rising into his mouth. He presses his hands on top of the headboard and brings his face down to hers; wood knocks against the wall.

'Mum, if you don't see Pearl…'

She tries to answer but he presses a finger to her mouth.

'… I swear to Christ, I'll let them burn you up and put your ashes out with the bins. You'll never be with Dad again.'

He takes the damp washcloth from the bowl and presses it to his own eyes before wiping it across her forehead.

'I can't do it no more. I got to go clean. That Rosie ruined everything. She was cursed. First your dad dying, then how she turned you. I tried to block it out, tried to do my best for Pearl, but Rosie was always there. It's all poisoned,' she snarls; her false teeth drop together.

'You're everything to Pearl. I won't have you ruining her memories, making her think she's done something wrong. Do you want to be buried with him or not?'

He picks up the ring from the blanket, picks off a fleck of lilac wool, places it on the bedside cabinet.

'What do I tell her?' Her breath whistles between her teeth.

His fist clenches, water drips from the cloth warm as piss. He throws it to the floor.

'Tell her you love her, that you're proud to have been her mother.'

He realises too late that he has used the past tense, as if those forces his mum is always talking of have already carried her away.

'John.' A tear swells at the corner of her eye.

He brushes it aside with his knuckle. 'I'll keep my bloody fingers crossed, if that'll keep you happy, Mum?'

She nods.

'Get in here,' Jack calls out.

Pearl trips across the room, buries her face against his mum's starched nightgown. He stands at the end of the bed.

251

'Jack, let's show Mum how we've been training.' Pearl sits up and rolls her sleeve above her elbow – a row of red dots fading into white lumps near the crook of her arm. Jack takes a cigarette, lights it, sucking down to inhale the smoke. He dabs the glowing end of the fag on to her forearm, pulls it away quickly. His mum studies Pearl's face, expectant.

'I did feel it a bit more that time. I really think the practice is helping. We'll get better together, Mum.' Pearl lies down alongside her.

'God forgive us.' His mum strokes Pearl's hair but stares straight at him.

He doesn't care if she thinks he is the one who will burn; it couldn't be any worse than the suffocating staleness of that closed-up bedroom, and the ashen colour of her dried-up skin.

SIX

Friday night was cold as hell: like being locked in the back yard on Christmas Day when he was ten and frost had drilled its way into every bone until the pain made him howl; stray dogs had chorused him. Jack drew his coat tighter, tried to stop his teeth clacking together. On his third cigarette and still no sign of Vincent. He stamped life back into his feet. Beer barrels and crates of empties cast long shadows into the alleyway like fingers trying to hook him. The smell of yeast and rotting wood was thick in the air. Jack flicked the butt away. It sparked against the wall, hissed in a puddle; dark shapes moved across the surface of the water. Two men stood at the mouth of the alley. Jack held the smoke inside, the last brush of warmth tickling his throat. Above the drone of buses on the street, the echoing clip of footsteps, a chattering of starlings swarmed through the air.

'Thought you weren't coming.' He held out his hand.

'I'm always good to my word. How's the fighter?' Vincent kept his hands in his pockets.

'Tucked up in the warm. Looking good, though.' Jack blew on his whitening fingernails.

The Thin Suit stood behind Vincent. No coat; two red hands hanging down as if he was burning from the inside. He reached into his pocket, pulled out a lighter. His face illuminated from underneath as Vincent sucked down on the glowing cigar; lines etched around his mouth looked as if they were never stretched by smiling. Vincent beckoned Jack closer with his free hand. 'Harry is already in there, so we're all set to go. Just make sure your fighter follows through.'

'It's in the bag.'

Jack tapped his foot on the flagstones. The cold couldn't get him now. Soon he would have leather gloves and Georgie in a new fur coat pressed against his side to keep him toasty. He almost didn't want the fight to be over so soon; he wanted to feel the tingling, like a shot in the arm, spreading through his body.

Vincent's cigar tip smouldered.

'Don't forget to keep your distance in there. The last thing we need is prying eyes.'

Jack nodded. That red circle was all the light left; the evening had slipped away. The boxes and crates melted into the darkness of the wall. Jack shrank his arms and legs closer; it was like standing at the bottom of a grave, feeling the sides closing in.

'Should be filling up by now.' The Thin Suit tapped his watch.

'Always looking out for me.' Vincent gave a wave; ash fluttered to the floor.

The Thin Suit followed a step behind; Jack waited for a few minutes more, hacking at the black moss between the cobbles with the heel of his shoe. Silent as Camberwell New Cemetery. His mum and dad had a joint plot, stacked on top of each other: *Here lies...* No one had thought it funny when Jack suggested the stonemason stop right there.

He felt his way down the steps to the back entrance, fingers slipping on the sodden bricks. A cloud of steam wafted upwards as he went inside. The smell of beer dripped from the ceiling; puddles of water lined the corridor. Jack was glad he wouldn't need to drink from the tap any more – members' clubs all the way for him. A row of hanging light bulbs led to the makeshift changing room. Frank sat on a stack of empty crates, lacing up his boots.

'Where've you been, Jack?'

'Don't worry, just checking everything's in place.'

'Have you seen my opponent?'

'He's down the end of the corridor, and he ain't exactly your opponent tonight. You're on the same side, remember?'

The rounded ceiling of the cellar room was so thick that barely a noise permeated down from the pub above. But Jack knew it was all happening. The ring set up, benches laid out, and glasses full. He took a seat opposite the barrels, moving the chair to the left; getting away from the glare of the wall lamp. Jack prodded Frank's boot with his foot.

'Ain't much of a talker tonight, are you?'

Frank's fingers looped bows into the laces. 'I'm getting ready.'

'Where's Bert?'

'Checking the ring.'

Frank went on methodically tightening the laces through each eyelet. He was absorbed in the routine; somehow Jack hadn't thought he would bother with it tonight, but he supposed it was a hard habit to break. Frank's eyebrows knitting together as he rolled the top of his socks over his boots. His right eye had a thick padding of scar under the brow, nose shunted a little further back into his head, ears puffed up, and dents on his left cheekbone.

Frank rubbed his hand across his face. 'Marks of the trade, hey, Jack.'

'Everything costs these days.'

Frank lifted his chin into the light. 'Have I paid enough?'

'Come on. I read that letter – this is the best way.'

He went back to his laces. A puff of smoke and dust spat upwards into the air above the lamp: another moth had got too close. Jack watched the ash fall and hoped Pearl hadn't got to Frank, singeing his wings before the big fight.

'It's good to be on edge before a bout. And this is just like any fight – better even. We know how this has to end. Just put on a good show and remember to count the bells. I know you can count to five.'

Jack checked his watch, counted off another three seconds. Frank rubbed his head. 'There's something I got to ask – '

Jack cut him off. 'We won't get it wrong, but you're right, we need to follow the routine. I'll get your gloves.'

He stood up, felt the weight of all those men stomping around the pub above him. They would all be watching, checking for any sign. He opened up the bag; the gloves were icy cold. Jack's nose twitched as he worked the leather, nostrils drawing in sweat, a metallic ionisation: the smell of a fight brewing. All those years before had been building to this one night. Jack licked his lips: the taste of butter on his toast, real chilled milk in his tea every day, whisky that hummed with smoke and peat, the brush of silk against his skin. Everyone would know his name: Jack Munday.

'Jack?' Frank stood with the bandages in his hands.

'Let's get those on.'

He picked up the white roll, held the boy's hands steady, wound the bandages tightly about his fists. The white lines made Frank's hands look bigger, great big square palms and thick fingers. Hands that were made for fighting, but they would find something else to do. The knuckles protruded as Jack bent Frank's hands into paws. He tried to think of what he would buy first; he might even go to Oxford Street, new department stores opening all the time: a tailored suit or maybe even a car, a black Ford Consul to start with and working up from there. Jack didn't need to look as he worked the bandages around; the image of those bright blue veins and creased pink palms was imprinted on him.

Bert manoeuvred his round body between the barrels as he came into the cellar. He slapped his hands down on Frank's shoulders. 'Ready to weigh in, and get them bandages signed off? Time to teach that upstart a lesson. Getting top billing with you, the cheek. I've never even heard of him.'

Frank glanced up. 'Jack hasn't told you?'

'Frank's a bit nervous, not quite feeling it, ain't that right?' Jack tugged on the bandages.

Frank nodded his head, stared at the white ends flapping and waiting to be tied off. Bert rubbed the red pinch his glasses left on his nose. 'I can mix you some tonic up. Get it down you after weigh-in.'

'He'll be fine. Come on. We're up next.' Jack herded them out of the cellar towards the scales at the end of the corridor, then it was up the narrow steps where the ring was waiting.

The noise erupted like a hailstorm when Frank came up. The crowd parted for them, feet shuffling and eyes black in the dimness. Pillars held the roof up, and a thin carpet slid about under the stomping feet. The place was so packed Jack couldn't even see the bar, but the men had pints in their hands; splashes ballooned on his suit and beads of beer glistened on Frank's arms. The men were waiting to see him win or to see him crushed by the newcomer; most of them didn't care which. Always was someone waiting to knock out a champion and leave him in the dust, and always was a fool waiting to be beaten down for the nerve of thinking they stood a chance. It made Jack want to laugh until his cheeks ached. The crowd pressed up against the benches in front of the ring. The noise was just as jumbled; Jack couldn't make out words, only the thumping of voices. He held open the ropes.

'We're all going to get what we want out of this. Make it look real,' he whispered into Frank's good ear.

Rich already stood in his corner, shoulders jumping, feet moving on the canvas as if he was running through the fight in his head. The ropes snapped back into place and Jack sat down on the benches. Every muscle in his body tensed, but there wasn't room to stretch out his legs. He drummed his fingers on his knees, waiting for the bell. Programme read, announcements made, gloves shaken, back to corners. Thud thud thud in time to his heartbeat. Finally, the only sound left was the ringing of metal. But Frank hadn't heard it; how could he have? Jack rubbed his ear. Frank stood inside his corner, hands drooping low. Close enough to see the purple dusting above his kidney, the dark-shaded muscles under his ribs; still enough to see him breathing. Bert was in front of Jack, right by the ring, staring through the hole of Frank's legs.

Jack broke the silence. 'Get out there.'

A cheer went up. Rich strode forward, stretching but not landing, head tilted. And still Frank didn't move. The first hiss slithered over the canvas. *Don't let it end this way*. Rich tightened his guard, shuffled closer then circled off again. A bottle bounced off the ropes and smashed in front of the first row. Jack kicked glass from his shoes. Frank edged forward but his arms remained loose at his sides. The noise filtered down to Jack as if he were lying at the bottom of the swimming baths: pops and clangs exploding against his ears. The referee was walking towards Frank. If he touched him on the shoulder that was it: technical knockout. The rows of benches swayed around him as if they had been hit by a wave. Spider jumped up, appearing further down the row, the shiny thread of his checked suit catching the light.

'Kill the darkie, Frank.'

One day someone would have to squash that Spider, but not tonight. Jack stood up, knees shaking. *Don't freeze now, boy: guard up, head down, hit hard*. The stamping of feet on the floor rattled Jack's brain against the sides of his skull. A balled-up programme flew through the air, hit the side of Rich's face.

'Get back on the boat or smack him one,' a man in a white suit shouted, waving his arm.

'Only boat I've ever been on is the Woolwich ferry,' Rich shouted back.

His neck set hard, the muscles poking down into his shoulders. He spun and lunged at the ropes, fighting to get into the crowd. He bounced back like the thrown bottle – enough to make him catch a breath.

'Let him have it,' Jack shouted between his hands; and he didn't care which one of them heard him. Throw one punch, that was all it would take. He gripped his hand around his throat, hoping Frank would remember their signs. An

258

elbow jabbed Jack in the spine and he sat down, winded. Rich let go of the ropes, swung back towards Frank's corner, muttering under his breath, shaking his head as he pulled back his arm. His fat gloved hand landed square between Frank's collarbones. The force pulled Frank's arms together and in reflex he hit out. Rich was ready for it: knees bent, calling Frank on. A cheer as Frank led with his right, making contact on Rich's upper arm. It was the permission he had been waiting for. Rich grinned, dipped his head, and threw a sharp swing that caught Frank a blow on the temple. Frank rocked forward, a patch of red hair turning black as treacle at the roots. Blood flicked on to the canvas, enough to feed the crowd. But it was too early to fall. Frank's knees locked. Jack relaxed his hands, uncurled his spine.

The bell for the end of the first round; Jack leapt up to Frank's corner. He wiped Frank's face with the towel, his breath steaming through the cotton. All the mouths crammed into that low-ceilinged room gasped at the stale air, no windows or draughts to refresh it. Bert knocked against him as he moved to the other side of Frank.

'I see what's going on. Glasses or no, I'm not that short-sighted.' Bert scrubbed a sponge over Frank's shoulders.

The crowd stamped and called; no one seemed to notice the fighting had stopped – for a moment at least. Jack opened the pots as Bert rubbed Vaseline into a graze on Frank's cheek. 'Need-to-know basis, that's the deal. Only me and Frank needed to be in on it.'

'I know about those sorts of deals. Make sure I'd turn up so it looked real, more like it.' Bert shook his head, bending Frank's neck to the right. 'This is it, Jack, I'm out. After this fight's done, we're done. My reputation's a clean one. I mean to keep it that way.'

The bright lights above the ring even washed out their shadows; cut off from the crowd by a tide of voices, scraping wood and breaking glasses. Bert worked a cotton ball up under Frank's left eye.

'I should wallop your backside, Jack. I don't believe you even see what's coming to you.'

'Lay off. It ain't personal. I've seen you all right, ain't I? You'll get your cut. Don't think I was going to short-change you.' Jack knelt down in front of Frank. 'No freezing again. What got into you?' He put his hands on Frank's knees, blocked out the crowd behind him.

'I thought I... was going to sick up... my lungs. Do you think... I'm yellow?' Frank swiped sweat from his forehead with his arm. 'Jack's got it... all worked out, Bert. I can't... keep fighting. I've got a future... to think of.'

'That's the first sensible thing I've heard anyone say.' Bert picked up his box and the bucket.

'Head down, hands up, look out for that left hook.' Jack laid it out in front of Frank but it was all for show: no self-respecting manager would give up the opportunity to talk to his fighter between rounds. He had to keep to the routine. But Jack couldn't help looking over his shoulder at Rich in the other corner.

'Your folks would be proud.' The words slipped out.

Frank's eyes turned dark as the cobbles in the alley outside: cold and wet. The bell rang. Frank roared out of his corner. He didn't seem to hold back, and Jack was looking for it. He tuned into the roar of the crowd behind him. Spider gave him the thumbs-up as he pushed out of the row, making his way across the room. It was the fight that everyone hoped to watch: a night that would be talked about for years. Jack lost sight of Spider moving behind the bookies' runners. Even they were twitching, licking pencil stubs, tilting back hats; they usually made an art form out of lounging against walls.

The bell for the fifth round sounded. Frank took a step and Rich was there. Arm out, red-gloved fist hurtling for Frank's head. And Frank ran straight on to it. The crunch of bone as his cheek caved couldn't have been any better if they had planned that bit too. Frank stood tall like a tree balanced in place by a single splinter. His boots were wrapped together at the ankles, just as Jack had showed him, and he fell forward as Rich jumped back: a deafening thud like a side of beef hitting the butcher's slab. The referee got down on one knee beside him; the crowd cheering. The countdown began. Two. Fluid rushed to fill the void, Frank's eye swallowed up by the swelling, a pulsing life of its own. Head on the floor. Four. Gloves lifeless. Six. Spit and blood pooling on the white canvas. Eight. The twitching legs were still. Nine. Knock Out. Frank played his part to perfection.

The referee grabbed Rich's arm and held it up in the air, high enough to touch the ceiling. So what if none of the cheers was for Jack; so what if those fools didn't know both those fighters in the ring were his? He had to shove past the row of backs that crowded Rich's corner. Frank lay still, alone on the canvas, one bloodshot eye swelling shut; rolled on to his back, knees up. Bert reached him at the same time as Jack. They dragged him to standing, and it wasn't for show. Frank's legs were shaking; his neck hung limp.

'I didn't… expect it'd feel… this bad.'

Bert shook his head. 'Always hurts worse when you can't fight back. And the extra sting, that'll be pride biting you in the arse.'

'Don't listen to him, Frank. Money softens all blows.'

Frank's feet shuffled on the spot and Jack remembered the day he had bought him those boots. The smiles, the promises; it'd all seemed so easy then. Rich jumped on to the pub floor; arms were slapping his back and hands trying to shake the big red gloves. No one was looking at the ring.

Bert dropped the kit bag beside Frank's feet.

'I'm leaving you to it. I'll be by the gym to pick up my share on Monday. Good luck with everything, Frank.' He patted Frank on the shoulder. 'You're good in the ring, but out there…' he pointed into the room '… you got to learn to be a fighter.'

Jack held out his hand. Bert turned away, hauled himself out between the ropes and bumped his way through the crowd. Frank stood and watched. Jack picked up the bag. 'We don't need him no more. Let him go.'

'Spider's gone too, Jack. He was up by Vincent.'

Frank bowed over the ropes, spat blood out of the ring; it mingled with the broken glass on the floor.

'What's Spider up to? No, don't tell me, I wouldn't want to know.'

Jack climbed out first, helped Frank down the steps. They made their way through the press of people. A few kicks were aimed at the back of Frank's legs. They stuck to the edge of the room. The celebration was going on in the main bar; the door swung open and Rich was magnified behind raised glasses, gloves hanging around his neck. Jack's spine stiffened at the sight of it. *There's no such thing as second place in boxing* was what his dad had said after his first loss. Jack opened the door to the stairs.

'They… hate me.'

'Everyone hates losing. Small change is all they parted with.'

'I feel… like I… lost something.'

'No, you didn't lose nothing. You gave it away.' Jack gave Frank a little push to get his legs moving. The lightbulb swung above them. Frank's arms trailed by his thighs, heat rising off the horsehair and leather gloves. The door was still open to the pub, and laughter followed them along the underground corridor. Frank sat on the chair, back slumped, legs kicked out in front. His swollen eyes flickered over Jack's face then dropped back to the gloves.

'Give them here, Frank. Just don't touch the trousers.'

Jack unlaced and eased off the gloves. The smell of salty skin and hot leather was like sitting next to a racehorse. So familiar he could pinpoint it in a packed changing room. He pushed the hands away.

'All done. Just remember, when the pain really kicks in tomorrow, why you done this. For you and Pearl.'

Frank nodded. 'For Pearl.'

The trail of greying bandages spiralled from his wrists down to the black floor. Rat-prints crisscrossed the dusty barrels, the wood slick with their sickly-sweet spit; a scratching came from the corridor. Jack crossed his ankles to deter any strays from making a bolt up his legs. But it was the Thin Suit who stepped out of the tunnel, his shadow straight as a blade.

'Thought Vincent said we were meeting up at the club tomorrow.' Jack moved out of the corner; a length of grey bandage unravelled on the floor between them.

The Thin Suit batted brick dust off his sleeve. 'I'm here to collect your fighter. We want a word.'

'This ain't about what happened at the beginning of the fight? A bit of show, getting the measure of his opponent, that's all.'

'Vincent wants to make sure your boy knows what's expected of him now.' The Thin Suit swung an arm down to pick up Frank's bag, threw the trousers and jumper straight at him.

'I didn't mean... nothing, I just got – '

'Keep quiet, Frank.'

'It's nothing for you to worry about, Jack. This is between the boy and us. You understand how it works.' The Thin Suit kicked the gloves towards Frank. He eased his bruised body into the clothes; held on to the barrels to inch his hand down towards the gloves.

Jack slung his coat over his shoulder. 'I'll bring Frank by with me tomorrow.'

The Thin Suit shook his head.

'It's... all right, Jack. I'll sort... it out.'

'Well, if you say so. I best get back to Pearl, she'll be waiting. I'll tell her you'll be round later. We'll put a nice spread on for you. You done good.'

Frank wrapped a scarf around his neck, stuffing the ends down into his jumper. Jack felt the Thin Suit's eyes on him all the way up the stairs. He surfaced into the alleyway. The

263

cold nipped at his skin; the smell of coal dust and traffic soot stung the insides of his mouth and nose. He made his way to a bus stop around the corner, hoping he wouldn't have to listen to anyone discussing the fight. Two fat women waited on the pavement, baskets and headscarves, bodies hunched inside pre-war winter coats. The first bus came, but it was only going as far as Tower Bridge; no point changing more than he had to. Frank would be walking round the corner any minute; they could go together. The women got on; a man with a young son came to stand by the wall.

The boy kicked a can up and down the gutter as his dad peered at the racing news under the flickering street-lamp. All Jack had to do was get on the bus, lose himself in the rush of late-night drinkers and be home in less than thirty minutes. Frank was old enough to look after himself. Another bus went past, but none of them was right. Jack couldn't seem to get his feet to work. Frank was probably too tired to walk quickly – always trailing behind. The man shoved the young boy up the bus steps, the conductor's hand hovered above the bell wire, but Jack waved it on. He sprinted back to the pub.

Jack slid past the overturned bins. Edging along the wet wall, the noise growing louder: the slap of leather on the ground, grunts like a hungry dog foraging. A light came on, the attic window from the pub providing a spotlight; no moon or leaking street-lamps reached that far. The sharp lines of the Thin Suit's grey flannel cut through the centre of the alleyway. The black mound on the ground had to be Frank – down again. If the Thin Suit left it at a quick kick then he and Frank would get the next bus, even if it was going to Tower Bridge. The kick came. The Thin Suit pressed his nose against the black shadow.

'Get up, Frank,' Jack murmured.

But Frank couldn't hear him. The second kick never came but the Thin Suit slammed his foot down on to Frank's right hand, grinding in his heel. Frank screamed but no one on the street stopped: coats buttoned-up, marching into the wind.

The starlings were back, screeching and twisting in a dark cloud above the pub, hundreds of them. Jack banged his head against the brick.

'Fucking idiot.' His breath fogged but no sound came out.

If Jack broke them up it wouldn't make it any better for Frank; it was the way this sort of business went. He and Frank hadn't even seen any of the money yet, and they never would if Jack interfered now.

The Thin Suit worked up the ribs, rooting with the toe of his shoe, as he spoke. 'Hesitation is bad for your health. Can't have you making any plans for a comeback, can we?'

His back was to Jack; intent on what he was doing. He was enjoying it, Jack could tell by the relaxed swing of his arms, the cocked angle of his head. Jack knew that posture, knew what it was like to be curled up on the floor. He kept close to the bricks, edging around a row of barrels; holding his breath as rats skidded across his shoe out towards the light of the street. It was too late for Jack to do anything now, it really was. The Thin Suit raised his foot again, this time over Frank's left hand; he was going to break every bone.

'This puts you out of harm's way, for your own good.'

A spike of light pierced up into the alley; the Thin Suit's foot paused in mid-air as the back door to the pub banged open. Vincent stood in the doorway. Jack crouched down, puddles illuminated in front of him. Spider came out from behind Vincent, climbed the steps, shoulders swaying; his shiny suit looked as though it was shrinking around him. He stood next to the Thin Suit, pressed his knuckles to his knees, peered over at Frank.

'I need him with one good hand.'

'It's not fucking up to you.' The Thin Suit pulled up to his full height, a good six inches above Spider.

'It's my say-so. Leave the lad be now,' Vincent called up.

His shadow displaced the pool of light around Frank – lying flat on his front, face turned to the side. The Thin

Suit cracked his neck to the side as he inspected Spider. He snorted twice, turned and went down the steps. Vincent's cigar smoke crawled up the black brickwork.

'That boy's lucky to have a mate like Spider. He's brought to my attention just how useful a strong pair – well, one hand – could…'

The door slammed shut on the rest of the words. Jack needed to stand up, his joints throbbed, but Spider was still in the alleyway.

'Help us up, Spider.' Frank drew his knees up under himself.

'All I ever do is bail you out, Frank. You owe me this time, no getting around it.'

'My hand. It's smashed up.'

'He was going to break every bone you were born with before I turned up, and now you're moaning about one pissing hand. So much for gratitude.'

Jack wanted to bash Spider's head between the ridged bin lids, but more fool the boy for taking on a debt to Vincent – it would be called in soon enough. Spider stood up, lit up a cigarette, the orange flame reflected in the shimmering threads of his suit. Puddle water soaked into the cuffs of Jack's jacket, a chewed cigarette butt floating towards his fingers.

'What are mates for, eh, Frank? You just got to worry about getting on the mend because I've got us work lined up. First job's not far off. I've fixed it good. Shouldn't really say much now but Vincent thought it was spot on too. That new department store they're finishing on Oxford Street, we'll strike it rich there. What was I always telling you?'

'I never thought it would come off.' Frank tried to lever himself forward on his elbows.

Spider reached down, grabbed the back of Frank's belt and pulled; the cigarette clung to his lip. Frank made it to standing, swaying forward, staggering up against the wall, his left shoulder taking the weight. Jack's muscles tightened; any minute now cramp was going to shoot up from his feet into his thighs. He rocked slowly on his heels, loosening the ligaments in his legs. Spider prodded Frank's bag up to the wall with the toe of his shoe.

'Never had enough faith – not you, not that manager you signed up to. I did it without any of you. And look who's offering the handouts now. '

'I ain't said I'll do it, Spider.'

'There'll be something you need and you'll come looking for me to provide it. Same as always. Now you know what it'll cost you. Here, get yourself a cab back, I'm good for it.' Spider jiggled his pocket, pushing up a handful of coins; poured some into Frank's bag. He jumped down the steps, two at a time, and went back into the pub.

Frank never should have hesitated, shown indecision. It wasn't Jack's place to save the boy from himself; if he went round doing that for everyone then he would be six feet under himself by now. But he couldn't go back to the house without Frank, couldn't face Pearl's questions. He eased himself up, stepped out into the middle of the alleyway and walked towards Frank.

'Came back to see what was taking so long. What happened to you?'

'He got me with a low blow before I saw it coming. Help me, Jack.'

He rushed forward, grasping hold of Frank's shoulders to keep him upright; the dead hand swung free. They fell back against the bins; lids rolled to the floor. Jack couldn't look at the red and white pulp hanging from the end of Frank's arm. Out of the corner of his eye it looked as if a boxing glove had shrunk around his fist, no fingers to be seen in the swollen mound.

Frank pressed his forehead to the bricks, left hand gripped around his right wrist. 'How bad?'

'I'm no doctor but Pearl can't fix that up, it's going to take a hospital this time.' Jack scooped up the bag, pulled it over one shoulder and pushed the other shoulder under Frank's armpit.

267

'Will you come in with me?'

'Let's just get there first.'

Jack wrapped his other arm around Frank's waist, supporting him, wobbling to walk upright. They staggered out into the street like payday drunks. Frank was heavy, dragging him down, making the sweat build under Jack's jacket. But everything would work out: Frank would heal. Jack had got his hand trapped in the door hinge when he was younger and it wasn't even noticeable now, just a small hollow groove in his index finger. *Don't put your digits in the door, boy*; Jack must have heard his dad say it a hundred times and never listened until that last time when his dad got his brothers to slam it shut – it was a lesson well learned.

They reached the bus stop, had it to themselves, and Jack propped Frank against the pole. 'Won't be long now. Get you squared away.'

'But we did it, didn't we, Jack?'

'Too bloody right. We fooled them all.' He laughed; stuck out his arm to hail the oncoming bus.

'I've the fare in my bag.'

Jack shook his head. 'I've got this one.' He didn't want anything from Spider – let him go hang.

SEVEN

Newton straightened the buttons of his janitor's overalls, standing in the middle of the grey corridor as if he was delivering important news to Jack and Pearl.

'My shift's done for the day. Thought I'd check on the patient and drop him off something to read. I'm sure my Jimmy could come by too, be some spiritual comfort for the boy.'

'He don't need any last rites.'

Jack took hold of Newton's elbow and moved him aside. *Delinquency, Prostitution: the Paths to Gonorrhoea* flapped behind him on the hospital noticeboard.

'Frank said the doctors told him he was healing well.' Pearl clutched the edge of Jack's sleeve.

A wrinkled couple went past, averting their eyes, pretending to study a prescription.

'Course he is. Hurry on in, visiting time won't last long.' Jack waited for her to go through before he turned back to Newton. 'Tell your chaplain son we don't need his services. But if I ever find myself at death's door I'll be sure to look him up.'

'Sorry to hear you lost the fight, Jack. Never mind, there'll be others.'

Jack didn't bother to reply. The shuffling step of Newton retreated down the corridor. Let them think what they liked: he was coming back with an even better deal. Not that the people around there would be able to afford the entrance ticket. Jack pressed his hands to the ward door but he didn't push straight in, his reflection spooned back at him in the brass plate. That hospital was where they all ended up: stretched out on a steel tray, marble floors sucking all the warmth from the world.

In the ward, heads lolled on pillows, faces slack, no fight left in them. Pearl stood at the foot of Frank's bed but in front of her Spider was bent over, his hand gripping Frank's shoulder. Spider grinned at them, the scars on his face contracting. He stroked the striped pyjama jacket back into place.

'Don't mind me, Jack. Patient's doing well. But I don't think we've been formally introduced, though I've seen you around.' Spider nodded at Pearl. 'Ain't you going to do the honours, Frank?'

'Pearl, this is Spider.'

Pearl's arm jolted at the elbow as he shook her hand. Frank reached out to pull her away but his good hand couldn't stretch that far. Spider released her and she sank on to the edge of the bed. Jack took the empty chair. White crescents marked her hand as if something had bitten down hard. She didn't notice, but Frank rubbed her skin with his thumb.

'Well, I'll leave you to your visitors, mate. Remember, I'm here if you need anything. Jack, see you soon. We're bound to run into each other at Vincent's club. Seems he was looking for young blood after all.'

Spider sauntered past the nurse's trolley parked at the bed opposite, scooping a handful of pills into his pocket as he went. Jack glanced back at the face on the bed.

'You're looking better already, mate.'

Frank managed a smile, but it wobbled at the edges. His skin picked up the green of the blanket, the yellow of the walls, as if the bruises from the fight were dripping out and staining his whole face.

'Maybe he's having too many visitors. Shouldn't it just be family? He still looks a bit grey around the gills.' Pearl stroked the side of Frank's cheek.

Jack caught the silvery flash of fish scales. Hospitals were enough to make anyone sick. The blue curtains billowed slightly, taking a ghostly form, as someone walked past the beds. 'Don't worry, Pearl. Getting better all the time, ain't you, Frank?'

'I've had me hand broken up.'

Frank tried to move along the bed but gave up and twisted his head to the side. Pearl prodded the pillows into place so he could lie straight.

'I shouldn't have let you do it. Should have known something like this would happen with Jack involved.'

'I shouldn't have stopped to think about it...' Frank rubbed an arm across his face.

'Frank's old enough to make his own decisions. Ain't that what you told me? I got him away from that lump, took him to the hospital, didn't I?'

'What if they come back for you, Frank?'

'Spider said he's fixed it. It ain't about that, Pearl. But did you talk to them at the factory?'

'They said they ain't hiring at the moment.'

'Not hiring one-handed workers, you mean. Who's going to give me work when I'm like this?'

'It'll heal.' Pearl rubbed his arm.

'Can't have spent the fight money already, Frank.'

'It ain't enough, Jack. Not for what we need. What about a job training?'

'Give us a chance, it'll come, but first I've got that new fighter to set up.'

Frank tried to reach for a glass of water on the cabinet; it crashed to the floor. 'What am I going to do?'

'I've got it, don't you worry none. It's only water.'

Pearl mopped up with a flannel from the bedside cabinet. But she glanced over at Jack, waiting for something more. Through the gap in the curtain Jack saw red tulips wilting in a vase, a card wilting next to it.

'Come stay with me, Pearl and Georgie when you get out. We'll get something better sorted for after Christmas. We won't be short of a bob or two from now on.'

Jack took the glass Pearl handed him and filled it with water, holding it up to Frank's lips; a drop ran over Frank's chin.

'Maybe I ain't fit for work but Spider says he's got a job for me.'

'We agreed to the fight to get away from all that. Something will turn up, Frank. I know it will. Maybe Georgie can get you hours at the pub until something better comes along.'

'How am I going to pull pints or lift barrels with this hand, Pearl?' Frank waved the bandaged lump; it looked as if a trainer had gone mad with the wrapping. 'You deserve more, more than what I can give you here. I did everything Jack wanted; now there's something he can do for us. Borrow us the money for the boat passage – all them other things we'll need to make it out there. We've got to go to Australia like he said. Start again.'

Jack shook his head. 'What you on about? I didn't mean nothing by that. I was angry then, that's all.'

'But you were right, Jack, and I've been thinking on it.'

Pearl pressed her hands together. 'We can't leave here.'

'If Jack won't help us I'll have to ask someone who can.'

'There are medicals, Frank. I can cheat mine, but how are you going to hide that hand? We need to get you better before anything else.' Pearl reached for his leg; he kicked under the blanket then went still.

'There's always someone out there can get you what you want, for the right price.'

He cradled his bad hand in the crook of his elbow. Jack knew who he was talking about. 'Spider and his lot are only out for what they can get.'

'I know all about that. I had a good teacher.' Frank's teeth bit at a dry flake of skin on his bottom lip.

'Jack's right about them. We don't need to be going nowhere. Let's just get through Christmas.'

Jack smiled. She didn't even want to leave the house. All Frank's talk of leaving London would sink away soon.

'We'll put the bed up in the front room again. I slept there myself when Mum was poorly. Tell him, Jack.'

'You'll have Pearl and Georgie fussing over you. Front room's the best place. You can get to the kitchen and outside to the lav easier from there.'

'I can't even piss straight.'

A nurse pushed the medicine trolley along the ward; the squeaking wheels seemed to cut right through Frank: eyes squeezed tight, lips pressed shut. Coughing started up on the other side of the curtain, a rolling rattle like a butcher's bike on the cobbles. Pearl ran her hand over Frank's forehead, fingertips trying to loosen the deep furrows between his bruised eyes.

'He's just trying to help. Jack will see us right, won't you?'

'Course. It ain't just a one-off. It's all working out for me. I don't forget my pals.'

'I earned the money from that fight. I ain't some lame dog you can lay out in front of the fire and throw a bone to. Me and Pearl, we'll make our own way.'

Frank slumped against the pillows, the sides pressing up against his ears. Pearl's hand dropped on to the blanket. The sound of coughing surrounded them. A silver head poked out from the green blanket on the next bed; blood speckled the sheet turn-over. Jack shivered.

'These places always give me the screaming abdabs. Why do old folk hack so much?'

'Just wait until you're that old.' Pearl prodded his leg.

'I ain't never getting old. I'm going to stay young forever.'

Frank winced as he shifted to his left. 'I feel dead already.'

'Frank!'

'I'm sorry, Pearl. I'll come round. I just need some kip. Pain keeps me awake all night.'

Pearl laid her head on his chest; it moved up and down as she spoke. 'Wish I could pass on some of what I've got.'

'You're the only one who always knows how I feel.' Frank lifted his wrapped hand and placed it on top of Pearl's.

Jack tried to study the old newspaper folded on the cabinet; he shouldn't have come with Pearl, wasn't sure how she'd talked him into it. He wanted to get up and walk out but the nurse in the pale blue uniform blocked his way, the trolley pushed up by the end of Frank's bed as she saw to the bloke on the left. Jack picked up the paper; underneath sat a brown book, spine cracked, page edges crumbling: *Boxing* by A.J. Newton.

Pearl tapped his arm. 'Let's go. Frank needs the rest.'

'Take the book with you. I'm done with it all.'

Jack slipped the small book into his pocket. 'I'll see you soon, then, Frank. Get that bed sorted for when you're out of here. And don't worry about Spider and that lot – '

'Whatever you say, Jack… It's always been whatever you say.'

'I'll see you tomorrow, Frank.' Pearl stood at the end of the bed.

Jack wanted to get out into the corridor. The way they looked at each other left a void in the room; it happened that way sometimes, the way a fractured gas pipe could suck the light and warmth out of the streets around it. Jack remembered how it felt. The curtains clung against his legs as he left. He kept his head down, didn't want to catch sight of any of those limp faces on the beds; he was meeting Georgie later, time for some shopping. Pearl followed him out of the ward.

'I'm worried about him. Does he seem different to you?'

'It's the stuff they've got him on – he'll turn about. Be out in no time. And he's got Christmas to look forward to.'

'This is the same colour as we painted the kitchen.' Pearl ran her finger along the wall as they walked along. 'I remember you bringing me here for all those tests. I never understood why you were always so angry with the doctors.'

She touched his arm. He couldn't help staring at her hand: the long fingers and curved nails, so familiar, so like Rosie's.

But she was only warning him to step aside for a man in a wheelchair, the bottom of his left pyjama leg pinned under his thigh.

'I know you tried, Jack.'

She let him go. Jack had to double-step to catch up. He wanted to share something too.

'Do you know, since I told you – '

'You didn't tell me – '

'Since you found out, she hasn't been with me as much. She used to be all I'd think about. Like how smoke can hang in a room for weeks, clouds of her each day.'

'Opening a window's best way to clear smoke. But some things hang around for a long time. Like you. Persistent, Jack, that's what you are.'

'A Munday trait.'

'In those pictures, they've all got dark eyes.'

'Her eyes were same colour as yours, like smoke.'

'Do I look like her?' Pearl stopped to study her face in a notice framed on the wall.

'Sorry, that face is all me.'

'Thought so. Oh, well, could be worse.' She ran a finger down to the tip of her nose. 'Georgie said you're handsome, but she'd never tell you because it'd go to your head.'

'She did, did she?' He tilted his head back but they had passed the glass.

'How'd she die?'

Jack took a breath; Pearl had a way of getting in the hits without him ever seeing them coming. They passed under the hanging sign for the mortuary; even the air felt frozen in that spot.

'I know what you want, Pearl. Some fairy story about her lying peaceful like Sleeping Beauty, all Hollywood curls and – '

'I only want to know what happened.'

He knew all the questions she had inside; he had been through them all himself, but none ever led anywhere other

275

than back to that night: dropping the match, bumping heads – something to be laughed about at any other time except that moment on Albany Basin. He wiped his sleeve across his forehead; Pearl handed him her handkerchief. What she needed, he could never give back to her, like his thumbnail that never grew back, like his dad never coming back up from that cellar; just as he could never save Rosie, no matter how many times he woke screaming and kicking against the tangled weed of bedcovers.

'She drowned. I don't need to tell you it was my fault like everything always is.'

'What did you do, Jack?'

'I didn't do enough.' He tapped the side of his skull. 'Best leave it buried.'

'No, best start finding a way to dig it up. I have to know.' Pearl stepped outside.

He scrubbed his face, lips puckering against the white cotton. If he had been anyone but who he was then perhaps he could have mashed the words into something Pearl would want to hear. He stuffed the handkerchief, with its embroidered P, into his jacket. Pearl reached over and rearranged the damp cotton into a V in his top pocket.

'Only one question, then, for now. Would things have been different with her still around?'

'Everything, Pearl. That's the worst part of it. Getting up each morning, seeing you, seeing the house, and knowing how it should've been... How it should've been so good.'

The wind knocked against him, leaves spinning around their ankles. Pearl raised her voice above the clanging bells of an ambulance pulling through the gates. 'What about you and Georgie?'

He knew what she meant: how other good things had come, sprouted like moss on places where there was no soil to grow on, no nourishment for them. But he wasn't about to start digging around in all that.

'She's expecting me to meet her at Brixton Market by half past. We're getting some odds and sods for the house. Want to come?'

The ambulance doors were yanked open: a body dropped on to a trolley, men in short white coats hurrying it away. Pearl linked her arm through his, down the steps and through the tide of orange leaves.

'It's like me and Frank. I can care for him and not stop caring about you.'

'Frank, Frank, Frank, Frank!' He nodded from side to side as he slid his arm around her neck, covering her mouth with his hand.

'Persistence. I get it from you.' Her lips vibrated against his skin as she spoke.

'It's a good job he's coming for Christmas if you and Georgie are going to be ganging up on me.'

Pearl laughed; it felt like butterflies dancing on his fingers.

EIGHT

Jack stood by the fireplace, elbow at a right angle, the way he had seen Gary Cooper do in *High Noon* at the Odeon. A framed print of a cottage hanging above him – one of Georgie's Brixton Market finds. The collection of Munday faces lined the hallway now, and as long as Jack never looked left he could pass every day without seeing them.

Rich sat in the armchair, moved to the window, net curtains gone, and the last full moon of the year soaked into the polished leather of his shoes. Let the whole street stare in; Jack wanted them to. He picked up his glass and settled back in the new armchair, on tick from Courts. Rich lifted his glass.

'To Jack. Manager Number One.'

'You liked the Camberwell gym, then?' Georgie rearranged her crossed legs, perched on the arm of Jack's seat and the leather squeaked.

'Jack's got it set up good.'

Ice cubes tinkled, accompanying the low hum of the new refrigerator in the kitchen. Jack fingered the tip of the cigar poking from his pocket, an early Christmas gift to himself.

'I'm glad we could toast our partnership. I've got meetings set up after New Year, hand-picked a few opponents. Launch you proper like, get you away from cheap pub fights.'

Rich ran his finger around the edge of the glass. 'No Irish, no blacks, no – '

'All welcome in the world of boxing, my friend.' Jack raised a toast.

Rich tipped up the last of his whisky, taking in the room over the rim of the glass; he rubbed the frayed collar of his shirt. Jack could tell he was impressed, and he didn't seem to notice Frank's bedding rolled up beside the dresser. Georgie tapped his arm.

'We've got mince pies. I'll fetch them out. Jack, give us a hand.'

In the kitchen she bent down to check the oven, cocooned in the buttery steam, her cheeks glowing.

'How many pies you got, that you need my help?' Jack opened the English Electric refrigerator, not to get anything but just to hear the motor kick in again.

'I don't – only wanted to know how long he's staying.'

'You don't like him?' Jack snorted.

'You're tipsy, Jack. I like him fine, but Frank and Pearl will be back from the pictures soon. Are you going to tell her about the letters from your sisters or just wait until we're all out on the street?'

'All them letters they keep writing, those envelopes stuffed with papers from their solicitor, just mean they ain't got a leg to stand on. If they could have done it without my signing we'd all have been out on our ear before now. Let them huff and puff. Now I can't exactly throw Rich out after bringing him all this way to see the gym. Where's your festive cheer? It's Christmas come end of the week.'

'Too right. I've got to pick up the beef in the morning, and I wanted to wrap some presents tonight.'

She closed the oven door with her foot; a wave of spicy heat barrelled out into the space around her tight crimson dress. He dropped his mouth in mock surprise.

'We're doing presents?'

'I've seen you carrying brown parcels upstairs. What you got me?'

'The back of my hand.'

'You don't fool me, Jack. Here, take them.' Lifting and blowing on her fingertips, she piled the pies on to a china plate.

'I'll pick you up a present from Simmonds' on the corner later.'

279

He winked. But under their bed upstairs sat a rabbit fur coat in a pink box, for Georgie; and for Pearl a silver frame with his picture of Rosie inside – she deserved to see some light again.

'Rich'll be gone before dinner.'

Jack carried the tray through, placed it on the table, and every time he went into that room it was like stepping into someone else's life now – in a good way. He'd never thought he would be the sort to invite people round, for Christmas drinks of all things. *It ain't so easy walking in someone else's shoes*, that was what his dad used to say. Well, Jack wanted to walk the rest of his days through this new life. He rocked back on his heels, breaking in the oxblood brogues. Georgie stood next to him, her dress sucked in between her legs by the draught of the fire. Rich ate a pie in two bites, pastry settling on his lips.

'Tasty. We're spending Christmas at the wife's mum's. She can't bake a pie for toffee.'

'With the fights I'll be setting up, you'll all be able to eat out at a fancy hotel next year.' Jack blew air on to a pie before sinking his teeth in.

'I hope you're right, Jack. I've been holding out for it. Vincent's kept me on a promise long enough. But I don't want to get turned over like your boy was.'

'Maybe Rich's right and you should find another backer, Jack. After what Vincent done to Frank, I don't like the thought – '

'It's all going to pay off. No one needs to worry about nothing. We're worth good money to Vincent. Long as you don't eat too many pies, that is. I'm expecting you to put in some proper training, not spend January sweating off the weight.'

'I'll be training. But I'll take one for the road. I need to get back to help bath the twins.' Rich stood up. 'Don't forget what I said about the States, we could really be on our way.' He spun his hat on his fist, bounced it on to his head.

Georgie and Jack filled the doorway to wave him off, the only people on the street. But Mrs Bell came out on to her step, shadow thumping the pavement. She held her elbows in her hands, big breasts stuffed between.

'Have you seen me cat? Not a sign of him since yesterday. I'm awful worried. It ain't like him to miss his tea.'

Georgie pointed at the twitching net. 'Checked he's not trapped in that room upstairs?'

Mrs Bell shook, her curlers bouncing. 'I've got some Cardinal will bring up that doorstep for you.'

She twisted swiftly at the waist, not waiting for an answer, and slammed the door. Georgie sidestepped up against Jack, pressing her chin to his shoulder to keep out of the wind. 'Who cares if she thinks we're slovenly? I'm not getting on my knees to scrub no steps.'

'The wrecking balls will clean this street up for good soon. But she must be worried about her cat. Never even mentioned the negroid coming out of our house.' He laughed and wrapped his arms around her silky dress. 'Let's get warmed up inside. Probably got a short while before Pearl and Frank get back.'

'Ain't that Pearl?'

Hair flapped behind the running figure, not close enough to see the face, but Jack made out the yellow jumper jumping through the puddles of streetlight.

'She's going to trip.' He cupped his hands and shouted, 'Slow it down.'

Pearl's shoes smacked against the pavement. Jack stepped out of the doorway. Snow was in the air, a rush of oxygen before a dumping, opening his nose and mouth, and he felt light with it. Steam from Georgie's breath clouded around him. He braced himself. Pearl crashed against his ribs.

'Is he here?'

She squeezed her hands around Jack's forearms. Damp fronds of hair stuck to her face as if she had just got out of a bath.

'What you talking about?'

'Come inside. Where's your coat got to?' Georgie reached out but Pearl didn't move.

'It's Frank I've lost.'

Jack moved backwards, bringing her closer to the door, but Pearl pulled against him. She bit down on her lip, staining the front of her teeth pink.

'You're bleeding.' Georgie held out a handkerchief.

Pearl wiped the woollen sleeve across her mouth; a smear of red soaked into the yellow.

'We're not a hotel. I'm locking the door if he ain't back by ten. We've had a nice evening of it, bit of a drink. I ain't got time for games.'

'He said he wanted to get me a Christmas present, but I saw him get into a van with someone. I've been outside the Odeon for an hour. He never came back. All the shops are shut by now.'

'Well, I don't know where he's got to. Maybe he's out having a drink with the boys. I said he could stay here, didn't I? What more's he want?'

'Maybe they've taken him, going to finish what they started with his hand.'

'No one's taken him. Come in and warm up. Anyway, Frank said Spider had seen to it, remember?' Jack looped his arm around her, scooping her up the step and into the house.

'Spider, it must be something to do with him. I saw them at the hospital, more than once, whispering together. Frank said it was nothing to worry about. But you saw him yourself up there – he was scared.'

Her pupils contracted under the brightness of the hall light. Frank wasn't his problem; he had done everything he could for the boy. Had even been about to risk a beating from the Thin Suit before Spider stepped in. Jack closed the front door but chilled air had already entered the house, as if the new refrigerator were leaking ice. Georgie rubbed her hands together, warming them up. 'What would he have to be frightened of, a big fighter like him?'

Frank lying curled up in the dirt of the alleyway – Rosie, Pearl, Georgie, his mum, even his dad did it once – anyone else would have stepped in to stop the beating. But it had to be Spider: those white scars and pin-prick eyes.

'Do you think we should telephone the police from the pub?' Pearl blinked up at Jack.

'Frank won't thank you for that, whatever he's up to.'

'Jack's right, Pearl. Frank's a big boy.'

'But you promised me everything would be all right, and it ain't. I know it. When are you ever going to do enough for anyone but yourself, Jack?'

He was ready for it this time. Pearl blamed him for everything too: Rosie, his mum, Frank. They stood in single file, filling up the narrow hall, the fingers of the coat-stand poking towards them. Frank's training jumper wilting on top of the rubber wellingtons and umbrella with the broken spine. The boy couldn't say no to anything, that was his problem, and Spider was the sort who always got his way. He kicked the black boots aside.

'I've an idea where they might be.'

'Please get him back, Jack. He wouldn't lie to me like this unless it was something bad.'

'We'll sort this nonsense out, nothing to worry about. I'll get my coat.'

He wedged his foot under the gap at the bottom, to lever the cupboard open. Spider was nothing but a snivelling rat, couldn't even keep his mouth shut. Jack had overheard his grand plan so it was a sure bet a hundred others had heard it at some point too. If they hadn't got themselves collared already they were probably stuck halfway up a drainpipe at that big department store of his. The door swung outwards into the hallway, Georgie's face framed above him, her chin resting on the sloping edge.

'It's hanging at the back, Jack.'

He bent down to get inside; he used to be small enough to stand in there. Once he'd even managed to crawl under the upside-down stairs, but his dad had waited by the door all afternoon, cracking the leather strap in his hands, until Jack's bladder ached so bad he had to slide back out again. He reached for the coat, knocking over a wobbling pile of old blankets, wool and cardboard toppling into the hall. He scooped the mound back into the cupboard, fingertips prickling against fur.

'You can tell Mrs Bell she can stop looking for her cat.'

Under a mothballed overcoat lay the ginger tom, paws curled up, head pressed into the jumper beneath, set hard as the icicles on the pipes outside. Georgie peered over the side; he raised the coat a little higher.

'Guess he got through his nine lives.'

'Oh, Jack. That's bad luck.'

'Just hurry up.' Pearl banged the wall.

'Jack will fetch Frank back.'

He fitted his arms inside the tight woollen sleeves. 'It's not enough to give the boy somewhere to stay, I have to go and fetch him home by the hand.'

'Not on your own, you don't. I'm coming too.'

Pearl's hands were on her hips, the way she'd stood as a child when she heard about a broken bird or trapped dog. On to the highest roof, through the smallest hole – she'd always found what she was looking for, even if the scars had taken months to heal.

'Let's get this over with.' He pointed towards the door. 'Frank will have some making up to do, and not just to you.'

Jack stopped in front of Georgie, a trace of sugar around her mouth, lipstick caught on her front tooth.

'Don't take all night, Jack. There'll be some Christmas cheer waiting for you, if you're lucky.'

'It's only black cats bring bad luck. We'll be home in no time.'

Their faces nearly touching: her freshly bleached hair, white as bed linen; her lips bright red against her powdered face. Pearl pressed against Georgie's back. 'Let him through.'

'In Cousin Alf's car we'll be there and back in an hour. He won't even know it's gone.'

He winked at Georgie. She stepped to the side, face in line with those family photographs.

'Keep some of those pies warm for me. And don't go sniffing around after any presents.' He kissed her on the ear, a small copper hoop catching against his teeth. 'I'll be right back, love.'

'I love you right back, Jack.' She smiled, twisting her earring back into place.

He held her arms down against her sides, didn't want to let her go, but Pearl was calling him again.

Georgie yelled after them before the door banged shut, 'He keeps the key under the bar, on the left by the till.'

The breath froze in Jack's mouth, the salty taste of the Thames turning and the silky feel of soot from smoking chimneys. He took Pearl's elbow, held her back from breaking into a run, the yellow wool of her jumper crackling with black frost.

NINE

Headlight beams diluted by the glowing lamps of Oxford Street, a hundred setting suns hanging in the fog. Jack turned off the road. He climbed out of the old Morris Oxford: rusted around the window frames, rainwater pooled on the roof. It didn't look as if it could make it across the river, but there they were, hidden behind row upon row of bricks, black with dirt. Pearl stared up at the building. Scaffolding stretched high out of sight, thin poles laced like a spider's web. A black Ford van was parked in front of them with its wheels on the pavement. The rest of the street was empty; only a stray dog raised its head, eyeing them from the alley opposite.

'Better hope they've done with their little job, because he'll be in trouble if I get hold of him.'

'How do you even know about it, Jack? Don't tell me – that's another one of your secrets.'

'I can't do nothing right, can I?'

'Frank wouldn't do something like you said.'

'When you want something bad enough, you can furnish yourself with a thousand reasons why it ain't wrong. Now wait here.'

'No.' The word ricocheted off the wet tarmac.

He stepped backwards into a puddle, the place full of them. 'I ain't playing. Stay by the car.'

Drips from the scaffolding planks thumped on to Jack's head; wind rattled the winches and rigging ropes. He swiped a hand across his face, flicking drops to the floor. Maybe this was exactly what Pearl needed, to realise that Frank was a waste of muscle and Jack was right about everything. He pushed against the glass doors, stepped over a broken lock; a dustsheet brushed his face, and he swallowed a yelp. But it wasn't black inside as he'd expected. The lights of Oxford Street formed gluey pools at the front of the building; counters covered in white sheets blushed like cold milk. The windows were covered over with brown paper, but a gap ran along the bottom, and legs walked past outside. They couldn't see him: the space was three times the size of the gym. If Jack had left Frank to the booths he wouldn't be there now shivering in his coat and no hat, slinking around like Mrs Bell's cat. He should have locked Pearl in her room and waited up for Frank with his dad's old leather belt.

He patted his arms across his chest; nothing else moved on the ground floor and he picked his way through packing boxes towards a side staircase. Flecked concrete steps, air chilled to the level of a morgue. Jack's teeth started to chatter, he tensed his jaw as if for impact. Someone was up there; streaks of lightning glanced across the steps. He went up on tiptoe to muffle the clack of his shoes. Everything in the stairwell was stripped smooth as boiled bones; his hand slid along the polished wooden banister. Voices filtered down, low like the rattling of windowpanes as buses passed. Jack took the steps two at a time. A distorted double echo followed him up. Stacks of planks and pots of paint littered the landing; the smell of white spirit caught at the back of his throat. Pale beams like early morning sun striped the floor; Jack stepped out. The lights vanished. Blackness so thick it felt like the floor was bouncing under him. He groped for something to hold him up; before he found balance he was caught in a circle of white.

'What the fuck's he doing?' Spider's voice came from behind the torchlight.

'Jack?' Frank's voice sounded further away.

Jack squinted into the bright beam, but more footsteps came up behind him on the stairs. No time to twist the torches off. Pearl rushed out, kicking a tin of paint that rolled over the floor.

'Frank, it's me.'

Frank's torch flashed across the ceiling and walls. Patches of light sliced through the darkness like blades: cutting open empty cabinets, stacked boxes, covered clothes rails. He let it settle at his feet, his face still hidden. Jack blocked Pearl's way, and the light scattered around him.

'Could have been the night watch up here. What you playing at, Pearl? He's here – happy? Now let's get going. Frank, get down them stairs.'

Frank aimed the light at Jack's face. 'You can't tell me what to do no more.'

'It ain't me you're in trouble with.' He held his hand above his eyes.

'There's no trouble. Come home, please.' Pearl turned her head from side to side, trying to find Frank's face in the darkness. It was a vast half-filled space of a room, nothing finished, shapes and forms hidden under dustsheets like hunched people waiting to jump out.

'It's a bloody charabanc.' Spider spun his light on to Pearl.

The tin of paint rattled to a halt against a cabinet; Spider's shoulders jumped up to his ears. Frank rammed Spider's arm aside, gripping his own torch, the bandaged lump of his other hand bulbous as a match head.

'What you doing here, Pearl?'

'Jack knows all about what Spider's making you do…'

'How does he know?'

'It ain't really important how, is it?' Jack shrugged.

Frank's torch settled on a flat glass-covered display, spilling a yellow glow around them. 'I asked Jack to borrow us the money to get out of here and he said no. I'm doing this for us, Pearl. Spider's sorted out everything we need.'

'You won't get nothing if you don't get rid of them. Now, or the deal's off.' Spider shoved Frank out of his way, cracking the display apart with his torch, reaching in; dragging out a fistful of watches.

The lights lapped against the walls. Pearl strained forward; Jack kept a firm hold on her.

'Please. You don't need to do this, just come home with me. I don't want the money.'

Spider dumped two bags, fur tufts poking through the tops, into Frank's arms, stuffing the watches inside. 'I want the bloody money. I'm owed. What was it you said, Frank? A new life? Some such shit.'

He bent down and started opening up crates, spreading out the contents with his foot: cufflinks and tie pins. The floor around Spider looked as though a child had emptied out its toy box; the whole department store looked half-done. That was what worried Jack: unfinished business.

He took a step towards Frank; a white dust-sheet billowed as he moved. 'Enough chat. Pearl said she wants you home, so we're going.'

'When did you start to care about what she wanted?' Frank balanced the bags in his arms.

The dust, the darkness, it made Jack's eyes ache; the heat of Pearl's breath against his neck; the scratching and scraping of Spider still rooting on the floor. They didn't even know Jack was there: kids playing in the road, unaware of fallen tram cables and rushing buses; those sorts of games always ended in tears.

'Come on, lads. Just take what you've got. Trust me, there's such a thing as pushing your luck.'

'Want those passports and medical certificates, don't you, Frank? I won't let you kibosh it now. I gave Vincent my word on this job.' Spider banged his fist on his puffed-out chest; the scars criss-crossing his forehead glowed.

Jack rubbed his chilled hands together. 'So the man himself sent you on an errand. Ain't that nice. Better finish up and run on home to him, then.'

Spider cracked open the lid of a box; a sea of nails and screws spilled out. 'You old ones talk about bloody rules and codes. It's all changing, Jack. You didn't need Frank no more but I fixed him up. Vincent won't be too happy about you sticking your nose in here.'

Spider had one thing right – Jack did feel old. He rubbed the side of his head, a dull throb spreading from his spine into his skull. The whisky had worn off, and water was soaking up his sock into his trouser leg. He wanted to be in bed, warm against Georgie's body.

'I ain't got time for this. Enough messing. Frank, let's go.'

'Why don't you shut it?' Spider pulled something out from under his jumper, pointed it at Jack.

It wasn't his hand – a black gun stuck out from the end of his fingers. A wave of sickness made Jack sway: his dad's souvenir Luger.

'Stop pissing about, Spider.' Frank smiled but his lips didn't cover his teeth.

Jack grabbed Pearl's arm; something in him kicked to make sure she was behind him; the wooden handle of the Luger shining, the silver eye at the bottom of the clip glinting.

'It ain't loaded, Jack. I loaned it from your place this morning. It's just for show. Spider, tell him.'

'Don't think I'd be stupid enough to do over a place and not come kitted out with the right tools?' Spider laughed, curling his finger around the trigger.

In the dim circling torchlight their small shadows made them look like cut-out puppets putting on a show.

'You never said nothing about bullets to me.'

'Remember who's in charge here, Frank.'

Spider stared at Jack along the bony barrel of the pistol. Jack stepped backwards, taking Pearl with him. Spider shook his head. 'Did I say you could go?' The torch on the floor angled up at his face, deepening the scars into black lines. 'As you didn't want to leave first time, you'll stay and help us with the safe, old timer. Don't think about wandering off now.'

Spider held the toggle arm of the pistol, pushing twice to get it down. Jack remembered using both hands as a boy to get enough strength to pull the trigger. But it was Spider's smile that made Jack's leg muscles shake and his tongue too big for his mouth. Nothing to fear until a smile appeared; he'd seen it in the ring, seen it on his dad.

'Pearl, go and wait outside. We'll be down in a minute. Where's this safe, lads?'

The floorboard creaked as she took a small step backwards.

'Did I say *she* could go? How about you all start listening to me?'

'Don't point it at her, Spider.'

'You ain't the big champion no more, Frank. I could put you down, any of you...'

Jack couldn't look away, but he raised his hand up to his neck, gripped the base of his own throat. Frank saw it, those hand signals to finish and get out. He barged sideways into Spider, bags rolling from his arms, loud as the thud of feet on canvas. Legs knocked away. The tangled mess tumbled to the floor, fur coats swelling around them, bandages unravelling, watches skittering away. Frank didn't cry out as Spider smashed the heavy handle of the pistol into his shoulder and then again across his cheek. Torchlight twisting over ceiling and walls, lighting them up with a flash like the end of a picture reel. Pearl skidded down on to her knees in front of them. All Jack had to do was keep her back and he couldn't even do that – nothing but a fluff of yellow wool left from her jumper. Spider between him and Pearl.

Spider cracked the barrel against Frank's arm but it slipped from his hand, crashed to the ground and slid past Pearl, spinning on the floor. Jack reached the middle, the air filling with fur and wood shavings. Frank threw his weight against Spider, a shoulder smashing into his neck. Jack couldn't find an in, couldn't reach Pearl. Spider's fingers groped for the gun, pinching it away as Jack's thumb and forefinger grabbed at it. Pearl's skirt flapped against Frank's legs, he was trying to push her away. If the gun went off she wouldn't even know she had been hit.

291

Jack lunged, catching her around the waist and swinging her to the side. Spider kicked at Frank's right hand, low blows. Jack circled, coming at them from behind this time. He pressed his weight in between them. Spider wrapped his hands tighter around Frank's throat, knuckles cracking as he squeezed, the gun forgotten. But Jack saw where it went. Pearl stood up, arms out in front of her. The black barrel absorbed the light, shapes shifting along the matt metal. She pointed it towards the floor as if it was too heavy to lift. Frank gasping for air, Spider crouched over him, putting all his weight into the suffocating grip, his knees clamped to Frank's ribs.

'Always knew you wanted to fight me, Frank. Always knew I'd fucking finish – '

A sliver of white like a trapped Jumping Jack firework; glass in the cabinets shaking. A scream, just one. Pearl dropped the gun. Frank rolled over, pushing up with his good hand. She hugged him around the waist, thrusting her face into his chest. 'Are you hurt?'

'No.' Frank held on to her.

Jack felt his tongue drop down into his throat as he remembered to breathe again. His body throbbed, but he wasn't hit.

'She done me.' Spider crumpled over. Blood pumped up, black between the fingers he'd wrapped around his thigh, soaking into his dark clothes. The scars on his face whitening, disappearing, as the blood ran out of him.

Pearl didn't look up. She tried to catch her breath but it came out as a hiccup of words. 'I never meant it.'

'It was an accident, Spider. I'll get you to a doctor. It'll be all right, Pearl.'

Frank coughed as he rubbed at the darkening fingermarks on his neck. But Pearl wasn't making a sound: not crying, not sobbing. She was frozen in that moment, going over the decision in her head, watching every frame like flicking backwards through a photo album; Jack knew because he had done the same. He kicked aside the watches, faces smashed, hands bent, and picked up the Luger: lighter and smaller than all those years ago. The beam of torchlight on the floor glinted against Spider's eyes, black as the furthest corner of the room. Jack's shadow fell across him. Frank wiped a spot of blood from Pearl's chin with the edge of his shirt.

'He's going to be all right, ain't he?'

'What you fucking whispering, Frank?'

'We'll get you help, Spider. It's just your leg. A thigh's best place to get injured – all that flesh. It'll heal right up.'

'Just a leg… Vincent'll finish you off, Frank, and them both.'

Jack stepped over Spider, standing in front of Frank and Pearl. 'Half of Oxford Street will have heard that shot. Soon it won't just be us up here.'

'You and Pearl need to go, Jack.' Frank straightened up, let go of Pearl's hands. 'This is my fault. I'll see to Spider.'

The torch lay abandoned at his feet. Jack gave it to Pearl. He smoothed the hair around her face, turned down the edge of the blouse poking out from the yellow jumper. She held the light under her chin, making her skin transparent.

'I can dress it, stop the bleeding.'

'She'll pay…' Spider huffed up air and spit as he leaned against a display case. 'My leg…' He screamed, wet and throaty. *Raise your guard and go for the clinch*, that was what the trainers said to do if a fighter knew he was losing. Jack patted the gun in his pocket, straightened out his jacket. He walked back towards Spider.

'Where's the stuff you owe them?'

'Not telling… nothing.'

Spider's trouser leg was black, sticking to the floor. Jack took another step but held his foot in the air.

'You're going to want to tell me.'

'Toss off.'

He lowered his foot down on to Spider's knee – a deep howl filled the open space.

'What you doing, Jack?' Pearl flinched.

'I need to make sure you get what you're both owed, Pearl.'

He stamped his foot down again. Spider's leg felt soft, as if all the stuffing had been pulled from the bag. His torso slumped in on itself, head nearly touching his knees; Jack's heel sank lower. Spider's head bobbed then jerked back as if he had fallen asleep on a bus. Jack raised his foot.

'Under van seat... pull matting. Won't be no use to you less you get me out. Get goods to Vincent.'

Jack rubbed the sole of his shoe on the floor. It left a stain; a rubbery string of bile rose up over his tongue.

'I'll do it. But you two have got to leave.' Jack wiped his lips on his sleeve.

Pearl's voice was almost a whisper. 'What will they do to us?'

'No one's going to know you were here, Pearl.'

'We got to call an ambulance.' Her bottom lip hung low, the words falling out.

'Say you heard shooting, but anonymous like. Promise me you'll do it that way. Leave the van and take Cousin Alf's car back – you'll have to help Frank steer.'

She nodded. Spider's breathing tripped over itself. Frank stepped towards the dark puddle seeping into the floorboards. 'What about Spider? You'll need help to get him out of here.'

Jack put his hand against Frank's chest, felt the thud of his heartbeat, the familiar mustiness of his sweat. 'You can't afford to lose this one. Who's your family, him or Pearl?'

'I'll call the ambulance. We'll use the service lift, it'll be quicker – looks chained up from the outside but we can squeeze through.'

'Good, Frank, thinking for yourself. Always were good at the preparations.'

'They'll come looking for us, Jack.'

'Then you best not be there. You two are going to get those tickets and get on a boat. This ain't your fault, either of you. Remember that.'

He herded them towards the lift, blocking out the pool of blood crawling up the sheet around a display cabinet.

'Don't fucking leave,' Spider screamed. 'Bobbie Black's – take me there.'

'I'll tell the police I done it, won't even mention Vincent. I'm the one brought you here.' Frank slid back the door of the lift, holding the gates as Pearl stepped inside.

'With a broken right hand? Who'd believe that? I never did tell you about the real McCoy...'

Pearl clutched hold of the gate. 'I'll go, but you have to come with us. We can collect Georgie. We can all go. Please. Don't stay here.'

Jack tucked away a strand of her hair, his fingertip slipping into the hollow behind her ear. The toes of her support shoes touched the edge of the lift; the platform dropped slightly with his weight. Jack wished Pearl were small enough to gather up in his arms, just once more. Time had passed but those debts still needed to be paid. Frank unlaced her fingers from the metal.

'... best fighter there was in his day, used to send other fighters in his place – two or more McCoy fights taking place on one night. People started asking for the real McCoy. Understand me? I came out with Spider. It was my rob. Who wouldn't believe me?' Jack slammed the gate shut and thumped the button. 'I'm the real McCoy.'

Pearl and Frank were segmented by the diamond-shaped gaps. She opened her mouth to speak but Jack cut her off.

'This'll be the only good thing I've ever done for you. Promise you won't never speak about it. Won't never ask no one about it. And you won't never come back.'

Pearl nodded; the white parting of her hair disappeared as the lift clanked down. The chains vibrated. *Dad*, he was sure he heard that word. It was the only thing he could give her: a fighting chance.

Jack went over to the legs sticking out from behind a sheet.

'Didn't I say it'd all end in tears? I should have listened to myself.'

'I ain't crying…'

'What's your name, your real name?' He crouched beside Spider. With only one torch, the department store was nothing but a small circle of yellow around them: a few nails, a paint lid, clumps of mink fur, the ripped handle of a bag.

'Spider's what they call me.' Snot fizzed around his nose. 'They'll be calling you lot dead when Vincent finds out.'

'No one knows Pearl was here except you. Vincent won't care who takes the blame for this, long as it ain't him.'

Spider dragged himself sideways with one hand, heading towards the steps. But it was a long way; he stopped, coughing for air. Jack stayed low, slid up next to him. Spider kept one hand clutched to his leg, tried to hold Jack back with the other.

'When's help…?' His voice broke around the words, tears blocking the corner of one eye.

'I'll help you.'

Spider's shirt was streaked with dirt, his hair flattened at the back as if he had just woken up. Jack pressed his knees against Spider's back and the boy shifted slightly, their bodies in a clinch. He moved his hand to Spider's forehead; the boy was cold as the floorboards.

'It's going to be all right.' Jack stroked the spiky hair, but he wasn't talking to Spider.

He wrapped his other arm around Spider's boxy chest, pinning the boy's arms; the blood pumping faster now, nothing to stop the flow. Spider's body heaved for breath, struggling to be let loose, but there was no referee to make Jack step away; he swarmed the boy. Jack's hand slipped from the hair down to Spider's face, pointed eyebrow hairs pricking his palm, fingers gripping the boy's lips shut. No room for the mumbled words to get out or the air to get in. Jack held him tight; felt like a lifetime until the squirming stopped. But he had to be sure. One, two, three… he closed his eyes and kept count. On eight, Spider's head lolled forward, all the fight gone. Nine. Ten.

Jack loosened his fingers; no movement. He lowered his face to the boy's, catching the smell of cigarettes and buttered toast still on Spider's lips, but no breath. Jack had seen dead people before, laid out and stiff in their coffins, but not like this, not when he could still hear their voices ringing in his ears, still smell the soap flakes on their clothes and hair cream on their heads, the skin heavy and spongy like clay. Blood stuck between the cracks of Jack's fingers. He let go of the body, the dead weight toppling it to the side. No one left to call him a liar now.

Jack took the cigar from his top pocket. He smoked and waited. His legs cramped in the cold, but he stayed close to the body. Halfway through he heard them: the rattle of bells sliding off the street and into the building, running feet on the stairs.

'Stay where you are,' a voice shouted.

It was all Jack had ever heard: *keep your place, don't do that, remember who you are*. But for once he was going to do what he knew was right. Light was cutting between the cabinets; it nearly had him. Jack turned the Luger in his hand, the metal grown cold.

'Put the weapon down,' another command.

A second beam settled on Jack, and he was sure they could see him clearly now. The coppers would get their man, and Vincent would have his silence. He waved the gun in his right hand.

'I done it.'

He knew why Rosie did it too, why her body had curled around Pearl's like a spring dropping back into place then pushed the baby out into his arms. He was doing the same for Pearl this time round. Jack had carried that night with him: the crushing fear that he wouldn't find Rosie; but he had forgotten the most important thing. He remembered now, because for a moment, this night, he felt it again. Pearl saying his name: *Dad*; and earlier too, standing in front of the oven: Georgie bending over and lifting her head to half-smile, absent-mindedly pulling out a rack of pies. Sharp moments of happiness like illuminated silhouettes caught by a struck match. More torchlight spiralled up the stairs. Jack pointed the gun out at arm's length for them all to see then dropped it to the floor. The cigar was nearly out; he wanted one more taste before he was down for the count. Footsteps thundering towards him. Jack slid out the paper book of matches; the pages caught between his bloody fingers but he kept his grip. Smelling-salt rush of sulphur, sparking orange: he finally saw it again – turning the corner into Albany Basin and Rosie standing there.

TEN

'Took your time.' Rosie steps out from under the footbridge. 'I've been waiting for you, Jackie.'

The match fizzles and falls to the floor at his feet, the air smells of washed-out bonfires. She leaves the dampness of the tunnel, battered laundry box hanging from her hand. Drops of rain shine silver in her hair; pale light from a barge on the other side of the Basin lengthens her shadow. Jackie clutches the yellow wool of Pearl's blanket. He swallows down cold air as he tries to bring up the words.

'Mum said you'd gone.'

He presses one hand to his side; a sharp pain like a kidney punch kicks inside him. Pearl moans, twisting her body, straightening her shoulders, all jangled from the running. Rosie drops the strap of the cardboard case and plants her hands on her hips.

'And you believed your mum over me? You thought I'd do that?'

'No, but I checked the tram stop and the buses, then I remembered here. Was under that bridge where you told me you was expecting Pearl. But Mum's all wrong about that family ring…'

'Jackie, I don't need no ring from some dead relative. But we could have been in that house forever. We needed money for rent up front, that's why I took her train fare.'

She smiles, beckons him closer; her coat snaps against her legs as the wind rises and circles off the black water. He kisses her, Pearl sandwiched between them.

'Christ but you had me scared.'

Pressed against Rosie now, smelling her chilled skin, creamy like morning milk, he doesn't understand how those doubts fingered their way inside him. He breathes her in: the grass of Peckham Rye, sweet fermenting apples.

'I've got us a place in the flats beside Camberwell Green. The man says if I bring my *husband* by later we can have it. If he likes the look of you.'

She wrinkles her nose and grins.

'Who wouldn't?'

'You charmed me – must be there's something a little bit magic about you, Jackie.' She kisses him again, breathing into his mouth between the flicks of her tongue. Pearl lets out a cry, a low-pitched warning.

'She's getting too big to be carried around.' Jackie shifts her weight higher up against his chest.

'She'll start crawling in her own sweet time. Don't like it when you bang down on your backside, do you, poppet? She must be freezing, give her here.'

Rosie scoops the yellow bundle out of his arms, opening her cardigan to fit Pearl inside. Jackie wants to curl up and mould himself against Rosie's ribs too. She stamps her feet on the muddy cobbles.

'So, what was it took you so long to come after me? I'm half frozen out here.'

'I had to pick something up after work.'

And this is the moment; he knows he can't wait any longer. Jackie kneels, because he has heard this is how it should be done. He sinks into a puddle; grit and stones poke into his shin, and the sticking discomfort helps him keep the tears from filling up his eyes.

'Dropped something by the looks of it… what you doing, Jackie?'

'Marry me forever?'

She laughs, hand covering her mouth. Those fingers of doubt are crawling back, pinching at his cold skin. 'Did I get it wrong?'

'The *marry me* bit was good…' She gets down on her knees too, steadying herself with one hand on his shoulder, Pearl slipping to her other hip. 'Forever goes without saying.'

His hands are level with her face; he closes his fingers around her iced cheeks.

'Yes.' They say it together.

The lights from the barge go out, coughing and spitting from onboard; the back of the warehouses block out moonlight and city light.

'Bloody hell, I nearly forgot.' He digs in his pocket and comes out with the jewellery box. 'It's not tin, look.'

He strikes a match on the sole of his shoe and holds it to the ring; the flame brightens the gold plating. Her breath comes in short gasps. 'It's beautiful. Put it on me.'

'Its bad luck, ain't it?' He rubs the top of the green leather with his thumb.

'That's old wives' stuff. What happens happens.'

She presents her hand. The ring fits perfectly, gliding over her blue-tinged knuckle. Jackie rubs her skin between his palms to warm up the flow of blood. The wedding band throbs with friction. Breath steams and condenses on their eyelashes; Pearl sighs.

'There's a boiler on the landing outside the flat. Hot water when we want it. The bedroom's a bit damp but the old woman lived there before probably never cracked a window. It'll clear up.'

He drops the match; down to the last one in the book now. He lights it and holds it high.

'How much?'

'We can get by, with your money from the factory. I can take in some work. And it's closer to the gym. Trust me.'

'I do. Mum's going to be angry as a mad dog.'

'Let her huff and puff – what do we care? Ain't that right, little one?' Rosie nuzzles her forehead against Pearl's.

The flame starts to flutter, striking their shadows down on to the wet path. The water in Albany Basin laps behind

301

them as a rat squeaks and splashes into the water. The cardboard case tilts slightly against Rosie's thigh; her coat pokes outwards, and her feet are too close to the mossy edge. If the match were to fall now they would try to stand, brushing the spark from her blue flowered dress, feet catching in the case handle – falling – the iron mooring ring cracking apart the back of her skull, blood and mud and hair, before the Basin would swallow her down and only release her a week later. But it isn't that time yet. The surface of the greasy water isn't ruptured into purple and silver streaks; Pearl snores quietly, yellow wool tucked in the warm folds of Rosie's arms; the bargemen are settling down for a good night's sleep; the metal hook used to fish overboard cargo still rests on deck. Only the stem of the match is hot as hell, sizzling closer to the tip of his missing thumbnail. Jackie will have to let go soon. The silhouette of his wife and child burn into him; and, in that moment, he feels himself the luckiest man alive.

EPILOGUE

My watch ticks, drawing my eyes from the open Bible. Less than a minute left. The print on the page floats up towards me, black specks like bouncing rain. I should read it out, but the words are not right. Pierrepoint coughs; he does not like the rhythm of these hangings to be altered. Procedures must be followed before that rope is dropped, and we are coming to the end of them all. The men stare at the greening crucifix on the opposite wall, but Jack is not looking there. He still studies the ceiling, or perhaps he is thinking back to some other time.

Our paths must have crossed growing up, running the same streets. Standing here, watching the pulleys being cranked, I am sure that is why he told me everything. No grassing – the constant cry over bomb sites and back yards; Newton's son knows the rules.

No windows, no noise from outside, but Jack closes his eyes and tilts his face as if he feels rays on his skin. The envelope postmarked *Victoria, Australia* sits in his top pocket; he showed me the tinted photograph of Pearl and Frank standing together in front of a corrugated hut, blurred hands waving: the black and red flash of a student nurse cape, a pencil behind Frank's ear and sawdust on his sleeves – solid and shadowless outlines in the bright New World sunlight. *To Dad Love Pearl & Frank* neatly printed in blue ink across the right-hand corner. He replied to each letter, reading his words over and over until the paper wore thin at the folds, but he never posted the replies. They will be wrapped in brown paper, packaged up with his knitted bedsocks, ounce

303

of tobacco, shaving mirror, snapped comb, silver-framed picture of Rosie, title deeds to the house (a result of the only letter he did send, to his sisters), and sent by boat to Australia come the end of the day.

The younger man steps forward with the white hood; it billows as he lifts it into the air. Jack stands with his back stiff, a soft rush of breath from his mouth. I reach for his shoulder. The hood slaps my arm, droops and hangs still. Pierrepoint blinks twice – telling me this is not how things are done. But I do not move away; I squeeze the rough material of Jack's shirt. This is his final chance to tell the truth to someone other than me, to save himself.

'Do you have any last words?'

He flexes his wrists, fingers locking as he holds his own hand. 'I done it for her.'

My arm falls down to my side. The hood comes again. And that is when he sees it; before the whiteness seals him up. Floating specks of dust in the light, each one a moment from his life balanced against another – this time he really sees it. After all, it is the longest fight there is, life. Jack has known knockouts in the first round and long agonising defeats in the fifteenth: no reward, no prize purse. It is only the fight itself that is important: finding the strength to make it through. The noose fits over his head; wisps of greased hemp stand up – thin and bright as baby hair. The cotton hood trembles as Jack breathes, sucked into a shallow O between his lips.

The Bible in my hand feels heavy. I know the words by heart, but now they are not enough. The pinioning straps are checked – securely fastened. The last time I visited Jack, before he was moved to the condemned cell, he opened this Bible, ran his finger across the lines. 'Maybe I printed these words at the factory, maybe my dad did,' Jack said. He told me then he wanted to return something that was mine. *Boxing* by A.J. Newton, printed in black ink down the spine. I had heard the tales from my father, but I never thought there was much truth to it until Jack pushed the book across the scrubbed table. Silver pencil trails score the dusty pages, trickling through the margins. Rich's wins and points totalled in columns on the back leaf, the date for his title fight at White City written in capitals: two weeks from today.

I rub my fingers across the black leather of the cover, close the scarlet-edged pages. We all step back from the spot where Jack stands; only Pierrepoint keeps beside him. When they post the notice of death on the prison gate it will be on plain white paper. Usually a crowd gathers, pushing to examine the small type. Georgie said she would be there to read Jack's name, to finally accept he was not coming home. She has not missed a visiting day, but this will be her first without Jack. Only on the last visit did he make her cry, telling her she would find someone else some day because that was the way things always went, whether you wanted it or not – and he knew because it had happened to him. She told me Jack would always be printed inside her. I offered to persuade her not to come; he laughed at that. Instead he asked me to take her for champagne and oysters after Rich's title fight, said that night out was the only promise he ever made her. She is waiting out there now on the rain-licked cobbles. Pierrepoint removes the safety pin, places his hand on the metal lever. Nothing now can stop the clack and scroll of the typewriter from printing that name, the name he was born with: John James Munday. Only one thing left.

'Be of good courage.'

The platform drops. The rope cracks tight about the prisoner's neck. The body shakes, slowing to a sway, until only the scuffed oxblood brogues circle from left to right. The grey shadow of the doctor appears in the room below. He presses a stethoscope to the prisoner's chest. But Jack has nothing more to say.

Turn up the lights, sweep out the ring. This fight is done.

Acknowledgements

I would like to thank the following people for their care and attention in getting this book made: Ed Wilson, my agent, and Candida Lacey, MD at Myriad, for their vision and belief in Jack; Holly Ainley, my editor, who didn't pull her punches and always hit the mark (in a friendly, non-violent way); Linda McQueen and Dawn Sackett for having great eyes for detail; Leo Nickolls, for the lovely book design; and all at Myriad Editions. It has been a pleasure to work with you all.

I also want to express my gratitude to early readers of *The Longest Fight* – Robin Lindsey, Elizabeth Silver, Hatice Özdemirciler, and in particular to Linda Anderson and Derek Neale whose feedback and advice was invaluable. Thanks are also due to my family and friends for their encouragement and support.

MORE FROM MYRIAD

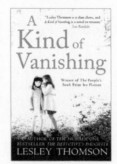

MORE FROM MYRIAD

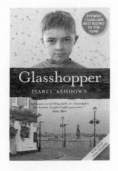

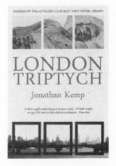

MORE FROM MYRIAD

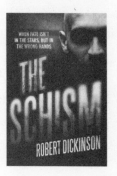

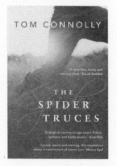

Sign up to our mailing list at
www.myriadeditions.com
Follow us on Facebook and Twitter

About the author

Emily Bullock won the Bristol Short Story Prize with her story 'My Girl', which was broadcast on BBC Radio 4. She worked in film before pursuing writing full-time. Her memoir piece 'No One Plays Boxing' was shortlisted for the Fish International Publishing Prize 2013 and her short story 'Zoom' was longlisted for the Bath Short Story Award 2014. She has a Creative Writing MA from the University of East Anglia and completed her PhD at the Open University, where she also teaches creative writing. Emily Bullock lives in London.